8/09

|||||||||||||||||||||||||||||||||||

Perfect Life

ALSO BY JESSICA SHATTUCK

The Hazards of Good Breeding

Perfect Life

A NOVEL

Jessica Shattuck

W. W. NORTON & COMPANY

NEW YORK · LONDON

For information about permission to reproduce selections from this book,
write to Permissions, W. W. Norton & Company, Inc.,
500 Fifth Avenue, New York, NY 10110

For information about special discounts for bulk purchases, please contact
W. W. Norton Special Sales at specialsales@wwnorton.com or 800-233-4830

Manufacturing by Courier Westford
Book design by Kristen Bearse
Production manager: Julia Druskin

Library of Congress Cataloging-in-Publication Data

Shattuck, Jessica.
Perfect life : a novel / Jessica Shattuck.—1st ed.
p. cm.
ISBN 978-0-393-06950-1
1. Fertility, Human—Fiction. 2. Parenthood—Fiction. I. Title.
PS3619.H3575P47 2009
813'.6—dc22

2009015080

W. W. Norton & Company, Inc.
500 Fifth Avenue, New York, N.Y. 10110
www.wwnorton.com

W. W. Norton & Company Ltd.
Castle House, 75/76 Wells Street, London W1T 3Q

1 2 3 4 5 6 7 8 9 0

To Helen & Tilde

Perfect Life

Prologue

LATER, AFTER EVERYTHING, after Neil had come and gone again from their day-to-day lives, Laura had a memory of that other time, a million years ago it seemed, when they had all been college students, living in that cushy, all-American holding pen for almost-adults, reading books and being cooked for, drinking five nights a week, and worrying over nothing more than term papers and social gaffes.

The memory was of one of those gray November-in-New-England days with the heat banging and ticking in the radiators and wind rattling the windowpanes. Laura and her roommates had spent the day entirely in their suite, taking refuge in the insufficient comfort of smoking cigarettes and listening to melancholy CDs.

Their rooms were at once slovenly and decorous—full of glossy prints of Victorian paintings, Indian tapestries, and once-decent furniture inherited from Laura's great-grandmother, now strewn with discarded shoes, full ashtrays, half-empty beer bottles, and crusty plastic dining room dishes. No one ever cleaned. There was a general atmosphere of simulation. They were all aware of those four years as a kind of oblique practice for Real Life.

It was Laura herself who had brought up the subject. *Children*— the idea had been so vague, so hazy as to seem almost make-believe. Children—those loud, exotic, intimidating creatures who existed in an altogether different universe. They never saw them. Later, when

Laura was pregnant for the first time, she would suddenly be aware of them all around her—mothers and babies, pregnant women, toddlers—a ubiquitous presence that her eyes had up until then simply dismissed.

But at the time of this memory they were still invisible, theoretical at best.

How many children do you want to have? she had asked, the question arising from—what, some article she had been reading? Boredom? Elise and Neil had looked at her blankly from where they sat on the sofa, engrossed in a game of hearts.

Jenny, the former high school debater and prom queen, had a certain and immediate answer: *Two. A boy and a girl.*

Not two-point-three? Neil had asked, raising his eyebrows. At that time, he was Jenny's boyfriend, if the casual, friends-turned-lovers nature of their relationship could be labeled in those terms.

But Jenny had disappeared into her bedroom to get ready for something, a meeting or a summer job interview, maybe—Jenny was always getting ready for something, even then.

And you? Laura had turned back to Elise and Neil.

I don't know. Elise had been disinterested—of the three girls, she was both the brainiest and the most abstracted. *I've never thought about it.*

I can see you having an only child, Laura had pronounced. It was the kind of thing she liked to do back then—make things up and see her own imaginings as premonitions. *A sweet little boy who gets really into something unusual like . . . fencing. Or ping-pong.*

Hm. Elise had shrugged. *Okay.*

What about you? Laura had poked Neil with her toe.

None.

Why not? Even in Laura's twenty-year-old mind, the idea of having children, however theoretical, was a given. Of course she would have children. Of course someday she would be a mother—it was already a part of who she was.

Why would I?

Because—I don't know—isn't that the whole idea?

What—like some giant hall of mirrors? Have children to have children to have children . . .

At that moment Jenny had come back out of her room, having exchanged her T-shirt and sweatpants for a snug black sweater and skirt.

Well, I guess you two won't be starting a family, Elise had pronounced, with her usual foot-in-mouth frankness.

Jenny had not missed a beat. *Guess not.* She'd smiled glibly, shrugging on her jacket.

There had been a lag in Neil's response. This was what stuck out in Laura's mind now, so many years later. In that momentary pause, she had glimpsed on his usually imperturbable face a look of . . . what was it—hurt? Or something more complicated—a kind of recognition that despite the unique brand of cool he so effortlessly, even accidentally embodied, despite the air of promise, talent, and exceptionality that surrounded him, for Jenny, he was still someone to be summarily dismissed.

Well, he had said, *I guess that settles it.*

Part One

1

IT WAS DURING THE HOMILY that Laura caught sight of Neil.

She was sitting toward the back of the church—a calculated move, given the ticking time bomb of her two-year-old daughter, Miranda, and her own dislike of churches, which always made her think of death, of futile human striving, of everything in life that was sad. All those grim carvings of saints and the ubiquitous gory specter of the crucifixion—as if she did not think of her own mortality—her children's mortality!—enough.

But the service at St. Bernard's this morning had been unavoidable: it included the christening of her college roommate, Jenny Callahan's, baby. And it was important to Jenny—the societal ritual of it, the fact that it was taking place in this tony suburban church. Laura leaned against the hard back of the pew and tried to focus her eyes on the world *outside* the window, on the tiny buds of leaves, the heads of crocuses, the yellow forsythia. Surely this would bring her closer to God than the melancholy drone of the priest's voice.

It was considering this that she saw him. Not God, but Neil Banks. The sight of him gave Laura something like an electric shock.

He was not supposed to be there. That was obvious. Not because the christening was small or intimate (quite the opposite: big and public was how Jenny lived her life these days) but because of the arrangement, which very specifically precluded any such casual dropping by on Neil's part.

He was standing outside the last window on the right, affecting the look of a casual passerby and wearing a beaten leather jacket despite the warmth of the day. He looked skinny and his hair had turned from sandy blond to a premature sandy gray.

Laura glanced at her husband, Mac, who was surreptitiously checking his BlackBerry as Miranda attempted to climb onto his shoulder, panting slightly with the effort to work quiet mischief. Beside them, their six-year-old daughter, Genevieve, sat coloring, her head bent in concentration.

"Be right back," Laura murmured, almost hoping Mac wouldn't hear her, and slid out into the aisle. She ducked her head as if somehow this would render her less visible and kept her eyes on the carpeting with a vague, hopefully respectful, expression plastered on her face.

Once through the heavy oak doors and in the cool stone foyer, she felt a quickening of excitement and a breath of relief. Outside it was spring. Unseasonably warm, even muggy. An apple tree beside the church was blossoming, fallen petals frilling daintily over the damp black earth beneath. Everywhere there was the faint stench of winter rot—crumpled apples and defrosting dog shit, mud and unearthed metal. Laura filled her lungs with it and felt suddenly free—free of her husband and children and even her "spirited" dog, Cocoa, who was usually at her side when the children weren't. Free of her obligation to be an enthusiastic friend, to coo over the baby and make chitchat with far-flung family members and acquaintances. It was as if, for a moment, she could be a college girl again—a bright and lucky twenty-one-year-old, skipping class.

Was it the weather or seeing Neil that brought this feeling back?

She traversed the soggy grass on tiptoe, careful to keep the pointy heels of her new shoes from sinking in. Around the corner of the church she could see him, still hovering at the window, looking up toward the knave. He had lit a cigarette and the tarry, indoor smell of it muted the springiness of the air. From behind, like this, he looked unchanged—a boy, really, rather than a man.

Laura hesitated for a moment, aware suddenly of her own altered form: baby belly she still hadn't lost hidden under the blousy top she had bought to conceal it, boring hair, the beginnings of lines between her eyebrows and at the edges of her eyes. But she was still pretty, wasn't she? This was something that she took for granted— that somewhere between adolescence and adulthood she had developed a confidence in (possibly mistakenly, she sometimes thought, looking at photographs of herself in her glasses, or her dingy bathrobe, or with her children in the unflattering overhead light of the playroom they seemed always to be photographed in, but it was a confidence nonetheless).

She drew a breath. "Neil."

The figure at the window whirled around and for a moment the look on his face was so hostile, so defensive—like an unfriendly, startled dog—that Laura stepped backward, sinking one heel into the mud and teetering wildly off balance.

Then a softer, sheepish look came over Neil's face.

"Jesus. Laura," he said, throwing his cigarette down and grinding it under his heel. He cast an eye around as if maybe there were other, more menacing figures waiting in the wings to apprehend him. "I'm not supposed to be here."

"I know." Laura was struggling to assimilate this Neil—an older (now that he was facing her she could see this), more downtrodden Neil—with the one she had been thinking of as she stepped out of the church.

"How are you?" He stepped forward and hugged her, and in the quick, slightly rigid embrace, he became himself again, the Neil she knew. The Neil she and Jenny had pulled months' worth of all-nighters with in college, drifting in and out of parties, downing drinks in divey bars. The Neil who had, for instance, shown up years ago at her father's house on the Vineyard with a trampy sixteen-year-old, coke-addled girlfriend, looking for a place to stay.

"Good," she said breathlessly. "I'm good. God—it's been such a long time!"

"We're old and gray," Neil said, grinning.

"Don't say that!"

"No, but you look great, Lo." He struck a match and lit up another cigarette.

They were silent for a moment and, inside, the organ struck up a new hymn. The groan and snap of the congregation rising was audible.

"What are you doing here?" Laura asked, reminded suddenly of the weirdness of his presence.

"Ha!" Neil took a drag on his cigarette. "That's funny."

"No, I mean, of course—but I thought you weren't supposed to— All the agreements and papers and legal stuff Jenny had you sign . . ."

Neil glanced over his shoulder back through the window. "What's he like?"

Laura put a hand to her throat—a habitual gesture of nervousness. It was only now that it occurred to her that finding him out here was not just surprising, but bad. And that she was now enmeshed in it—guilty by association. Would she have to tell Jenny she had seen him? Or somehow take responsibility for hustling him away? Neil was not really someone she could imagine herself hustling anywhere.

"Cute? Healthy? As smart and charming and funny as his daddy?"

"I wouldn't call Jeremy so charming or funny," Laura said firmly.

"Yeah. Right." Neil's eyes stayed on Laura's face. "You're a loyal friend, Lo Lo. You always were."

Laura thought of her husband and children for the first time since stepping outside. Mac would be wondering what on earth had happened to her. And Miranda might be making a scene—from inside the church she could hear crying.

"No, you're right, though." Neil hunched his shoulders forward. "I shouldn't be here. I was just in town and I ran into Nelly McCormack and she mentioned it . . . Stupid, though. I'm an asshole."

Laura looked directly into his eyes. "No, you're not."

Neil met her gaze and his eyes looked tired.

"I should get back . . . " she said. "My kids . . ."

"Right—of course." Neil shook his head. "What is it—two of them?"

"Two girls." Laura smiled weakly.

"Wow."

The weird disjuncture of time seemed to wash over them both. "Really, you look great, Lo. I'm glad you came out."

"Are you around for a while? Or just the weekend?" she said. "It would be nice to catch up—"

"Nope, not allowed—I think I signed something about that too."

"What?" Laura exclaimed.

"No—I'm just kidding. I'm sorry. Look—call me. Here." He reached into his back pocket and pulled out a beaten wallet, fished around to procure a card, which he handed to her. *Neil Banks, game reviewer*, the card read. *Los Angeles.* "It's my cell number."

"Neil Banks has a business card," Laura said, raising her eyebrows.

He smiled. "Times change."

Laura pushed her way back through the crowd that was now exiting the church, smiling faintly, trying not to appear flustered.

Once inside, she could see Miranda's curly head bouncing up and down beside Mac, who was scanning the doorway with a frown.

"Mommy, Mommy, the baby got a bath from the mister! The

baby got a bath from the mister!" Miranda shouted as Laura approached. Genevieve's dark eyes looked predictably concerned.

"What happened to you?" Mac asked reprimandingly, his big, handsome face wearing an agitated scowl.

"Where were you?" Genevieve asked.

"Where you?" Miranda echoed giddily, bobbing against the back of the pew.

"I was just . . ." Laura put her hand to her throat. "I had to get some air." There it was. She had not really decided, but now it was clear that she was going to keep Neil's presence to herself.

"Are you sick?" Genevieve asked.

"No, no, no—I'm fine," Laura said, scooping Miranda up off the pew and starting down the aisle, hiding her face in her daughter's warm, child-smelling neck.

"Can we get out of here now?" Mac trailed behind her with Genevieve in tow. "Do we really need to go to this lunch?"

"Mac." Laura shot a glance over her shoulder at him. "Of course we have to."

"Let's see if we can find Jenny, shall we?" she whispered into Miranda's ear.

"No." Miranda shook her head. "No, no, no." But Laura plowed ahead, sweeping her agitation under the convenient charade of social purpose.

When Jenny had first told Laura of her plan, Laura had been absolutely dumbstruck. Jenny wanted to use Neil's sperm to have a baby? It was like the Pope wanting to have the Dalai Lama's love child.

"Why Neil?" Laura had asked, gape-mouthed.

"What do you mean, *why Neil?*" was Jenny's response. "You *know* Neil is brilliant."

"But you don't even know where he is now. And he drove you crazy!"

"I'm not asking him to be my boyfriend," Jenny had said testily. Of course, being Jenny, she had a plan. A very specific, very bold plan. Neil would sign away all rights to the child—there would be contracts and lawyers, and she was working with a top-notch fertility clinic that had navigated every which kind of arrangement before. And Jeremy, *poor Jeremy*, as Laura and Elise, their other college roommate, always referred to him on account of Jenny's bossiness, would adopt the baby upon birth. They would never tell the child that Jeremy was not his biological father. The proposal was improbably absolute.

"But why would Neil agree?" Laura had asked mildly.

Jenny's answer had been maddeningly smug. "He will," she said. "I just know. He'll recognize the opportunity."

And despite the fact that Laura knew Neil too—that, in fact, she almost felt she knew Neil *better* because, unlike Jenny, she had not dated him—Laura believed her. That was the thing about Jenny: she envisioned the way her life would go, and life cooperated. Never mind that Neil had been lost for years to anyone who had known him in college, had been absolutely no-email-address, no-forwarding-number *gone*; Laura did not doubt for a moment that Jenny would find him. And drag him out from whatever rock he was hiding under, dazed and bedazzled, into her plan.

2

JENNY WAS NOT PLEASED with the way the day was unfolding.

She had been up long before Colin or Jeremy were awake, checking to be sure the cleaners had polished the silver and dusted the champagne flutes, and that the white Portuguese lace tablecloths she had ordered were in fact the right size for the rented tables. They had, and they were. But the hand towels had not been replaced in the bathroom, and Jeremy had left his sweaty glass of brandy on top of the piano, leaving a whitish ring of condensation on the glossy mahogany that she had no idea how to remove.

There were forty people expected for lunch after the service: a combination of family and friends and a few prominent members of the St. Bernard's committee who she had had to schmooze in order to arrange for Colin to be baptized there. She wanted everything sparkling, smooth, and orderly. If there was one thing she had learned in her career, it was that sloppiness and spontaneity breed unease. Organization and foresight, she liked to tell new hires, were the key to making people comfortable. It was like child rearing, actually. She had read Weissbluth and Ferber: to raise a well-adjusted child one must have clear boundaries, consistent routines, and order. And it had paid off! At six weeks Colin had begun sleeping through the night.

So in the wee hours of the morning Jenny had slaved away picking out platters for the caterers, organizing the coat closet, distributing bowls of roses to prominent locations around the apartment, dispensing with emails. By the time Colin's first cries bleated out over the monitor she had attached to her hip, everything was under control. And then there was Colin! So sweet and smart and miraculous, lying against the blue and white circles of his baby sheets like a little prince.

He was a fairly serious baby and not at all chubby, which was, of course, completely logical. She was a rail herself and always had been. But there were moments, for instance looking at Elise and Chrissy's smiley, roly-poly twins, when she wished Colin was just a little plumper, had a few of those baby fat wrinkles and folds under the chin. Which was silly. It was much healthier for him to be just as he was—a long, lean little man, well on his way toward crawling, with a strong, well-coordinated grasp.

Singing the "Good Morning" song they had learned in his baby music class, and watching Colin clasp his little hands together in that sophisticated way of his, Jenny had felt the kiss of promise that this would be a really successful day.

But then things had began to unravel. Colin was cranky, and halfway through his breakfast of pears and rice cereal he began to fart violently and shake his head. By the time Maria had arrived to help dress and ready him for the service, Jenny's breasts ached with milk he wouldn't drink and Colin was a fussy mess. Meanwhile, Jeremy emerged from the bedroom looking pale and unhappy, certain he was coming down with the stomach flu. "Not allowed," Jenny barked. "And not a word to our guests." Jeremy skulked his long, thin body off to shower looking truly miserable and Jenny had a moment of remorse, but what was she supposed to do? Cancel the whole baptism? Serve the lunch with Jeremy notably (and off-puttingly) upstairs sick in bed? Half the guests had children themselves and would surely flee at the mere mention of a virus. Thank God for Maria, who had such a wonderfully calm, reassuring way about her, and had Colin calmed down, dressed, and bottle-fed in half an hour flat.

Jenny pumped (what was the big deal women kvetched and moaned about? Jenny didn't mind the efficient hiss and clutch of milk being expressed from her breasts), dressed, and brought Jeremy a cup of tea and a tablespoon of Pepto-Bismol as a gesture of apology. He continued to make an overblown show of how badly he felt, sighing and resting in between donning articles of clothing as if he were an old man or a rehab patient, but Jenny bit her tongue and straightened his tie with a smile. Men were always babies about being sick—they got sick less often than their wives and children, but when they *did* succumb to whatever ordinary cold or flu was going around, they acted as though it were the plague. Jenny herself was strong as an ox—Jeremy got sick at least twice as much as she did, much more than your average husband, and it had begun to render him downright wimpy. What had become of the fierce, brilliant, and tireless software genius she had married?

Despite the crankiness and stomach flu, and the flurry of last-minute phone calls from disorganized friends needing directions, the small Callahan-Sharha family made it out on time. And Colin looked perfect in the sweet white sailor suit she had bought for a small fortune at a little baby boutique on Newbury Street last weekend.

But then, just before the babies (he was not the only one being christened) and their entourages were called up to the front of the church, there was an enormous rumbling from Colin's little belly and a greenish, snotty-looking shit, unlike any she had seen before, spread like some sort of evil seaweed up the back of the fancy French muslin. It was a cliché in its predictability. Jenny had of course thought to have a second outfit on hand, but the timing was terrible. In moments, the shit spread rapidly onto the blanket she had under him and the crisp DKNY dress she had picked out for the occasion. And Colin began to wail as they headed forward with his godmother, Elise (thank God it was steady, responsible Elise she had chosen and not Laura, who would have begun to laugh), and Jeremy, whose already long, pale face was now looking almost as green as the shit threatening to envelop Jenny's entire outfit.

Jenny was not usually given to self-consciousness, but carrying her little wailing, smelly bundle up the steps to the grand and imposingly proper knave of St. Bernard's, the church she had just kissed more Brahmin ass to get into than a Beacon Hill debutante, she began to sweat. The lunch, the reception, had all begun to seem like an ordeal. She wanted to kiss her sweet little baby and hand him off to Maria and go for a run—or take a nap.

Now, standing outside the church, greeting people with a wide smile plastered across her face and a freshly changed Colin perched on her hip concealing the smear of shit along her own waist, her enthusiasm for the day was gone.

"Beautiful, beautiful baby," a waspy old crone in a Chanel suit cooed, leaning in to chuck Colin's chin—a grandmother of one of the other babies, maybe? Or simply a baptism enthusiast? It was enough to start Colin squirming and fussing again, arching his back in protest.

"Are you giving your mother a hard time, dear?" chimed one of the smug church-board housewives.

"It's his mealtime." Jenny smiled tightly. "And he likes his lunch, don't you, Colin?"

"Aha!" the woman raised her eyebrows condescendingly. You almost had to admire these preppy New Englanders; they were so well versed in the ways of making a person feel small. Growing up in the no-man's-land of Central California, Jenny had never encountered such skillfully veiled sniping and passive-aggressive finesse.

"See, there she is!" This was Laura now, emerging with Miranda straddled awkwardly on her hip—she was too big to be carried, really, but Laura always obliged her. "That was beautiful! And how is the little man holding up? It's a lot to take in, isn't it—and you've done such a stand-up job!" This was addressed to Colin, who responded with one of his rare, unreserved, openmouthed smiles. Jenny felt a swell of warmth toward her old friend. Laura could be such a birdbrain, but she was a genuinely sweet person. And Jenny was shrewd enough to recognize there were very few of these in her life.

Laura kissed her on the cheek, ignoring Miranda's cries of protest. Jenny lifted Colin away from her waist for a moment.

"Shit," she said. "Everywhere. Total disaster."

Laura's eyes widened comically—she looked especially pretty today, a little flushed and particularly bright somehow. But just as Jenny was beginning to remark on this, she was swooped down upon by one of the coworkers she had invited. Why had she ever invited anyone from her office?

See you at lunch, Laura mouthed amid the fawnings of the young woman, and faded back into the throng of people, taking with her the first glimmer of good humor Jenny had felt since dawn.

And naturally Colin began, once again, to wail.

On the way back to the apartment after the service, Jenny drove, Jeremy sat morosely in the passenger seat, and Maria and Colin snugged into the back, an unlikely and silent foursome speeding along Storrow Drive toward the Back Bay. The new house Jenny and Jeremy had bought in Wellesley was not ready yet. The contractors were behind schedule and because of this, the fledgling family was still holed up in the brownstone duplex on Clarendon Street. No yard and no parking. It was not where Jenny had imagined her first winter with the baby would be. Or, for that matter, where the lunch after the christening was going to be. But there it was. You could only manage your own part of every operation. And the apartment on Clarendon was beautiful, Jenny reminded herself. It was small for hosting forty people, but light and airy, and you couldn't beat the address.

"Did you tell Neil about today?" Jeremy asked, cutting through her musing.

"What?" Jenny nearly swerved out of her lane. She and Jeremy did not talk about Neil.

"I think I saw him." Jeremy was staring straight ahead.

"Neil lives in Los Angeles, if you remember," she said icily, shooting him a reprimanding glare. Maria was sitting right there in the backseat.

"I think I saw him," he repeated.

"I'm sure you didn't," Jenny said forcefully. Was Jeremy losing his mind? "Can we discuss this later?"

Jeremy continued staring straight ahead through the thin spheres of his rimless glasses. "I just need to know, Jenny: did. you. invite. him?"

Jenny glanced over at him again. He was enraged. Quietly, burningly furious. She could not remember the last time she had seen him this way. It was easy to forget how hard this was for Jeremy. He was infertile. He was, biologically speaking, raising another man's child. An unusual swell of sympathy rose in her chest, despite the absurdity of his question.

"I didn't," she said in a kinder, softer voice. "I swear to God, there is no way he would have been there." This was true. There was honestly no way. No one even saw Neil anymore these days. She had practically had to hire a sleuth to find him.

Outside the car, cyclists and Rollerbladers sped down the narrow strip of park between the river and the reflecting pool like apparitions of health and well-being walking on water. On a regular Sunday morning she and Jeremy would have been running out there among them.

She almost reached out to him. "I think you were hallucinating."

"Hm." Jeremy grimaced.

In the backseat Colin began to wail again, and then there was a choking, sputtering sound, followed by helpless baby coughing.

"Oh, baby!" Maria exclaimed. "He just throwed up, poor little one."

"Shit!" Jenny banged the steering wheel.

And Jeremy rolled down his window.

3

THE ROOM NEIL WOKE UP in was almost offensively flooded with light. Bright, dirty spring light, alive with dust and microorganisms. It illuminated sticky beer stains and a crowded ashtray, the humidity bubbles on album covers strewn around the floor. Neil was in Boston, in his old coworker Johnson's "wreck room," sleeping on a futon without a sheet. Johnson was an ass. He lived like an ass. With pretensions to some ridiculous hipsterdom he should have outgrown. The turntable and the vintage record collection. The tiki lamps and P-Funk posters. It was humiliating to be staying here. Because how far removed from all this was Neil, really? It drove that question home.

Neil sat up gingerly, trying to touch as little of the grubby mattress as possible. There was a bad smell coming from the radiator, which was banging and hissing despite the apparently pleasant weather outside. Neil shook his head and rubbed his face vigorously to bring the blood up to the surface. His cheeks felt scratchy and rough. He knelt to fiddle with the screw top on the radiator valve— it looked ancient. And predictably, it was stuck. In wrestling with it, his arm grazed the metal of the first coil and he jerked backward in surprise. The thing was fucking hot. He settled for opening the window instead, and a rush of cool, refreshing spring air blew in from the improbable cliff behind the place. For a moment it reminded him of California, of San Francisco specifically, where such rugged pieces of geology cropped up with regularity—evidence that the land was bigger than the city. That the quirks and foibles of the earth's surface were not so easily dismissed.

This cliff was dirty, though, like the light coming through the window. It was brown with decomposing leaves and twigs and whatever scrappy, unbeautiful vegetation made a home for itself on the steep incline. There were bits of junk caught all along its snarly surface—ballooning plastic shopping bags worn thin and holey by the winter, faded silver candy wrappers, shards of beer bottles, a pair of pants, a toilet seat . . . East Coast geology for sure—intact on account of human sloppiness rather than some insurmountable metal of its own. Hell, it was probably just a solid wall of poorly designated landfill.

Neil sighed aloud and rifled through his duffel bag for a clean pair of boxers and a shirt. From the next room there was the sound of music with a pounding electronic beat and the shriek of female laughter, a loud snapping groan that sounded unmistakably like a body—or two?—hitting the bed. It was eight a.m. on a Monday morning. At thirty-five, Neil was too old for this. He might have sold his soul to take over Johnson's job at ZGames, trading his years of maverick game-review writing (the ridiculous self-importance of the label, even in his own head, made him smile) for the steady pay of being a game company hack, but this didn't mean he had sold his adulthood, to boot—or did it?

He pulled a clean T-shirt over his head and tried to block out the sound of the bumping headboard. Forget shaving. He was going to get out, get a cup of coffee, make the most of this morning back in the town he loved to hate—and drive away the blackness he could feel circling around him, waiting for an opportune moment to sink its talons into his head.

Letting himself out of the triple-decker Johnson lived in—the triple-decker he, Neil Banks, would officially live in if Johnson and his girlfriend Kirstin ever got on with their plans and cleared the hell out—Neil was greeted by the pleasant, greasy smell of dough and plantains frying. There was a Cuban place on the corner that Johnson had described as a good place to get a "cup of joe" (had he always talked like this?) and Neil headed there, resisting the urge to stop in the convenience store across the street for a pack of cigarettes. It was one of his resolutions now that he was thirty-five. He would cut back on smoking, try to avoid the gravelly voice and hacking, phlegmy cough his father and his grandfather had always had.

The neighborhood was better than he had expected. He had never come here during his time at Harvard, so it was relievingly free of associations—had none of the bookish redbrick Victorian architecture, none of the historic cemeteries and cobbled alleys that now made him feel at once regretful and angry, lucky and failed. It felt almost like New York, with its litter and bodegas and general treelessness. This was good.

"Coffee?" the round, elderly woman who approached Neil's booth, once he was seated, asked with a thick, presumably Cuban accent. "Meelk? Shooger?"

Her un-Boston-ness was good too. The morning was turning around. He could make a life here for himself for a little while. He could survive the return to his homeland. He could, maybe even, make it feel new.

He ordered eggs and bacon and toast, relishing the freedom to eat bad food. For the last three years he had been macrobiotic, due to living with his now ex-girlfriend Jane, and this morning the act of ordering something full of saturated fats and carbon compounds felt liberating. This was the kind of thing he had to look forward to.

Out on the street a group of delinquent teenagers slouched past, skipping their morning classes, calling out to each other too loudly, mock-fighting. Their soft rolled vowels and dropped *r*'s were disturbingly familiar. Shades of New Bedford, the Massachusetts town

Neil had grown up in and spent the rest of his life trying to escape. He pulled his laptop out of its case, and despite the ugliness of being The Guy in the Café With His Computer, turned it on.

The connection was slow: the Yahoo! log-on photo of the girl with her tongue sticking out stared at him for long enough that he had time to notice the faint rise of taste buds on her unnaturally long tongue. It was his least favorite of the surely focus-group-tested snapshots that served as guardians of the entrance to Yahoo! mail. (Was there some subliminal message he was supposed to be picking up from the girl's squinty expression, or the antics of the pizza-devouring teenagers who sometimes greeted him? Had this girl known that she would become so anonymously, irrelevantly famous when the picture was taken? These were the tedious questions his brain fussed over every time he checked his email.)

Seventeen new messages. Amid the usual junk and freelance-related back-and-forth, one from Laura. *Hey*, the subject header read. He opened it. *Just wanted you to know I didn't tell Jenny that you were there. Or anyone else for that matter. It was good to see you though. Are you in town for a while? Want to have coffee with a boring and exhausted mother of two? Or a drink?*

It made him smile. Laura was exactly the same. Jenny had become a nightmare, that was clear, and Elise, well, he had glimpsed nothing of Elise, but Laura was just as he always thought of her. Pretty, spacey, sweet. It was almost tempting to say yes.

But it was too dangerous. It had gotten under his skin already, The Situation, as he liked to think of it, and Laura was too close to it. He had been so aggravated, so emotionally raw after his visit to the church yesterday that his ulcer had come back. As well as the old itch of eczema on the joints of his fingers, the insides of his elbows. The electric charge of bitterness that had coursed through him standing at that window had taken him by surprise.

He had gone to the baptism out of a sense of curiosity, a removed, entertained feeling, like it would be some sort of lark. But trying to see through the thick, distorting historical glass of the church window, he had felt the profound exclusion he was, apparently, for the rest of his life to endure. He could not even *see* what the baby looked like. His own genetic material, possibly the only mark he would leave on this earth, and he had to stand on the wrong side of a melting glass window watching him be used in this spiritual charade.

The crowd of people in attendance had been blandly but expensively dressed, and carefully coiffed. He had watched them casting glances over their shoulders the whole time to see who else was there. This was the world his baby would be raised in. An intellectually meager, provincial world of fat-cat Americans with no more sense of their own privilege than a herd of Christmas turkeys saved for the zoo. The anger this raised in him was unexpected. And it scared him. He had enough work already keeping the blackness at bay.

Before he could think twice he deleted Laura's email from his in-box. The waitress cleared the messy remnants of bacon and eggs, the pile of soggy home fries. Outside, pedestrians marched past the window—more teenagers, a few old women, a man in a construction hat. And babies—one snuggled invisibly deep in a carriage, another red-cheeked, smiling, up high in a giant, outdoorsy-looking backpack, another absolutely tiny, just a pair of pajamaed legs sticking out of a carrier, a flash of white knit cap. For what seemed like the first time ever, Neil really looked at them. The future. Suddenly he understood.

4

FOR LAURA, GETTING OUT THE DOOR with the girls every morning was like launching a rocket ship. It took a mad push of activity—gathering snacks and sandals and extra pairs of underpants, special teddy bears and piano music and show-and-tell objects (where, oh, where could that pebble from the beach in Maine last summer be?) and jackets, and of course her own keys and phone and wallet and, if possible, cup of coffee. Laura had never been an organized person and this was exaggerated and exposed by motherhood, which seemed to demand an inordinate degree of foresight and planning.

"My leotard, we forgot it," Genevieve announced this morning, stricken, as Laura turned off of their street.

"I have it—in your bag," Laura said, glancing at her daughter in the rearview mirror. Genevieve was such a worrier: the smallest things were capable of sending her into fits of doubt and antic fretfulness. Laura lived in a constant state of vigilance against loose ends and sad stories, anything to do with death or orphans, and all manner of hurry.

"No, it was on the sofa. I put it there," Genevieve insisted, her features tightening with concern.

"But I got it—I picked it up and put it in your bag," Laura countered, masking her own sudden uncertainty: *had* she left it on the sofa?

"From the sofa?"

"*Yes*, Vievee. From the sofa!"

"*I a Yankee doo doo, a Yankee doodle doo doo*," Miranda sang out from her seat beside Genevieve, oblivious to the crisis. "What Yankee doo doo, Mama? What Yankee doo doo?"

Genevieve looked fretfully out the window.

Had Laura been like this as a child? She felt, somehow, genetically responsible for Genevieve's worrying, although she was not sure why. She was not a big worrier now. But she had no mother to offer information on her childhood self. Annabelle Trillian had died when Laura was nine. And without a mother's narrative to represent, or even *mis*represent, whatever her childhood self had been, it remained elusive—both more present and less clear than other people's.

It was a relief when Laura had both girls, finally, out of the car. This morning was a "work morning," at least theoretically, which meant that she was to go home to her study and use her brain. She was due, according to the schedule drawn up by Charene, her energetic twenty-five-year-old editor at *The Beacon* magazine, to come up with twenty fall books to be vetted for the September issue. Last year she had somehow managed to parlay her long-outdated and never very impressive experience as an assistant editor at a New York publishing house into a job writing a monthly books column for *The Beacon*. It was both something she took pride in as the occupation that separated her from being a full-time stay-at-home mom with all the identity-obscuring predicaments this position was fraught with, and a task she hated.

Laura shut the door behind her and stepped over the obstacle course of discarded jackets, sippy cups, and stuffed animals that Miranda liked to arrange in little rows all over the house, snuggled under T-shirts and pajamas. There was half a banana perched on the front hall table, its peel dangling off the side like a wilted bloom. Laura did not even think of picking up. It was the kind of thing Mac did not understand: how could she walk into a mess like this and not be compelled to at least push its contents into the coat closet out of sight?

Coffee and handbag in hand, she marched straight upstairs to her little study on the third floor. At her desk, she began sorting through the pile of books, looking over jacket copy for the umpteenth time, as if these nuggets of marketing might reveal more upon second inspection. What on earth interested readers of *The Beacon*? She had no better idea now than she'd had when she started.

But there was a more pressing question, which made it difficult to focus: should she call Neil? All afternoon yesterday and all morning today he had been on her mind. Not front and center, but in the back somewhere beneath the ordinary tasks and preoccupations, the mundane business of assembling meals and brushing teeth. Like an alarm clock, ticking, poised to startle her awake.

She had emailed him after the christening and gotten no response. But he might not be online, considering that he was away from home; his card suggested he was still living in LA. So if she really wanted to see him, she should call. Laura hated calling people. The pressure to be witty and the sense she always had of barging in—appearing suddenly in someone's head, preceded only by the invasive trill of the phone ringer—was inhibiting.

But she *did* want to see Neil. Their encounter at the church had left her wound up—charged with that kind of energizing nervousness that came with flirtation. It was surprising: had she been flirting with Neil Banks? Old friend, father of her best friend's baby? No, no. She dismissed the idea. She had just been talking—happy, after so many years, to see him. But in that five minutes, she had tasted the promise of presenting herself anew, dredging up the best and most interesting parts of herself for his appreciation, and it had given her a rush: here she was, Laura Trillian, in all her specificity.

Outside the window of her study a landscaping crew was using electric hedge clippers that sent up an annoying racket. Laura got up to pluck her eyebrows in the bathroom mirror. The face that looked back at her looked bored. Decidedly. So what if calling Neil meant enmeshing herself in a situation about which she would have to lie to Jenny? It was unrealistic of Jenny to have expected Neil to be out of sight, out of mind, forever. If she were not having lunch with Jenny today she might not even think of it as a transgression. And what was life about if not to grab opportunities? To seek out new experience, complication, adventure? These were not tenets Laura usually lived by. But they spoke to her now. Or anyway, they provided cover. There was a stirring of something long dormant in her gut: a kind of thrill that in a certain way served as a warning.

She rifled through her wallet, found Neil's card, and began dialing the number. On the other end there was that plaintive unsatisfying bleat of a cell phone ringing. But then—of course, of course—the click of voice mail.

"Neil," Laura began breathily, suddenly unnecessarily confused, "Hi! It's Laura. I just thought I'd see—I don't know if you got my email since you're not home . . ." She could hear her own voice prattling on, taking on a slightly formal diction and then thanking him (thanking him!) in close, as if he were a professional contact from whom she had just asked a favor or something. How silly. She hung up and shook her head in an effort to leave the whole episode behind. Whatever.

She would go downstairs and make a cup of tea and refocus. Put on her *Beacon* magazine hat for the remainder of the morning, which now seemed, unfortunately, to be all of one hour before she had to leave to meet Jenny.

Jenny liked to meet for lunch at the café of Louis Boston, that odd Old World establishment that reigned magisterially over one end of

Newbury Street. It was near Jenny's office and had valet parking for Laura's benefit. (How glamorous Laura always felt climbing out of her car in the cobbled driveway! This was one place she did not have to don the mantle of shame for driving Mac's SUV.)

Climbing up the steps and into the stone mansion the store was housed in, Laura felt a tick of excitement at being a part of a fashionable—or at least as fashionable as this dowdy city ever got— lunching world. She scanned the narrow, blank-walled room for her friend, who was, of course, already there, at a table in the corner. Jenny was always on time.

"Hiii." Jenny stood to kiss her hello, overriding Laura's babble of excuses. "You look nice—what's this? New?" she plucked at Laura's jacket, which *was* new—short and black and cropped in the current style. *Very*, according to the salesperson who had talked her into it, *Jackie-O*.

"I went ahead and ordered the mussels to start. To share," Jenny said. *"Bueno?"*

For all her bossy, pragmatic ways, Jenny was good company. There was the comfort of shared history (their friendship had spanned almost half their lives now), and there was the refreshing straightforwardness of Jenny's opinions, which were never couched in niceties or apology and were always uniquely her own. Unlike the earthy Cambridge mothers Laura had met in the parks and playgrounds of her neighborhood, Jenny was never judgmental or concerned with political correctness. And unlike the preppy, moneyed wives of Mac's coworkers, Jenny was never cagey, ignorant, or oblique.

Laura sipped her own glass of Pellegrino, and tried not to feel guilty about the fact that she had just, under two hours ago, called Neil without—still—having told her friend she had seen him.

"I don't understand what's gotten into Jeremy," Jenny was saying. "He's so tense all the time and so whiny—if I have to hear one more thing about his knee, it's going to put me over the edge! Really! It's not like he hasn't seen twenty doctors about it already . . ."

"Is it his work, maybe?" Laura offered. "It must be hard—"

"Ugh." Jenny dismissed this with a wave. "Of course it's hard. Launching a software company is hard. But he's good at it. It's *the* thing he's good at. And the stakes aren't even high anymore. I mean, if he fails this time around, it's not like anyone will think he hasn't got what it takes . . . No, no. You know what he asked me yesterday?" she leaned in closer over the steaming plate of mussels.

"What?" Laura asked gratuitously.

"If I had invited Neil." Jenny almost hissed.

"Neil?" Laura felt a bolt of adrenaline shoot through her. "Why?"

"Ugh." Jenny sank back in her chair. "I have no idea."

"Well, did he—I mean, he just thought you would have?"

"He thought he saw him or some ridiculousness," Jenny snorted.

There it was. Laura could feel her face growing hot. She should have told Jenny. Or should—it occurred to her—tell her now.

"I think this nonbiological father thing is catching up to him—I mean, maybe he wasn't really focused on it when it was happening, with his whole IPO happening at the same time," Jenny continued.

"Actually . . ." Laura made herself say, and Jenny stopped.

"What?" She had a quizzical look on her face. Clearly something in Laura's tone must have been off.

"Actually . . ." Laura hesitated, and then found herself veering away. "I think that's very normal. I mean, that he'd have complicated feelings, you know, at something like the baptism."

"Oh, I know. I'm not saying it's abnormal for him to have complicated feelings about it. All that focus on Colin and parenthood . . . It's just he needs to deal with it."

"Mmm." Laura nodded. She had just as good as lied to her friend by not offering up that she had seen Neil. That in fact Jeremy was not crazy. And why? What was compelling her to keep this to herself?

A very tall, nervous waiter delivered their salads with some mumbled, unnecessary information regarding the frisée, which was a replacement, or was being replaced. Laura nodded and smiled, grateful for the distraction. Jenny did not register his presence and kept talking. Jeremy had not even wanted to invite his mother to the baptism. Had acted like she wouldn't be interested, like it wasn't a big deal . . .

Laura shook her head and murmured vaguely. What was becoming clear to her, as Jenny spoke, was that there was something selfish in her own secrecy. It was not about protecting Jenny. She wanted Neil to herself.

". . . I mean, don't you think?" Jenny asked, snapping Laura back into the conversation. Laura had no idea what she was asking.

"Mm." She fretted her brow. "Well, how is he with Colin these days? Does it affect how he feels toward him—or acts toward him, do you think?"

"Oh, you know Jeremy," Jenny said with a sigh, accepting this as a response. "He's always a little preoccupied. But no more than usual. With Colin, I mean. He's sweet with him when he's not too tired to, you know, take him for a walk or whatever. He likes to watch basketball with him."

"That's cute," Laura said.

Jenny shrugged. "Colin's usually just sitting next to him, in his little Bumpo seat. But he seems to like it," she added—was it hopefully?

"Oh." Laura pictured this: wan, abstracted Jeremy on the sofa, and Colin, serious little baby that he was, beside Jeremy in the molded plastic seat Jenny claimed he was so enamored of. It was a little sad, actually. Her own deception about Neil began to fade into the back of her mind.

"Jeremy's just not that big on physical affection," Jenny continued. "When was the last time you saw us snuggling up in public? But he *is* a decent father—God knows, I think about, you know, like, Andy Fesenden, who can't even make it home for his kids' birthday parties—"

"Oh, I know—he's sweet with Colin. I've seen him," Laura offered.

"You have?" Jenny leapt at this. "You think so?"

"Of course." Laura grasped for specifics—had she actually ever seen Jeremy, for instance, holding Colin? "He's so calm."

"He is calm. That's true. I probably shouldn't be so hard on him. I know it's difficult. Logically. I mean, I'm sure it is for anyone . . ."

Underneath this, there was an unusual agitation in Jenny's voice. Laura knew her friend well enough to hear this. It was inevitable, wasn't it? She had made an odd choice marrying Jeremy. Laura and Elise had pondered it many times. Maybe it was Jenny's strong personality—she needed someone as pliant, as full of negative space, as Jeremy was. Or had this been obscured during their courtship, which had occurred at the pinnacle of Jeremy's success as an entrepreneur?

"But what about you?" Jenny turned the subject abruptly. "How are the girls?"

"Oh, fine—the usual . . ." Dutifully, Laura recounted a few cute stories, and some complaints about Genevieve's sleeping, which was infamously disordered. As she talked and picked over her salad (was this really what fava beans were? she had ordered in a state of distraction) she felt a growing unease. There was something not right about the way Jeremy seemed these days. Jenny and Jeremy's marriage, which had always been enigmatic, seemed suddenly and contagiously grim. And in the middle of this, sweet little Colin—so small, so earnest, and so fragile. There was something about him— or really about babies in general—that filled Laura with a sort of teary enthusiasm. That gave her a longing to protect, coupled with the knowledge that at some point, inevitably, protection would fail. Little Colin would have to enter the wide world of false starts and indecipherable conclusions, mysterious causes and effects. So would her girls, those two little bundles of nerves and energy, highly specific collections of experience and genes.

"She'll be okay," Jenny said, making a worried, sympathetic face. "All kids have their issues." And Laura realized her eyes had welled up.

"I know," she said, laughing and wiping her eye with the back of her hand. "I don't know why I'm crying."

And for a moment they were both quiet against the din of chatter and clinking cutlery that echoed through the high-ceilinged café.

5

NEIL LISTENED TO LAURA'S MESSAGE with a feeling of resignation. He would have to call her. She seemed, for whatever reason, to really want to see him.

He slid the phone back into his pocket. He was at ZGames getting his orientation tour and network passes, meeting his "team." Corporate America had finally sucked him in. The door to the development offices opened and Joe, the painfully shy and breasty young man who had just given Neil the studio tour, reappeared.

"They're ready to see you, sir," Joe mumbled, wiping the tiny bangs of his haircut back with his forearm. He looked positively subterranean—like a chubby, earth-grubbing mole, pale from lack of exposure, and faintly damp.

"Not this 'sir' business again," Neil chided, gathering up his jacket.

"Sorry, sorry—I know, I'm just—" the poor boy fumbled, shaking his head.

"That's all right." Neil fell into step beside him. "They have my caviar blinis waiting?"

Joe swiveled his head around, alarmed. "I don't know—did you—"

"No, no—just joking, Joe." Neil shook his head. The kid's nervousness was beginning to rub off on him. Here he was making stupid jokes. But you just wanted to do something, anything, to shatter the earnestness—the reverence this kid had for the whole enterprise here. Treating Neil as if he were Nelson Mandela or something, talking about the level designers, programmers, sound editors, and the like as if they were involved in something world-changing—a brilliant new art form or a format for brokering peace. Not an elaborate form of escapism with a low overhead. This was why Neil hated the game industry, and hated himself for proving to be just as susceptible as ignorant idiots like Joe to the cloying, disorienting madness of the escape it produced.

He followed Joe back through the pretentiously hidden door to the cube zone—a hive-like terrain of institutional carpeting and giant, flashing, humming flat-screen monitors, walls decorated with promotional posters for games like *Time Quest*, *Fangun*, and *Raven's Alley*, arguably among the most highbrow outputs of the industry: action-adventure titles with dark, apocalyptic storylines and obscure meta-references to scientific precepts, biblical prophecies, and, of course, Games of Yore. These were technically splendid productions, best loved by scornful, above-the-riffraff gamers like himself, which made them all the more despicable in Neil's mind. Outside, the world was happening: plants were growing, birds were singing, people were killing each other and being killed. Governments were blundering and lying and leading or misleading people into spirals of material consumption, waste, war, and even genocide. And people themselves were stumbling on despite insurmountable obstacles, scraping together bowls of rice to feed whole families, living in squalor, but even so, caring for their wounded, their young, their infirm . . . And here—here young men sat around feeling smug about understanding level seven of *Maelstrom*.

He suppressed this chain of thought as he entered the conference room behind his faithful tour guide, who practically quivered with the excitement of coming face to face with Rod Emerus, founder and president of ZGames, owner of two Lamborghinis and an actual, "antique" (could such a tasteful, delicate word really apply?) iron maiden.

The man was bald and unashamed, apparently, having left a ring of healthy blondish hair, clownlike, around his pate. He had on a pair of black jeans, pale sneakers, and a dark blue button-down shirt.

"Banks," Emerus said, ignoring Joe completely. "Good to finally meet you."

He had a crisp, slightly nasal voice, and did not rise.

"Likewise." Neil extended his hand and was shocked to find it left hanging, like something obscene—body part that it was—between them.

Emerus waved it away, rifling through the documents in front of him. "I don't shake," he said, without looking at Neil. "Germs."

"Ah." Neil thrust the offending hand back into his pocket and tried not to notice the conspiratorial, whoa-this-guy-is-crazy look Joe was casting in his direction.

"So you're a hotshot game reviewer, but you've never shipped a game before," Emerus said, looking, apparently, over Neil's résumé.

"Nope." Neil decided to take a curt approach to the meeting. Fight fire with fire.

"Well, Johnson really talked you up. Sit down, sit down." Emerus gestured irritably at one of the expensive Aeron chairs at the glass-topped table. "Neil Banks, Steven Closter." He nodded his head between Neil and the lanky, curly-haired young man seated beside him whose presence Neil had not fully absorbed. "Steven is our lead designer. You'll be working closely with him here."

Briefly, the two men made eye contact—a kind of tacit assessment of each other. Steven Closter was wearing one of those decidedly hip black-framed pairs of glasses and—of course—a vintage heavy metal T-shirt that hung thinly off his jutting collarbones.

"Steven has experience with 3ds Max and MotionBuilder and he's a great level designer. But he's got no imagination for storyline. Dragons and riders of the apocalypse and commandos, blah, blah, blah. Nothing new. That's where you come in."

Steven wore an awkward, self-deprecating smile plastered acidly across his face through the disparagement.

"I'm thinking *big* for Pro II," Emerus continued. "And *new*. I don't want a solid return on this. I want another breakaway. Pick up where we left off, but then take it to a whole new place—a new world. I want a fresh look, fresh characters, fresh premise— connected, but new. That's why I'm taking the chance on you—no baggage. No previous games to echo. I want to set a whole new paradigm for sequels. It's a challenge." He looked at Neil here for the first time. "But it's an opportunity. Could put your name in the books forever."

Neil tried not to let the self-loathing he felt creep up through his mask of impassivity.

"Joe?" Emerus said, acknowledging his devotee for the first time. "You're all done here."

Joe reddened and murmured some sort of thanks or apology and scrambled out the door.

"I've read your reviews and I'm familiar with your column, of course. And I know you've got a critical mind. High standards. But my question is: Are you up to this? Creation?" Emerus looked at Neil.

The word jarred him with all its primordial echoes.

"Yes," Neil said, quashing this.

"All right, then." Emerus rose. "I'll leave you two to get to know each other."

And with that Rod Emerus made his exit, leaving a sort of

schoolboys-in-detention feeling in his wake. So. This was what it had come to. Neil Banks in charge of creating a game company home run. He took a breath and pulled his chair closer to the table, tamping down the panic, scattering the crows.

Hold your nose, he told himself. *Close your eyes. Dive in.*

He returned Laura's call from the parking lot, eager suddenly for some reminder of his actual life. And Laura was that: a reminder, in fact, of the *best* part of his life. His college years had held such promise and potential. They were so *fresh* and *new*, in Rod Emerus's terms, untouched by the blight of failure and disappointment, of self-doubt and the general dinge-ing of the world.

"Hello?" Laura sounded a little out of breath when she picked up.

"Laura. It's Neil."

"Oh!" she exclaimed in what sounded like great surprise, and for a moment he wondered if he was confused. If maybe she hadn't ever called.

"Am I getting you at a bad time? You sound—"

"No, no. It's fine. I'm just driving. I just had lunch with Jenny, actually."

"Oh." A wave of regret washed over Neil. He should not have called.

"Shit!" There was the sound of traffic in the background. "I don't know why I said that. I don't mean to stress you out. I just—ugh. Just a funny coincidence, I guess," she finished lamely.

"Yeah." Neil did not try to make it easier for her.

He stared out the windshield at the row of precisely placed shrubs on the traffic island in front of him. The anonymity of their proportions, of the cedar chips below them. He could be anywhere.

"Neeeeeil." Laura's voice on the other end of the line was wheedling, familiar. "Please don't get freaked out. How long are you here for?"

"A year," he said flatly.

"What?"

"A year," he repeated. "I'm working."

"Here? Where?"

"Boxborough. At a game company. It's a long story."

"Boxborough!" Laura exclaimed, as if that, of all things, were the most outlandish.

A posse of sparrows skittered noisily by—sparrows, the same plain, co-opted breed of nature as the bushes.

"Neil?" Laura said. "Are you there?"

"Yup."

"Well, do you want to have coffee sometime? Or a drink? Or you could come over for dinner, of course, but the kids can be such a handful . . ." She let her voice trail off.

"Sure," he found himself saying. "I could use a drink."

Back in Johnson's apartment, Neil was greeted by the relieving sight of packed bags. There was a note on the floor scrawled in Kirstin's girly handwriting, which read: *Out to the movies, back for dinner. We're leaving tomorrow—whoo hoo! Bet you can't wait.* Followed by a smiley face.

He poured himself a glass of water from the dubiously sanitary Brita pitcher and held it up to the light as if the toxins (what exactly was he looking for anyway? lead? bacteria? mold?) would be visible. So many years of living in California had made him fussy—full of troubling, useless information about pollutants in the environment and the assault they waged daily against the human body, the toll they took on his blood, his cells, his fragile, gradually decomposing DNA. The water looked murky. He took a big tepid swig.

Then, delighting in the unexpected boon of having the place to himself, he sat down at the kitchen table with his computer, fully intending to oblige Steven Closter and check out *Faunacy*, a game they were supposedly going to "wet their pants" competing with.

But the conversation with Laura had affected him. It confirmed why he had known, to begin with, that it would be better not to be in touch. It made him think about the baby. About *his* baby. The baby he had signed away all rights to see or know or influence in any way. Starting with his name—Colin. The name of a pale, invalidish, dandy. What was it—Irish? or Scottish? Neither Jenny nor Jeremy was either, which made it pretentious, to boot. Not a name he would ever bestow on his son. *His* son. He had a son out there in the world. *In what sense of the word?* the therapist he had seen in LA had asked when he mentioned it (only *mentioned*, because it had not been an issue, was certainly not what he was seeing the therapist about). A *"son" is a societal construct, isn't it?* she had pressed. *A role to play in a family unit.* Neil had looked at her with disdain. No. The baby was a son in the one way that was unambiguous.

Of course, this was not how he had thought of it beforehand, when Jenny came to him. What had he thought? It was a good question. He hadn't been thinking. That was the kindest answer he could come up with. His head had been shoved up his ass.

Jenny had appeared in LA two years ago with her proposal. He had not seen her since, God knows, her wedding three years before or so. How had she found him? She had talked to someone who had talked to someone who had seen Tom Frick . . . And so Neil's elaborate obfuscation of his own existence had proved, with no more than a few simple conversations, to unravel.

She had shown up with no warning. She knew him well enough to know that lead time would be to her disadvantage. And so one day, emerging from his basement studio (that little cave of a room set into the hill below Jane's house), Neil had come across her, sitting outside his front door in the shade of her chauffeured car.

"Aha!" she'd said, springing from the backseat with her familiar sure-footed athletic bounce. "I had a feeling if I waited you'd appear."

He was taken aback—no, alarmed. There was Jenny Callahan in front of his home. His eyes blinked in the bright sunlight and he was aware of having not yet brushed his teeth or changed out of the T-shirt he had slept in. The greasy, lived-in smell of it rose off him in the heat.

"What've you been doing?" she asked, stepping forward to kiss him. "No one's seen you for ages."

"Maybe that's on purpose." His own voice sounded sullen and paranoid in his ears. Her presence raised something like panic in him. She did not belong here. She did not belong in this new reality of his.

"I know!" She boxed his arm lightly. "But you can't hide from me."

And, standing there with the sun blazing off the whitewashed stucco, and with those unshy California flowers in his yard offering themselves up to it, garish and bold, he had felt utterly, unusually, naked—a delicate shade-growing fauna, shutting itself away in the face of Jenny's brilliance.

Later, sitting in the cool, wood-paneled interior of Nelson's, a salad parlor frequented by the combination of hipsters and entertainment industry lackeys that made up Neil's neighborhood, he had begun to adjust to her presence. Here she was: Jenny Callahan, ex-girlfriend, college athlete, rising corporate superstar. How incredible that he had ever dated her—that he had been in love with her! How incredible that they had ever even been friends. She was wearing a suit. Lemon-yellow and short enough to show off her legs. Around her neck she had an expensive-looking lavender scarf. The effect was very LA. She had always been a chameleon. It was one of her many skills.

They ate giant vegetable salads full of sprouts and shredded carrots and tahini, which was clearly not Jenny's kind of food. She picked through hers like a surgeon, selecting only the least exotic ingredients and mainlining saccharine-sweetened iced tea. Mostly she talked and he listened. This was what she did now, this was where she and Jeremy lived, this was who they saw, this was the deal. Neil honestly had not seen the request coming. He had sat and listened with the finely tuned attention of suspense. Was she asking him to be godfather to her unborn (unconceived?) child? This was the closest he got, and it seemed so outlandish and unreasonable—weirdly more so than her actual request when it came—that he discounted it. Maybe it was the element of surprise that had been so effective.

"And you want me . . . ?" He had left the question gaping, like his jaw, and stared at her.

"Unless you've completely lost your marbles or something."

He could see, for the first time, that Jenny was nervous. The slight rapidity of her breath, the picked-through salad, the intensity of her expression. And he began to laugh.

"You're not supposed to laugh, Neil." Jenny put down her fork and leaned forward, elbows on the table. "You *know* I've always thought you were brilliant."

"Ha!" Neil threw his head back. "That's a good one."

"Would I be sitting here if I didn't?"

"You're serious."

Jenny nodded her head.

Behind them a raggedy waif who looked suspiciously like an Olsen twin was being ushered to a table at the back, creating one of those feathery LA stirs.

"Of course, there are tests you'd have to go through, forms to fill out—family history and all that, and then you freeze the sperm six months—I'd want to do this entirely by the book of the clinic I'm working with—but if it checks out—yes. Yes, I am serious."

Neil put his own fork down. "Wow."

He drank down the rest of his water all at once.

"I don't want to have kids," he said finally.

"I know. You always said that."

Behind them, the restaurant's signature talking parrot began squawking. *"Roast beef, corned beef, ham and swiss on rye."*

"Jesus." Jenny looked up at the bird in its giant dog crate of a cage and gave it a withering frown. She turned back to Neil. "That's why I thought you might do it. I'm not asking you to be a father. Jeremy is going to be this kid's father. One hundred percent. This would be between us exclusively. In fact, I don't want you to do it unless you're willing to sign away all responsibilities and rights."

"Whoa—I'm not even on board yet, Jen—"

"I know. I'm just laying it out to you, all right? I'm just giving you the info so you can think about it. Talk about it. Whatever. There are counselors at the clinic . . ." she waved her hand to indicate . . . what? That the emotions these people were trained to discuss were beyond the purview of their conversation? "What I want is total anonymity on your part. Of course, Jeremy and I know who you are, but I wouldn't want the child to know. Jeremy would adopt the baby. We wouldn't tell him—or her—that there was anything at all unusual about the way he came to be. Just the norm—mother, father, baby. No siblings. No baggage about biological parents and adopted parents or donor parents or all that bullshit. Clean. Simple. You get the picture." She was slightly breathless at the end of this.

"Look . . ." she leaned forward. "I know it's a lot to ask. But I also know you don't want kids, Neil. And if you think about what that means—I mean, to *really* not have offspring, to dead-end your own genetic material . . ." She shrugged. "You aren't a romantic. You are the most clear-eyed person I know. And this is a clear-eyed thing I'm asking you. There's nothing warm and fuzzy about it. Nothing ambiguous."

She sat back, seeming to have exhausted herself. "Don't give me an answer now."

And it was sitting there watching her, Jenny Callahan, agitated and wanting something—*needing* something—from him, that began to plant the seed of his consent. Here was this woman whom he had once loved, and whom he had, in a way, come to despise. A woman who had embraced the lowest common denominator of the American dream—the pursuit of wealth, at the cost of any more complex ambitions. When Neil had dated her, she had wanted to be a lawyer at one of those nonprofits that advocated for women. She had been passionate about creating opportunities and broadening the horizons of children growing up in the kind of forgotten, working-class nowheresville she and Neil had. Had that all been a pose—a stepping-stone to achieving financial success? An outcropping of the unapologetic pragmatism he both hated and envied? Whatever the case, here she was, *wanting* something from him. The woman who had broken up with him because he wasn't good enough, wasn't headed for success enough, was sitting here because, it turned out, at heart she *still* believed in the promise and potential that had once defined Neil, that had once made greatness, or its foreshadowing, a part of who he was. It was a shock—and a thrill—to recognize this. Of course, the *yes* wasn't arrived at then and there, but he could trace the beginning of it to this moment, if he was honest with himself. He could trace it to this thread of naked egotism.

But the thing was, what did he think of while he whacked off in the little air-freshened room full of pointedly new porno magazines and a heavily curtained window? Not the child. Of course. Not the favor he was doing or the life he was bestowing. (Who could think of that and still "produce"?) Not of Jane, or the sexy waitress at Nelson's whom he'd had an escalating flirtation with. Not the rubbery bodies on the pages before him. He thought of Jenny. Not lovingly or longingly. He thought of fucking her. Hard. Of driving himself into her taut, Stairmastered body—splitting open her ambitious, eerily composed, successful self, and, like a Trojan horse, injecting the seeds of disorder into her world. It was a violent, intense fantasy, and the venom of it left him shaken. Had this always been there, between them? Walking out of the sterile clinic, he was still reverberating with shock. Was this something terrible he had done? It was not exactly premonition, but a kind of fear that came over him.

And then he had "forgotten." The sample of sperm he had provided had been split into vials by some masked and white-gloved worker, spun and separated, and shipped off to the cryobank's frozen chambers, where the sperm would wait the requisite time to be tested and declared HIV-free. If it took, the fertility clinic would send him a notification; this was the one term he had insisted on. Otherwise he had signed all rights away, including the right to make himself known to the child. This, the grave, damp-faced clinic lawyer had explained, was unusual. There was no binding legal precedent. He had raised his eyebrows significantly, inviting Neil to press further, but Neil had no interest. He understood what Jenny wanted. And at the time he wanted nothing more than to oblige. The clinic itself was clearly skeptical that it would come to anything, with only one sample.

The months passed and Neil immersed himself in the feverish, disorienting netherworld of *Underdog*, an eerily addictive first-person shooter he was reviewing for GameQuarter, and, alternately, into the research project that was his real passion: writing a biography of Albert Sorenson Jones, a mid-nineteenth century explorer of Africa whom Neil had discovered in the course of his now-abandoned dissertation work. All thoughts of those small vials of sperm disappeared under the consuming obsessions of his everyday life.

Until suddenly, improbably enough—a thin envelope from the Pacific Fertility Center arrived, bearing tidings that a child of his had been born into the world.

Part Two

1

BACKING HER OLD VOLVO into a litter-strewn space in front of her house, Elise Farber felt the sweet rush of relief and anticipation that homecoming evoked in her—this was joy, wasn't it? The delight in burrowing back into this cozy little hole in the universe that was truly her own. She did not take this for granted. It was a rare and lucky thing. She knew this not just theoretically, but absolutely from her life before Chrissy, which in comparison had been lived on a flat and desolate stretch of firmament, with no cracks, no openings to find foothold. Here, in the cozy three-bedroom house on Cottage Street that she and Chrissy had bought four years ago, she had learned what it meant to have a haven—not just a place of respite but a place of restoration. She loved coming home.

As soon as she opened the door, the cat, Calliope, pressed out past her legs and James, the bolder of her two boys, cackled with delight, throwing his chubby arms up in the air.

"Have you been chasing Calli again?" Elise asked, bending down and scooping him up. He laughed harder and kicked his small legs against her middle—his new mobility was as urgent and addictive as a drug. He could not be contained. She set him back down.

From the kitchen came the reassuring, reasonable sound of Diane Rehm on NPR, and the rich smell of Chrissy's signature braised pork with prunes.

"Hi!" Chrissy called, clattering something on the stove. "Did you pick up the wine?"

The wine? A cloud moved over Elise. She had forgotten. Not just the wine, but the reason she was supposed to get it. Claire Markowitz and her child, the fellow sibling of Donor #176, were coming over for dinner.

"I'll go get it right now, I'm sorry—"

"No, no. It's fine. I found some, actually—in the basement."

Elise slipped off her shoes and rounded the corner into the kitchen, where Chrissy stood poised over a steaming Dutch oven. She wore an apron over her khakis and polo shirt, and her thick dark blond hair was loose around her shoulders. Everything about Chrissy was round—her face, her breasts, her belly—even her elbows managed somehow to be round rather than angular: it was one of the things Elise loved. Her lack of sharpness. She was the cozy, comfortable mother Elise had never had, in the tedious, dampening language of talk therapy. Elise could see this, but it was not all.

She kissed Chrissy's hot ear, trying to tamp down the sense of dismay rising in her. She had promised to put a good face on for the night.

Chrissy had discovered Claire Markowitz on the Internet—she was a woman who had been inseminated with the sperm of the same man Chrissy had. Which made her son the half-sibling of Nigel and James, one of the eleven(!) children sired by the apparently prolific—and robust—outputs of this half-Jewish, half-Colombian donor with the almost perfect verbal SAT score that Elise and Chrissy had spent so long deciding on. Elise was not particularly curious about Claire Markowitz, or her son, or any of the other families Chrissy's research had turned up. In fact, she was instinctively repulsed by the whole idea of the Donor Sibling Registry. She found its name repugnant: as if the children of sperm donors were animals to be registered and assigned numbers. But Chrissy had been determined to join, and to ferret out information from it, and then to email this woman, Claire Markowitz, who apparently lived not more than ten miles away, in Lexington. To what end? Elise had teased her. Tonight, apparently, was the answer.

"Where's Nigel?" Elise asked, noticing him as she said it. He was sitting on the floor behind the counter amid a florid pool of toys, happily chewing the tail of a stuffed dog. Unlike his brother, he had not yet begun to toddle around.

"Hi, bear," she said, squatting down beside him and sinking her face into his silky, baby-smelling hair, an act that he rewarded with one of his big, delighted smiles. Sweet Nigel, Elise felt a swell of appreciation for him. More than James, Nigel seemed to accept Elise as a close second, if not equal, to Chrissy. He was a little slower and less independent than his brother, and from the start more of his care had been left to Elise. She had cuddled him in their queen-sized bed, and fed him bottles, because unlike his brother, he did not unequivocally reject anything but his mother's breast. But this was not to say he didn't prefer the comfort of his mother's milk, his mother's smell, and touch, and voice—all the innate biological markers that attached him to Chrissy, and not Elise.

"All right," Elise said, rising and resigning herself to the night, "I'll go get changed. Do you need the table set?"

"That would be great," Chrissy said, with a look of appreciation and—was it apology?—in her eyes.

As she was pulling on her sweater upstairs, the phone rang.

"Colin had a fever," Jenny said into Elise's ear, almost before she had said hello. "That's why he was such a mess at the christening. I hope everyone doesn't just think he's a whiny, fussy baby."

"Of course not," Elise said. "Poor little guy." She glanced at her watch—she could not afford to get sucked into a call with Jenny right now.

"You know he's not usually like that," Jenny said.

"I know. But he wasn't being so—"

"Ugh. He was awful!"

"He wasn't. But what would it even matter if he was? Babies get fussy," Elise said impatiently.

"I know, but he doesn't. Usually."

"I know, but Jen? I can't—"

"I just have to find a way to let all those church-board bitches know what a prince he really is," Jenny interrupted.

Elise laughed, although she knew that in fact Jenny was half serious.

"I can't talk right now—we have guests coming." As soon as she said it she realized she didn't want to tell Jenny about Claire Markowitz. And with this realization came a clutch of uneasiness. Why didn't she want to tell Jenny? Why did the fact of this woman make her feel in some odd way ashamed?

"Oh? Who's coming?"

Elise hesitated. "No one," she said briskly. "Just some woman Chrissy knows. Can I call you tomorrow?"

"Of course!" Jenny said brightly. "Just spread the word."

"The word?" Elise repeated blankly.

"About Colin!"

Despite herself, Elise smiled. "You are completely crazy, you know."

Jenny gave a gleeful hoot of laughter. "Not crazy—careful."

When Elise answered the door, the woman standing on the steps was older and more bohemian than she had imagined her to be. She had long, frizzy hair loose around her shoulders and a sort of caftanish jacket of nondescript ethnicity. Her eyes were big and slightly buggy, but sorrowful.

But Elise didn't take any of this in at first. Her eyes went straight to the child she was holding. Who had the same dark hair, dark eyes, and funny little adult nose as James and Nigel.

"Welcome," Elise said, extending her hand in the slightly jocular way she tended to use when she was uncomfortable.

"Thank you." The woman smiled nervously. "You must be Chrissy."

"Elise," she corrected, as Nigel crawled around the corner and grinned up at their visitors happily.

"Wow!" the woman exclaimed, staring at him. "This is totally—Wow."

Elise scooped Nigel up, tongue-tied. And for a moment there was nothing but the sound of a car alarm beeping on the street.

"Justin—" Claire looked to her son, who was staring from Elise to Nigel impassively, "this is . . . is it Nigel or James?"

"Nigel," Elise said, blowing on his chubby belly to make him squeal.

"Nigel," Claire Markowitz repeated. "Amazing." And she bent to deposit her son on the ground.

"No, no, no! I don't want to get down!" the boy shrieked in a surprisingly loud and unpleasant voice. He was how old—three and a half? Four? This was an age Elise knew nothing about. It looked intimidating.

Chrissy bustled out from the kitchen wiping her hands on her apron. She looked flushed and rosy with excitement, especially pretty. Watching her, Elise felt a kind of pride—Chrissy was so appealing! And so natural! Immediately she made the boy feel comfortable, made him smile and slide down off his mother's hip and allow himself to be led into the kitchen holding Chrissy's hand. But there was something else Elise felt too: a stab of jealousy. Chrissy shared something with this woman—a total stranger—that she and Elise did not. They had borne the same man's children, for almost nine months they had lived with this same stranger's multiplying DNA.

"Oh, it smells delicious!" Claire was exclaiming. "Are you a good cook? I can't do anything in the kitchen. Justin and I just live on Whole Foods prepared stuff, don't we?" She smiled manically at Justin, who was careening a toy train around the playroom, much to the twins' wide-eyed amazement.

"It's actually pretty good, though," she continued defensively. "I mean, it's not full of preservatives or anything—it's all good organic ingredients."

"Oh, we love Whole Foods," Chrissy offered supportively.

"It's really important that Justin get a lot of fresh fruits and vegetables for his health, you know—and we have to stay away from wheat because of his allergies. I don't know how we'd do that without Whole Foods. What did people used to do?"

She was a skittish woman—her whole body emanated an anxious unsureness. But Chrissy, who usually had little tolerance for this sort of person, did not seem at all bothered. She shook her head soothingly and offered Claire wine and helped direct Justin to the bathroom. Elise herself felt utterly tongue-tied.

"So I've been telling Justin that he and Nigel and James all have the same daddy, right?" Claire chirped in a jarringly loud voice, when Justin emerged from the potty. "Wait—did you wash your hands? Always make sure you wash your hands after wee wee. Can you reach the sink?" She hustled her son back into the bathroom. "Oh, good—there's a stool, look, just the right size for you."

Chrissy looked over at Elise and smiled. The smile was content, not conspiratorial. She was in a magnanimous mood. Elise tried to absorb some of her partner's evenness rather than be irritated by it. She tried, genuinely, not to care that Claire Markowitz had just shouted something about the boys all having "the same 'daddy.'"

"What sort of work do you do?" Elise asked when Claire and Justin emerged from the bathroom. This was both to wrest the subject away and to break her own silence before it gathered enough steam to render her mute, something that had been known to happen.

"Oh, I work at the Stadner Institute," Claire sniffed, apparently disappointed by this switch of topics. "I'm the research program director."

"Ah." Elise nodded, waiting for more, but apparently this was to be it.

There was a little squeal as Justin snatched a toy from James.

"And you're a scientist?" Claire continued. "Is that right? Sorry, do you mind . . . ?" she slid the bottle of wine toward herself and refilled her glass.

"Mm-hm." Elise nodded, the gloomy prospect of explanation in front of her. She was a biochemist who worked in a transgenics lab. And she was not one of those scientists who loved making their work come alive for the layperson. She did not revel in breaking it down into simple, elegant metaphors and terms. What she did was transfer genes from one species into another to achieve specific outcomes: currently she was transferring genes from humans to goats. The bald, shocking explanation of it either made people recoil in horror, or light up with a million questions, all new and fascinating to them, but not to her.

But Claire Markowitz was not, actually, remotely interested. "Do the boys go to day care? Or have a sitter?" She asked, sipping her newly refilled wine glass.

"They're home with me," Chrissy said, sliding the pork out of the oven.

"Oh, how wonderful that you have the time for that . . . I wish there was some way for me to work less—I mean, not that I don't love my job . . ." Claire burbled on.

The idea that they would have to spend another at-least two hours with this woman seemed suddenly oppressive. Elise took a sip of her own wine and sat down on the floor beside James.

There were a few things she remembered about Claire Markowitz from the research Chrissy had acquired Googling her. She had graduated from Sarah Lawrence College in 1984 and from the UMass School of Social Work fifteen years later. She was the owner of a basset hound, who apparently ate some sort of very fancy raw-meat dog food that was delivered—this was how the information had cropped up online—weekly. She also had some hypochondriachal-sounding syndrome called Raynaud's phenomenon and was a contributor to the *Circulatory Disorders Journal*, although, Chrissy had reported cheerily, her contributions to it dated back to before the time she would have conceived Justin. *You found all that out online?* Elise had asked Chrissy, incredulous. Elise was apparently living in the Stone Age of Internet use.

Watching Chrissy nodding along to Claire's monologue, murmuring appropriate queries and assents, Elise felt distance opening up between them. The fascination with Claire and the donor siblings was unlike anything that had arisen between them before. She *understood* Chrissy. And Chrissy understood her. It was one of the great beauties of their life together, this rare and sustaining feeling of being *known*.

But she did not understand this. She did not *know* what it felt like to bear Donor #176's children. She did not know, even, what it felt like to be a mother. Chrissy rejected this. *Of course you do*, she said. *You and I are both Nigel and James's mother.* But this was false, and Chrissy knew it. Didn't her desire to connect with Claire and her son prove this?

Dinner was chaotic. Justin did not like pork. He did not like prunes. He did not like rice, or broccoli, or cheese, or the kind of yogurt "with pictures on it" that Nigel and James would slurp up by the gallon if given half a chance. And Claire was neither strict with him nor go-with-the-flow about his dinner: yes, maybe a few chicken nuggets would do the trick (they didn't), or maybe some of that lentil soup Chrissy offered to defrost (ditto), or, sure, if it wasn't too much trouble, steaming some carrots and edamame might be a good idea. Nigel and James, who were voracious eaters, looked on with wonder and pounced on Justin's rejected foods whenever they could reach them. Meanwhile, it was getting late. Elise had to be up at five-thirty tomorrow morning to get to work before the lab meeting. And the boys would be loopy with exhaustion all day if they didn't get to bed soon.

But Claire wanted to talk about the long and winding path that had led her to the sperm bank (an early, unhappy marriage, a slew of loser boyfriends, a sojourn in the Peace Corps in Guatemala), and the "almost spiritual" event that had ultimately deposited her there. (She had been looking through her baby pictures with her mother . . .) She asked almost nothing of Elise and Chrissy, assuming, perhaps rightly, that the decision for them had been more obvious.

Justin had retired from the table and the wasteland of untasted edibles at his place, and sat on the floor dismantling the twisty-limbed baby doll Chrissy had bought for the boys as a nod toward gender neutrality. It was not a popular toy. But all the same Elise felt protective of it.

"Oops," she said, picking its head and trunk up and leaving Justin brandishing one leg. "I think that dolly might need her legs." It was the first thing she had uttered in some time and the sound of her voice seemed to startle them all.

"Justin!" Claire exclaimed. "That's not a nice thing to do to that doll!"

Nigel began to cry.

"Oh, no! I'm so sorry—I've talked your ear off. We have to let these poor people get to bed," she said, addressing the pouting Justin, toward whom Elise was developing a pronounced dislike.

And they began the slow process of departure—jackets and cell phone and handbag found, dump truck "borrowed," kisses and hugs bestowed. Claire Markowitz seemed to have penetrated deep into the marrow of the house.

"Okay," she called over her shoulder, as she scurried down the sidewalk after Nigel. "I'll divide up the list and email you three of them. Divide and conquer, right? Bye-bye."

Elise and Chrissy and the boys waved from the doorstep.

"The list?" Elise asked, raising her eyebrows.

"Oh, that." Chrissy pushed her hair behind her ear and immediately Elise knew the list was going to be something she wouldn't like. Something Chrissy *knew* she wouldn't like.

"We just thought maybe we'd get in touch with the others and see if they were interested in setting up some sort of email connection—you know, like a list serve." Chrissy tossed this off as she was heading up the stairs with Nigel, her back to Elise.

And standing there, at that moment, looking after Chrissy's solid form ascending the stairs, Elise felt biology—her love, her life's work—rise up between them like a transparent but impenetrable scrim.

2

JEREMY WAS DRIVING JENNY CRAZY. The stomach flu had turned into an endless migraine and an irritating dry cough. And his complaints were incessant. Or actually, not so much his actual complaints, but the hangdog look he wore around the house and the general torpor with which he approached everything from dinner at the Hendersons' to a trip to the cabinet store. *Buck up*, she wanted to say. She wanted, physically, to shake him, almost. This was not the Jeremy who had started up a mobile phone software company from the bedroom of his first postcollege apartment and sold it for twenty million dollars. This was not the Jeremy with whom she had biked across New Zealand and hiked up Machu Picchu.

The new Jeremy, for the first time in his life, did not seem ambitious or driven. His start-up had seed funding from a group of platinum investors, a great board, and a proven technical team. But Jeremy was home by seven every night. He talked about "waiting and seeing" when she asked how the beta installations were going. He wasn't jumping out of his skin in suspense. He wasn't even getting up early to check the user blogs.

This morning, for instance, when she came back upstairs from her half hour of early morning email he was still in bed.

"Jeremy," Jenny said sharply from the doorway. "Jeremy Markingham." This was his middle name and Jenny liked to use it in jest. This morning she was not joking, though. It just gave her a few more syllables with which to wake him from his trance.

He stirred under the covers and groaned.

"It's six forty-five," Jenny said.

"You go ahead," he mumbled.

Jenny put her glass of water down on the dresser. "What do you mean? You're not going to be able to do Sugarloaf if you don't step it up."

"I don't think I'm going to run it this year."

Jenny stared at her husband's form under the sheets incredulously.

"Since when?"

They were both committed runners. Every year since they had first met they had run the Sugarloaf Marathon together. Every year they trained for the preceding three months together. Running had been, in fact, a major part of their courtship, their honeymoon, their first years of marriage.

"I'm going to take the year off." Jeremy's voice was muffled and his narrow face was turned toward the wall. All she could see was the mess of pale blond hair, soft and straight as a doll's—completely wasted on a straight man, she liked to joke—on the gray satin pillow.

"That's it?" Jenny asked. "You've decided?"

"Mmmff," Jeremy said into the pillow.

"Well," Jenny said coldly, stripping off her nightgown and pulling on her jogging bra. "Thanks for telling me."

"I *am* telling you," Jeremy said, rolling onto his back to look at her. He shaded his eyes from the overhead light.

Jenny yanked on her running shorts.

"I don't feel up to it, Jen."

"That's because you're out of the habit." She glared at him.

Jeremy held her gaze inscrutably.

"I just don't get it," she said.

Jeremy sighed. "I'm sorry, Jen—I didn't know you'd mind."

The unwittingness of this infuriated Jenny. She could run the marathon alone, that was not the problem. It was the loss of the activity—*their* activity (any half-respectable relationship book or advice columnist would tell you couples needed an activity they shared, wouldn't they?) that bothered her. And this whole thing— this new malaise that had settled over Jeremy—was becoming a real problem. It was all about Colin, she was sure. Jeremy had seen none of the fertility center counselors, and read none of the infertility literature she had encouraged him to. He had done nothing to deal with the feelings that she was sure were now rising up in him, poisoning his well-being and his energy.

Jenny had been convinced he would refuse to let her use Neil's sperm, but when she girded herself to bring up the idea—the conviction, really, because as soon as she had thought of it she had known it was right—Jeremy had listened quietly, asked a few questions, and agreed. They had been in the restaurant at the top of the Hancock Building, looking out over the spread of glittering land and smooth black water that was Boston at night, and Jenny had been nervous. She had picked the restaurant because it was the scene of their first date and she had wanted the meal to feel equally consequential, to bring up this memory and resonate for him, almost as if it were an alternate way of conceiving a child. But the conversation had felt hollow. Her own voice detailed her thinking, offered up facts and figures as if she were giving a PowerPoint presentation, and Jeremy meticulously cut, speared, and ate his venison in silence. A known donor, she explained, was like a guarantee—sure, sperm banks offered profiles and SAT scores and, in some cases, even pictures, but what was to stop the donors from making things up? Some banks offered employee impressions, but they were just that: impressions. Who *were* these people selling their sperm? With a known donor you knew what you were getting—family history, emotional disposition, intelligence. She heard her voice speeding through the reasons like a motor. What she did not explain was that the very idea of inserting an unknown person's sperm into her uterus was almost pathologically repelling to her.

"And you're sure he's the best person?" Jeremy had asked when she got to Neil. Jenny had launched into her answer, carefully reasoned and rehearsed. Neil was brilliant. He had gotten a summa on his undergraduate thesis. He had pulled himself out of New Bedford by his own bootstraps. He had gotten two 800s on his SATs without even studying—these were facts. He had misapplied himself since college, but that was fine, because the natural ability was there. And in a way it made things easier: after all, their worlds were completely different, they were unlikely ever to intersect. His parents were both alive and, she would confirm, cancer-free. Plus—she threw this in as extra enticement—he looked something like Jeremy. This was a stretch.

"Okay," Jeremy had said, picking up his napkin and wiping his mouth.

"Okay, Neil?" she had asked.

Jeremy had looked at her—his head tilted slightly, and something unfamiliar and inscrutable in his eyes. She would always remember this. "Okay, whatever you want, Jen."

His acquiescence threw her: he knew very little about Neil other than that she had gone out with him in college. He had only met him twice. She would have liked to continue somehow. To reach over and draw him out: what was he thinking? But she had a sudden uncharacteristic problem. She did not know how.

It was not until later, in the engrossing rush of her workday, that Jenny was able to put the matter of Jeremy's frustrating malaise out of her head. She had a meeting scheduled with Eric Watson, head of worldwide marketing for the large pharmaceutical company she worked for, and she had been looking forward to it with suspense. Entering his office, her Triple Venti Latte in hand, she felt the shimmer of excitement that accompanied a conquest. In her twenties these had been largely of the romantic variety; now, as a mother and a married woman, her conquests were professional. The rush was surprisingly similar, though, both kinds linked, at root, to ambition, that underrated stimulant.

"So what do you think?" she said, closing the door behind her.

"Cut right to the chase, hunh?" he said, grinning. "No 'How are you?' No small talk?"

Jenny shrugged, grinning back. "We've got work to do." She had an instinctive rapport with Eric Watson. He was a big man, with the bearing of an ex–football player and a surprising Boston accent. He was a man who had pulled himself up by his own bootstraps. And he reminded her of her father, or what her father would have been if he *had* pulled himself up by his own bootstraps.

"All right," Eric said, throwing up his hands. "So what do *you* think?"

They were choosing an advertising agency to help bring Jenny's baby, her brainchild, the project she had been plotting, scheming, and pushing for during the last six months, to life.

"Ogilvy," she said firmly, settling into the chair opposite Eric's desk.

"Why's that?" he raised his eyebrows and leaned back in his chair, hands behind his head in one of those stylized gestures of confidence that he actually managed to pull off.

Jenny outlined her reasons.

She had thought them through carefully, and, as with anything to do with the project, she was convinced she was right.

For many years, Genron had been marketing Setlan, a ubiquitous SSRI, prescribed with roughly the same frequency as Prozac. For two of those many years, Jenny's job had been to promote Setlan, which was, at this point, basically a self-selling drug. It was a steady but unchallenging job that had left her with no room to make a splash.

And then she had given birth to Colin, and with him, a brilliant idea. She had looked around at all the women in the mothers' group she had dutifully joined and seen a potential market—large, easily accessible, and full of potential. All these women staggering around like sleepwalkers or mugging victims, joggling infants on their squishy last-ten-pounds hips, making do with decaf coffee and minimal sleep. Women who would never previously have set foot outside their homes without a blow-dry and a spray of Chloé were now going out in sweatpants and spit-up-stained T-shirts. They were full of unfamiliar feelings—feelings they wanted, ad nauseum, to discuss, or placate, or denounce as unfair. And they felt duped! This was an unspoken undercurrent—motherhood was not what they had been promised. After so much hard work being pregnant, sacrificing good cheese and caffeine and alcohol, not to mention their previously fit and trim bodies, the daily experience of infant care was not the joyous reward they deserved. They *needed* something, Jenny could see. They were ripe for a marketing campaign aimed at their particular quandary.

Yes, of course, of course, Setlan and Prozac were already available to them. But these came with certain stigmas and associations. And these women were used to a greater degree of specificity—they didn't run in aerobics sneakers, after all; they didn't use body lotion on their faces. They had a name for their problem: postpartum depression. Now they needed a solution specifically aimed at it: Setlan PPD. They would not even need to come up with a new drug: just new packaging, and a campaign. The plan was brilliant in its simplicity.

Eric listened to her tick off the reasons that made Ogilvy the best ad agency for the job, nodding at intervals. "All right," he said, laying a big hand, palm down, on his desk. "You have a deal. But it better be good, for that price."

Jenny was just opening her mouth to respond when Eric's secretary, Violet, stuck her head in. "Your babysitter's on the phone," she said apologetically. "I figured I better get you."

"Go on, go on," Eric said, waving her out. "We're all set."

Jenny picked up the phone at Violet's desk.

"I'm sorry for bother you," Colin's nanny, Maria, said. "I just wanted to know where is the baby's binky toy. I am looking everywhere for it—"

"The binky toy?" Jenny asked, sighing.

"From the stroller. Always it hangs on the stroller. But today—nowhere."

"Ohhh, the pacifier clip—right—that thing. No." Jenny rolled her eyes at Violet, who was sitting at her computer. "It must be there. I didn't take it off."

"No. I look everywhere."

"Maybe it's stuck behind the seat?"

"No."

Jenny could picture Maria standing there shaking her head, insistent. Colin was probably sitting at her feet, dressed in about seven hundred layers topped off by his fanciest clothes.

"I don't know, Maria. Maybe Jeremy took it off," she said, although this was almost unimaginable. Jeremy mucking around with the stroller? Even in his current state the idea was preposterous. The whole conversation was ridiculous.

"Okay. I use a string to tie a new one, Okay? From his hat?"

"I don't think that's safe," Jenny said.

"Then he will lose," Maria said stubbornly.

"Well, bring a few, then," Jenny said. "Don't we have a bunch in the drawer?"

"I find two."

Jenny sighed. "I don't know, then, Maria. You'll just have to do what you can."

"Okay, Jenn-eefer," Maria said brightly. "Sorry for disturb you."

Jenny hung up the phone.

"Binky emergency?" Violet quipped.

"There's always something," Jenny said, rolling her eyes.

But it was unsavory, actually, picturing that pacifier and the little clown clip Colin loved to chew on missing. Had some vagrant been rifling around in the stroller? Another reason why they should, by now, have been safely settled in Wellesley. The city, even the Back Bay, was no place to raise a baby.

Jenny's own childhood had played out entirely in a bland but dependably safe subdivision of DeSoto, California, a semirural suburb of Fresno. It had not been a compelling place to grow up: as soon as she was able, she had been desperate to get out. But it had been comfortable, distinctly all-American, and stable. It was not entirely new, like those soulless bedroom communities springing up outside of LA where you heard about latchkey kids becoming neo-Nazis and spending afternoons high on crystal meth. But it was certainly not old either—not even in the California sense of the word. It had been established in the 1940s to house the workers of the local canning plant, and the homes that lined the mathematically plotted streets bore a resemblance to the functional, boxlike houses of military bases. But someone had had the bright idea to paint DeSoto's homes cheerful, outlandish colors: pink, turquoise, fern-green, vermilion . . . And this had become a source of pride in the community—a kind of wildness otherwise absent in the conservative town of industrial and agricultural workers. It had, Jenny always felt, provided an inspiring example of scrappy all-American spirit. She imagined discussing this in interviews sometimes. Or drawing on it in business school commencement addresses she would, someday, be invited to give.

As a girl, in her peach-colored house on Pine Street, she had imagined she would become a veterinarian when she grew up. It was an ambitious career, in the spectrum of careers held by members of her family. Her father was a foreman at the canning plant and her mother stayed at home and raised her four children. Her grandmother worked, to Jenny's embarrassment, in the local grade school lunchroom. And her oldest brother, whom she had worshipped as a handsome, popular football player when he was in high school, had gone on to become a threshing machine operator. Veterinary school had been a brainy, upwardly mobile aspiration applauded by her mother, who was ambitious for her bright, winning fourth baby. "Promising" was the word most often bandied about on Jenny's report cards, and Jenny had felt the crisp anticipation of its syllables, and the pressure.

Which was one of the things that made DeSoto seem, in retrospect, to have been a good place to grow up. Jenny had been recognized. She had stood out as exceptional among the mediocre-minded children of this homogenous community. The system for recognizing and categorizing had been simple and effective. Unlike the vagaries of urban education—the rowdy, unacceptable public schools that ground down so many bright, capable young people before they ever had the chance to shine, or the precious, coddling private schools full of rich kids whose genuine, innate level of promise was obscured by expensive tutoring and extracurricular commitments, trips to China, and parental connections, DeSoto had been truly—purely—democratic.

Not that Jenny would want to raise her own children there. That wasn't the point. Colin had come into the world with a full freight of assets in his favor. He didn't really need to be recognized for his pure smarts. Honestly, he didn't even have to be so smart (although, of course, Jenny knew he was). No, Colin already had so much Jenny herself hadn't had; his upbringing was going to be an entirely different story. He would go to private school, and they would take exotic, enriching family vacations to Europe, Asia, or even Africa once a year. By the time he was old enough to remember anything, they would have a beach house. Colin could be one of those rich kids she saw at the Wellesley Sports Club pool, slouching their tanned bodies under baseball caps, lazily tossing lacrosse balls, talking about what a drag it was to accompany their "'rents" to Provence.

And, of course, he had his own uniquely successful set of genes—genes she *knew* set him up for success in the world of culture and enterprise. Neil had screwed up, it was true, but his brain—his intelligence—was top-notch. And he possessed a rare sort of thoughtfulness Jenny had once heard a German word describe: *weltschmerz*. It was something Jenny did not have, but that she recognized. And, for reasons she could not explain, could not understand, really—reasons having to do with the quivering, shimmering sense of aloneness she felt running on the rubble-strewn beach near her in-laws' house at dawn, or the draft of sadness things like her grandmother's girlhood needlepoints raised in her as a child—she saw its value. *Weltschmerz*—it was something she could not pass on, but which she understood was in some way necessary for greatness, talent, and success beyond the world of money. And she wanted Colin to have opportunity for this too.

From Jenny herself, Colin would inherit all the sharpness and pragmatism he would need. It was the marketable half of the hand she had been dealt, and came exclusively from her mother. Judy Callahan was the kind of woman people referred to as a "force of nature." She had run a day care out of her home while raising her own four children and served as an amateur livestock judge every time the state agricultural fair came to DeSoto. She put together three hot meals a day and did not own a dryer or dishwasher. Even now, at age sixty, she was training for the Boston Marathon—as if she couldn't come to visit her new grandson without achieving some unrelated, fantastical personal objective! She drove Jenny crazy. But Jenny was not blind; she knew where she came from.

Which did not seem to be from her father. What had she inherited from this big, quiet canning plant foreman with hands like slabs of meat and a face as flat, ruddy, and impassive as a statue's? It was as if she had sprung solely from her mother. Her father was handsome in an impressive, oversized way and was well liked by the community, which he soldiered uncomplainingly to aid at his wife's behest, showing up to help bolster the sinking WWII memorial or sand down the decrepit, splintering jungle gym at the park. He was a chain smoker, he played poker. Every Friday night. With a group of loyal and devoted friends who called him "Motor"—in reference to what, Jenny could not imagine. At home and with his children, he was all but mute.

Safe, comfortable, smelling of smoke and machine oil and shaving cream, he had been a wide lap to climb in, a strong set of arms for boosting. Jenny had lived in a state of constant embarrassment about her loud, demanding mother, but for some reason—his sheer bulk? or the dignity that comes with silence?—she was proud of Frank Callahan. And even now, in her adult life, she had some deep-seated respect for this unknowable man who remained entirely fixed in his own world. He was afraid of flying and had never come to visit her in any of her East Coast habitations. Which was maybe for the best: her pride in him had never had to accommodate the vision of his bulk perched on one of the spindly chairs at Clio or sleeping in her sleek, Zen-inspired guest room.

It was only fleetingly and occasionally (maybe once or twice) that

Jenny had allowed herself to stumble on the idea that this man she admired and loved possibly more than any other on earth would exist in an entirely different world from the man she was raising her son to be. They would not speak the same language. Even the simplest nouns would be attached to such different things in their minds: *kitchen, school, transportation, meat.* Forget adjectives, which were subjective even within a given socioeconomic bracket. They would be left with nothing but the hugest and most basic precepts: *ocean, light, sickness, death.* Would this be enough?

3

NEIL WAS HOPING it wouldn't be there. That he would reach into his pocket and find it empty, or filled with the usual detritus of matches and change, maybe a scrap of paper or two. That the murky memory of last night's escapades would prove to be a dream. But his fingers brushed immediately against the chunky plastic and the sticky rubber nipple at the end. Shit.

He shoved it deeper down, hoping there was no weird bulky outline of it visible through the leather of his jacket. He thought, for a moment, about pulling it out and tossing it into the corner garbage can—blood off the hands, evidence destroyed, etc. But this seemed creepy. Creepier even than having taken it in the first place. After all, it belonged to the baby. To *his* baby. It had the boy's saliva on it— minuscule traces of his own DNA.

So he shoved it down, patted his jacket, and tried to shake the thought of it. He was meeting Laura here at a bar she had suggested, a new place with an anonymous, modern look—booths with black leather benches and low light, a shiny, stainless steel bar. At least it wasn't some "old haunt" from their college years—the fetid, beer-smelling Bow and Arrow, or the dirt-cheap, carpeted second floor of the Hong Kong. He would have been unable to take that. How did Laura stand it, living here? Everywhere he turned in Harvard Square there was some ghost memory that made him cringe.

For himself at the time? Or for himself now? Both, probably. No deconstructing. Deconstructing got him nowhere.

Laura was late. That hadn't changed, apparently. Neil sipped his beer and winced slightly. He was still hung over from last night. Johnson's fault. All of it. Including the pacifier. (What would he do when Johnson wasn't around to blame?)

To celebrate Johnson and Kirstin's last night in Boston, they had gone out in the Back Bay. An unlikely place for them, sworn hipsters that they were, but they had a friend who was the bartender at this "swanky" place who could hook them all up with free drinks and a good table. Kirstin and Johnson were giddy with excitement at their imminent departure—ZGames had made them rich enough to follow their dreams: his to try his luck "acting" in a reality TV show (*Isn't that an oxymoron?* Neil had asked. *All the world's a stage*, Johnson had drawled in his new game-company-personage voice), and hers to make a name for herself in soft porn. So they had set off, the three of them, Johnson and Kirstin making out like teenagers on the subway ride there, Neil glum with the knowledge that he would have to get absolutely wasted to tolerate the night.

And once there, the champagne had flowed to their table as if they were Puff Daddy and his entourage, and at some point lychee-nut martinis and a bottle of Glenlivet entered the equation, and a too-tall, birdy girl named Saryn, whose small breasts pressed erectly against Neil's arm with the same insistence as her monologue about being a postfeminist feminist, until finally Neil had gathered the force to break away, bid goodbye to Kirstin and Johnson, who were somehow leaving for the airport at six a.m., separate himself from Saryn, and stagger out into the damp calm of Boylston Street after hours.

It was just unfortunate that he had walked past Clarendon Street on his way to the train. Otherwise Neil would not have thought of it. But in the fog of drink the address had stood out in his mind

with clarity: 43b Clarendon Street. He had studied it on the back
of that birth announcement, unpacked the implications of it many
times. There was a lot you could tell about a person—about a life,
about what *kind* of life—from an address. This wasn't just a Victorian conceit.

But five minutes later, standing in front of it, he did not find it
that revealing, actually. It was a brownstone. Expensive, no doubt,
and well kept. Drapes in the upstairs windows and shutters below, all
dark. A wrought-iron railing, alarm system, an ugly, too-shiny brass
knocker and doorknob combo indicating bad taste. It had probably
been recently renovated: granite countertops, open layout, whirl-
pool tub, etc. Nothing he would not have already guessed. Until he
caught sight of the stroller tucked away under the front steps. Which
seemed unlike Jenny. On closer, albeit drunken, inspection it turned
out to be locked, bicycle-style, to the railing. That was more like her.
Although it hinted at cramped quarters. Clearly they were not long
for this space.

The stroller itself looked expensive—sleek and well designed, it
rode high on a set of thick mountain-bike-like tires, and was covered by a neatly fitting clear plastic rain shield. Inside it was lined
with fleece. And there was the pacifier, attached to its brightly colored string of plastic beads and ducks. The one truly personal thing
he had come across. And looking at it from what seemed like a
great height in his spinning, drunken state, Neil was overcome by
how little it was, and how silly, and how totally, blissfully primitive
the creature who used it must be. How undifferentiated by taste
and preference and preconception. Here was this bright, chewable
thing—why not suck on it? He didn't care if it was decorated with
ducks or pigs, if it was pink or blue, if it was cheap or expensive. He
had no prejudices or social expectations. Tabula rasa and all that.

And suddenly Neil wanted to have some *influence* on this little
malleable being who would grow up to be a person with opinions

and attitudes and a distinct point of view. What had he been think-ing, letting Jenny have his child with no strings attached? With no place for himself in the drama of its unfolding life? And it stung suddenly, bitterly, that she had wanted it this way—that she had wanted not only total control but secrecy—as if his genes were good enough to pass on but his person, the man he had become, was too shameful to acknowledge. He had been so busy imagining himself some sort of eugenic infiltrator, seeding her obliviously privileged American life with his own self-conscious complexities and doubt, that he had overlooked the insult inherent in her plan. She had come to him for his promise and potential, but he himself was no fitter or more appealing in her eyes than he had been when they'd broken up.

From Beacon Street there was the thundering of a truck lurch-ing along, and beyond this, on Storrow, the thin rush of traffic. The streetlight shone a pale, dappled light onto the sidewalk through the tender new spring leaves.

Neil climbed down the two steps to the shadowy nook the stroller was parked in, and before he knew it, he had unzipped the clear plastic cover and opened it up, let the cool night air into the cozy bubble—boy in the bubble, he thought, and felt as though the baby were actually in there and he, Neil, the baby's father, was helping him out. But of course the stroller was empty. Except for the pacifier and its colorful clip. Lurching slightly, unsteady and suffused with bitterness, Neil had yanked it off.

Now, sitting here, gingerly sipping his beer in this sleek pizza bar Laura had chosen, he could see this was completely crazy. What was he, a college prankster? Living in this town was a bad influence.

Laura appeared at the same time as the basil and prosciutto piz-zette (couldn't they just call it pizza?) he had ordered. She launched into a wave of apology, gesturing animatedly, undeterred by the hovering server who danced around her in an effort to keep the pizzette out of harm's way.

"But it's so nice to see you!" Laura finished, beaming genuinely and kissing Neil on the cheek. Even after all these years, her smile, her protests, the way she shrugged off her jacket were familiar. It was reassuring. So much had changed, but his old pal Laura Trillian (or had she taken Mac's name?) had not.

"So where're the kids?" Neil said. "Help yourself." He gestured to the pie.

"Oh, no, I'm fine. A glass of chardonnay?" she directed this last at the server as if it were a question. "With the sitter. Thank God. Tuesday nights. Usually I take a yoga class."

"And you blew that off for me?"

"Of course!" Laura grinned.

She was still so pretty. A little rounder and fuller, a few lines around the eyes, but she didn't have that severe, timeworn look that so many women her age were beginning to.

"So how old are they?" he asked.

"Six and two."

Outside the window on the sidewalk a wild-haired man pushing a cart full of bottles clattered past.

"That must keep you busy."

Laura rolled her eyes. "I can't complain." She leaned forward a little. "But what about *you*, Neil—where have you been all these years? What have you been up to? I can't even believe how long it's been!"

"Nothing," he said, keeping his eyes fixed on the homeless man's slow progress. "Honest to God. Nothing."

"You were in that PhD program," Laura said helpfully.

Neil groaned. "Let's talk about your kids."

Laura groaned in imitation.

"Okay, we're even."

They both looked out the window for a moment. A pair of bespec-tacled men, locked in earnest conversation, followed the homeless man. Scientists, or academics—Neil felt the usual twinge of regret.

"So how is it, living here?"

Laura looked startled. "You mean Cambridge? Why—because of school?"

Neil nodded.

"It's all right. I mean, I do like it, as a city, and I'm used to it now—I didn't want to move back, but then . . . you have these pre-conceptions about everywhere else in the Boston area you know, after having lived here. And Mac wanted to live out in Lexington or Dedham or somewhere suburban . . ."

Neil watched her hands move. Slender, delicate fingers and rings—interesting rings, a silver frog on one, two flat green stones on another. There was nothing processed about Laura. Nothing polished or filtered. She had always been that way. It was part of why it had seemed so unlikely that she would have married Mac. The guy was so stylized—so aware of his presentation. All that Tommy Hilfiger–type preppy crap he wore, for example. Mac Elias. Why affect the posture of some superannuated breed of New England aristocrat when you had a much more impressive credential? Mac was a real all-American success story—a Greek immigrant's son turned business success. Neil had met him only once or twice ages ago, when Mac had first started dating Laura, and Neil remembered him as a handsome guy, arrogant and broad-shouldered, the kind of man who looked likely, behind closed doors, to have a bad temper. Laura would have liked him for his difference from the whole insular New England WASP culture she had grown up in, not his (at best) tenuous status in it.

She brushed her hair behind her ear as she talked. Neil had been wrong, he could suddenly see—she *had* changed a little, or maybe just sharpened, become more of who she was when he had known her. The sadness that had always shadowed her resting face was more pronounced, even under the smile. Her mother's early death? The relative isolation of her childhood? He did not know what its roots were, but it dogged her now, even as she waved her hands animatedly.

What about him? Did he like LA? Did he just hate being back? Wasn't he just a little bit curious about any gossip? What Elise was up to, for instance, or Abe Sorenson—and how, by the way, had he seen Nelly McCormack? Were they in touch?

Neil answered her questions—omitting the fact that he had not just run into Nelly McCormack, but had slept with her—and finished his beer. Laura was on to her second glass of wine.

"And Mac?" Neil asked. "He's good? Enjoying life these days?"

A more closed look came over Laura's face. She shrugged. "He loves his work."

"Which is what again?"

"Commercial real estate. Development."

"The glory of strip malls."

Laura frowned. "What's that supposed to mean?"

"Nothing. Honestly. I love 'em. America's least-celebrated innovation."

Laura gave him a skeptical look and sipped her drink.

They were silent for a moment. Next to them at the bar a pony-tailed blonde with too much makeup on flirted with two entranced college boys.

"So is it weird for you, Neil?" Laura ventured suddenly. "Having this baby out there—I mean, are you okay with it—having no connection? I was thinking about that after I saw you, and just thinking . . ." She trailed off hesitantly.

"It was weird?"

"No." Laura looked alarmed. "No, not at all—just that . . . you seemed a little sad at the christening."

Neil felt his back grow rigid, an on-demand exoskeleton. "I don't think about it much."

Laura nodded, looking unconvinced.

"I mean, now that I'm here, though, it's true, it's kind of in my mug. More . . . I don't know—" He broke off.

"More what?"

Neil shifted his gaze up to the corner of the ceiling. "I don't really know what I was thinking."

"Well, it was a wonderful thing you did for Jenny," she said hesitantly. "And for Jeremy, of course. I mean, you gave them this . . . amazing baby."

Neil took a swig of his beer—his second, which was not giving him a buzz, just adding to the toxic feeling he had left over from last night. "No," he said, putting the glass back down. "That's the thing. I didn't. I gave them some sperm."

Laura looked . . . was it reproving somehow?

He hid his face in his last sip and slid the empty glass over the table. "Want to see something?" he said impulsively.

Almost as soon as they stepped outside, though, Neil regretted the impulse. What the hell was he doing? Trying to guarantee some new spot for himself in Laura's mind as a weirdo? As poor-Neil-he-really-kind-of-lost-it? He tried to think if there was something else he could, plausibly, have led her out to take a look at. He could think of nothing. Certainly nothing that would seem even marginally apropos. They picked their way along the bustling sidewalk of Church Street and onto quiet, shadowy Brattle with its Old World air of refinement, history, and money.

"God, it's great to have spring here," Laura said, throwing her head back. The breeze stirred her hair. "Did you miss it? Out in California? That particular relief, you know, that comes with New England spring?"

"I don't think so." Neil shrugged. "I don't know. I guess I'm not a weather person."

" 'A weather person,' " Laura scoffed. "Unlike me."

"No, I mean, I just don't noti॓it much. It's a bad thing. It probably indicates some kind of psychological handicap. Or self-absorption. Probably that."

They had reached Neil's ancient, pre-autolock VW. It was a shocker that it had made it all three thousand miles east. Neil leaned against the door, hoping, maybe, she had forgotten they had come out to see something.

He was parked in front of one of the street's huge historic mansions, the doors of which never seemed to open and close. But at this moment a light came on in an upstairs window, sending a splash of yellow over the immaculate lawn.

"So what is it?" Laura asked. "What are you showing me?"

"Oh, it's stupid."

"What? No way. We came all the way out here."

Neil sighed and turned the key in the door. The glove compartment fell open with a thud, spilling papers and manuals, bottles of Advil and crumpled foil packages of cigarettes and beef jerky. Neil rummaged through this, aware of Laura outside, leaning against the car. And there it was. He backed out and handed it to her, his heart pounding unexpectedly in his chest.

Laura took it gingerly, squinting to make out the white letters on the faded carbon copy. "Your birth certificate?"

Neil pointed to the hour of birth: 11:40 a.m. And weight: six pounds, ten ounces.

Laura gave him a quizzical look.

He handed her the grubby square of thick blue card stock, printed at the top with a gold baby rattle. Colin's birth announcement. It had come to him, as promised, but with no note, no picture attached, nothing personal at all. *Colin Callahan-Sharha. Six pounds ten ounces. October 8, 11:04 a.m.*

Laura did not look up for a moment. Then she handed him back the papers. It seemed possible that she would say nothing—would shame him with silence, as if his possession of this document were unspeakable.

"Life is weird, isn't it?" she said, looking straight at him. And her eyes were large and kind—not critical or pitying. A sudden fierce impulse came over him: he wanted to kiss her. He wanted to be gathered up into the sweetness of her upturned face. There was a scattering of freckles across the bridge of her nose that seemed suddenly beautiful. Had he ever noticed these before? Had he ever thought of her this way?

"What?" she said, concern crossing her face.

The sound of her voice startled him.

"Oh, nothing. Just that you're right."

Back at Johnson's apartment, Neil dove into the research project that had been so burningly consuming to him for the last several years. It had begun as a spin-off of his dropped dissertation—a study of resistance to King Leopold's reign of slaughter in Africa. In the course of his thesis investigation, Neil had come across the mid-nineteenth-century American explorer Albert Sorenson Jones, self-proclaimed American hero turned detractor, seminary student turned adventurer, idealist turned . . . middle-class everyman. Jones had gone into deepest Zaire with his moral hackles up, a blustery drinker with a penchant for self-promotion, a self-made man from a poor farm in southern Vermont, renowned for his riflery and poker skills, with ambitions to make a name for himself and American rectitude around the world, to map undocumented swaths of the continent and change the appalling colonial treatment of "Negroes." And then, after his five years there, about which relatively little was known, he had resurfaced in, of all places, Mobile, Alabama, a different person. Thinner, milder, and by all measures reduced. He had opened a blacksmith shop and begun publishing maudlin poems about flowers and teapots.

What had happened to the man? What had eaten his idealism and his swagger? It was not hard to imagine. The sheer horror of Africa had certainly broken even stronger, better-prepared men and sent them running, or worse, made them accomplice to its evil. God knows Neil had read enough André Gide and Joseph Conrad. But this man—Albert Sorenson Jones—was, to Neil, different. He was, for one thing, boldly and unabashedly American. He had wanted to build a hospital, which seemed to express a very particular American kind of ambition and idealism. And when the project had failed— the circumstances of which were largely unknown—he had come out diminished rather than broken. His fate was mawkish rather than tragic. The day-to-day of Jones's travels was documented minimally and contradictingly in the journals of two members of his exploring party and in his own hotheaded missives, sent from the road and published in his hometown newspaper. The mystery of this fascinated Neil.

He had discovered Jones only after his own exploration of the "dark continent," where he had gone ostensibly to research his dissertation but had instead ended up teaching English and hitchhiking like some college-year-abroad student. It had been the end of his dissertation. The end of any academic ambitions. And his return to California had been the beginning of a new Neil. So in this way, he felt a kinship to Jones. Two ugly Americans, full of pride and lofty ideals, inexplicably changed by Africa, rendered weirdly mediocre, small, and insignificant upon return. What had happened to *Neil* was that he had seen real poverty and desperation. In the scheme of all-things-Africa it was very little. He had not seen the bodies of macheted victims of the Rwandan genocide. He had not seen the raping and maiming of Congolese women. But he had been hit over the head with the infinite sorrow, injustice, and sheer brutality of human life. And moreover—by his own cowardice and privilege. He was an American, traveling through the world wrapped in a bubble of impenetrable luck and affluence. And some fundamental flaw in his character had prevented him from breaking out of this, or pulling anyone else in. He had written a few impassioned editorials, which went nowhere, and he had tried to keep in touch with a few African friends. But he had joined no noble NGO, had signed up for no Red Cross relief work, had lobbied no one for aid. So this burning sense of his own privilege sat holed up inside him like a cancer.

Was this what had happened to Jones?

Neil had toiled away for the last few years on this as if the answer would free him. He hunted up ancient census documents and grocers' tabs, read and analyzed the unimpressive poetry Jones had written upon his return. And he pored over the spotty and often contradictory journals of Jones's teammates and the literature on other, more prominent explorers of the time.

Sitting in Johnson's kitchen, though, reviewing his own copious notes, Neil had trouble concentrating. In the transition from his subterranean office studio beneath Jane's house in Silver Lake to his new home on the opposite coast, something had been lost. He could feel the spark of relevance slipping from his grasp. Better to close up the work, in that case, cap his pen, and give it a break. Because without it—without Jones—Neil would be lost.

4

SUNDAY MORNINGS WERE A "THING" in the Elias household. This was what Laura would hear Mac say when asked, for instance, to play golf by one of his friends. "I'd love to, buddy, but I've got this family thing." At moments like that Laura could not, honestly, remember why she had married him.

In any event, the "thing" was to be together as a family. To cook pancakes or go out for brunch or take a walk or do some sort of activity that would keep them all entertained. Which was a challenge. A walk, for instance, was out of the question at this point. Genevieve hated walks. And brunch was impossible with Miranda. But they made do—the "thing" served its purpose. Without it there would be almost no time the Eliases were all together.

This morning the "thing" was a trip to Drumlin Farm at Genevieve's request. She had developed an obsession with horses and somehow gotten wind of the fact that the mare at Drumlin Farm had just given birth. Laura did her best to quash this interest of her daughter's. *Please don't become one of those horsey girls*, she prayed silently at night while tucking her in next to the giant stuffed pony Mac had given her for Christmas. Possibly it was already too late. Possibly her sensitive, intelligent little girl was bound to be sucked into the stolid, humorless world of scraping hooves, braiding tails, and thumping up and down on a horse's back in a pair of sweaty nylon pants. But Laura hoped there was time to turn this around—

to impress upon her, for instance, that horses sometimes kicked people and nipped fingers, and were not always as smart as they were cracked up to be.

Mac pulled the car into the parking lot and ferreted out a space in the shade. He was weirdly particular about this sort of thing. Keeping the car cool and clean (no snacks!) was an imperative, no matter the cost.

"Piggies, piggies, piggies," Miranda chanted. "Are we going to see the piggies, Dada?" It was maybe the four hundredth time she had asked.

"What piggies? You think they have piggies here?" Mac asked, feigning bemusement.

"Yes! Yes, they do! They do, they do!" Miranda shrieked, as he hoisted her up out of her car seat and over his shoulder. She adored her father.

Behind Laura, Genevieve was fiddling with something in the little purple bag she carried like a talisman, her head bent in earnest concentration.

"You brought your camera?" Laura asked, dismayed.

"I want to take a picture of the foal to show to Morgan."

"Mmmm. Does Morgan like horses?"

"Oh, she loves them," Genevieve said breathlessly. Another strike against Morgan, the sullen, large-headed girl who seemed to be Genevieve's new best friend.

Genevieve looked so earnest standing there, head bent, small feet planted squarely on the ground. Laura felt a swell of love for her, and contrition at her own controlling impulses. Of course Genevieve should be interested in whatever she wanted, be friends with whoever made her happy, and take pictures of baby horses to share with them.

"C'mon," Laura said, tilting her head toward the barns. "Let's go before your sister scares the animals to death."

And so the Eliases made their way around from sheep to goats to chickens (Laura's least favorite, those dirty squawky creatures she preferred not to associate with anything she ate) to geese to pigs, and finally to the long-awaited horses. The weather was heavy—the sky white and still and the air cool but humid. The stench of animal shit rose pungently from the earth. "I smell somebody's dinner cooking," Miranda announced generously. She sat on Mac's shoulders, in heaven, her tiny pair of jeans hanging off of her, baring half her bum.

Mac checked his BlackBerry as they walked. It was a subject of contention between them, an obvious metaphor for something larger and less concrete. Not just his constant distraction, but also his inattention—to his wife, to his family, to his home. He was out at least four nights a week traveling or finessing deals over filet mignon at Locke-Ober. Once a week, no matter what, he drove to Worcester to have dinner with his mother, a proud inscrutable woman who had never forgiven Laura for being an American and refused to speak English in her presence. Even when Mac was home in the evening, he crawled into bed after Laura was asleep, having watched some college basketball tournament or football game until the bitter end. She could barely remember the last time they had made love. All the mothers Laura knew talked about being taken for granted, unappreciated, and frequently left holding the bag. But these criticisms did not begin to cover Laura's status in her marriage. It felt often as though she were invisible to Mac. As though she were completely looked through. What went on in his mind? Did he have any idea what went on in hers? She had tried to draw this out—to have at least some sort of discussion about what was missing—but initially Mac had put an end to such forays with a bear hug and good-natured nuzzle: *C'mere, Henny Penny, no more worrying.* And now any vague gesture in the direction of reflection or inquiry was met with a stony-faced, beleaguered blankness: *Not this again.* He traveled so often and worked so late, the questions had occurred to her: Had he . . . ? Would he ever . . . ? And no intuitive answer presented itself to her. Oddly, the uncertainty seemed to change very little for her. It was part of what they were.

She walked into the stable behind Genevieve and her eyes fell upon it immediately: a dead chicken, lying in the corner of the stall Mac and the girls were stopped in front of.

"Mac," she said. "Mac!" more loudly. It was imperative that Genevieve be shielded from this or there would surely be some torrent of upset, and, knowing Miranda, she would probably run over and start sticking her fingers in the dead chicken's eyes. The thought made Laura's skin crawl. She had the childish sensation of wanting to tiptoe, to connect her body to as little of this dead chicken's final resting ground as possible.

"Mac!"

He turned toward her, Miranda's fingers twined in his hair.

"D-e-a-d-c-h-i-c-k-e-n," she spelled. "I think we should keep moving."

"D-e-c—what?"

Dead, Laura mouthed, and angled her head toward it with a grimace.

"Oh, yeah?" he raised his eyebrows and took a step toward it as if in fact she were pointing out an attraction.

"No—I mean—" Laura began in exasperation, but why was she surprised?

Miranda saw it first, of course. "Chicken!" She bounced on his shoulders. "Lie down chicken!"

"Where?" Genevieve spun around from the big black horse she had been holding her hand out to. "Oh, no! Is it dead? What's it doing here—oh, no, it's all twisted—" her voice began to take on a panicked edge as she shrank backward against Mac's legs.

"Looks like someone got in horsey's way," he said cheerfully.

Genevieve looked at her father aghast. "You think the horse—"

"No, no it probably just got old and ..." Laura tried to backtrack, but tears were welling up in Genevieve's eyes.

"Should I pluck you a feather, Vievee? for a souvenir?" Mac taunted.

"No! no!" Genevieve shrieked.

"Oh, it's so—it's so yucky, Mom—I don't want—I want to get out—"

And so it began, the sobbing and dismay, Genevieve's battle with her own disgust over whether to walk past and on to the stall of the much-anticipated foal. The final, tearful decision to let Laura carry her, hands over her eyes, past the chicken's remains and to the foal, who, it turned out, could no longer be concentrated on let alone photographed on account of his proximity to the body, and then the glum walk back up the hill, toward the lot, throughout which Mac was oblivious, first playing tag with Miranda and ultimately talking on his cell phone ("Just a minute, ladies ..."), while Genevieve plodded forward, eyes downcast.

Laura had met Mac through Jenny, who had been in his class at business school and had painted an almost messianic picture of his business prowess. He was seven years older than Laura and had sent her flowers after their first date, a gesture so old-fashioned and paternalistic that Laura would have been creeped out by it if she hadn't, in her own paternalistic way, chalked it up to his background. He had come up through the Worcester public schools, a star football player who worked nights at his father's restaurant, and had a grandmother still living in a village on the Peloponnesus. He had taken her to fancy restaurants and Broadway shows, and told her how beautiful she was with such straightforward fervor that she felt herself to be some sort of Aphrodite. Unlike her own aristocratic family members or the various witty and jaded New Englanders Laura had dated throughout college, Mac was not self-conscious or ironic or conflicted about his feelings, and this was compelling to her in its novelty.

Their courtship had been fast. Based on some indecipherable criteria that became *less* rather than more clear to Laura as time went by, Mac had made his mind up right away that she was the woman he wanted to marry. His certainty was appealing. And something of the motherless daughter in Laura had leapt toward his uncomplicated, almost sexist air of protection. They had been married in her home turf of Boston, but in his Greek Orthodox church. They had spent their honeymoon on Santorini. When Laura tried to account for her happiness during this adventure she could think primarily of one thing: luxury. As a self-made man with new access to money, Mac was much more generous, and much more comfortable splurging, for instance, on a private cruise of the harbor at sunset or a fifty-dollar bottle of champagne, than anyone in Laura's old New England family or circle of acquaintance ever had been. It felt exciting, transgressive even, and had, for a while, manufactured the necessary thrill.

The drive back to Cambridge from Drumlin Farm was silent. Genevieve looked moonily out of the window and Miranda whined about the lack of snacks. Mac made arrangements for the meeting he was flying to that night. The *Wee Sing Silly Songs* CD chirped out a torrent of inanity it was nearly impossible to think over.

"Are you going to have time to put together the climbing thing this afternoon before you leave?"

"The climbing thing?" Mac asked as if the modular, "simple assembly" jungle gym his mother had given Miranda for her birthday were not something Laura had asked him about practically every night that week.

She shot him a look.

"Oh, right—the climbing thing. Sure. Sure I will, babe."

"It'll take a while. An hour at least."

"No problem." Mac patted her knee.

Laura could hear the anxious needling in her own voice. The wife, the nag, the worrier—it was a boring story. *Why play it out, then?* her shrink had asked her. *Find a new narrative.* But the new narrative—a local handyman who could take care of the various sundry chores she seemed always to be waiting on Mac to get to—was apparently galling to Mac. His all-American pull-yourself-up-by-your-bootstraps upbringing made no accommodation for a man who hired someone else to replace window boxes, clean gutters, build swing sets. So the projects piled up, irritating Laura daily and diminishing the general quality of life in the Elias household.

Laura was about to bring up Duane, the handyman, and plunge headlong back into the same conversation they had had a thousand times before when her phone rang. It was a 310 number. Her heart gave a quick lurch in her chest.

"Hey—do you have a ladder I could borrow?" Neil asked, almost before she had said hello.

"What do you mean—what for?"

"It's a long story. But I need it sort of soon."

"The ladder?"

"Exactly."

"I climb," Miranda began to say from the backseat.

"I don't know—Mac, do we have a ladder? What kind of ladder?" she said back into the phone.

"Regular. Stepladder," Neil supplied.

"Of course," Mac said as if it were insulting to imagine they might not. "Why?"

"Yes," Laura said into the phone.

"Can you possibly bring it over here? Or could I come get it?"

"I'll bring it," Laura said hastily.

"Soon? I don't mean to be a pain, but there's this dog, you see, I have to get into the yard, and the fence—"

"An hour?" Laura felt the blood rising to her cheeks. Here was her escape from the day. To Neil. Her heart skittered a little. She did not even pause to wonder why he needed it.

"Perfect. Thanks, Lo. I knew you'd hook me up."

She hung up the phone and tried to affect a nonchalant expression. They were just entering Cambridge, the three blunt red high-rises of the Rindge Avenue projects lording a particular dreariness over the return.

"Who was that?" Mac asked.

"Oh, a friend." Laura tried to say it breezily. "Someone from that mother's group."

"Asshole." Mac scowled at a driver to his right.

"So do you mind if I go over there—drop the ladder off after I bring Vievee to Morgan's house? Miranda'll be napping—"

"No! No nap!" Miranda wailed.

"Sure," Mac said over this. "You know what I'll be doing."

"What?" Laura asked.

"Building the climbing thing."

When Laura arrived at number 420 Center Street—a grubby triple-decker in a part of Jamaica Plain she had never been to—Neil was waiting on the steps. The problem was immediately apparent. There was a dog barking hysterically from the other side of the fence to the right of the house.

"Lo!" Neil sprang up immediately. He was agitated, clearly. His eyes barely rested on her before scanning the back of the car for the ladder, and taking it in with obvious relief.

"Is that your dog?" Laura asked doubtfully.

"No, no." Neil ran a hand over his head. "But I'm taking care of it. Supposedly."

"I won't ask how it got in there."

"Through the apartment—the back door. It lives on the first floor. But I lost the key."

Together they wrestled the ladder out of the car. In Neil's wiry arms it looked heavier than it had in Mac's and for a fleeting moment Laura had the fear that maybe he couldn't manage it—there was something fragile about Neil in a way that almost embarrassed her. But he proved capable, and in a moment he had disappeared over the side of the solid fence.

There was much excited whining and nail-scrabbling from the dog, whose name, apparently, was Amos (unfortunate, she thought), and gruffly affectionate commanding to sit and chill out from Neil.

It took what seemed to be an unusually long time for him to come back around to the front, crazy-looking spotted mutt straining on its leash ahead of him through the door.

"Sorry," Neil said, yanking on the dog's leash to prevent himself from being pulled down the steps. "He threw up all over the rug."

"How long was he . . . stuck?"

"Not that long. Since last night."

" 'Not that long'?" Laura bent to pat Amos, who went wild with gratitude.

Neil shifted his weight guiltily. "Want to come for a walk with us?"

Jamaica Pond was particularly beautiful in the weird April heat. The new grass looked suddenly brilliant, and the water pleasant and fresh, inviting enough to swim in. Mothers pushed strollers and pale, winter-skinned young people—so many more of them than Laura was used to seeing in her own sedate, even elderly, neighborhood—lounged on picnic blankets and discarded jackets. A group of Dominicans were setting up a supersized barbecue on some picnic tables and a flock of Canadian geese milled around on the grassy bank nearest busy Jamaica Way, oblivious to the speeding cars.

It was so easy talking to Neil! And so much fun not to talk about children and sleep and husbands or plans or the books she was supposed to be writing up, but instead to talk about people from the past, and the article in the *Times* about that Pakistani nuclear physicist, and about Africa—Neil had lived in the Congo for a year, had taught English and written for some journal or something. He was not forthcoming about it, but she drew out a few particulars. (He had encountered fleeing Hutu rebels? And spent time in a diamond mine? It filled her with a kind of awe—his connection to this place that was otherwise only a symbol in her mind, a metaphor for disaster and chaos and the evils of global enterprise.)

And then somehow she found herself talking about her secret work, a project she hid and hadn't talked about with anyone—not even Jenny or Elise: her mother's tapestry.

The tapestry was what had kept Annabelle Trillian busy during the final, awful year of her life. She was an avid needlepointer and had been from girlhood, but it was unlike anything she had worked on before: a giant, fabulous, and unlikely depiction of a monk in battle with a unicorn. And it remained unfinished—its threads hanging off the shelf in Laura's guest room closet—a status that weighed on Laura more and more as the years passed. But for it, and the existence of her daughter, Annabelle would be remembered only obscurely as the sickly but supportive wife of Sir Adam Trillian, world-renowned economist and academic. And this would be a betrayal, not only of Annabelle, but of herself. Laura had been ten when her mother died of bone cancer, and her own memories of Annabelle were limited, but internalized—consecrated, even—as the deepest, truest part of herself. And so finally, after all these years, Laura had dug it out and was trying—ineptly—to finish it.

The violence of the image Annabelle had chosen was surprising, and the physical dimensions were enormous—it filled a six-by-six-foot square. Most outrageous were the colors she had selected. These were not the subdued reds and greens and golds of the famous Metropolitan Museum tapestries, but instead the loud, garish, and beautiful colors of Mexican weaving. The unicorn was not white, but electric blue. The monk was wearing brilliant red, his face and arms were orange. The crown of hair on his head was yellow. For a sweet, soft-spoken, and conservatively raised English girl these were radical choices.

"Wow." Neil nodded when Laura described the image. "A unicorn doing battle with a monk. That's pretty heavy."

Laura glanced over at him. He seemed genuinely impressed, not mocking.

"It's weird, isn't it? You think of them as friends, right? Unicorns and monks and maidens and all that."

"But this was an evil monk, maybe."

Again Laura darted a glance at him. "Maybe."

A shirtless man on Rollerblades whizzed by, leaving a trail of aftershave smell. "I wonder why she chose it," Neil said, and something in Laura leapt at this. He understood.

"I don't know—that's why, I guess, I want to finish it. Even though it seems so . . . silly."

"Silly?" He looked at her. "It's not silly. You should. You have to finish it."

They were silent for a moment and Laura groped for some sort of segue. Something that would take the conversation out of this place she harbored an age-old, childish sense of apology for. The sadness of it, she felt, was awkward for others. "It's made me think about unicorns, you know," she said cautiously. "I mean, they're so silly to us now—they got so co-opted by sixth-grade girls with purple bedrooms and rainbow T-shirts, but they're interesting, if you can get past that. They're sort of the first chimeras—half horse, half rhino or narwhal or whatever."

"Which idea is older, the unicorn or the centaur?"

"The thing is, they're not like centaurs—they're the opposite because they're supposed to be so innocent. Centaurs are scary. Or corrupt. They're always making off with maidens and all that. But the unicorn, it's like the fact that it's a fusion, that it's a genetic freak of nature—that's what makes it so pure."

She half expected Neil to look at her as if she were crazy. She had never shared this train of thought with anyone else.

"Like it's innocent because it's *not* pure. Because it's mixed."

"Exactly!"

A new flock of geese landed, squawking, at the edge of the pond beside them, honking and fussing.

Neil nodded thoughtfully. "You think she was thinking about that?"

"My mother?"

He nodded again.

"I don't know." Laura frowned. "I don't know what she was thinking."

She could feel Neil's eyes glance over at her, but she kept her own focused straight ahead.

"You'll get there," Neil said, shoving his hands deep in his pockets, and for a moment, Laura loved him.

It was nearly four when they arrived back at 420 Center Street. Mac would be leaving soon; Genevieve would be arriving back home. Miranda would be hungry. Kaaren, their Danish au pair, would be earnestly, stubbornly even, preparing some sort of health food the girls would reject at dinner.

"Can I just grab a drink of water quickly?" Laura asked, aware suddenly that she was desperately thirsty. Amos had settled down and ascended the stairs calmly beside Neil, panting.

Neil opened the door to his apartment and started down the hall toward the kitchen.

"Not mine," he said, gesturing at the poster of an outrageously clad, white-fur-boot-wearing George Clinton.

"Not mine," he repeated, passing the grubby Tibetan Tonka scroll. "Nothing's mine."

Laura followed, thinking of her own house filled with things, her things, all at some point selected or inherited or given. Things she was on some level judged by. Here was Neil, free as the college student he had once been, able to shrug off worldly associations. Laura, on the other hand, was tangled up in objects. Diffused by ownership. Was she really someone who owned an electric bread-maker and floor-to-ceiling drapes?

In the kitchen, Neil poured her a glass of water, and Laura gulped it down—she was so thirsty! How had she gotten so dehydrated? It felt as though there wasn't enough water in the world to quench this thirst. She drained the glass.

As she put the glass down, a sudden shyness overwhelmed her. They were alone and silent for the first time—no more fellow pedestrians and joggers and Dominican picnickers to keep them company. Even Amos had left to flop down, panting, in the living room. Under the whirring of the refrigerator, she could hear the rapid tap-tap of his tags against the bare floor.

"Thanks," she said. "Whew—"

And she was about to continue, remark on the thirst that had so suddenly overwhelmed her, and bid him adieu, when she looked at

Neil. With a sudden electric jolt of realization somewhere between terror and delight, she saw where all this was headed—the heady conversation, the happiness, the freedom, the *thirst*. It froze her against the counter, mute, eyes wide, heart careening dangerously in her chest.

Neil took the glass out of her hand, which was still, unwittingly, wrapped around it, and pushed it across the counter. And then he bent toward her, one hand somehow behind her, on her neck, trembling slightly—or was that her? And his lips met hers—dry, a little scratchy, an awkward connection that gave way with a rush that reminded her perversely of nursing, the sensation of milk letting down—the body suddenly rising and catching a rapid, commanding current. She felt herself give in to the thrill of being taken over, not by Neil, but by this. She bobbed headlong downstream on it, into an unknown future of shipwreck or salvation, spared for the moment at least, from her mind.

And then Amos barked.

Laura jumped, and the edge of the counter dug into her back. Neil pulled away, startled. The barking escalated.

"Jesus Christ."

Neil went down the hall toward the living room and shouted at the dog. Laura stood frozen, heart pounding; the place where Neil's hand had been at the nape of her neck tingled.

From the other room came the sound of Amos's frightened whining: what was Neil doing—killing him? And then Neil reemerged. He looked disheveled.

"Fucking dog," he said.

"What was it?" Laura asked. And for a moment it seemed as though the current was lost. But Neil ignored the question and kissed her again. And with determination, single-mindedness, they jumped back in.

Lying on Neil's bed afterward, Laura felt suddenly awkward—more than awkward. Terrified almost. The afternoon sun was bright. Her skin was pale. She was aware of the stretch marks on her stomach, the hair on her arms, the lines around her eyes.

Neil, lying on his back beside her, looked good despite his T-shirt tan and the awkward in-between growth of straightish hair on his chest. He was thin, his hips were shockingly narrow, and he was muscular—taut in a way that defied aging. His arms were folded behind his head and the hair in his armpits was dark. Men's bodies were allowed so much freedom! She felt envious of his abandon. There was nothing to be ashamed of, no effort at containment.

She sat up and pulled on her bra—a clean one, thank goodness, blue and reasonably sexy—and then quickly followed it with her T-shirt.

Laura tugged her skirt up over her hips.

"Are you okay?" Neil sat up.

Looking at him, Laura had a flash of strangeness. Who was this man? Did she even know him? What had she just done? She was married. She had children. She felt like throwing up.

Instead, she nodded.

"Shit! Are you freaked out?" Neil pulled on his own clothes: boxer shorts and jeans, no shirt.

Laura did not move from her place at the edge of the bed. She felt frozen.

Neil crouched in front of her. "Lo," he said, trying to peer up into her downturned face. "Lo Lo." He put his hands on her knees. "I'm sorry—I didn't realize—"

"Don't—there's nothing to apologize for. I wanted . . ." She lifted her eyes. "I'm not doing anything I didn't want to do." Saying it was somehow a great relief. It was true. It was bad, maybe. Terrible, even. What a terrible mother! What a terrible wife! But true. The self-recrimination bounced tinnily in her mind. She would make it up to her children. She would do something special tomorrow— take them to the museum, or the ice-cream shop, be a fun, energetic mother. But her children seemed a million miles away. And Mac— Mac— She drew a hard wall down over the thought.

Neil's hands dropped down to her ankles. He was still looking into her face with concern and tenderness, and in this he became once again Neil, her old friend, the least strange person she knew.

She began to laugh, just a little bit, and then more.

"What?" Neil looked confused.

"You look so worried!"

"Me?"

She nodded, still laughing, aware she must seem a little hysterical.

"I'm not," he said, rocking back on his heels.

And Laura fell backward against the mattress, feeling the warmth of his hands on her knees.

"It's so strange," she said. And Neil pulled himself up, sat on the mattress beside her, looking down.

"Is it?" he asked.

Looking up at him, his strange/familiar face, the almost eerie blue of his eyes and the stubble along his jaw, she felt suddenly completely calm.

She wanted him to kiss her. Silently she willed it. With every piece of her brain and body. Had she ever wanted something so simple?

5

ELISE OWED HER GENERAL MIDLIFE HAPPINESS to Chrissy, her true love, soul mate, and liberator from the unrewarding confines of her scant relationships with men. But second to Chrissy as a catalyst for her sense of fulfillment was her work as a biochemist.

Elise had always been weirdly good at math and science and, growing up as a St. Anne's School for Girls field hockey player in a Detroit suburb, this aptitude had been a dirty secret rather than a source of pride. It was not encouraged by the St. Anne's school culture or by her mother, who was determined that Elise be a popular, social young lady, at home in the provincial middle class of Farmington Hills in a way that she, as the seventh child of a strict and humorless German minister, had never been herself. And as a quietly compliant girl, Elise had tried to quash the satisfaction that came with her aptitude. But it had always been there for her—the secret pleasure of studying the intricate double helix of DNA, of fathoming the crazy infinite order and predictability hovering everywhere inside the messy confines of life. So when Elise finally gave in to her own natural inclination and began PhD coursework in molecular biology at Boston University, she felt freed. Dormant nooks and crannies of her brain suddenly buzzed with energy and life.

And now here, six years later, she had found, for all intents and purposes, the perfect job in which to apply this excitement. The Pharm, as the transgenics lab where Elise worked was known, was owned by Genron, a giant pharmaceutical corporation, but the Pharm's task lay in the very earliest stages of drug development—the exploration of possibilities rather than the execution of market strategies, which made the science relatively pure. Elise owed her job at the Pharm to Jenny, who worked in product marketing at Genron, and who had put Elise in touch with Harold Rangen when he was looking for bright young scientists to pluck from university labs.

The specific mandate of the Pharm, and of Elise as a staff scientist there, was to develop pharmaceutical-grade human proteins in the milk of its herd of fifty transgenic goats—goats born of unfertilized eggs that had been harvested and injected with human genes, fertilized, and then implanted in surrogate mothers. The proteins, once successfully expressed in the milk of the lactating goats, were then extracted, purified, and readied for use in various drugs. It was a brilliant process, really—so much neater and cleaner than the traditional method of growing pharmaceutical proteins in bacteria or fetal cow serum. So much less icky and so much more sustainable.

For Elise, there was a great thrill in watching a human gene be so efficiently and calmly swept up into a goat embryo's developmental process. She was a pioneer in the age of biology—that ever-nearer time when the intricate workings of life itself would drive the bulk of innovation and progress. Just as the borders of the sociopolitical world had broken down already and a child growing up in Moscow could listen to music made in California and wear clothes made in India and eat rice grown in China, so the boundaries of the animal world would break down too. Already goats could have human genes, humans could have pig hearts, corn could have bacterial DNA. What was next? The possibilities of borderless biology were thrilling to Elise.

The ability to make this work, to predict exactly how the goat's biology would shape itself around the introduction of a human gene, was so satisfying. *Like dumping flour, water, and yeast into a bread machine and having bread in the morning,* Chrissy had said glibly when Elise first described the process to her.

There was another way to look at it, of course, which was, as Laura had so innocently put it when Elise had first described her work, *taking the miracle out of the miracle of life.* The comment had deflated Elise, although Laura had certainly not meant it to. Elise was not a religious or spiritual person. But the sanctity of miracles crossed into the realm of her secular belief. Wasn't it beautiful—and even necessary—to leave some things unexplained? So she saw the miraculous in the very nitty-gritty of the predictable—the fact that somehow the equations she and her coworkers came up with matched what actually happened. The sheer incredibleness of the cellular order that again and again made a + b = c.

This evening, Elise had a particular work-related errand to attend to that filled her with a little pitter-pat of excitement. She was going to stop at the barn on her way out to check in with Emanuel, the Pharm's veterinary surgeon. The barn was connected to the lab by a long, windowed corridor and Elise headed down this and into his office, which, unlike the body of the barn where the animals lived, and the operating room where he infused the oocytes, had no "scrub-in" policy, which meant she could enter without showering, scrubbing down, and donning a whole freshly washed and sterilized shower cap and suit.

Emanuel was a tall, sad-faced Brazilian man, with the grave demeanor of an undertaker. Hunched behind his computer, bathed in bluish light, he looked awkward and gigantic, his shoulders too wide, his neck too long. He started when Elise rapped on the door and looked up with a comically surprised expression.

"Am I interrupting?"

"That's all right," Emanuel said, composing his features back into their usual dignified and somber expression.

"Any news?" Elise asked hopefully.

"Ula?" Emanuel frowned. "Nothing."

"Nothing?" Elise blanched. She had not until that moment real-ized how completely she had assumed she would find the opposite. "Not even colostrum?"

Emanuel shook his head.

Ula was Elise's pet "project." As work on the blood plasma pro-teins that she had been hired to develop had become streamlined enough to seem downright routine, she had begun her own private experiment, using the same process to produce a baby goat whose milk would, hopefully, contain a different plasma protein—one that could be used to cure a rare but devastating blood disorder if she could develop it.

So far, Ula, the goat injected with this new genetic construct, had developed in sync with her peers. She suckled fiercely and played goofily and was every bit as shiny and glossy and healthy as any of the other transgenic goats. Last week Ula had hit nine weeks and had begun the routine injections of synthetic hormones to induce lactation. Which meant that by now the milk should be in. But there was nothing.

"That's weird, isn't it?" Elise asked.

"Unusual," Emanuel corrected.

"What do you think it is?"

Emanuel shrugged. "It happens sometimes. It's hard to say."

"But you're not giving up," Elise said, feeling an unexpected pitter-pat of fear.

"No. Not yet," Emanuel said in a way that was not very reassuring.

"Well, I believe in her," Elise said, in what she had meant to be an ironically emphatic voice, but it came out sounding just as urgent and honest as she really felt.

Emanuel smiled wanly. "We'll see what happens."

When Elise arrived home she was stunned to find Claire Markowitz sipping a cup of tea with Chrissy in the backyard. The boys were puttering (or, in Nigel's case, *sitting*) around with toy gardening tools, sifting, digging, and eating dirt, and Justin was throwing sticks over the fence at the neighbor's dog.

"Hi," Chrissy said, smiling as if there were nothing unusual about this. She did not get up from the table where she and Claire were sitting.

"Hi," Elise said quizzically.

"Wow! Is it end-of-the day already? I had no idea!" Claire Markowitz babbled by way of greeting. "I didn't mean to stay so long."

Elise walked over and kissed Nigel and James on top of their heads.

"We forgot Justin's lunch box over here so I came back to pick it up," Claire continued.

There was a wounded yelp and bark from the other side of the fence as the good-natured mutt Justin had been throwing sticks at leapt away from a direct hit. Justin yowled with delight.

"That's not nice, Justin. Stop that," Claire said, rising.

She was wearing a loose-fitting, faux-African printed leisure suit and looked even more scattered than she had the other night. There was a smudge of black paint or dirt or something on her cheek.

"No!" Justin shrieked as she approached, which made both of the boys look over in surprise. Claire wrestled the stick out of his hand. "Come on, now, Justin, we've got to get home and see about dinner."

"Do you want to stay?" Chrissy asked, and Elise shot her a fierce look.

"Oh, no, no—that's all right. We've imposed enough already. We have to get home and feed poor Camembert, don't we?"

Camembert? Elsie thought incredulously. Could this be that basset hound whose special raw food had appeared on Chrissy's Google search?

"Stop by anytime," Chrissy said graciously. "Will you come see us again?" she asked, leaning down to Justin, who glowered but nodded. "Oh, good. Next time we can make cookies."

"Nice to see you," Elise said, not exactly coldly, but certainly without warmth.

"Oh, right! Yes, of course!" Claire said. "So nice to see you again, Denise."

"Elise," Elise corrected.

"Oh, I'm so sorry! Of course! Of course . . ." the woman began a fit of harebrained apologizing as she made her way out, colorful muumuu, lunch box, and at least four handbags flapping, Justin dragging his heels.

"What was that all about?" Elise asked when Claire was safely out of earshot.

"Claire's visit?" Chrissy said, raising her eyebrows in some approximation of surprise. Then she narrowed her eyes coldly. "She's our friend, Elise. It's not a sin to have a cup of tea with her."

"I didn't say—" Elise began, but Chrissy had already turned and, gathering up a few discarded sand toys, disappeared into the house.

"Come on, boys," Chrissy said with a note of . . . what? Proprietariness? "It's dinnertime."

It was later, on the phone to Laura, that Elise identified the feeling the incident had given her.

"It feels like I'm being punished," she said. "Like I've done something awful—like lied or had an affair."

"Why?" Laura's voice sounded unduly alarmed. "Have you—"

"Of course not! That's what I'm saying. I don't understand what I've done."

"Right. Of course." Laura was silent for a moment.

Elise poured herself a glass of milk, wedging the phone between her shoulder and her ear. The boys were asleep. Chrissy was at her beloved book group.

"It has to do with this donor sibling thing, I think. Chrissy is mad that I don't want to be a part of it."

"Hmmm," Laura said thoughtfully. "Why don't you?"

"Because"—Elise shut the door to the fridge—"I'm not."

"Not what?"

"A part of it."

"Yes, you are," Laura said. "They're your boys too."

"Not that way." Elise stared at her reflection in the window. Short hair, sharp bones, glasses. Her eyes were inscrutable—dark pools of shadow. "Not biologically."

"But—" Laura began, and then stopped. "Hmm," she conceded. "But I'm sure Chrissy understands that that's complicated . . ."

"I don't know." Elise sighed.

"Well, have you talked with her about it?"

"Of course! I mean, I've told her I don't like seeing the boys as members of some weird biological pod, circling around this all-powerful, missing progenitor."

"Well, okay. You've told her *that*—but I mean have you talked about what it means to *you, personally*?"

"I don't know what you mean," Elsie said stubbornly. Although actually she did.

She had not wanted to share her feelings on this thorny subject with Chrissy. To give them voice would have dragged them out in all their divisive egotism, would have made them real. The fact was that there were times in those early days when Elise would come home to find Chrissy and the boys in bed sleeping like a litter of kittens, the room close and purring with their synced breaths, and she would be hit with a feeling of exclusion that was stronger than anything she had experienced since grade school. There were times even now when Elise felt the cold slap of outsiderness, coming upon the three of them crouched together on the living room floor building a block tower or constructing a train track. All at once she would feel her apartness from them—not only her workday absence, but the warm circle of blood that they shared, wholly unconnected to her own.

"I'm just saying it couldn't hurt."

"Really?" Elise said archly, and then sighed. "Anyway."

They were silent for a moment.

"I'm sorry—I haven't even asked—is everything— How are *you* doing?" Elise drained the glass of milk.

"Oh, fine. Fine. Just normal. Everything's, you know, normal."

Laura sounded overly breezy, actually. It was unlike her not to issue at least some small complaint.

Behind her, Elise could hear Chrissy's key turning in the lock.

"It's getting late," Laura said. "Go to bed. You'll feel better when you wake up."

"Okay." Elise felt a swell of warmth for her. Laura was a good friend. At least she had a good friend, even if Chrissy was falling out of love with her.

"Goodnight, sweetie."

"Goodnight."

She placed the phone back in its receiver and stood for a moment, watching Chrissy's reflection in the window—sinking onto the sofa, pushing back her mane of hair, looking normal, the anger and hostility washed away. Where had it gone? Who was this newly volatile woman she was married to? And then, warily, maybe a little petulantly, she turned around.

"Beanie," Chrissy said. "I'm sorry I was such a grouch."

Chrissy was the only woman Elise had ever been with, a fact that was occasionally troubling to Chrissy but made perfect sense to

Elise, who had not considered herself gay when they met. She had spent her life up to that point as a heterosexual, neither delighted nor disgusted by the opposite sex. In high school and college she had partaken in the requisite amount of hookups (largely with semi-outsiderish boys—acceptable, but not particularly appealing to the mainstream—or to herself, for that matter). And for the most part she had been uninterested in sex. She was willing to partake in it for all the obvious social reasons; it was really not that different from her willingness to smoke nasty-tasting cigarettes outside the Mini Mart in the humdrum Detroit suburb she had grown up in, or feign interest in bands whose music she found grating. It was all in the name of fitting in, which had for a stultifyingly long time been her primary MO.

And then she had started the PhD program in molecular biology and met Chrissy. It was hard to separate the two revelations of her life, both of which had occurred within two months. She had been scooping out portions of lasagna at a soup kitchen—an unlikely activity which she had been dragged to by Laura, who was experiencing one of her regular fits of volunteerism that she good-naturedly shamed her friends into joining. Chrissy had been the supervisor—the tireless women's shelter advocate who turned the motley crew of volunteers into a functioning body of workers, and who, after the meal was served, went around from table to table checking in with the homeless women, asking after kids and husbands and job interviews with genuine interest.

Elise was spellbound by Chrissy's quiet competence, her gentle voice and odd mix of humor and earnestness. She had shown up at the shelter every Sunday and Wednesday for the next few months. Until finally she had been able to name the attraction and admiration she felt for this woman, for what it was. Love. But Chrissy was a woman! The idea that she could love Chrissy was so radical it had filled her with a heady, terrifying excitement. The revelation had been cataclysmic, but at the same time utterly, smoothly perfect—

like the clink of a delicate dominolike machinery slipping, one piece after another, into place. She only doubted it at all because it seemed too perfect to be right.

Chrissy, on the other hand, had come out at the very beginning of her wholesome, self-actualizing sojourn at Macalister College in Minnesota. She had been in two serious and long-term relationships with other women, had checked out the lesbian bar scene, participated in gay rights protests, and been a peer counselor to other, less confident gay youths. Her lesbian identity existed entirely apart from Elise. *How could you not want that?* she had pressed before they moved in together. Elise had had to work to convince her. Her love for Chrissy was a thing unto itself. It was everything, not part of a sexual experiment. In Chrissy's presence Elise felt defined. She was no longer the mismatched collection of attitudes and experiences that made up her life, but something purer, truer, and more coherent: an individual. She saw more clearly. She thought more clearly. And for some reason—this was a central and sometimes disturbing mystery to Elise—Chrissy loved her. Chrissy gathered up the scattering of bits and pieces that had heretofore been Elise Farber, and palmed them into a logical and desirable shape.

And this firm and unifying grasp was the most certain thing in Elise's life.

6

THE TASTE OF VICTORY WAS SWEET. Sweeter even than Jenny would have imagined. Lying on her desk was a white cafeteria plate containing a sleek lacquer-red box that looked like a cross between a compact and a cigarette case, modern but not mod, shiny but not slick. She pressed the hinge and opened it to find four neat lines of beautiful robin's-egg-blue pills, each in its own little compartment. She lifted the red foil packet and slipped one of the pills onto her palm. It was the loveliest, most alluring color she had ever seen. And the size was perfect: not too big to swallow, but not the usual, apologetically minimized, wish-me-away size most psychopharm drugs came in. This was a pill that fairly sang of happiness.

She picked up the phone immediately, heart beating in her throat.

"Your baby's here," Watson's strong voice boomed over the line two minutes later. "You like it?"

"It's beautiful. I want to pop it in my mouth right now."

Watson laughed.

"So was it worth hiring them or what?"

"You win. You win."

She could imagine him shaking his head, throwing his hands up. The idea for the birth-control-style package had been hers exclusively. In the face of much resistance from her male colleagues, she had insisted Genron hire a top-notch consumer product design firm, one that had never been used by any pharma company before, to come up with a prototype. Her instruction: to create a pill and a package that did not connote "medicine." Something that would make it easy to see if you had missed a day, and that replaced the stigma of antidepressants with the sly sophistication of "family planning." And the firm had come up with several unimpressive ideas: a shiny yellow star-shaped pill in a Pez-dispenser-like container, a clear box full of tiny pink beads, and then a row of more typical beigy oblong pills in a case like a pencil, which Watson had favored. But now this: The fruit of her labor! The most beautiful pill and packaging she had ever seen.

"Who wants a pill the color of a Band-Aid?" she taunted.

"Not new mothers, apparently."

"They don't want a Band-Aid. They want happiness. They want bliss."

"Whoa, there. You're scaring me. No. But Jennifer . . ."

She could hear him shifting gears—here came serious Watson. Intimidating Watson. The Watson who had built this place to what it was today.

". . . the focus groups loved it. Nine to one. I've never seen anything like it. Just—bam. So we're gonna move this thing fast. The FDA boys are all over it and it shouldn't be a problem. The factory's ready to go. And you and me—we have things to discuss."

" 'Things'?" Jenny's heart beat a little faster.

"I'll pass you back to Violet. You have lunch plans Friday?"

Jenny glanced at her calendar. Laura. "Nothing I can't change."

"All right then. You like steak?"

The other half of Jenny's inspiration had not been executed yet. It was the ad campaign itself, which had come to Jenny quite literally in a dream. She had woken up one night around three a.m. with the idea in her head, fully intact, as if it had been planted there—by God, or some computer chip, or some archetypal mechanism of the human brain. *You deserve* . . . she saw in bright, cheery yellow writing. *You deserve to be happy, you deserve to enjoy your baby, you deserve to sleep* . . . Wasn't that what every middle-class American mother felt?

The writing was transposed over an image of a woman lying on the grass—an attractive woman, not too beautiful, but healthy and smart and happy, holding a baby aloft above her, smiling into its blissful, gurgling, cooing face. And then in bold, bright font, the list of things that she deserved: happiness, love, affection, the ability to be carefree, to sleep, to look good, to feel good—the ability, above all, to be *herself.*

Jenny was not unsympathetic. Hell, motherhood was nuts. It did not fit logically into the modern, well-educated, career-driven woman's life. What preparation had they been given for the physical demand of it; the lifting and carrying and lugging? The sleep deprivation? The odd combination of worry and tedium that dominated every day? Maybe in simpler times, when women grew up learning how to cook and garden and keep house, to take care of brothers and sisters and grandparents—maybe then the routine of caring for a newborn had slid right into place. When a woman's primary aspiration was to achieve reproductive potential—not some more elusive form of recognition, monetary or otherwise.

Jenny was sympathetic to this plight, but she was different. She had her mother to thank for this. Judy Callahan, bossy, demanding, domestic genius that she was, had schooled Jenny early in the day-to-day running of a household (dishes, laundry, casseroles—at age eleven Jenny had been responsible already for her own wash and for putting dinner on the table once a week). And she had trained her only daughter to help her with the day care she ran out of her living room.

So Jenny had grown up changing diapers, freezing teething toys, and ignoring the irrational screams of infants. She knew to regard the latter as expressions of the normal kinks in their new little bodies—the coughing sputters of engines being, for the first time, turned on. She did not try to assess the emotional implications of Colin's crying jags, or pinpoint the elaborate physical causes of his fussing (the "allergies" so popularly discussed in mothers' groups and message boards online). This was a great advantage, she realized, watching other women trying to apply their finely honed anlaytical skills to their babies. No wonder they turned to therapy in droves!

At home, Colin was sitting in his sleek, modern-design high chair in the hideous "Heartbreaker" bib Maria had bought for him, serenely eating sweet potatoes off a spoon. His mouth, his nose, his hands, and the tray were frighteningly clean—Maria kept a wet cloth diaper on hand to wipe up every smidgen of food, a habit Jenny worried would make Colin persnickety. In her experience, babies were supposed to eat like maniacs and leave their high chairs covered with food from head to toe, ready for a bath.

"*Hola.*" Maria looked up at Jenny's entrance with a worried expression on her face.

"Maria," Jenny said, "let him make a mess!" but Maria's expression stopped her.

"Mr. Jeremy is upstairs. He come home before an hour, not feeling so good. He look"—she made a frightful face and drew a hand down over her features—"so white—like a ghost! I ask him if I can bring him anything, but he want—"

"He's upstairs?"

Maria nodded.

"Hi, baby," Jenny said, turning to Colin, who looked at her impassively and then refocused on the spoon Maria was holding, stopped midair. He was not the most satisfying baby to come home to. She leaned over and planted a kiss on his head despite her irrational sense of wounded pride.

Upstairs, Jeremy was lying on his back in bed with the shades drawn and the sheets hiked up to his chin. He did look frighteningly pale. His eyes were closed, but they opened when Jenny sat down on the bed.

"What's going on?" she asked. "Are you sick?"

Jeremy closed his eyes again. "I feel weird."

"Weird how? Do you need to go to the doctor?"

"I went."

"You went? What do you mean, you went? When?" Alarm coursed through Jenny.

"Yesterday."

"You didn't say anything! What did the doctor say?"

"He didn't. He didn't know what the problem was."

"Oh." It felt hot and stuffy in the room with the blinds down and windows closed. Outside it was beautiful—a clear, bright spring day. "Do you mind if I open these?"

Jeremy winced slightly and turned on his side, away from the windows.

"What's going on? Does it bother you—the light?"

"A little."

Jenny stared at her husband, his bony body outlined under the sheet.

"Jeremy," she said. "What did the doctor say? Was he concerned?"

Jeremy didn't open his eyes. "He's running some tests."

The stuffy dark of the room seemed suddenly oppressive. The green carpeting, the drapes, the thick burgundy sheets—they had to get out of here, get settled in their new, airy, spacious house. "Tests," she repeated. And for the first time she considered the fact that possibly her husband might not simply be a malingerer.

7

THE STORYLINE OF *PROMETHEUS SYNDROME*, the game that Neil
had been hired to add to, was pretty much standard gaming fare. A
benevolent race of highly evolved beings from the planet Xanadu
find themselves under attack by a cunning and selfish alien race. To
preserve the secrets of their peace and enlightenment from being
extinguished they hide a digital tablet in a distant galaxy on a backward and uncivilized planet called Earth. This planet is ruled by a
foolish, rudimentary species called human beings, who are confined
to their own infinitely fallible bodies and do nothing but blunder
around trying to make money and driving nasty, planet-destroying
automobiles.

Ultimately Earth becomes the battleground-du-jour of the epic
struggle between warring factions of the universe. The digital tablet,
of course, seems to be the only prayer the compromised and beleaguered earthlings have for surviving the crossfire of the nasty aliens
running amok on their planet. First they have to find it, and then—
here was the premise for *Prometheus II*—once they have found it,
they have to decode it, protect it from their adversaries, and decide
whether to put its powerful contents to use.

Neil saw multiple problems in this foundation. What the hell
was a "digital tablet," and whose imagination did such a thing really
appeal to? Furthermore, what gamer would decide not to use its
contents once they were decoded? And the earthlings who came

across this thing in a sea cave off the island of Madagascar (this was where Johnson had left them at the end of *Prometheus I*) were a tiresome group of geologists who said things like "Wass up, bro?" and "Gotcha" all the time. The enemy characters were downright juvenile: a shape-shifting alien princess who favored being a swimsuit model as her disguise of choice, a two-headed dragon, a greedy, toupee-wearing human physicist, and, of course, the headless nymphomaniacs from the planet Praxis.

Neil's work began with tackling the digital tablet. This was clear. From here everything else would flow. His idea for the fix came out of his conversation with Laura. What if in fact this digital tablet turned out to be alive? What if, instead of some computerized scroll of commands and information, it was an animal— a unicornlike chimera? Maybe suspended in some sort of frozen amniotic fluid à la Woody Allen in *Sleeper*. It would be a specimen whose very cells held the key to freedom and power—a sort of biological Rosetta stone. There was so much possibility that came with this. There would be those who wanted to kill it to get at the answers, and those who felt the secrets it held could be accessed only through its life. And there would be the fertile, and not-yet-completely-exhausted-by-the-gaming-industry, substance of DNA to unpack. It would point *Prometheus Syndrome II* into the timely green current of scientific exploration, sweep it away from the graying detritus of physics and computers, of outdated cultural artifacts like PalmPilots and the movie *TRON*.

"What *kind* of creature?" was Steven Closter's predictably nonplussed response to the idea. "Like a rhinoceros?" he said, snickering. The man was a savant. He had no imagination and no sense of the profound.

"I was thinking more like a dachshund," Neil said, and enjoyed the uncertain look on Steven's sarcastic face.

Rod Emerus was, also predictably, more enthusiastic. "That's good," he said, giving Neil a shrewd look. "That's exactly what I'm talking about. You read *Scientific American*?"

"No."

Neil found himself, once again, in the awkward position of sitting directly across the conference table from Rod, which was intense—too intense for nine a.m.—given the man's penchant for prolonged eye contact.

"There was an article about the domestication of biotechnology in last week's issue. Check it out."

"I will."

"What else?"

"About the game?"

Emerus nodded irritably.

"Well, an overhaul of the enemies. Less focus on the aliens. Get rid of—"

Emerus waved his hand. "Right. Fine. I meant anything else profound. Fundamental."

Neil hesitated. "Yeah," he said, although he had not really thought this through. "Breeding."

Emerus raised his eyebrows.

"Genetic engineering. Something they learn from this animal—this living key to the universe. Making things."

Emerus continued his penetrating gaze and Steven Closter looked from him to Neil and back again like someone observing a tennis match.

"I like it," Emerus said, knocking his pale knuckles on the table. "All right, then." He rose from his chair, which made rude squeaking noises. And beside him, Harry Fontaine, his nervous, bespectacled assistant, rose as well.

"The marketing—" Harry began.

"Right. Cancel your *Warcraft* face-off matches or what have you. You have a meeting at two with the ad sales team."

And with that Emerus and Harry left the room, leaving Neil squirming with shame at being included in this kind of industry joke. As if he were spending his afternoons engaged in online role-playing games! The fact that, come to think of it, he sometimes did only made it worse.

Back at his desk, there was one message and two caller ID calls from Laura. Neil felt suddenly overwhelmingly tired. Here he was in Boxborough, Massachusetts, writing a computer game and having an affair with a married woman. He could practically see Jane pushing up her glasses in that reproving way of hers, chewing on an end of her dark hair, shaking her head. Five weeks of being unattached and this was what he was doing with himself. He had an urge to simply drop his head onto his arms at the cluttered fiberboard desk he had been given and go to sleep. But it was only his first week on the job. This could be misconstrued. So instead he grabbed the pack of cigarettes from his jacket pocket and headed out into the sun.

Breeding. For a minute there he had actually felt a flash of excitement. A burst of true enthusiasm for his work—as if this genetic engineering he had thought of adding to the gameplay was in some way important, would actually have some power to, what—reflect? transform? hold currency in?—the real world. Ridiculous. He had to catch himself with shit like that or he'd end up just like Steven Closter, or even Joe, that poor, snuffly, ass-kissing kid who had toured him around on his first day at ZGames. Delusional. That was what it was. All-American delusional, getting caught up in the minutiae of something as small as a video game without considering its frivolity, its utter insignificance, in the larger world. Better to stick to researching the life of Albert Sorenson Jones—this, at least, was fundamental. Someone's life. At least just a little bit, it mattered.

The landscape of the office park ZGames stood in the middle of was absolutely deadening: manicured, anonymous, deflecting of the elements so that even the lovely peculiarities of sunshine (the way it filtered through leaves or glanced off of sideview mirrors, the way it glowed on a pelt of grass) were deadened. The sun became just one thing: bright. The grass became just one thing: green.

Neil closed his eyes against this, sitting at the round carved-granite table beside the entrance on a rounded carved-granite bench. Had there ever been a less inviting place to sit? But he was simply too tired to walk around. He smoked for a full minute like this, eyes shut.

When he opened his eyes there was a girl in front of him, lurking off to the other side of the mirrored-glass entrance and trying to light a cigarette of her own. She was short and petite, with blunt-cut, chin-length brown hair. Her manner of flicking the lighter, cupping her hand (unnecessarily in this windless cul de sac) in front of her cigarette, radiated energy. Neil sat up straight and jerked his arm—his dead-looking, pale arm—off the table and onto his lap.

"Sorry," the girl said. "I didn't mean to startle you." She had a slight accent and a novice's way of almost sucking on the cigarette now that it was lit.

"No, no," Neil protested for no reason. "That's what I get for sleeping in public."

"But you weren't sleeping," she said with a smirk. "You were smoking."

"Right." He said, feeling inexplicably annoyed.

"You work here?" she tilted her head toward the building.

"I do."

"And this is where you have to come to have a smoke?"

"Beats the men's room." Neil stood and ground his cigarette out under his heel.

"America," she said, rolling her eyes and sucking on her cigarette again.

"Hm." Neil shrugged noncommittally. "Enjoy," he said curtly, heading back in through the mirrored doors. Something about the girl's obvious derision galled him. Not that he disagreed with her— it was a hideous place to have to smoke. For that matter, it was a hideous place to have to work. But still. He had felt implicated in her critique—a *part of*, rather than *apart from*, this monstrous example of the American quotidian.

He walked through the cool, featureless foyer to the back of the building and into the parking lot. He would have to call Laura from here. It could not be done from his desk—or from the front of the building now that the girl was there.

"Neil," Laura said when she picked up. Her voice was breathy, full of delight.

"Lo," he said.

"Hi."

An early-season cricket chirped from the bushes behind him.

"What's up?"

"Oh." Laura sounded taken aback.

He could imagine her straightening, frowning a little. She was so transparent, Laura. There was no contrivance in her, and no game. It made him feel almost sorry for her—how did she manage in the world?

"I don't know . . ." she said. "I guess I just wanted to tell you—to make sure you knew—you know, that I'm not freaked out. I know you thought I was. You were probably worried I'd go cuckoo on you or something. But I'm not. I'm just"—she paused—"happy. That's all. That's what I called to say."

"That's sweet," he said, smiling despite himself. They were silent for a moment.

"And you . . ." she said. "Do you feel—are you okay . . . ?"

"Oh, yeah. I'm fine."

In the hiccup of silence that followed, he realized he was supposed to offer something more here, something positive. "I'm glad. I had a great time with you."

"Good."

There was another silence. This one tinged with awkwardness.

"Do you want—I guess we didn't really talk about 'the future.' " He hated himself for saying it so ironically, so Johnson-esquely, with such obvious quotation marks.

"Ugh," Laura said. "God forbid."

"Right." Neil laughed. "I just mean . . . do you want to get together again—I mean, for coffee or a drink or whatever? Not—"

Laura laughed. "Well, no. Yes. I'll take 'whatever.' "

"Okay."

Abruptly, the cricket's chirp shut off. Neil began shaking a new cigarette from the pack out of habit, and then stopped himself, shoved it back.

"I'm in this crappy parking lot right now—you should see it. It's like"—he paused—"post-human. Can I call you later?"

"Of course! That sounds awful. Post-human."

"It is. All right—I'll call you after work."

"Okay." She sounded a little sad.

"Lo . . ." he said impulsively. "I love you."

"Oh!"

"All right—talk to you."

He closed his cell phone and shoved it into his pocket. Now he'd really done it. What a fucking mess. He meant it. He loved her. She was so sweet, and so good, and so pretty. But those words—they were dangerous words. He should know better. Thirty-five years old and behaving like a twenty-one-year-old. Behaving like an idiot. Maybe he was not capable of navigating this world on his own after all. For the first time since he had left her, he actually felt some nostalgia for Jane and her psychiatrist-like sensibilities, the aura of frankness and control she exuded, that, if nothing else, he had been able to crawl up and be absorbed into.

The moment he stepped into the conference room he knew it. Almost before he saw her. The marketing girl. Of course. That was who she was. It was as if, on some level, he had known the cigarette break would not be the last he saw of her. She was sitting at the table with ZGames' own intrepid promo team—a tall, blond, but unattractive duo who looked more like brother and sister than coworkers. Heidi and Ulrich, his brain supplied. These were not their real names: Neil vaguely remembered being introduced to them. But Heidi and Ulrich was good.

Beside Heidi, the marketing girl looked downright pretty, although she wasn't.

"You!" she said, laughing. "The sleeping smoker!"

He was reminded of her accent—Eastern Europe. The rest of the group looked at him. "A joke," she said. "I met him coming in."

"This is Galena Ibanesku," Heidi said with a smile frozen on her face as if to acknowledge this bit of repartee would have been untoward. "Neil Banks, Steven Closter."

Galena rose to shake their hands.

"Galena's here to talk with you about an exciting new opportunity we all have here," Ulrich said.

"Exciting, hunh?" Steven mocked, and for once Neil felt a twinge of appreciation for him. Had they no shame, these marketing people? How could they honestly adhere to this tired language of hyperbole so widely mocked that it had for years been fodder for improv groups and *Saturday Night Live* skits?

"Well, *we* think so," Ulrich replied huffily. "And you would too if you thought about where your next paycheck was coming from."

"Okay," Galena said in that blunt Eastern European way of hers. "Okay. No squabbling."

This did not seem to be an auspicious start for the meeting.

Heh, heh, heh, everyone laughed uncomfortably.

"So," Heidi plowed ahead, still smiling. "Galena is here from Genron, which has just signed an unusual new product placement plan with us that I think you will find very interesting to integrate . . ."

Neil's brain remained stuck on Genron. That was Jenny Callahan's company. This girl, this Galena, probably knew Jenny. Possibly worked with her, even. The idea was startling—an intrusion of one mental space into another. And it seemed, somehow, to connect the girl to the baby. *His* baby. The thought pinged through Neil's mind like an alarm that had been wound all this time, waiting, springs loaded, to go off.

"Do you want to take it from here, Galena?" Heidi was saying, still smiling plastically.

"Sure," Galena said. She had an aggressive way about her, not at all like most women in marketing whom Neil had encountered. Except for Jenny. She was, in this, a little *like* Jenny, actually. "You are maybe wondering *why* Setlan," Galena said. "Why computer games as a marketplace for Setlan? But the answer is not so difficult to understand. You see . . ." She opened a folder and distributed a set of news articles neatly copied and stapled. The first of these bore a headline that read "Survey Finds High Incidence of Depression in Computer Game Players."

"Oh, boy," Steven groaned. "The evil, depressed, disgruntled gamer rears his ugly head."

"Not evil, not disgruntled," Galena chided flirtily. "The numbers here"—she gestured at the next page, which showed a simple chart, courtesy of *The New York Times*—"show us that there are many people playing computer games who need some kind of psychological help. They are turning, maybe, to these games as a way to escape reality, or their own feelings. You are familiar with the *DSM-IV*?"

Steven shook his head and Neil nodded mutely, the specter of the baby—his baby, Colin—still looming over all else in his mind. Jenny would have pictures of the baby in her office. Glossy eight-by-tens, probably professional, for the world to see. And yet he, Neil, the biological father of this child, had never seen him. Never laid eyes on his little face.

"The *DSM-IV* is the diagnostic manual used by mental health clinicians to diagnose mental disorders. In more than one survey, computer gamers were more likely to fit the *DSM-IV*'s criteria for depression and mood disorders than their non-game-playing demographic counterparts. So this is a logical market for Setlan, which is the most commonly prescribed medication for depression, with over thirty million users in the United States alone. We think if you can integrate the medication into the gameplay in some way—"

"Ha!" Steven reared back in his chair. " 'Pick up some meds with that ammunition,'" he said in a fake game-show-host voice.

Galena ignored this and plowed ahead in a bulldoggish, unsmiling, and unmarketinglike way. "If you can integrate the drug into your gameplay in some way this will be worth a certain amount of advertising dollars from us because the player's attention is guaranteed. If you integrate the drug into an in-game advertisement it will be worth a smaller amount of advertising dollars. We will be working out the particular dollar amounts with Carter and Martin"— she nodded her head toward the blond promo team—"once we see the finished product."

"Man." Steven shook his head. "Meds."

"You don't need to worry about that element," Ulrich, or rather Martin, said smoothly. "You just worry about the creative angle and we'll take care of the rest. Galena has brought along information to share with you . . ."

Neil tuned out the man's insipid, smiling drone. It was a double whammy, really. The reminder of Jenny—of the baby—here in this previously completely irrelevant place, and now Setlan. Not only that he was completely enmeshed in the inane and unselfconscious world of computer games, but that he was now also supposed to play the creepy role of product marketer for, of all insidious things, a psychotropic drug. A drug, in fact, that he had long despised for its ubiquity and its premise: that happiness and well-adjustedness was within everyone's reach. Was, in fact, the norm. He had truly been bought. If there had been any question, any grain of hope that perhaps his role here at ZGames was not actually corrupt, not actually a signifier of total sellout on his part, it was gone.

"Neil," the girl, Galena, said, leveling her gaze at him. She had apparently just finished explaining the various pieces of literature now lying in front of him. "It's Neil, is that right? You look unconvinced."

Steven, Heidi, and Ulrich all turned to look at him.

"Unconvinced?" he asked, taken aback. The girl's intensity was confrontational. She looked ready to spring across the table and tear his throat out, lift her face heavenward with a mouthful of flesh.

"You don't look like you like this idea."

"No, no," he protested instinctively, and then shrugged. "I'm not a fan—" he began, and then reconsidered. What was the point? He wasn't about to stage some moral battle over this. He had sold out. Period. "Doesn't matter," he concluded.

There was a moment of strained smiling on Heidi and Ulrich's parts, interested spectating on Steven's, and intent, challenging staring on Galena's as they waited to see if he would say more.

"Well," Heidi said finally, just as Galena opened her mouth and then shut it again, still staring at him, "why don't you boys look this over and see what you come up with and we'll take it from there?"

And with that cheery instruction from Heidi, the meeting was adjourned. There was smiling and hand-shaking all around. Steven, it seemed, had a basketball dialogue going with Ulrich and a condescending flirtation with Heidi.

"Excuse me a moment," Neil could hear Galena saying to them as he made his way out the conference room double doors. And then, as he had—hoped? dreaded? was it normal to have no idea which?—she pressed out the door after him. "So you're suspicious of pharma," she said, somehow managing to plant herself between him and the elevator bank.

He had no choice but to meet her gaze. Glittering, sharp, slightly mocking—he knew what he would find there. It was—honestly, *absurdly*—the story of his life. She wanted him. For God knows what reason, or what signal he was giving off. This Albanian whip-cracker was interested.

The recognition made him tired already. He knew what would happen. He would try to walk away. God knows, he tried. But something in his trying was defunct.

8

LAURA WAS AT THE FOOT of her daughter's pink, princess-inspired bed trying not to think of Neil.

"Will you sit with me?" Genevieve asked anxiously as soon as Laura turned out the light.

"Of course," Laura said with a sigh, and let her head rest against the wall.

Her daughter was a fearful sleeper. Frightened of ghosts and monsters and burglars, giant tractors and rabid squirrels. For years Laura had kept up the charade of an argument over sitting with her. All the books and doctors and friends she consulted were in agreement: Genevieve had to learn to fall asleep alone. But this proved impossible without torrents of tears and screams and protests that Laura herself was not capable of withstanding, and so now she sat with Vievee, for the most part in secret. (Mac would find it ridiculous—or worse, would find it *coddling*, which in his book was tantamount to abuse.) She waited until Vievee's little hands finally unclasped from the fretful fists they made around her sleepy bear, and her breath grew deep and even, and sleep overcame her body like a drug.

Laura's compassion for her daughter was clearly on account of her own childhood memories of being left alone at night in the nether regions of the tall brick house she had grown up in. It was a narrow five-story brownstone on Beacon Hill: the house, in fact, that her father, Adam Trillian, had grown up in so many years before. It was full of ghosts—cold, disapproving ancestors and disgruntled cooks, housekeepers, and nursemaids. After her mother died, Laura had imagined her as a protector—a kind spirit from the other world who sat on her daughter's bed and kept the others at bay. But it was not enough, always, to reassure her.

And here Adam Trillian had also been of no help. He had stocked his daughter with sophisticated reading: Steinbeck, Dickens, and the Brontë sisters when she was only ten, and Poe (why Poe for an impressionable, motherless young girl?) for her twelfth birthday. He had taken pride in her voracious reading, and boasted jokingly to friends of his daughter's sensitivity. But as a caretaker, he was remote and oddly formal. He had been much older than Annabelle Trillian when they married, and was sixty when Laura entered her teens. He was the product of an older, more formal era, which had ill-prepared him to reassure his imaginative ten-year-old that she would not be carried off by evil spirits in her sleep.

Tonight, sitting in the dark, with Genevieve's warm, innocent body curled up beside her, Laura's head was full of thoughts of Neil. He had sounded so funny on the phone at lunchtime, so . . . distracted. And then suddenly announcing that he loved her! What did that mean? It was Neil, after all. She was not naïve enough to ascribe some usual sentiment to those words. Of course he loved her in a way—they had known each other for so long! But did he *love* her? Was he in love with her? Had he been for all these years? The idea made her heart beat fast with excitement. It took her by surprise— had this wish always lurked somewhere in the back of her mind? Or was it something uniquely here and now—an alignment of circumstances and trajectories that had given birth to some completely new electricity? Honestly, she did not know. But no matter what, she had to be careful. She knew Neil well enough to know that.

When he had called her after work, his tone had been inscrutable.

Mac was out of town, she had volunteered shyly. And Kaaren was there all night. *Should she—? Would he want—? She could come over* . . . This had been left inconclusive. Did he pine for her touch the way she pined for his? The patch of skin on her neck that he had passed over still prickled and thrilled when she thought of this.

Finally Genevieve was asleep. Laura maneuvered herself gingerly off the bed. She stood for a moment in the hallway, thinking, until Cocoa, fearless Cocoa, back from the country (otherwise known as Mac's sister's place on the Cape—a haven Laura took every opportunity to ship the manic dog off to), frisked toward her down the hall. Laura bent absently to pat her and Cocoa licked her face and breathed hot dog-food breath into her ear.

She would take her out, Laura decided. It would give her time to think, to clear her head. Downstairs she pulled on a cardigan—it was still chilly after dark these days—and let herself out.

The night was damp and fragrant with the smell of lilacs, which grew lustily along the peeling garden wall. They were Laura's favorite flower and she stood for a moment appreciating the fact that she had inherited such a healthy, blooming old world garden from the previous owners of her house. She'd barely had to lift a finger to enjoy such luxuries as delicate, blossoming mock orange bushes, white climbing roses, clematis, and, of course, the lilacs, which were profuse and widely admired. This was the kind of neighborhood in which people admired lilacs. Distinguished elderly couples walked by after dinner to see them, and neighbors asked what sort of fertilizer she fed them, and who did the pruning, smugly aware of the quaintness of their conversation. This was exactly the sort of thing that drove Mac crazy about Cambridge—he had wanted to buy a newer place somewhere less fusty, like Weston or Chestnut Hill, but Laura had fallen in love with the house on Fayerweather Street, and while in most of their life decisions she was quite pliable, in this she had stood fast.

And so the house, with its odd, painted sandstone façade, and long, elegant shuttered windows, became hers. It was so serene and peaceful, with its flat, pinkish-beige-painted stone front, its slate roof, its crumbly, English-looking garden wall.

"It's like you," Elise had said when Laura had first taken her by to see it. "If you were a house, this would be you."

"How do you mean?" Laura had asked, although she understood it was true.

"I don't know." Elise had shrugged matter-of-factly. "Beautiful, but a little sad."

The neighborhood was quintessential old Cambridge: liberal, disheveled, and discreet. Boring, Mac pronounced. And he was right. But Laura liked this about it. There was a sense of moderation inherent in the beautiful, expensive old houses, with their minimally landscaped yards and well-made but neglected fencing. There was something commendable, if contrived, about the frumpy L. L. Bean style of the rich people who lived there: elsewhere, their economic counterparts would be wearing Hermès and Chanel, driving Lexuses, renting shares in private jets, but here they drove their Volvos and flew commercial. It was an assertion of values, which, however righteous, Laura could respect. "Hypocrites," Mac would say as he watched them unload their paper bags of overpriced groceries from the local gourmet shop, but Laura didn't mind. What was hypocritical about spending money on food rather than bling?

Tonight the pavement was wet from the light rain and Cocoa pulled sharply at her leash, hot on the trail of fresh and interesting city smells. The streetlights threw misty pools of light, buzzing with the first intrepid insects of the season. Should she go to Neil's? Would he want her to? More importantly—she reminded herself— did *she* want to? It wasn't just some game they were playing, after all. It was an Affair. It was the deepest, darkest form of deception and emotional calumny a person could perpetrate within a marriage.

Within a family. The thought of family—her girls, sweet, sleeping girls—laid a tentacle of cold and slippery panic on her shoulder. She shook it off, sped her footsteps, tugged violently on Cocoa's leash. The dog yelped indignantly and tore her nose away from the stinking pile of shit she had been absorbedly snuffing. No, Laura would not think about this right now. She would not stop and consider.

And so back at home she found herself dialing the number from her cell phone, her heart beating madly, the glass of bourbon she had poured joggling slightly in rhythm with each thundering heartbeat.

"Lo?" Neil said, and she blurted it out without even really hearing him. Certainly without trying to read his tone.

"Kaaren?" she asked moments later, rapping lightly on the au pair's bedroom door. "I have to go out for a bit." She had not even stopped to think of an excuse and felt her face coloring. "Just wanted you to know in case, you know, something is wrong. I have my cell phone."

The door opened and Kaaren's stern Scandinavian face appeared in the crack. Kaaren was a good person, a perfectly fine, relatively unobtrusive, responsible young woman, but for some reason Laura had not managed to establish a comfortable rapport with her. Maybe it was her seriousness. Or her general air of reproof. (In Denmark, it seemed, people were much more efficient and less frivolous—more direct and unhampered by demonstrations of humor or politeness.) She almost never smiled.

"You want me to do something?" Kaaren asked bluntly.

"Oh, no, no," Laura protested. "Just wanted you to know—you know, in case. I mean, maybe if you leave your door open a crack in case one of them wakes up. But they won't—they were so tired."

"Okay." Kaaren continued to look at her expectantly.

"Just drinks with a friend. Having a hard time. Her husband . . ." Laura made a vague gesture and rolled her eyes as she began to back toward the steps.

"Ah," Kaaren said. "Okay."

And then, feeling guilt creeping up again, Laura ducked down the stairs and grabbed her keys, her wallet, and, at the last moment, a newer, sexier pair of underwear that she shimmied into under her skirt.

It was later, lying on Neil's bed, flat on her back, breathless, that she realized she had forgotten to feed Cocoa.

"Shit," she said aloud.

"What?" Neil rolled onto his side next to her.

"I forgot to feed the dog."

"You have a dog?"

Laura nodded. "She's a pain in the ass."

Neil rolled onto his back and laughed.

"What?"

"Just that this"—he waved his arm to encompass the scene in general—"seems to be bookended by hungry dogs."

"Hm." Laura sat up. "Is that good or bad?"

"I don't know—hungry dogs, going to the dogs, getting dogged—doesn't seem too auspicious."

Laura shifted on her hip to look down at him. "That's not funny."

"Biting the hand that feeds, let sleeping dogs—"

"Neil!"

"I'm sorry. It's just, as a metaphor—"

"Well, it's not a metaphor. It's just a"—she groped—"circumstance."

"Un-hunh."

"What? It's no more a metaphor than, say, the weather. Which has been fine. Or, like, the parking. Which has actually been easy. Surprisingly easy." She pushed her hair out of her face. "Do you always do that? Look for metaphors in everything?"

"Not voluntarily."

"What was that program you dropped out of? Rhetoric?"

Neil groaned.

"Okay, okay, I'm sorry." She put a hand on his belly and gave it a pat. His skin was smooth and dry and warm.

Neil wrapped a hand around her wrist and pulled her down, laughing.

"You like to be gloomy," she said.

"Is that news?" Neil managed to spin her around and lie on top of her now, nuzzling her neck. "You knew what you were getting into."

"I did?" Laura said into his hair, feeling—what was it?—a hint of foreboding?

Pulling up her skirt sometime later, snapping her bra, preparing to go home, Laura was reminded of this again. It was nearly one a.m. She hoped Kaaren and the girls were sound asleep. And off in his hotel room in Louisville . . . She didn't finish the thought. A wave of anxiety welled up in her.

"What is Jenny's job now?" Neil asked, apropos of nothing.

"Jenny? Marketing. At Genron—it's a—"

"I know. A pharmaceutical company. I mean, what exactly? Is she still a product manager for that heart-disease drug she was in charge of when she paid her visit to me?"

"Oh, no. She's been promoted. She works on coming up with new drugs now. And Setlan."

"Fuck me," Neil said with real force, and Laura turned to look at him.

"What?"

"Nothing," he said, then sighed, and sank back against the pillows now propped up against the wall. He reached for his pack of cigarettes, shook one out, and lit it. The dirty smell of cigarette smoke filled the room.

"Why 'fuck me' then?" she asked.

"Ha." Neil gave a bitter and humorless snort of laughter. "Just figures she'd be pushing that shit. I should've seen it coming."

Laura frowned and began buttoning her blouse. "I get it—you're anti-antidepressants."

Neil looked up at her in surprise and then shrugged insolently. "No, I mean, whatever floats your boat, I guess. Just as a cultural force—as an arbiter of normalcy—" He broke off, taking a long drag on his cigarette. "So she's a big shot now? At Genron?"

Now it was Laura's turn to shrug. There was something ugly about Neil's tone. "She's done well. I don't know what her title is."

Neil leaned his head back against the wall. "I'm sure she'll run that place someday."

Laura scrutinized him, sitting there, shirtless, cigarette smoking dangerously from his hand between the bedsheets. He looked scrawny suddenly, the bones of his ribs visible. "Neil," she said, sitting back down beside him. "She's still Jenny. She's still the girl you used to know." She hesitated, and then continued tentatively. "And she's a good mother. Colin will have a good life."

She expected derision—a snort of sarcastic laughter or some declaration that that was not what he was thinking about. But instead Neil blew out a long stream of smoke and looked back at her, and his eyes were both cold and hurt. "In what sense?"

Sitting there, Laura had a sudden strong desire to return to the comfort of her own orderly, unascetic house and sleeping children, even her by now surely desperate, needy dog. "Many," she said finally. "In many senses."

But Neil did not look convinced. Did not look, in fact, like he had even heard.

9

GALENA CALLED NEIL three times before he answered. It was funny how people still did that in the day of caller ID. She didn't mind, maybe, that her determination was obvious. After all, she seemed to have no self-consciousness to speak of—a product of being Albanian or whatever, probably. No question: she was what someone like Johnson would call a "ballsy chick."

The place she had suggested for a drink was predictably characterless: one of the glossy new eateries that had sprung up in the South End since Neil had been away.

Neil hunched forward in his leather jacket and fought the impulse to go back outside for a smoke. He had two barstools. That was a good thing. If he gave this up and had to drink his whiskey standing cheek-to-jowl with this crowd of done-up twenty-somethings he would just about croak. It was a great word: "croak." Croaked. So full of comical indignity. He was already croaked, wasn't he?

It was fifteen minutes past eight when Galena walked in wearing jeans and an unflattering, stretchy brown shirt. She scanned the crowd boldly, spotted him, and started across the room. You had to hand it to her: she was completely uninhibited by her lack of fashion sense and minimal natural beauty.

"Hi," she said, slipping onto the stool he pushed out for her. "What are you drinking?"

"Whiskey."

"Good." She nodded approvingly. "Another one of those," she said to the bartender. No please and thank you. No apology for her lateness. She perched on the stool with both feet squarely on the footrest below her and her hands clasped in her lap like a child.

She was entertaining.

He took another sip of his drink and waited for her to speak.

"So have you always worked at a game company?" she asked. "Do you like to play computer games?"

Neil laughed.

"What?"

"Nothing. Let's just get right into it. No, this is my first time working at a game company. Yes, I guess I like to play computer games."

"Hunh," Galena said, looking at him appraisingly. "In Romania, where I'm from, computer games are mostly for teenagers. I mean, teenagers who have computers. Or who go to the game rooms—where they have the big video game machines."

"Here too." Neil shrugged. "Mostly for teenagers and losers like me."

"No!" she said it fervently. "I did research on this. If this were true we wouldn't be making deals with those idiots in your office. There are lots of adult men who play them too."

"Depressed adult men, apparently," Neil said.

"This is true," she said cheerily, and took a hefty swig of her drink.

"It's very American, I think," she continued. "Adults playing games like this. In my country—no, in most countries—they sit around and drink beer and talk. Or play cards."

"They do that here too."

"No. Not the same way. Here they drink beer at a bar. Like this. Or a party. Not just in their backyard or living room or on the corner. It's not the same."

"I don't know," Neil said doubtfully, but the prospect of a debate with her about cultural drinking habits was unappealing. "What about you?" He turned the subject away. "Have you always been in marketing? Do you like reaching consumers?"

She gave him a curious look, but did not seem to grasp the sarcasm. "I just graduated from Harvard Business School last year. I like my job. Genron is a good place to work."

A shadow fell over Neil at the mention of it. He would have to ask her about Jenny now. He would not be able to stop himself. "Why?" he asked, holding back for the moment.

"It's a very important company—and the drugs I work on are really breaking new ground. Also the people are smart and the benefits are excellent."

She sounded like catalog copy. Neil nodded and then let loose. "Do you know Jenny Callahan?"

"Jenny? Of course!" Galena's whole face sharpened and illuminated. "Why? Do you know her? She's my boss."

Neil shrugged, he hoped, nonchalantly. "I used to. We were friends in college."

Galena practically careened forward toward him. "She is an amazing person. I really think she's incredible. All of the things you learn in B-school about managing people and making decisions, she just *does* it . . ." she gushed, and Neil downed the rest of his drink. Of course she was a fan of Jenny. She was a little mini-Jenny. And Jenny always had a retinue of sycophants.

"Are you still in touch?" Galena asked.

This stopped Neil midsip. He had blown it, it occurred to him suddenly. Now Jenny would know he was in Boston. "Not really," he said. "Not for a few years." But then, fuck it. He was allowed to be in Boston. It was a fucking free country. Let Jenny know he was around here. For all he knew, Laura had spilled the beans already anyway. He pushed away the thought of Laura, which threatened for a moment to bring down an avalanche of guilt.

"So you were friends in college," Galena said, giving him another of her frankly appraising looks. The transparency of her skepticism went a ways toward defusing the gloom that threatened to overwhelm him.

"Incredible, hunh?"

"Unlikely. But college is like that, isn't it? Everyone's in the same milieu."

"Did you go to college here too?"

"Penn."

"Well, Jenny was always in her own 'milieu,'" Neil said, flagging the bartender down and ordering two more whiskeys.

"One cider," Galena amended, again making him smile. "Do you have Woodpecker?" She turned back to him intently. "Why? What was she like in college?"

Neil threw his head back in a posture of deep consideration, though the word had actually already popped into his mind. "Pragmatic," he said. "She knew what she wanted when the rest of us were just bumbling around in the dark."

"And what was that? What she wanted."

The whiskey tasted sharp and rough on Neil's tongue and was beginning to give him a pleasant loose feeling in his joints. "Well, for example, she wanted to try out acting one time," he began, and felt himself warming to the role of raconteur. Galena was an avid audience. The bright café lights and buzz of chattery, dressed-up people had an air of festivity. So what if it was a bland scene? So what if it was Boston? The night was beginning to seem downright fun.

They tumbled into Galena's apartment at two a.m., ostensibly to listen to the Romanian pop music he had forced her to describe. ("Kind of like, how do you call it, that band from the eighties with long hair, Guns N' Roses, but more soft.") The apartment was in one of the new luxury high-rises that had risen over the last decade—a spacious one-bedroom with floor-to-ceiling glass windows and a tiny, off-the-living-room kitchenette.

Neil settled himself on the beige carpeting and waited for Galena to load the CD. The room was spinning slightly. It felt good to sit cross-legged on the floor and press his back against the wall. The music, when it came on, was utterly indescribable: a mix of super-market Muzak and husky tribal-sounding singing.

He was listening to this with his eyes closed when there was the sound of a door opening and shutting; he had lost track of Galena while he listened, and he opened his eyes with a start. The sight that greeted him was no less than alarming. Galena had changed into a shiny yellow negligee and matching thong and was coming, streak-ing out of the bathroom toward him. She literally threw herself onto him with a kind of high-pitched screech, followed by giddy laugh-ter, and bit his neck.

"Whoa, whoa," Neil started to protest, but this only elicited wild laughter as she started undoing his pants.

From there what occurred was barely human. Galena pulled out his poor unsuspecting penis and proceeded to go to work on it as if it were a hamster she was teaching, roughly, to stand. And the girl had energy! The same aggressive determination she displayed when hawking SSRIs to poor unsuspecting gamers, or looking for her date at a crowded bar, she applied to the sex act. She had plans and tricks and she was, by God, going to play them out! She was not exactly grim-faced about it, but there was a look of intense concen-tration that came over her in the midst of tricky maneuvers that was nearly militant. He had never felt so commandeered before. It was both exciting and horrible.

It was nearly five a.m. when he left.

"Hey." He nodded sheepishly at the doorman on his way out, hands thrust deep in his pockets, shoulders hunched. Galena was sound asleep, snoring riotously on her side of the fancy memory-foam bed.

Neil had a headache and a sinking feeling. What little he remembered of the night made him blush. And worse, gave him a pang of guilt as acute as a wave of nausea. Laura would be horrified to know of Galena. Devastated. Here she was, putting her marriage (the word itself was almost too outrageous, too horrifying, to think) on the line for him and he was dicking around with this Albanian twit! It was way too much responsibility for him. This was the problem with Laura wasn't it? She was so fucking fragile. She was so good. And so kind and sweet and pretty. It made him want to kill himself. He couldn't be held accountable for someone like that—fuck—it was like trusting a child with a Fabergé egg.

The street was quiet, still gray with dawn, and littered with broken bottles, papers, an abandoned shopping cart. One lone truck lumbered toward him down the avenue, metal body clanking and thundering like an angry beast.

At the corner of Boylston he was able to hail a taxi and slide into the dark cave of a backseat with relief. It smelled of cigarette smoke and faintly, under this, of bad breath. "Mind if I have a smoke?" He leaned toward the driver on his side of the scratched Plexiglas.

"You have one for me?" the man asked.

"Sure." Neil tapped two cigarettes out of the carton and felt a pleasant sense of kinship. He rolled down the window and inhaled the satisfying combination of tar and nicotine.

Galena was crazy. That was clear. Crazy in the kind of culturally sanctioned way that would not inhibit her from career success or social acceptance. But crazy nonetheless. He would have been wise to head this whole thing off. But she was so fucking determined! It would have been like trying to fight off a pit bull. Sitting there on the tattered vinyl of the cab, he found himself smiling. You had to hand it to the girl: she knew how to get her way.

When the taxi arrived at 420 Center Street, Neil ascended the stairs to the third floor on tiptoe as if it would have been terrible to wake his sleeping neighbors, who really could not have cared less who came or went. The disaster that greeted him upon entering was no less shocking than his night had been. There was water all over the hallway floor and the P-Funk poster had slid down the wall into a colorful pool at the bottom. From the kitchen there was a gentle, almost peaceful rushing sound. Neil stood for a moment, gaping in the doorway, letting the water spread onto the dirty carpet in the foyer in a brown, soggy stain. Then he splashed along the hall to the kitchen—the heart of the mayhem. Here, the water spread in a wide fanlike pattern from a hole where the wall had simply given out. Bits of plaster lay in a soggy mess on the stovetop and across the beige linoleum. One of the dinette chairs lay on its side. The flow had clearly at some point been more powerful than it was now. Neil turned around and was tempted to simply walk out, lock the door behind him, and disappear. But he made himself go to the bedroom—wet as well, but not as impressively so—throw a few of his things from the floor onto the bed, grab his computer, and shove it in his backpack before he left.

Clearly some major artery of the building had burst and rendered his already tenuous home uninhabitable. Could there be a more apt metaphor for the general state of Neil Banks's life?

The building would need to undergo extensive repairs, his fast-talking landlord informed him when she called him back that afternoon. They had surveyed the damage and would need to get a whole slew of specialists—plumbers, plasterers, cleaners, insulators, all practitioners of ancient underappreciated trades—to take care of the problem. "How did you not notice until morning?" she barked irritably as if the break in the ancient piping were somehow his fault. He would not be able to live there for the next two weeks. No, it was impossible even if he didn't mind having no running water. Even if he didn't mind the mess. Liability. He could deduct it from next month's rent.

It would have made sense to ask Steven Closter for a couch to sleep on if Closter wasn't such an ass. Neil had nearly come to blows with him over the living "tablet" in the game—the creature the group of geologists would discover, and which held all the secrets of enlightenment in its cells. It should be a monster, Steven had suggested. Something really terrifying and bogus. It should have three heads and be pickled in some kind of formaldehyde and look really nasty. This was all wrong. Neil had tried, at first, to put this gently. The creature had to be peaceful and alluring. It had to reflect perfection on a fantastical level. (He thought of Laura's unicorn, but this would never fly with gamers.) Steven had been so belligerent, so snotty in his derision of Neil's "arty" concept that Neil finally had had to give it to him straight. His monster idea was childish, clichéd, and unsophisticated. Neil would never put his name to it. The debate had ended when Joe, the breasty kid who had shown Neil around the first day, stepped into the cube in which they were arguing and offered tentatively that they should all take a smoking break.

So there was no way he was going to ask Steven Closter for a place to crash.

It was at five forty-five, with the specter of having to ask Joe to take him in, when Neil thought of Elise. He had not seen her yet. Had not looked her up or made any effort to get in touch since his arrival in Boston. But at one point they had been good friends: pot-smoking buddies with a kind of unlikely intellectual admiration for each other, to be exact. Something about the idea of putting himself in front of her, of letting her sharp gaze take him in, was intimidating: Elise's perspective had always had a certain moral acuity. But desperate times called for desperate measures and he needed a place to stay. And dialing the number, Neil felt, actually, a kind of growing excitement about seeing himself through Elise's eyes: being summed up.

It took no more than a call to information to track down Elise's number, and the woman who answered the phone sounded friendly—Elise's partner, probably. He imagined an attractive pixie-haired woman with a lot of tattoos. Elise was attractive herself in a kind of skinny, unstriking way.

"Neil Banks?" the woman asked. "Not her friend from college?"

That's me, he had affirmed, and the woman had sounded genuinely excited, even a little giddy. *I'm sure she'd love to see you,* she said, before he had even asked.

Elise's house was like something out of a movie—one of those cheery romantic comedies in which the heroine, a single mother or otherwise somehow handicapped woman, lives in the coziest, most creatively but inexpensively appointed house, which stands in stark contrast to the hero's own awful, rich, and mannishly neglected pad. The kitchen was painted a bright yellow and rosy orange. There was a bay-windowed sitting area with a love seat and a squishy, comfortable armchair. Brightly colored pots of herbs lined the windowsills, and the wall calendar—Wayne Thiebaud cake paintings—was full of jotted plans.

"Have you told Laura you're here?" Elise asked, sitting across from him with her arms folded on the white kitchen tabletop, holding a steaming mug of mint tea.

Neil hid his face in his own steaming cauldron of tea and scalded his lips sipping it.

"It's hot," Elise said. "Sorry." But she continued to wait for his answer.

"She knows," he said, looking away.

"She does? She didn't say anything. I just talked to her yesterday—"

"Maybe she was trying to keep it on the down-low. You know, with Jenny and all that . . ." It was the first time the subject of Jenny— implicitly of the baby, *his* baby—had come up since he had arrived. It felt, actually, relieving to mention. And like a viable excuse.

"Oh. Right." Elise frowned more deeply. "I never understood—" She cut herself off. "Well."

She stood up and selected an orange from the fruit bowl on the counter. "We don't have to get into that. For the moment." She looked at him appraisingly and then extended the orange. "Do you want one?"

Neil shook his head.

"So. Laura must be happy you've resurfaced. She's always been defensive of you—I mean"—she hesitated, but in typical Elise fashion, did not look embarrassed at the slip—"defensive of your choices. Like your choice to disappear. Or drop out of that program you were in that everyone thought sounded so . . . promising."

Again, at the thought of Laura and her kindness, Neil felt a searing flash of guilt. And self-hatred.

At that moment Chrissy walked in, saving the conversation from the precipice it had come to the brink of.

"Asleep," Chrissy said, sinking into one of the cozy-looking armchairs under the window. "Thank the Lord."

A palpable sense of warmth and good humor entered the room with her. She was immensely likable. Neil had felt this at once. Elise had certainly done right.

"They like to put up a fight," Elise explained, holding a section of orange out to her partner, who shook her head, rolling her eyes.

"This," Chrissy said to Neil, "is what Elise considers a satisfying dessert." She stood up and opened the freezer, pulling out a carton of ice cream and two bowls. "For you?" She lifted her eyebrows, and Neil nodded. When was the last time he had even thought of having ice cream?

"Why is it that children are so afraid of sleeping?" Chrissy asked, scooping a hefty portion into each bowl. "There must be something evolutionary to it. I mean, we spend all this time emphasizing needing endless hours of uninterrupted sleep a night, but maybe you're not really *supposed* to go to sleep until exhaustion just completely overwhelms you. And you're not really *supposed* to sleep in such a long chunk. I mean, back in the cave days it certainly wasn't what you were going for—a comatose, eight-hour opening for some woolly mammoth to come and turn you into a midnight snack."

"Mammoths were vegetarians," Elise said mildly.

"It's unnatural." Chrissy put the bowl of ice cream—chocolate with some sort of butterscotchy-looking swirls—in front of Neil. "Convenient—don't get me wrong: I'm all for bedtime—but unnatural."

"Maybe it's the new natural," he offered. "We don't run around chasing woolly mammoths over rugged plains and wrestling them with our bare hands all day . . . and so we need *more* sleep."

"Exactly!" Chrissy beamed. "It makes no sense!"

"Except our brains, though." Neil was enjoying himself. "We have so much to process, right? Cars, trains, cities, TV . . . I mean, we think more, we act less. Nobody sleeps well anymore. Our brains need it, our bodies don't. Bring on the Ambien."

"Mmmmm-hmmm." Chrissy nodded in exaggerated agreement.

"What is this, Chocolate Pot Brownie flavor?" Elise said.

"We have created a fundamental imbalance," Chrissy announced. Neil struck his fist on the table.

"Well," Elise said. "I think you might be on to something."

"Can we start a website?" Chrissy batted her lashes.

And as they washed their bowls, bade their goodnights, and

separated—on tiptoe—at the top of the stairs, Neil felt a hundred miles, a hundred days, from where he had been when he woke up: that anonymous luxury building and barren litter-strewn street, crazy Romanian sleeping above. He had come home. It was not his, but it was pleasant—more than pleasant. It was a sort of city on the hill.

10

ELISE STOOD AT THE THRESHOLD of the guest room surveying the scene. Neil had tried to make his bed—the thin quilt was pulled lumpily over the pillows and the sheet hung down like an unraveling hem. But he had tried. There was something sweet about this. In the corner, his duffel bag sat spewing boxer shorts and blue jeans, several hardback tomes: *Gottling's Directory of Nineteenth Century Explorers*; *Locating the Inalienable: The World's First Human Rights Movement*; *The Immoralist* by André Gide. It gave her an uneasy feeling. He was a lost soul, Neil Banks. But this was no surprise. She had seen that coming since they were twenty-one, crouched at the edge of her dorm-room cot, getting high. Poor Neil, her fellow refugee from the narrow constraints of their college social life. He was connected to her life as another person, it seemed, only he was still the person he had been then. Maybe if he had found the right woman to help him evolve into a grown-up self—but no, this was a silly, sexist answer. That was not a universal solution.

It was Saturday morning—Elise's morning to sleep late. On the weekends they took turns getting up with the boys at whatever ungodly hour they awoke and when Chrissy was on duty she got them out of the house early and off to the park or the river or the grocery store. Usually Elise came out and met them wherever they were. She didn't like the feeling of being left out, lounging around in bed while they were out having fun. This morning, however, Chrissy had left her cell phone lying here on the bedside table so there was no way of contacting her, finding out where they were.

Neil had apparently exited early too.

Elise would have to content herself with some alone time—read the paper or do something constructive in the garden, or begin to organize the Ula notes she had brought home from work. The little goat's milk had still not come in. The whole project was turning into a great disappointment. Elise was tired of thinking about this. She wanted to be with her family right now! She wanted to see Chrissy!

Downstairs she began tidying up the remnants of breakfast— Cheerios spread like stars across the table, half-eaten bowls of applesauce, and crumbled egg yolk residue. The matching high chairs looked like Jackson Pollock paintings, encrusted with a week's worth of food experiments. She was scraping at these when the doorbell rang, and thinking maybe it was Chrissy and the boys, she leapt to answer it. But instead, it was Angela Noyes, Chrissy's mother.

In the five seconds it took Elise to get to the door Angela had already cupped her hands around her face and was pressing it against the glass panel beside the door, peering in. She waved brightly as Elise opened the door.

"Good morning!" she chirped, peeking around Elise's shoulder. "I hope I'm not too early. Where are my little bunnies?"

Angela Noyes was a bundle of energy. Always cheerful, always chatty, always ready to get down on her hands and knees and push toy cars around the floor or roll up her sleeves and chop onions. She was never still. It seemed miraculous that calm, deliberate Chrissy could be her daughter—her mental and physical presence were so diametrically opposite from this.

"Out on the town," Elise said. "I'm not sure where. I just got up."

"Oh-ho! Your morning to sleep in? You girls are so funny." Angela shook her head at what, apparently, never seemed less than a miracle of nature to her, this ability to sleep late.

"Mm-hm." Elise nodded, trying not to feel irritation.

Angela was such a good woman. Such a well-meaning, industriously helpful grandmother. And unlike Elise's own mother, she was unguileful. She was never passive-aggressive or judgmental or indirect. And as a grandmother, she was ever-competent and straightforwardly doting. She understood how to enter a room without overwhelming the boys, how to play on the floor without bossing and directing, how to distract Nigel out of his tantrums, and most of all, how to be helpful. It was not fair to be irritated by her.

"Well, I just thought I'd stop by and see if I could take them out for a walk—give you girls a break for a few hours," Angela said. "I'm not due at Maryellen's until lunchtime." She glanced at her watch and then clapped her hands to her sides in her habitual, nervous what's-next gesture.

"Oh, that's so nice of you, Angela," Elise said. "I'd love to take you up on that if they were around." Although, as she said it, Elise realized that in fact she wouldn't. She had been so distracted from family life for the last week or so, and things had been so oddly, subtly tense between her and Chrissy—she wanted the chance to make it right, sink her teeth back in. *Just tell her*, Chrissy would say—had, in fact, been saying for years. *It won't hurt her feelings—she's not like that.* But that was just the sort of thing Elise's own stark and proper, Germanic upbringing would not let her do. "Would you like to come in for a cup of coffee?" she asked instead.

"Oh, that's all right, dear. You enjoy your quiet moments—I know how it is," Angela said cheerily. "I'll just drop by Sarah's and see if I can take the baby out." Sarah was Chrissy's older sister who lived in nearby Watertown.

"Are you sure?" Elise asked. But Angela was already turning on her sensible sneaker-clad heel and starting toward the street.

"Oh"—Angela turned—"and tell Chrissy that I'm just so excited about this picnic. I want to come too."

"Okay," Elise said automatically, smile fading from her face. She had not heard about any picnic. Immediately she knew it was something related to Claire Markowitz and the donor siblings. It sounded like a doo-wop band. Under other circumstances the thought might have made her laugh.

"See you soon, sweetie." Angela waved, climbing into her compact white Toyota Corolla, oblivious to the wet blanket she had just thrown over Elise.

Chrissy and the boys were still not back half an hour later, and Elise began to worry that they were off somewhere with Claire Markowitz. That this picnic, whatever it was, was actually happening at this moment, without her. An illogical feeling of panic gripped her. She had lost them. Chrissy had fallen out of love with her, would move out, take the boys, and life would never be the same.

She tried to eat an egg and toast, but had no appetite, and finally she called Laura.

Laura was not quite her usual reassuring self. She sounded distracted. Her knee-jerk dismissal of Elise's worry ("She's not at some crazy picnic, Lisey, its ten o'clock in the morning!") made Elise feel silly.

But as she was about to get off the phone she remembered Neil.

"You didn't tell me Neil was here," she chided, and Laura sprang suddenly to attention.

"How did you—did he call you? I didn't tell you because I didn't know if Jenny should—"

"He's staying with me."

"What?" Laura practically shouted.

"What's so crazy? His pipes burst or something."

"His pipes burst? You mean in the apartment he's staying in?"

"Of course in his apartment. Where else?"

"Oh, God. How awful."

"He doesn't seem too worried about it," Elise said mildly.

"I wonder why he didn't call me," Laura mused almost petulantly.

Elise was silent. There wasn't really anything to say to this.

"But he's okay," Laura said as if testing it out.

"He's fine! He's just . . . you know, Neil. I thought you said you'd seen him."

"I did. I mean, briefly. I just meant, he wasn't injured or anything."

"Good grief! You sound like a mother hen. How many people get injured when their pipes burst? Senior citizens, maybe. Very, very senior."

Laura did not laugh.

"Why are you so worried about him?" Elise asked.

"I'm not," Laura bristled.

Outside the window a blue jay began squawking.

"All right."

Elise hung up feeling worse than she had to begin with.

"What is it?" Chrissy asked the moment she arrived home. "You look upset." And her face was a picture of such genuine concern, and such sympathetic worry, that in an instant Elise softened.

"Ta tatata!" Nigel stammered enthusiastically, practically bucking out of the stroller in his excitement to see her.

Elise took the bag of snacks and sippy cups and diapers from Chrissy's hand and unbuckled Nigel's shoulder straps, hiding both her fretfulness and her relief in the act of liberating him, scooping him up, and bouncing him up the stairs.

"Of course I was going to tell you about the picnic," Chrissy protested later, when the boys were napping. "You have to stop acting like this is some sort of secret mission I'm conducting. Or some kind of . . . betrayal. Why do I have to feel defensive about wanting the boys to know their siblings, for Christ's sake?" She pushed her thick blond hair up off her forehead and looked at Elise.

Her exasperation gave Elise a guilty, cowed feeling. She was being unfair, maybe.

"It's just . . ." she began. "It's just that you're doing it all alone, I guess. I mean, without me." Saying it aloud made her feel even stupider.

"Agh!" Chrissy pulled her own hair straight up from the top of her head. "Because you don't like it! You aren't into it! That's not my fault."

Elise sat down on the bed. "Okay." She sighed. "Whatever."

And they were silent for a moment, Elise sitting and Chrissy standing at the dresser. Why had they ever had children? The question reared up in Elise's mind with shocking vigor. They were a lesbian couple, for Christ's sake. It was not what nature had intended. An incredible guilt washed over her on the heels of the thought. Sweet James and Nigel, their little chubby cheeks and dimpled limbs, their innocent, unwitting minds. What was she thinking?

From downstairs there was the sound of a key turning in the lock.

"Hello?" Neil's voice drifted tentatively up.

Chrissy jerked around and stuck her head over the banister beside their door. "Shhhhh, the boys are napping," she said in a stage whisper.

"Shit! Sorry."

Neil started up the stairs. Elise could hear the groan of the worn floorboards under his feet.

"Hi," he said, poking his head into the doorway. "Just picking a couple of things up and I'll be out of your hair."

"Don't be silly!" Chrissy said warmly. Elise, on the other hand, could only continue sitting on the bed wearing a tight smile. "You don't need to get out of our hair."

"Oh, that's all right," Neil began somewhat sheepishly, looking like the twenty-one-year-old Elise had known him best as—or younger, actually. Like a teenager. They were all getting older except for Neil, it occurred to her fleetingly. He was traveling backward through time, toward a state of greater and greater confusion.

"No, no," Chrissy said. "I was just about to head out actually. Groceries." She looked over at Elise impassively. "I'll be back by the time the boys wake up, okay?"

Elise stared at her.

Neil looked from one to the other of them uneasily. "No, really— I'll just—"

"Stay and talk to Elise," Chrissy said firmly. "She's been alone all morning."

That's it? Elise wanted to say. *You're just ending this conversation?* And if she were Chrissy she would have just said it. But she was too polite to say it in front of Neil. (Again her mother's cold, appearance-driven propriety reared its inhibiting head.) So she just sat and watched Chrissy disappear out the bedroom door.

"Shit," Neil said. "I came at a bad time. I'll just—"

Downstairs there was the sound of the front door opening and shutting behind Chrissy.

"Shit," Elise echoed, and sank back on the bed with a loud sigh.

"You okay?" Neil asked hesitantly. "Do you want—can I bring you anything?"

"A new start to the day?"

"Damn," Neil said forcefully, and there was real empathy in his voice. "I wish I knew how."

Elise hoisted herself up on her elbows and looked at him. It was actually kind of nice, the sight of Neil Banks, scroungy as ever, lurking in her doorway. "What have you been up to anyway?"

"Oh, just fucking things up. As usual."

It made her smile. And in response, Neil smiled too . . . sheepish, a little apologetic, and—what was it? wistful?—but a smile.

"How about a smoke?" he said, pulling a plastic baggie out of his breast pocket. In it was a fat, carefully rolled joint. "For old times," he said.

"Man!" Elise said, sitting up, incredulous. "That's a bad idea." But somehow she knew, already, that within five minutes she'd be out on the back porch with him, doing something she hadn't done for almost fifteen years.

11

JENNY STOOD IN FRONT OF HER HOUSE taking in the newly painted exterior. It was a pale, professional-looking gray with white trim and a handsome dark red door. And it was perfect—the L shape created by the kitchen and attached garage with the TV room and guest quarters above, the smooth, newly paved driveway with its little island in the middle, the perky dogwood sapling finally in place and promising to create an elegant, artful shade in due time. Victor, the house painter, had helped her choose the particular shade of gray to paint the house, and it made all the difference: it was neither too stern nor too bright, and unlike the garish colors Jenny had grown up with in DeSoto it called absolutely no attention to itself, reflecting instead the impressive size and newness of the house. It had the effect of professional gift-wrapping: neat, crisp, and promising, an important part of the overall effect.

Beside her, Victor stood looking up at the trim along the farthest west-facing window.

"I'll have them do that one again," he said, pointing, brows knit. "It needs another coat."

Jenny followed his gaze.

"You see?" Victor continued. "Where the sill meets the clapboard? It's not so bright as the others."

Once he said it, she could see—it was a slightly yellower shade than the sill next to it. She felt a swell of appreciation for Victor's skill and precision. She felt, actually, a general swell of appreciation for Victor, who seemed, of late, to be the most hardworking, responsible, and intelligent person she knew. Unlike the contractor, Phil, whom she had come to regard as a lazy, fast-talking slob, or the architect, who had come so highly recommended but proved to be too idealistic (and frustratingly slow), or the landscaper, who could not be trusted to mow the lawn without accident, Victor was shrewd, effective, and driven. He was a firm and demanding manager—she had seen him directing the crew of Mexican workers in his employ and you could tell they were a little bit afraid of him. He was a direct, to-the-point communicator.

Personally she knew little about him: he was Cuban, had four children, and could have been anywhere from forty to sixty. He lived in Malden. Beyond this she had no idea. But weirdly, she felt almost closer to him than to anyone else in her life lately. There was a happy comfortableness to their interactions, and a recognition of shared sensibility. In the last month, talking to him had frequently become the high point of her day.

"So what do you think?" Jenny asked. "Another week?"

"Two days."

"Really?"

"Of course." Victor looked offended.

"Great!" Jenny was delighted. There would be ample time for the housecleaners to do their job, and the phone company and computer consultant to come in and set everything up. They would not need to lose even a day of access with the move. And then they would be settled! Residents of pastoral Wellesley! Colin would have the whole giant backyard to learn to walk in. She and Jeremy could entertain without worrying about how people would park and whether the kitchen would be roomy enough.

She followed Victor up through the house to inspect the finished product of his work. The walls were an unobtrusive and refreshing white: cool, calm, and unlikely to interfere with any decorating she might do. Only in Colin's room and the bathrooms had she allowed herself the gamble of choosing a color. Colin's room was a pretty, muted blue and the bathrooms were dark red, dark green, and a kind of rich, eggplanty purple that Victor assured her he had just painted the president of Harvard's bathroom.

Walking through the house with its high ceilings and state-of-the-art fixtures and appliances, Jenny did not explicitly consider how far she had come from the peach-colored ranch house of her childhood with its cheap, accordion-style sliding doors and dingy shag carpeting, its unreliable stove and exposed laundry line. She did not congratulate herself on the personal success that had brought her to this place—the triumph of her own unlikely ambition that had led her to apply to Harvard to begin with, and strategically climb the corporate ladder. But she did feel suffused with a kind of peaceful satisfaction. For once her brain was not cataloguing improvements that could be made and angles that could be played. She was simply, truly happy with the fruit of all her planning, money, and labor.

It was, maybe fittingly, in the would-be sanctuary of the master bedroom that she got the phone call that burst this unusual contentment. It was Elise, and her presentation of the fact was typically straightforward.

"He's *what*?" Jenny barked, walking quickly across the cavernous room to the bay window. Victor had already discreetly disappeared.

"Living in Boston for the year. In Jamaica Plain. But right now, at the moment, he's—"

"What is he doing here?"

"Designing computer games. But what I wanted to tell you . . ."

"Designing computer games!"

". . . is that he's staying with me while they fix his apartment because there was—"

"With you?"

"Jenny. It's not a big deal."

"Oh, really," Jenny said acidly.

"It's a free country! Did you really expect that you would never, ever see him again? And why does it even matter? It's not like he's going to go around telling everyone—"

"He isn't?"

"Well, he agreed to the conditions. He knows the deal. It's not like—"

"You've *talked* to him about it?" Jenny could feel her rage mounting.

"No! I'm just saying he agreed. Right? I mean, that was your whole thing—personally, I don't know why—"

"Elise," Jenny said. "I don't really think we need to get back into this. I'm just surprised. I'm surprised that you would put him up, quite frankly, knowing—"

"He had nowhere to stay! Christ."

They were both silent for a moment. Jenny stared out the window. There was nothing to look at, really. Just trees and grass. A squirrel dropped from one branch to another. Whoopee. The stillness of the view would take some getting used to. She cursed Elise for bursting her bubble of satisfaction, making her see the negative for the first time that morning.

"Look," Elise said finally, "I know this pisses you off. But I really think it's unreasonable to expect Neil to be permanently lost in the cosmos. And I also think his being here is honestly not a big deal."

"Well, thanks for that thought," Jenny said coldly. "Can I call you later? I'm in the middle of going through some things with our painter."

"Okay," Elise said huffily. "I'm sorry to upset you. I just wanted you to know."

After this there was no more blissful enjoyment of her house.

Jenny went through the last few rooms with Victor and got back into her car.

The worst part, of course, was that she knew Elise was right—had been right all along. The arrangement she had struck with Neil was a stupid one. She had wanted to have her cake and eat it too. That was how Elise had put it at the time—the expression was vivid in her mind. She had wanted to *know* the baby's father, but keep him unknown to the rest of the world. It had not seemed too much at the time, or too greedy. It had seemed merely fortuitous: knowing the perfect, and willing, candidate.

Why not go to a sperm bank? Elise had asked, and for all Jenny's straightforwardness she was aware the answer had to be carefully put so as not to step on Elise and Chrissy's decision. She just liked *knowing* the person, she explained. Having a picture and a voice and a general sense—she just felt in her gut that Neil was right. The baby could realize all Neil's squandered potential.

Now, however, in the bright light of this Wellesley morning, with Neil having slipped back into her world—and so suspiciously silently!—the situation she had created did seem far-fetched. And worse, ridiculously fragile. *The truth will out.* This phrase occurred—loudly—to her. And made her feel duplicitous. She had not intended the circumstances of Colin's birth to feel so secretive. She had meant only for her little family to be *normal*, in the DeSoto, California, sense of the word. Throughout the whole struggle to get pregnant, the months of of peeing on ovulation sticks and taking her temperature and ultimately submitting herself to tests involving every sort of uncomfortable poking and prodding (there had been so many before they had even thought to test Jeremy!), she had wanted, simply, a child of her own. A family unit like the one she had grown up in.

Driving back to the office, she did her best to tamp down the irrational unease her conversation with Elise had inspired. But her mind kept going to Colin, sweet Colin, at home with Maria right now, probably napping, his little diapered bottom jutting up in that funny fetal position he slept in—she could almost feel the velvety fringe of dark hair at the base of his head. He was *hers*—the love of her life and her greatest responsibility. There was nothing to suggest that Neil's presence here in Boston was a threat to this, but somehow, all the same, she felt gripped by a kind of cold and primal fear. In her bullheaded creation of the perfect situation, the perfect familial construct, had she overreached? Had she left a crack that would allow disorder in?

Jenny arrived at her office just in time for her first meeting of the day. She had not even finished checking her voice mails when Galena Ibanesku, the hungry young project manager Jenny had assigned to the launch, knocked on her office door.

"Ready for the project meeting?" Galena asked with her signature breed of determined cheer.

"Isn't it a little early?" Jenny glanced at her watch irritably. It was now 10:27, which, by Jenny's American standards, she considered early. Galena had not caught on to this yet. She was steadfastly punctual, and the incorrectness of total punctuality seemed awkward to explain.

"It's ten-thirty," Galena said.

"Why don't you go ahead?" Jenny said. "I'll be right there."

"That's all right," Galena shrugged. "I can wait."

Jenny gave her a tight smile. Galena was exasperating—terribly intelligent, ambitious, and blatantly self-serving in a way that Jenny recognized as promising. But she had no social graces—absolutely no emotional IQ. And this morning Jenny felt particularly disinclined to deal with her.

Galena plopped herself down in one of the two faux-Eames

chairs across from Jenny's desk, while Jenny finished listening to her voice mails. From outside the door there was the tinkle of female laughter as Beth, Jenny's secretary, flirted with the FedEx man.

"I met someone who knows you," Galena said smirkily, when Jenny hung up the phone.

Jenny raised her eyebrows.

"Neil Banks." Galena pronounced it with satisfaction, and Jenny almost gasped out loud.

"Where?" she said, before she could rein in her lack of composure.

"He works at ZGames," Galena said. "One of the companies on our promo list," she added in response to what must have been an obviously blank look.

"Ha!" Jenny tried to strike an amused note. "Well, isn't it a small world. Shall we go?" She rose and walked quickly to the door to conceal the color rising to her cheeks. Was this some sort of a cruel joke, that in one morning Neil would suddenly have surrounded her?

"He said he went to college with you," Galena said.

"He did." Jenny held the door for Galena and involuntarily her eyes sought out the framed eight-by-ten portrait of Colin looking serious, and, in the light of this conversation, seriously like Neil. Was it possible—the thought accosted her with violence—that he would *tell* people he was the father of her son?

"He said you dated," Galena continued.

Jenny stiffened. "For about five minutes," she said. It came out sounding almost indignant.

"He's cute," Galena said, and Jenny saw suddenly—good grief—that the girl had a crush on Neil.

"Oh, he's too old for you," she said in genuine alarm. "And too—" *confused*, she had been about to say before she realized the danger of name-calling. Better to be utterly uninterested, unopinionated, and, most importantly, uninvolved.

"Too what?" Galena pressed.

They had almost reached the conference room and Jenny slowed her steps. "Nothing," she said, affecting a breezy tone. "Just too old; thirty-five-year-olds are dinosaurs."

"Ah, but men just get sexier as they get older," Galena chirped. And at that moment, Jenny felt a genuine rip of hatred for the girl.

"After you." She smiled, opening the conference room door.

At lunchtime, Jenny drove over to Mass General to go to Jeremy's doctor's appointment. He was getting the results of a CT scan. She did not really feel worried about what these results might be—but all the same, she was not looking forward to the appointment.

Once in Dr. Frager's office, though, it was clear immediately that the results were not good. She knew this immediately from the doctor's solemn face, the manner in which he touched the pen in the breast pocket of his shirt—like a child fingering the edge of a beloved blankie for reassurance—as he began to speak. There was a tumor on Jeremy's left kidney and another on his chest wall. A broader scan was in order—soon—as well as surgery to remove the tumors, which had the characteristics of renal cancer that had metastasized.

Jenny felt the blood rush from her head. She would have fainted if she had not been sitting down. She looked over at Jeremy with panic. He looked, actually, remarkably calm. The fear she had detected from him in the waiting room seemed, with the introduction of facts and information, to have given way to something both determined and resigned. His face was pale, but his jaw was set forcefully. "What . . . ?" Jenny blurted out. "But you don't *know* this is cancer, right?"

Both Jeremy and the doctor looked at her with, it seemed, a kind of apology.

"Until we have the pathology before us it is technically unknown, but I'm afraid research and experience suggest that a tumor on the kidney with these dimensions and characteristics is almost certainly some form of cancer, most likely renal, and the tumor on the lungs ..." The doctor's voice continued, gently but not reassuringly. Jenny could not really hear him for the rushing in her ears.

At some point in the midst of this, Jeremy reached over and put a hand at the back of her neck, lightly, smoothing his knuckles over the small bones of her spine. And the delicate intimacy of the gesture, the implicit reassurance, almost broke her. She was the one who should be reaching over to him, taking his cold hand in hers, pressing it comfortingly. How had she let it come to this? She could feel a ball of tears in the back of her throat that she had to swallow down, had to focus all her energy to repress, because if they came out she knew they would be ugly, horrible, primitive sounds—not so much tears as bellows and screams.

Jeremy's odd composure continued. He asked questions. Jenny had no idea what they were. He talked about biopsies and metastases and stages—clearly there had been anticipation here. How else to explain his understanding of the exact difference between stage three and stage four renal cancer and the inutility of radiation treatment under these circumstances? Jenny was silent—dumbfounded by her own complete ignorance.

She stared at her husband—his thin, angular face and the shock of blond hair falling forward. He looked thin. How had she missed this?

"Jen," Jeremy said, when they had left the muted corridors of the hospital and were out in the brightness of the evening. He turned to her fully for the first time. There was the movement of people in and out of the revolving doors, wheelchairs, hospital scrubs, the whistle of the valets parking cars. Sunlight glinted fiercely off of windshields and mirrors and traffic signs like the shards of some giant glass bottle that had exploded. "I need you to just keep on being normal. That is what I'm going to need," he said.

"How long have you been thinking of this—I mean, all those questions you had . . . ?" she asked, when finally they were seated in the car.

"I don't know," Jeremy answered, turning to face her. "I did some research."

"Why didn't you tell me?" she asked.

And the look on his face was quizzical—searching, even.

"I *have* told you, Jenny," he said.

"What do you mean?" she said, almost pleadingly, because of course she knew. It was a pointless question. There was no one here to fool.

Jeremy was wise enough to leave it unanswered, and he navigated the car out onto the street and then to Storrow Drive.

"Where are we going?" Jenny asked blankly. "I can't—you can't go back to work."

"Home," Jeremy said. Outside, the Charles River flew past, making Jenny wince with the memory of her lack of sympathy. Already the christening felt like ages ago. "I want to see Colin."

Jenny looked over at her husband in surprise.

"I just want to hear his laugh," Jeremy said, almost sheepishly. "It's so . . ." He seemed to search for the word. "Funny."

And Jenny felt a swell of love sweep over her. "You know—" she burst out. "You know how much I love you?" she asked. It was intended rhetorically. But as she sat, watching his profile, both hands on the wheel and hunching slightly forward, driving in that way she had always made fun of, she realized it was a more real question than she had imagined.

"Sure," Jeremy said, darting a glance at her. "I think so. I think I do."

And the gentle rebuke of his answer filled Jenny with a cold panic. This was not something that could be changed by protest, though.

12

NEIL HAD PUT OFF going to see his mother until it was absolutely inescapable. In fact, he had put off even calling to tell her that he was here—not only back East, but in Boston, in the state of Massachusetts—until last week. This was the beauty of having a cell phone. And, for that matter, a mother who never called.

Today was her birthday, though. It was something even the most callous, self-involved son could not ignore. To look at Lucinda Banks you might think she was turning seventy, but in fact she was only fifty-seven. The extra thirteen odd years on her face were not the product of hard living but a negative attitude, which was exactly what Neil wanted to avoid.

To Neil, the drive down to New Bedford from Boston was like being lowered down into a well. The elevated expressway sped over the warehouses of South Boston and touched down in Quincy, passing Corita's famous painted water towers, Ho Chi Minh's profile embedded subversively (or so it had seemed to him as a teenager, newly armed with the concept of subversion) in a long splash of blue, and as he sped past, Neil felt the rough texture of his childhood chafe at him—the walls narrowing, the world darkening, the deep black water at the bottom looming large. He was entering his own personal ground zero. The metaphor occurred to him with a wave of self-conscious irony. What a self-pitying asshole he was! So he had eaten TV dinners and Pop-Tarts and not joined the Kids

Hockey League because he couldn't afford the uniform. So his father was an alcoholic and his mother was depressed and his fourth-grade teacher had never heard of the Holocaust. This was hardly the stuff of tragedy.

This flurry of self-disgust did little to actually make him feel better, but he tried harder to see the beauty of Route 24. There were a lot of trees. It was green. So much greener than Southern California. And the road signs loomed large and cheerful, advertising every convenience a person could want. The bright pink and brown Dunkin' Donuts logo, McDonald's, Tiger Mart, Sunoco, and the smaller, more specific blue signs: Blue Notes Dry Cleaners, Amos' Pizza, Stop & Shop, Canton Primary Care . . . There was no excuse for hunger (figurative or literal) here.

Once he was actually on Main Street in New Bedford the green disappeared. The houses took on that particular working-class New England drabness—green siding, white siding, blue shingles, brown shingles, whatever the color, they were weathered to a dirty, equalizing gray. Two teenage boys with baseball hats pulled low made their way down the street, shoulders hunched as if facing a stiff wind. On the corner, a sassy-looking, feathered-haired woman leaned against a car, smoking, glaring at the passing cars like someone projected forward from 1983. A team of scrappy kids came whooping and hollering to the corner. New Bedford was a mean town. There was no way around it. No one looked healthy. No one looked glad.

Lucinda Banks still lived in the house that Neil and his brother had grown up in. It had been the primary windfall of the divorce, which had sent Neil's father off into a transient life of serial marriages and shabby, featureless apartments along the eastern seaboard. Alone in the house, Lucinda seemed determined to play anchor to John Banks's shiftlessness, becoming more and more a rooted fixture of the place, existing within a shrinking radius of her home. The house itself was changeless—brown sandpaper shingles and dark green, peeling trim. There was a covered front porch, which had sagged for as long as Neil could remember, and had always let very little light into the house. And in the small strip of grass behind the house there was a rusty white gas tank that Neil and his brother had pretended was a rocket when they were young.

Neil got out of the car determined to be easy and kind. His mother was a disappointed woman. She had been young and hopeful once. (Hadn't she? He couldn't remember this, but at some point it must have been true.) In the form of John Banks, a sick father, and thwarted aspirations, life had served her a meager and gristly meal. This was where her meanness came from. It was important to remember this if he wanted to make it through the visit unscathed.

He had not even raised his hand to knock on the door when it opened to reveal his mother in one of her classic nubbly beige cardigan and gray skirt getups that evoked a sense of wartime privation, her gray hair pulled back into a bun.

"Well, well, if it isn't my own Hollywood star," she said, smirking and nodding her head slightly.

"Hi, Ma," he said. In the largeness of his resolution to be easy and bring happiness and put aside his own gripes, he considered, for a moment, the possibility of kissing her on the cheek. But it was too outlandish an idea—was sure to freak them both out. So instead he nodded too, and ducked into the hall with its dank, cigarette-smoke smell and hideous brown-carpeted stairway.

"I would have put the champagne on ice, but then I remembered I don't have any," Lucinda cracked, leading him into the living room.

"Oh!" Neil said, remembering the fancy lemon and strawberry layer cake probably melting away on the front seat of his car. "I brought a cake for you. Hang on—I'll just run out and get it."

"A cake!" Lucinda sank into her armchair and lit a cigarette. But Neil could tell she was pleased.

Entering the house for the second time, cake box in hand, Neil had the chance to consider more completely what a museum it was. Nothing had changed. Not out of some desire of his mother's to preserve but out of utter indifference. Only the television was new. And the towering pile of crossword puzzle books on top of it—this was the preoccupation into which she now channeled her genuine and thoroughly wasted love of books and language. She was, after all, the source of Neil's own obsessive relationship with words.

"Jim and Sally coming over too?" Neil asked. Jim was his brother— the living, look-alike reminder of what Neil himself would have been if it had not been for the boarding school he had escaped to on scholarship.

Lucinda made a disparaging grunt. "I hope not."

"You didn't invite them?"

"I wanted you all to myself, my pretty. And"—she drew on the cigarette—"Sally would have insisted on cooking and I can't stand that garbage she passes off as food. Those kids are headed for fat city on the fast train."

"That bad?"

Lucinda rolled her eyes. "She doesn't like to come over here anyway." She sighed in what might have been her first expression of genuine emotion.

"Well, you gotta stop smoking."

Lucinda shot him a baleful gaze. "You're one to talk."

"How do you know I haven't given it up?"

"Ha! You don't think I can smell a smoker's sweat?"

Neil smiled weakly, leaning back on the sofa. "So how are you? What's going on here, Ma?"

"Well." She tucked her legs up under her in what struck him as a girlish movement. "What's 'going on' with me is that I'm teaching three classes now—how fabulous, right?" This was a reference to the after-school crafts program she had so disdainfully taught for the last fifteen years. "My blood pressure's down, and I'm seeing someone."

Neil's mind wobbled under the weight of this novel idea. His mother, Lucinda Banks, renowned bitter pill, *seeing* someone. For a moment he could only sit in wonderment, unable to think of anything to follow this with.

"My brilliant son, at a loss for words?" Lucinda said, lighting a cigarette. "It's about time, don't you think?"

"Who is he?" Neil asked. "How did you meet him?"

"No one you know. I met him at temple."

"Temple . . . ?" Neil blanched. The idea that his mother had gone truly crazy or joined a cult presented itself forcefully.

"Temple Beth Avraham—it's not right in town, I have to take the bus, but now—"

"A synagogue?"

"Yes, a synagogue."

"But you're not Jewish."

"Well, I should have been. I've always liked Jewish people."

Neil did not take this on.

"Bob says I've got a naturally Hebrew outlook on life."

"Wow." Neil nodded.

From outside there was the frightening rumble of one of New Bedford's Paleolithic-era buses. "Bob is the guy?"

"Bob is 'the guy.' " Lucinda glared at Neil. "Anyway"—she drew on her cigarette—"I just wanted you to know because I invited him for lunch."

"Wow," Neil repeated stupidly. "Has he met Jim?"

"I haven't had the chance to organize it."

"Oh." Neil felt a ghost of the old satisfaction mixed with guilt—that detestable, gloating competitiveness that his mother had always inspired. Without a husband to badger and manipulate, she had turned to her sons and played them with guilt and aloofness, with meager rewards and inconsistent punishments and the fickle sense of allegiance that passed for affection in their odd little family. One year, she had given Neil a dirt bike for Christmas and given Jim a winter hat. And after Neil had gone off to boarding school he had always been favored son. There was shame inherent in her approval, a flip side to any of the insufficient gestures of her love.

"But what about *you*?" she asked with sarcastic vigor. "Isn't it about time for you to start tying yourself down with a wife and kids?" She blew a stream of smoke out of her nose.

When Bob arrived, he proved to be surprisingly genial. Neil had pictured someone defective—a mute or a social misfit. But in fact he was simply older: seventy-five or so, Neil guessed. He wore a madras shirt and khakis pulled up high around his waist and a pair of wire-rimmed glasses nearly as large and square as Lucinda's. But he was sharper than he looked. His air of surprised, almost boyish innocence was belied by a kind of amused appreciation of absurdity that was downright likable. He was not, after all, as oblivious to Lucinda's jumpy crankiness as Neil had imagined he must be, but seemed instead to be entertained by it. And in his presence Lucinda seemed, in fact, to be able to smile, if not actually laugh, at herself.

She had taken pains with the meal—two tins of tiny hot dogs, a macaroni and mayonnaise salad, sliced ham with mustard, and two bowls of frozen vegetables: succotash and French-cut green beans.

I know how you love succotash, she said to Bob, who agreed heartily.

"So your mother tells me you're a screenwriter," Bob said, tucking into his favorite dish.

"Really?" Neil said in surprise, planning at first to call his mother on the fabrication. But then, looking at her sitting there, fork paused in the middle of her macaroni and lips parted in earnest expectation, he realized this was not necessarily a conscious error on her part. She looked, not sheepish or apologetic, but interested—and proud. As if she had been too shy somehow to ask him about this aspect of his life herself. Where had she gotten the idea? Had he, somehow, led her to believe it?

In the face of all this expectation, Neil couldn't bring himself to set things straight.

"Oh, sort of," he said. "Here and there."

Bob seemed to buy this ridiculous response. "You get to meet a lot of famous people? Actors?" he asked.

"No—I mean, LA isn't—" he began.

"Tell him about the time you met Sharon Stone," his mother interjected.

He stared at her. Had he really told her about this? One of those meaningless Hollywood celebrity encounters, in this case involving lost car keys and an angry valet? The vision of his life—or the way he had represented it to her—was becoming frighteningly pathetic. But he felt captive to his mother's odd state of thrall; she was, it occurred to him for the first time possibly ever, proud. Or proud of what she imagined him to be.

"Well, there's this place in Beverly Hills . . ." he heard himself begin to recount obligingly. And he hated himself for playing this role—it was a role, wasn't it? Doubt crept into his mind, accompanied by a real panic. It was just a son serving up what his mother wanted, he tried to reassure himself as he spoke. He was aware the story was losing something in the distractedness of his telling.

His mother nodded along as if it were the most interesting thing she had ever heard. And Bob tilted his good ear toward him and gave an unconvincing chuckle at the end.

"Now, which one is Sharon Stone again?" he asked, and Lucinda's face fell.

It was later, after Bob had left, after the fancy cake had been picked at and the leftover succotash scraped into the trash, that Lucinda turned. She always did—it had been naïve of Neil to think that somehow maybe this time he had escaped a direct hit.

"Bob says if a man isn't married by the time he's thirty-five he's not meant to settle down," she said from the doorway of the kitchen, where she had stood for some time, leaning against the doorjamb, smoking and watching Neil do dishes.

"Oh? Based on some kind of data he's collected?"

"Based on his experience."

Neil decided not to question this and waited warily for what would follow.

"I've *always* known you wouldn't settle down. You were never meant to have a family."

Neil kept his eyes trained on the dishes in the sink and said nothing.

"You're so—" she paused, possibly for emphasis—"*critical.* You're always thinking about what's wrong and how everyone else is screwed up—but what do you *do*? That's no way to make anything."

"Where's this coming from?" Neil asked, smarting under the blow of her words despite himself. "What did I say?"

"You don't have to say anything. I see the way you look. I see what you're up to. And it hasn't got you very far, has it?"

Neil froze, hands submerged in the dirty water of the brown rubber tub. And for a moment he was again the boy mocked for putting on airs, and a kind of desolation swept through him.

The kitchen was silent but for the sound of the water running.

Lucinda pushed herself off the doorjamb and came over to the sink, where she picked up a plate and began drying it. "That's all right," she said. "Not everyone has to be positive."

Neil shut the water off and turned to her finally, an unexpected rage making his voice shake. "Unlike you, I guess," he said. "You were always so . . . encouraging."

Lucinda shrugged, and finished wiping off the plate she had picked up. "The apple doesn't fall far from the tree, does it?" she said almost cheerfully.

But when she turned to face him finally, her face was not actually cheerful at all. "I'm just saying I *know* you, Neil Banks," she said looking him straight in the eyes.

And Neil looked back at her, wanting to challenge this, or something more complex—wanting, somehow, to undo it, but he could not.

All the way home those words resounded in Neil's head. She was his mother. She had brought him into this world. She *knew* him.

13

IT WAS EARLY EVENING when Laura spotted Neil sitting in his car outside her house. She and Genevieve and Miranda were taking Cocoa for a walk. The sight of Neil's face looking long, pale, and wretched (did he always look this way?) gave her an electric jolt of fear. He had not called all week, and now here he was, right in front of her. What on earth was he doing? Mac would be home in a few hours. Kaaren was cooking up "health burgers" in the kitchen. For Christ's sake—Genevieve and Miranda were at Laura's side!

"Neil," she exclaimed before she could master her surprise. Genevieve looked up at her, startled—she had been mid-description of her friend Morgan's new doll.

Neil himself looked startled, as if despite the fact that he had driven here and parked outside Laura's house he was actually surprised to see her. He raised one hand in a sheepish gesture of greeting.

"What? Who is it, Mom?" Genevieve asked, tightening her grip on Laura's hand.

"Just someone I know." Laura tried to affect a breezy tone. "I'll go say hi—why don't you see what Miranda is doing?"

Genevieve glanced at Miranda, who was noisily pushing her giant toy dump truck. "I want to come with you."

"Well—" Laura began to protest, but then realized this would seem, to Genevieve, unusual. "Okay." She started across the lawn, Genevieve beside her.

Neil rolled down the passenger-side window.

"Hey," he said sheepishly.

"What brings you here?" Laura asked with a tight-lipped smile.

"Me? Oh, just . . ." he glanced at Genevieve. "I was just in the neighborhood and I thought I'd say hi."

"Oh." Laura nodded robotically. Miranda, sensing some sort of disturbance, chose this moment to race over, sweaty hair flying, dump truck upended on the sidewalk.

"This is my daughter Miranda," Laura said, aware that a tone of slightly icy formality had entered her voice. "And my daughter Genevieve."

"Who he?" Miranda demanded.

"This is Neil," Laura answered before Neil had the chance to speak. "He went to school with Mommy."

Neil smiled and bobbed his head foolishly.

"Well, we're just walking the dog," Laura said. Sweet, sensitive Genevieve shifted her gaze down to her feet, and with a pang of regret Laura sensed that her daughter had grasped the implicit insult. It was just the sort of thing that would keep Genevieve coming back to the encounter: *Why was he there? Did Laura not like him? Who was he again?* She would hopefully unburden herself of her questions before Mac came home.

"He coming?" Miranda asked, looking nonplussed.

"Oh, no," Neil said. "No—I was just driving by. But it was nice to meet you."

Laura felt a wave of relief, and a slight pang of apology.

"I like your car," Genevieve startled her by saying.

"You do?" Neil grinned. "Thanks." He patted the dashboard. "It's a good car."

"Well." Laura raised her eyebrows. "You know," she added impulsively, "I have to pick up some dinner after this if you want to meet me for a quick cup of coffee."

"Yeah?" Neil said hesitantly.

"There's a place around the corner—Patrick's—"

Her eyes met his for a split second and in that he became again the man who made her insides turn to water.

"Really?" he said.

Laura looked at her watch. It was five. She had two hours before she could realistically expect Mac. She nodded.

"All right, then. Half an hour?"

"Twenty minutes."

He turned the key in the ignition and Laura clapped her hands to call Cocoa, who all this time had been busy digging a hole in one of the neighbors' flower beds. "C'mon," she said, tapping the girls' heads gently to pull them away from the spot where they stood staring like some sort of mummer's chorus. "Let's walk."

Sitting across from Neil half an hour later, Laura was all nerves and anxious glances. It was, after all, her neighborhood watering hole—a pretentious little wine bar with plate-glass windows and tall, spindly metal stools that made the people sitting on them seem bulky and awkward. Someone she knew was bound to walk in at any moment. It was not the place one would ideally come with the person one was having an affair with. But right now, right here, Laura told herself, Neil was simply an old college friend. There was nothing odd about this.

The truth was that she had pined for him over the last week, though. She had not called him because she was trying to practice restraint and maintain dignity. But it was incredible how physically she had wanted him. Craved him, really. The touch of his hand on her bare arm. The way he looked at her. The way he seemed to really see her. And to see something beautiful and interesting. Almost marvelous. It gave her an unusual, heady rush of self-regard.

Suddenly she noticed the men who glanced at her as she ordered her coffee at the bakery, or whose eyes she met walking down the street, or even at her daughter's school.

For the first time in ages she felt aware of herself as a woman— half of a basic, primal equation. It ran like a stream of constant background static through every interaction with the opposite sex. It was like having swallowed barium or whatever it was they gave people during those body scans—suddenly the markings of sex stood out on everyone around her, a bright electric blue that had been, until now, completely obscured. Here were all these people going about their complicated lives, organizing, planning, carrying out the details of their hyper-evolved upper-middle-class jobs, when really they were just animals, with bodies: fat, thin, clean, or dirty, needing oxygen and food.

She tried to sip her Pinot Grigio slowly and look unintimate as Neil explained the events that had brought him to her doorstep. A visit to his mother's, her new boyfriend, the depressing town of New Bedford . . . Laura tried to balance his slightly crazy intensity with her appearance of composure. "Right," she would say from time to time. Or, "Wow." And she both heard and didn't hear him through her own self-consciousness.

Neil had clearly been rattled by his visit to his mother. She had said something that had unnerved him—about children, or his children . . . *It had made him think of Jenny. And of Colin. How was Jenny going to raise him? Wasn't she just going to be one of those mothers who—*

This made Laura snap to attention.

"Neil," she said. "You have to *stop* with this. Jenny is not an evil person."

"Mm," Neil said, nodding his head without changing his expression.

"Neil . . ." Laura sat forward. "I know it must be *so* hard—I thought it was crazy from the start—" She cut herself off and hesitated for a moment.

Neil raised his eyebrows.

"But the thing is, it is what it is now. Right? You can have other children. I mean, you can have *children*. Period. You can raise them exactly how you want. You can ban television and home-school them."

"That's not the point."

"Oh." A wave of tiredness washed over her. "What is, then?"

Neil looked up at the corner of the ceiling and with his face profiled like this Laura could see the muscles of his jaw working. "The point is *this* boy. This child," he said finally. He turned his eyes to her. "He's mine. He's half of me and I don't know why I ever let Jenny just . . . *have* him."

Laura looked back at Neil for a long moment and around them there was the clink of glasses and the pop as the bartender uncorked a bottle of wine.

"Nobody *has* him, Neil. Not really. I mean, Jenny will raise him and love him and everything, but he's his own person. Not just half of you and half of her—the parts don't make the whole." She thought of her girls—of Miranda's wild shriek of laughter and bouncing, swaggering walk, of Genevieve's dark eyes and thin shoulders and unerring attraction to all that was sad and fragile and impermanent and her odd, passionate love of horses, and she thought of the way they both smelled when she buried her face in their hair and nuzzled their necks. "What the whole is . . . ," she said. "It's something else. It's not anyone's."

Neil kept his eyes on her face as if assessing this idea, taking it in. "But it's *influenced*—I mean, like, where you live, where you go to school, what your parents talk about—Colin is going to grow up in the Back Bay—I fucking hate the Back Bay—it's my least favorite place in Boston. Seriously—"

At that moment there was the tinkling bell of the door opening and the handsome, solid form of Mavis Haywood, social doyenne of the neighborhood and old family friend of the Trillians, entered.

Laura's face must have registered this intrusion and Neil turned to follow her gaze, at which moment Mrs. Haywood's own eyes alighted on Laura and brightened with interest.

"Laura Trillian!" she sang out, sailing down the long narrow bar to her and planting a kiss on the now-standing Laura's cheek.

"That's how I always think of her." She beamed at Neil. "It's just too fun a name to give up saying." She extended her hand to Neil, who took it without rising.

"Neil Banks," Laura said by way of introduction. "This is Mavis Haywood—one of my neighbors."

"And oldest friends," Mavis chided, as if the word "friends" at all described their relationship, separated by twenty years and an ocean-wide gap in understanding.

"Neil and I went to college together," Laura said hastily, feeling her face color.

"A Harvard man," Mavis said, running her eyes over him. "And do you live here too?"

"In a way," Neil said. He was making no effort to rise to the level of charm an encounter with Mavis demanded.

"He's visiting," Laura added, "for a year. Working."

"Ahhh." Mavis looked disdainful. "Well, your garden is looking lovely, as always. Those lilacs—mmm." She breathed with demonstrative vigor. "I'll leave you to your drinks. Nice to meet you—"

"Neil," Laura prompted too quickly.

"Neil." Mavis bobbed her head. It was difficult to tell what sort of look she gave Laura. Curiosity? Disapproval? Or was this just Laura's own paranoia?

It was nearly six-fifteen.

"I have to go," Laura said once Mavis had settled herself by the window with another sixty-something Cambridge lady. Mavis had known Laura's mother from the very beginning of her marriage to Adam, and yet she never spoke of her. She was a frustratingly inert repository of information.

"Right." Neil looked haggard to her. "Right."

Laura pulled out her wallet.

"Don't worry about it," he said, and then leaned in urgently. "Just tell me—is she a Republican yet? "

Laura looked at him blankly. "Oh. Jenny?" She recoiled, realizing what he was asking. His curiosity was awful. It was as if she were sitting across from a frenzied crack addict. And he was addicted to, what? To Jenny? To information about Jenny? Was it because of the baby or because of Jenny herself? Had he been secretly, all along, somehow in love with her? The idea filled her with a sudden dismay and loneliness. "No," she said. She mustered up her most withering voice. "And by the way, she's moving out of your least favorite place in Boston."

"Of . . . ? Oh, the Back Bay?" Neil said. And he did look a little chagrined.

"Where to?" he started to ask, but Laura was already standing.

"'Bye," she said, feeling the whole depressing mess of the afternoon hit her—Neil had come, not in the heat of passion, but in the heat of his insane obsession with Jenny.

"I'm sorry, Lo," he said lamely. "I'm just—"

"That's all right," she said tightly.

"You're a good person."

It had an ominous sound—like something said to someone you would never see again.

And outside, walking through the golden light of evening back to her house, along the trafficked but oddly pedestrian-free avenue, Laura felt tears swell in her throat and burn in her eyes. She was faced with the humiliating idea that maybe, possibly, her whole affair with Neil was part of some age-old desire he had to get back at Jenny, to even out some score that predated even Colin. Was it possible she had just been horribly, naïvely foolish? But she could not cry. She had made enough of a mess already. She had to go home, welcome her husband, bathe her children, and give some semblance of order to her household. She had to push all these contradictory feelings away and replace them with an even manner, a smooth and comfortable motherliness whose whole purpose was to make everything all right.

14

IT HAD BEEN A MISTAKE, of course, going to see Laura all addled after his visit to New Bedford. Like writing a response to an angry email the moment you got it. Or calling an old girlfriend as soon as her number popped up on your Google search. He had freaked her out. Clearly. And she had every right to be freaked by him, sitting there outside her house like some kind of maniac.

Neil blamed it on his mother. It had left him with this weird sense of urgency regarding Colin. For what, though? What exactly was he after? The urgency had faded, but the desire—deep, shadowy, and inescapable as a bruise—was still there. He *wanted* something.

Now, in the saner light of Elise's kitchen, his involvement of Laura in this seemed ridiculous and understandably alarming. There was something eminently rational about Elise that was reflected in her household, and under the cool clear light of the pendant lamp hanging over her kitchen table Neil could see that it had been unfair to lay this want at Laura's doorstep. He had taken advantage of something soft and forgiving in her, something that was itself needy. He would never, for instance, have thrown those questions at Elise.

At the moment, 37 Cottage Street was empty. Elise and Chrissy and the boys had gone to walk along the river. What a civilized and enlightened family thing to do! They had it good, James and Nigel. Hopefully someday they would grow into the kind of men who could recognize this.

Neil checked his messages. Three new ones from Galena. Christ! He was practically afraid of her. He would have to call her back today. The thought occurred to him first as a simple matter of obligation. He was not such a cad that he would sleep with a girl and not call her back. But then, as he girded himself for the conversation, a second thought occurred to him. A devious, unhappy thought that at another, better time in his life he might have dismissed. But here and now, it took hold. He could find out where Jenny was moving to from her. He could find out where his little son would live. Hadn't this been what he was after with Laura? But then, of course, it had been impossible to ask. Even Laura, with all her kindness and understanding, would have thought it suspicious. And Elise—forget it. He could already see the look on her face. But with Galena—what did she know of his relationship with Jenny? Why not ask for the address of an old friend in order to write a note?

Elise and Chrissy and the boys came home just as Neil was about to leave. Galena had suggested another trendy bar in her neighborhood. Which was fine. Thank God she didn't want some long arduous dinner with all the awkwardness of eating and sitting opposite one another and talking about the kind of real and serious things food seemed to require.

Chrissy and Elise and the boys entered, licking the dregs of ice-cream cones.

"Howdy," Neil said foolishly.

"Where are you off to?" Elise asked.

"Oh, just meeting a friend . . ." Neil shifted uncomfortably.

"Ahhh." Elise raised her eyebrows. She had always been able to see through him.

"Come on, boys, inside," Chrissy said, shuttling them past Neil. There was a marked coldness to her manner ever since the pot-smoking incident. He never should have offered the joint to Elise. He had gotten her into trouble.

Elise rolled her eyes in apology, but Neil could see that she was stressed.

"Going?" Nigel asked.

"Just for a little while," Neil said, and made a goodbye salute.

"Could you shut the gate?" he heard Chrissy snap in her new, crisp tone, as he jogged down the front steps, and he wished he could uncoil the tentacles of his bad influence from around the house.

Galena was waiting already when he walked into the bar—a narrow one with small booths and a long bar. She was standing at the far end, drinking a glass of red wine. There was nowhere to sit, Neil registered with an overwhelming surge of fatigue.

"Hi!" Galena said brightly, grabbing his wrists and standing up on tiptoe to plant a startling kiss on his lips. "It's too crowded," she said. "Let's get out of here." And despite the implications of this— they were a mere two blocks from her apartment, so it was not hard to guess where she was headed—Neil felt relieved. She put her wine glass on the bar and pulled him out.

There was no awkward charade about what to do next. "I have beer in my apartment," Galena said in her straightforward way. Neil appreciated this. No head games here. Not very Albanian, apparently.

In the sterile cube of her apartment, Neil looked out the floor-to-ceiling windows while Galena opened beers for them and microwaved bowls of fragrant-smelling mushroom soup she had cooked the night before.

"Here." She handed him his and sat down on the plush carpeting. "I don't like to sit at the table." Neil sat down opposite her and tasted the soup, which was delicious.

"Thanks," he said, and he meant it. It was actually exactly what he wanted to do. Sit on the floor and eat soup and drink beer.

"So how is *Prometheus II* coming?" Galena asked. "Have you given them guns that shoot Setlan yet?" she said, smirking.

"Just bombs. Setlan-loaded warheads labeled 'Make Love Not War.'"

"Kaboom!" Galena cheered delightedly.

Outside, a fire engine blared.

"No, seriously, you know I'll probably get promoted if you do," Galena said.

"Yeah?" Neil raised his eyebrows. "In that case, let's put it everywhere."

"Hey!" Galena kicked him in the foot in his least favorite type of flirting gesture. "I'm serious!"

"Oh," Neil said.

"Seriously, are you going to do it? I don't understand why you wouldn't—I mean, it's just a computer game, its not like we're talking about putting ads for Coca-Cola in Notre Dame."

"Right." Neil was getting annoyed with this line of conversation. Was she for real, sitting here and grilling him about the fucking product placement?

Galena put her soup bowl down and crawled across the floor to him. She took his bowl from his hand and put it to the side. Then she began to undo his fly.

"Are you kidding?" Neil asked.

Galena took her shirt off.

"You're seducing me to get Setlan put in the game?"

"What do you think?" She giggled.

"Man." Neil let his head drop backward to the seat of the couch. He could feel Galena's hands running up his chest. She attacked his neck, kissing it violently as her left hand slid down to his hip bone.

"Whoa!" Neil said, pushing her back.

"What?" she said. "Come on. I'm seducing you because I think you're cute."

"Do you always like to lead with work talk?"

"No," she said, giggling. "Just with you."

"Oh," Neil said, and, feeling as dirty and as compromised as he was—he submitted himself to her agenda.

It was afterward, getting out of her mod glass shower cabin and wrapping a towel around his waist, that he brought up his own agenda.

"So do you have Jenny Callahan's address? I thought I might get in touch with her now that I'm back East."

"Jenny?" Galena, who was still lounging on the bed, pulled herself up on her elbows, the surprisingly dark nipples of her small breasts pointing straight at him. "Do you have a thing for her or something?"

"God, no!" Neil stepped into his boxers. "Just old friends. You know."

"Jenny-dot-Callahan at—"

"I mean her regular address. Mailing address. I thought I'd write a card."

"A card?" Galena looked doubtful.

"Seems more . . ." Neil shrugged. "Appropriate."

"Romantic."

"No." In his jeans now, Neil sat down on the side of the bed. "Not romantic."

"No?" Galena shrugged. "Well, she just moved yesterday."

"Yeah?" Neil tried to sound surprised. "Where?"

"Wellesley." Galena stuck her tongue out. "I don't know why."

"The kid, I guess, right? Schools and all that."

"How do you know she has a kid?"

Neil stood up and busied himself with his shirt. "I heard that." He could feel Galena's eyes on his back from her position on the bed. It was silent for a moment.

"I'll get it for you," she said, and then giggled. "Lover boy."

Galena was nothing if not consistent, and as promised, she sent an email the next morning with Jenny's new address: 27 Belleview Road. *I didn't tell her I was giving it to you so your love letters can come as a surprise to her (:,* she wrote.

Neil was at ZGames, in the middle of a trying problem with the third level of *Promo II*, as it was referred to in development headquarters, and did not take much notice at the moment. Joe was sitting beside him, smelling of sweat and barbecue sauce and patiently guiding him through the intricate and exasperating workings of MotionBuilder. It was pissing Neil off that he was even wrestling with this thing: the job as detailed when he was hired had been more high-level than this. All concept, not execution. But as with most things in life, it had been falsely advertised.

Despite the smash success of *Prometheus Syndrome*, ZGames was cutting back on its programming staff and if he wanted to get this mock-up of *II* done right he was going to have to put together a rudimentary software sketch himself. Or rather, Steven Closter was supposed to put the rudimentary sketch together, but Neil didn't trust him. Their enmity was deepening rather than diminishing over time. The guy had apparently been calling Galena, who thought he looked, *What's the word for it? It means "like a penis."* Neil couldn't think of it. In any case, Closter had somehow discerned that she was sleeping with Neil. This threw strains of wounded manhood into his already rivalous relationship with Neil and resulted in an endless stream of sarcastic barbs that fell just short of open insult. Neil could tune them out, no problem.

But the two had begun attracting a kind of bated-breath audience among their coworkers, which was distracting. And stupid as his work was (it was a fucking *game*, Neil constantly reminded himself), Neil couldn't stand the thought of Steven's clumsy, angry brain sabotaging it.

The truth was, his growing enmity with Closter coincided with— was possibly even, if he was really honest with himself, *connected to*—his deepening investment in the game's story. He had solved the riddle of the creature, née "digital tablet." It would be a chimera. A creature defined genetically as a single organism with two distinct sets of DNA from two different zygotes. Or defined mythologically as a monster made up of different animal parts. And the chimera would be made up of more than two genetic frameworks: it would be made up of hundreds and thousands. It would contain a little piece—an infintesimal strand of DNA—from every living creature on the gentle utopian planet it came from. That was the secret. Right there in its flesh and blood.

It would look like a Sphinx, part woman, part lion. The Sphinx was a mythological creature that had always fascinated Neil. In ancient Greece it had represented a force of evil that strangled all those who could not answer its riddle. But in other cultures— ancient India, for example—it was a benevolent creature, capable of absolving man's sins. This was the kind of mixed bag Neil wanted for the secret. And he spent a good deal of time with the art crew, making his Sphinx both frightening and alluring. For one thing, she was going to be see-through, her glassy innards threaded brightly with strands of DNA like phosphorescence in night water. *Promo II* took place in the year 2300, after all, and was to launch in the year 2009. The Age of Biology was upon them. And this Sphinx—this Sphinx needed to represent it. The beauty, the intricacy, the potential, and the menace. The time when all progress and all salvation, all retreat and all destruction would come from mastering the forces of nature. Neil had conceived of the perfect title too—one he had not run by anyone yet. *Perfect Life. Prometheus Syndrome II: Perfect Life.* It actually made his heart race. Which was embarrassing, considering it was a stupid computer game, not his fucking magnum opus.

"Right there—just right-click," Joe was saying when there was a rapid, aggressive series of taps on the side of his cube.

It was Rod Emerus, in his signature CEO getup of dark shirt tucked snugly into dark jeans.

"Oh! Hi!" Joe seemed nearly to swallow his own tongue.

It was rare that Emerus made the trek downstairs and into the wretched cube world his creative team lived and breathed in.

"Can I have a word with you, Banks? In the conference room?" Emerus said.

"Sure." Neil nodded and then realized, as Emerus remained standing there, that the man meant immediately. "Now?"

"I understand there are some problems between you and Closter," Emerus said as soon as the conference room door was shut behind them.

"Oh," Neil said, feeling his heart sink. Feeling, really, *everything* sink. It was so incredibly *stupid.* How had he come to be involved in this?

" 'Oh'?" Emerus repeated. "Well, are there?"

"I don't have any problem with him," Neil said flatly.

Emerus dropped into a chair and regarded Neil frankly.

"I didn't think so," he said finally. "Well. He has a problem with you, I'm sure you are aware."

Neil nodded.

"Look." Emerus leaned forward. "Closter is an asswipe. We know that. I can't get rid of him, though, because he's been here too long. Too many stock options. You just go about your work and I'll handle him. You pick a new right-hand man—someone who knows his way around gameplay—and I'll find a new assignment for Steven."

"That's all right—" Neil began, but Emerus waved this aside.

"No. It's better that way. Consider it done. Is there anyone you want to work with?"

Neil tried to remember the other senior staff. Hal Offert, a nervous guy with thick glasses. Sung Ho, who liked to race ATVs on the weekend. And—he literally couldn't think of anyone else. He had been living in a bubble here, head in his work and then a fast exit at the end of the day. He could only vaguely conjure up faces.

"Joe?" he said finally.

"Joe?" Emerus frowned. "Joe Turnblum?"

Neil nodded.

"Joe is an intern."

"Oh."

Emerus was silent. A long, craggy vein on his forehead began to pulse with the working of his jaw. For a moment Neil thought he had been enraged by the ignorance of the suggestion.

"You think he can do it?" Emerus asked instead, though.

"I don't know—I mean, he's been teaching me MotionBuilder."

"All right." Emerus tapped his pen on the table. "I'll put him on it. With Sung Ho as backup." He shot Neil a hard look. "He owes you. Big time."

Neil nodded. "All right, then." He began to back toward the door.

"Wait," Emerus said. He tilted his long pale head to the side. "I understand you spent some time in Africa."

The question startled Neil. "How did you—"

Emerus waved this away. "I know everything. Don't bother asking how. Where were you?"

"The Congo," Neil said. "Mostly."

"Mmmm." Emerus nodded thoughtfully.

It was an unlikely line of conversation. Neil waited with interest to see what was coming next. Maybe the man had some phil-anthropic interest in the region? He had to do something with his money, after all.

"They had a civil war there, right? Militias and child soldiers and all that? Macheteing people's hands off? Rape?"

The line of questioning took Neil aback. He nodded warily.

"You see any of that?"

"Well, not right before my eyes. I mean, I wasn't in the villages when—"

"But the idea. You got the idea of it. The victims and stuff. The chaos."

Neil's discomfort was growing. "I guess so." He frowned. "I guess I 'got' it.' "

Emerus did not acknowledge the sarcasm in Neil's voice. He leaned forward on the table. "So I think you've got to work that into the gameplay. An Africa planet or something. That climate of vicious anarchy. Colored aliens, tribes, war crimes. Gamers love that stuff. Some little pocket of Africa-flavored hell in the galaxy. Level five, maybe."

Neil stared at him.

"Hey, I'm not saying anything racist. I mean, these people—these aliens can be pink, for all I care. Purple. Its just the idea of it—this primitive, twisted place you have to fight your way out of."

If Neil had had any pride left, any grain of idealism or hope or self-respect, he would have quit. Right then and there. The thought registered with a wild, internal shriek of defeat.

"Right," he said, and started for the door.

"Banks," Emerus said. "Don't look so glum. There's money in it—I promise you."

Neil had jotted the address Galena had supplied him with on the palm of his hand. *Old school*, he could hear Johnson's imagined voice taunting in his ear.

He had actually forgotten about it until that night, eating his microwaved pizza and leafing through a tome of collected essays on nineteenth-century missions in Central Africa. It was his first night back at Johnson's. The work on the kitchen ceiling was nearly done and it had become clear that it would be better for him to clear out of Elise's house. But sitting here under the fluorescent light of Johnson's kitchen, he missed the warmth of their household— missed James's cackle and Nigel's intent, observant stare. He had really formed a bond with them, hadn't he?

With his book open before him and greasy napkins strewn across the Formica tabletop, Neil was reminded of the address when he lifted his hand from the spot where it had been resting. There it was, backward, in smudged blue ink like some sort of secret code. Belleview Road. It had a saccharine sound to it. Was he really planning to write Jenny a card? He had been so focused on obtaining the information, he had not really formulated a plan. What would he say? *Why don't you see a lawyer and see if you can get visitation rights?* Laura had suggested. But this wasn't the point. He didn't want visitation rights. He wanted something both more obscure and more profound: he wanted respect. He wanted not to feel like some dirty secret.

And he wanted—if he was really honest with himself—Jenny to be thwarted in her plans. There was something almost supernatural about the way she always got what she wanted. How docilely he had submitted himself to her agenda, as if he were still the screwed-up twenty-one-year-old boyfriend who had let himself be persuaded to drive all the way to New York to bring her to a job interview, only to be kept waiting for four hours in the car. Who had gone out and spent his hard-earned cash on a rented tux(!) so he could accompany her to the Radcliffe Ball. She was the only person who'd had this effect on him. And it was dangerous—a threat to the very core of his own sense of who he was: unmalleable, strong-willed, eccentric. Not someone who just went along with other people's ideas.

He picked up the notebook Kirstin had left, in a naïvely hopeful gesture, for him to write down any calls that came for her or Johnson, and shoved it into his back pocket. He grabbed a pen and his car keys and wallet. He would just go. Just check it out. He could think of something to write when he was there. If he even wanted to write anything at all. And he could see the backdrop against which his son's childhood was to unfold.

Route 128 was reasonably empty; it was nearly ten and a weeknight, and Neil drove along with the windows open and the fresh, cool spring air battering his ears. At the Wellesley exit he turned onto Route 16, with its array of suburban conveniences—the ubiquitous roadside Chinese restaurant, the appliance showroom, the posh "free library," and, as he neared the center, the increasingly high-end boutiques and precious bakeries.

Finally he reached the corner of Pond Road and from there turned onto Belleview. At the end of the driveway to number 27, he edged the car to the side and idled for a few minutes, staring, before cutting the ignition.

The house was atrocious. Big, ugly, and showy. The kind of bland and squeaky new that characterized the homes of the B-list celebrities profiled on *MTV Cribs*. The clearing it stood in was cut into the wooded hillside like a brand.

Quietly, quietly, he climbed out of the car and shut the door behind him. He felt exhilaratingly vulnerable, standing so suspiciously at the side of this pedestrian-free suburban road. But no car passed and there was nothing but the sound of wind in the heads of the tall pines that lined the property. After a few minutes he started up the drive toward the house, his heart pounding. What would he say if Jenny or Jeremy or whoever came out and found him there, making his way up the drive? Would they call the police? He was in violation of the donor contract, to be sure. And of basic trespassing laws, for that matter. He registered these thoughts but didn't act on them—the thrill of transgression pulsed through him.

Neil kept to the trees and proceeded past the garage and up the hill behind the house instead of risking a walk across the front lawn. Someone was home for certain. There was a Land Rover parked at the garage door and there were lights on all along the backside of the downstairs.

At the highest point of the lawn behind the house, Neil stopped and crouched down on the newly turned earth at the edge of the woods. There was a fancy-looking swing set and jungle gym and on the flagstone terrace a forgotten baby contraption: something garish and elaborate-looking.

From here he could see inside the house clearly. There were no curtains and the only shaded windows were upstairs. The kitchen was fancy—granite countertops, Sub-Zero fridge, etc. The room beside it looked as of yet unassembled: a sofa still wrapped in plastic, two chairs, some heavy dark wooden furniture. On the roof there was a discreetly positioned satellite dish.

As he watched, he saw a form cut across the kitchen—a dark-skinned, Latina-looking woman in a red oversized T-shirt. The housekeeper, or babysitter. Of course. She looked tired—they probably made her work crazy hours—it was nearly eleven, after all. What was she doing in the kitchen, for Christ's sake? Neil watched as she rinsed a glass and filled it up with something from the refrigerator. She lived with them, maybe.

As he watched, Neil began to form a narrative. His son would be raised in this empty, materialistic environment by a hired nanny who was too tired and too pissed off to give him love. He would probably go to some provincial rich-kids day school and learn how to play tennis and lacrosse. He'd have a giant TV and game system in his room and never be encouraged to read books—Jenny had never been a reader, had she? And all this would be just as Jenny wanted it, just as Jenny had planned from the start: the privileged childhood that she hadn't had herself. The kind of soulless, unreflective reward that lay at the end of her consumer-driven version of the American Dream.

In the kitchen, the woman moved out of his line of vision and a few moments later he saw the blue shadows of a television flash out the windows of one of the downstairs rooms. Maybe this meant Jenny and Jeremy were out. The woman was babysitting. Which meant they would be coming back. At any moment. There would be a crunch of wheels up the drive and already they would have seen his parked car, be on alert for intruders or disaster. Considered in this light, his position here at the edge of the woods, peering down into the unprotected windows of the house, seemed truly creepy. After the first chill of repulsion, it struck him as funny. He was making a habit of lurking outside sleeping houses in the dark.

With some combination of panic and exhilaration, he began to make his way back down the hill, the loose earth skittering and sinking unevenly beneath his feet. Once back in the relative safety of the ditch along the side of the lower part of the driveway, he did not stop and look back. Twice he thought he could hear a car coming up the deserted road, imagined the sweep of headlights that would illuminate him there against the trees, the looks of fear and horror that would cross Jenny's face, and his mind leapt ahead to the patrol car, the police station, and then the inevitable drift of information back to Elise and Chrissy, back to Laura . . . And this sobered him. Made him pray in earnest, actually, that he could get to his car and get out before he was discovered.

And miraculously, because by this point he had imagined discovery so clearly it seemed inevitable, he made it back to his car without incident. He managed, even, to turn over the ignition, pull away, and drive to the end of Belleview Road undiscovered. By the time he reached the highway he was almost disappointed. There was no culminating drama to this bold lapse of judgment. And he had spotted neither mother nor child. But he had learned more. This was true. He had learned more about what he already knew.

15

CHRISSY WAS OFFICIALLY PISSED. Elise had pushed her over the edge: first with the endless wheedling over the donor sibling thing (she could admit it—she had been snivelly) and then with the regressive pot-smoking incidents. It was juvenile, really. Elise had turned herself into a sulky, rebellious teenager and Chrissy into a harried, aggravated mother figure. But now they were stuck. Elise could not find a way out.

She should have listened to Neil (it was a sign of the general ridiculousness of her actions that Neil occupied any kind of wise role) when he had suggested last week that maybe she should not toke up again, considering how mad Chrissy had been the first time. But Elise had wanted to. She hadn't bargained for the fact that the smoke alarm would go off, waking up the boys and disturbing the neighbors. It had elevated what would have been simply an immature act to an act of endangerment. Just remembering it made Elise blush. She was thirty-six, for Christ's sake, an established genetic scientist! And she felt badly about Neil, who had gotten the brunt of Chrissy's anger.

It was on the heels of this that Elise called Jenny.

Their snippy conversation had been weighing on her: not because she felt she had done anything wrong, but because in general, in life, she didn't like to leave that sort of loose end. And with Chrissy angry at her, the silence that had fallen between her and Jenny felt particularly sad.

So, Elise had sucked up her pride and called to apologize. She had expected a wound-up, hyper-organized Jenny, who would whisk past her apologies with a litany of things to be done. But instead, Jenny had sounded tired and unusually distracted. "Oh, whatever," she had said in response to Elise's contrition. "I don't care." Which was totally unlike Jenny.

"Did you get your basement cleared out?" Elise asked.

"No." Jenny sighed.

"Did you figure out the piano thing?" Elise asked.

"What? Oh, I don't know. We'll just see if it fits."

Jenny had been obsessing over this for weeks. "Are you sure you're okay?" Elise pressed. "You sound . . . different."

"Do I?"

"Yes!"

There was a silence and then the sound of Jenny crying. Elise did not believe her ears. "Are you laughing?" she asked.

And that was how she found out about the cancer. She was not supposed to tell anyone. Not even Laura. Not until Jenny and Jeremy had more information. And had made more decisions. *Such as . . . ?* Elise wondered, but she didn't ask. It was so incredibly terrible. And unlucky. It was terribly, terribly unlucky, just as Jenny had said. It was odd, Elise didn't really know Jeremy; even after his four years of marriage to Jenny he remained shadowy in her mind: thin, serious, brilliant . . . she had no sense of what he was really like. But weirdly—*horribly*, really—it was not as shocking to her that he would get sick as it was that this would be happening to Jenny. This seemed incredible, impossible even. Everything always went right for Jenny. It was like a central tenet of her person.

"What should I do?" Elise had turned immediately to Chrissy, of course, despite their current frostiness. As Angela Noyes's daughter, Chrissy always knew intuitively the right thing to say and the right way to be helpful. For the moment, it dissolved the ice between them.

"Bring her lunch," Chrissy had said. "Bring her something healthy and delicious to eat while she's unpacking. And then just listen."

And so on the day of Jenny's move, Elise checked the two columns her lab assistant, Prakash, was running, and left to pick up and deliver Jenny lunch.

At the fanciest food shop in Framingham, she picked up Diet Cokes and grilled chicken and spinach salad (Jenny would never eat something as bready and carb-filled as a sandwich) and headed off to Wellesley.

Jenny's house was bustling with movers and unpackers and a crew of gardeners putting the finishing touches on a terraced flower bed. A short, muscled man in a "Jesus Lives!" T-shirt was carrying a wing chair on his head, and two more workers grappled with the long part of a sectional sofa, sweat pouring off their foreheads despite the moderate temperature of the day.

The house itself looked even bigger and more gleamingly new than Elise had imagined. She had seen it once before, when it was not yet finished, and the unpainted shell had not indicated how formal it would look.

"Oh, that was sweet of you—you really didn't have to bring lunch," Jenny said, taking the bag from Elise and seeming more like her usual self. She was dressed in stylish workout clothes and had on lip gloss and her usual air of brisk efficiency.

"It's the least I could do," Elise said, which Jenny did not acknowledge.

"Give me five more minutes to direct these guys and then we'll break," she said. "Look around, if you like."

Elise did as told, and wandered while Jenny delivered calm, direct, but not particularly friendly instructions to the crew. The house was full of ostentatious nouveau touches like an upstairs gallery with a balustrade. The master bedroom had two giant walk-in closets that were each the size of the twins' bedroom. Yet, for all the space, there was no one room that seemed to promise a comfortable or logical place to hang out.

"What do you think?" Jenny asked breathlessly from behind her, startling Elise.

"Wow," Elise said. She had never been good at lying. "I hadn't realized how big it was going to be when I saw it before."

"You think it's too big," Jenny said, unconcerned.

"No, it's good to have—"

"It's not your style, I know." Jenny walked over to check the label on a large wardrobe box and frowned.

"You'll have plenty of room for parties," Elise said, and in saying it, she remembered Jeremy. The thought seemed to strike them both at the same time, and for a moment they were silent.

"Let's eat outside," Jenny suggested, leading the way back to the stairs.

"I'm sorry," Elise began. "I'm sure you're not thinking about parties right now. I didn't mean—"

"No. It's fine. We will have parties here," Jenny said with determination. "We just have to get through this next piece."

"Right."

Jenny opened some French doors at the bottom of the back stairs and led Elise out onto a flagstone terrace, ringed by a wide two-foot-high stone wall.

"And this next piece involves . . . ?" Elise let her voice trail off.

"Ugh." Jenny shook her head and took the bag from Elise's hand, began setting the salads and sodas and wax-paper-wrapped cookies on the wall. "I don't know yet exactly. We have an appointment on Monday to see the surgeon and the medical oncologist . . ."

As she spoke, Elise nodded along and tried to absorb and understand the information. It was not good. It did not sound good. But Jenny was "staying positive," as they say. Her voice had a clipped can-do tone with an edge of warning to it. *Do not press me on this,* she seemed to say. *Do not offer me your pity or your grief.* Elise tried her best to oblige. *That's good,* she said from time to time, or *That makes sense.* But she could see that she was not the right woman for the job. Laura, sympathetic, teary Laura, who was such an adept chameleon, so immanently able to pick up cues and adapt herself to fit them, was the one who should be here. Elise herself was too solid, too steadfast. She had inherited too much of her mother's reserve and social gracelessness. She could not fall into step with Jenny's necessary optimism with ease.

Behind them, on the freshly unrolled sod that spread up the hill to the woods, there came the chirp of a cricket. Already this artificial recreation of nature was being accepted by the world of insects, animals, and microorganisms. A squirrel darted across the green expanse from one patch of woods to another. All around them the grass was coming alive.

Jenny finished explaining the various treatment options and they both sat looking out over the lawn. The passing of time suddenly struck Elise in all its weirdness. Who would have thought, at age twenty-one, hanging out in their dorm room rehashing some drunken party or putting themselves through one of the quickly neglected exercise videos Jenny introduced to the room, that they would find themselves here one day, behind this McMansion, talking about the prospects of Jenny's husband's cancer? It felt for a moment as if they should have known. As if their innocence of the future had simply been stupid. And a little endearing. She wanted to say this to Jenny, but looking at her friend sitting there on the stone wall, knees pressed to her chin, she couldn't. What good would it do her? It was not practical or reassuring. If anything, it was tragic.

Jenny lifted her head and turned to face Elise squarely. "As a scientist, you see aberrations all the time, right?" There was a determination in her voice that Elise recognized.

"Of . . . ?"

"Whatever. One freak molecule that doesn't behave as predicted. Or one experiment that gets out-of-whack results. One, I don't know, *goat* whose milk for some reason refuses to express human proteins."

Elise frowned. Ordinarily, as a scientist, she did not really believe this. Even exceptions happened for their own logical, explicable reasons—some variable in process or makeup that would, if further studied, be revealed to have its own predictable, logical framework. But there was Ula, in whom, so far, Elise could detect no reason for her aberration. "Well, for the most part, there is order," she said. "And predictability. But it's true, there are exceptions."

"That's what I told Jeremy," Jenny said. "You can't just boil it down to numbers and averages. It's each individual case on its own."

Elise nodded.

There was a pause.

"I haven't been a very sympathetic wife, you know," Jenny surprised her by saying.

"That's not true," Elise protested, although of course it was true —she and Laura had often remarked on this.

But Jenny did not seem to be listening for any answer. "I have been selfish," she said.

Elise did not say anything this time. She waited for Jenny to turn back to her with her usual composure and suggest they move on to something else—dessert, maybe, or more unpacking. But she didn't.

A bird began to chirp loudly, almost rhythmically, in a nearby tree and the breeze rattled their sandwich paper. Jenny's gaze remained fixed. The skin around her eyes, Elise noticed for the first time, looked puffy under a layer of powder or concealer or whatever it was, as if she had been crying. It made Elise feel sad. Selfishly, it made her miss Chrissy.

"We're all selfish," Elise said finally. "It's in our genes."

Back on the Pharm, something had happened while Elise was gone. This was clear the moment she saw her research assistant. His round, transparent face was lit up with excitement as he walked toward her down the hall.

"Ula's milk is in!"

"It is?" Elise felt her own heart flip-flop.

"This morning. Plenty of it. I'm separating it already—I got it ready—"

"Where?"

"Over there—in number ten."

Elise threw on her lab coat and, trying to restrain her excitement, followed Prakash into the centrifuge room where number ten whirred away just as it was supposed to. There was nothing to see, of course, just the bright electric number indicating time and speed, but all the same, it was tantalizing. Inside the centrifuge, the raw result of her labors was waiting with all its promise and mystery, its complex challenges and particularity. This was what she loved about her work.

"So we'll use the same compound to cleave the protein?" Prakash asked, his own heightened interest as palpable as hers. And for a moment Elise loved him—her partner in fascination. A man who could speak the language of chemistry and biology and share her delight in its application. A partner whose unique scrawl of equations and formulas she could recognize a mile away.

The rest of the afternoon was spent in concentration preparing the various particulates needed to begin the purification. And Elise herself handled the sterilized and foil-wrapped beakers, the pipettes, the neat canisters of chemicals at her little-used bench. It felt good to be doing the work herself, collecting the amazing chalky substance at the bottom of the pipettes—it looked like no more than a smear of dried toothpaste!—from which all her work would stem. And she did not think of Jenny and Jeremy, or of Chrissy and their recent tension, and for the first time in ages, she and Prakash stayed at the lab late—watching the daylight fade to twilight and the computer screens begin to glow from the various empty offices like so many nocturnal creatures, opening their eyes.

When she arrived home the boys were already asleep and Chrissy was in bed. The light had been on in their bedroom window when Elise pulled up outside the house, but when she got to the door, Chrissy had switched it out. This did not deter her. The excitement of her work surrounded her like a bright, optimistic haze.

"Chrissy," she said, climbing onto the bed and putting a hand on Chrissy's hip.

"Mmm," Chrissy grunted irritably.

Elise was undissuaded. "Ula's milk came in," she said, and Chrissy rolled onto her back and looked up at Elise.

"And did it work?" she asked begrudgingly.

Elise nodded, grinning. "Like gangbusters."

"Congratulations."

"Chrissy," Elise said, lying down beside her, pressing her cheek against Chrissy's shoulder and wrapping her arm more tightly around her waist. "I'm sorry about getting stoned. I'm sorry I've been irresponsible. It was idiotic."

Chrissy was silent for a moment. "It's not just that."

The bright haze of elation surrounding Elise protected her even from this. "What? That I don't want to be a part of this donor sibling thing?"

"That you don't want to be a full part of the boys' lives."

Elise drew back in surprise. This stung. Even through the haze. "What do you mean?" she asked.

"That you make this not-biological-parent thing into a dividing point. Like you aren't as much a parent as I am. When you *are*. I would never have done this without you. They would not be here without you."

Elise stared up at the ceiling. *That's not true,* she wanted to say. *It's not me making it like that.* But she didn't. Possibly because of Ula, because of the hope and goodwill she had entered the room with, she tried to consider this objectively. Was this, after all, an alienation of her own devising? But how could she pretend that the fact of genetics and inheritance didn't matter, that the shared connection of DNA, of hard-wired traits and predispositions, wasn't important, when the whole point of the donor siblings was to honor the fact that it was? She was a biologist, for Christ's sake!

"It's just hard for me . . ." she sighed.

And to her surprise, this seemed to be enough. For the first time in what seemed like ages, Chrissy wrapped herself around her with real warmth. "I know, Beanie," she said. "But they really need you."

And in the relieving wash of Chrissy's forgiveness and the thrill of excitement over Ula, Elise managed, somehow, not to think again of Jenny and Jeremy. Her brain spun with thoughts of proteins and transgene expression vectors, of the DNA she had tampered with before Ula was ever born, the tiny, glassy egg she had injected and fertilized, dividing, replicating, and building according to plan. And what a plan it was: a whole creature! Warm body full of blood and bones and covered with a lovely glossy coat of hair, a whole intricately fashioned brain with its own set of imperatives and desires, and now, finally, milk—that perfect, mysterious substance from which life sustained itself. A distillation of the body's most basic needs.

When suddenly she remembered the role Ula had played in her conversation with Jenny. She had, in Elise's mind anyway, exemplified the possibility of scientific exception, deviation, that was so hopeful to Jenny: for example, the goat injected with hormones to bring on lactaction who didn't lactate. Except now she did.

16

IT HAD BEEN A WEEK since Neil had shown up outside Laura's house, when Laura and Mac went on a date. Mac had lost a deal in the Philippines and was around more than usual—home for breakfast and dinner. Yesterday he had even left work in time to go to Genevieve's weekly (and much-neglected) soccer game.

This evening, in a rare burst of creative—even romantic—direction, Mac had made a dinner reservation at the new restaurant of a swanky hotel downtown. Climbing out of the car and handing the keys to the valet, Laura had something like a flutter of nervous anticipation—it had been almost immemorably long since she and Mac had gone out together, just the two of them, to anywhere that could be even remotely described as romantic. And the unfamiliarity of the event coupled with the roaring sense of guilt it stirred up served as some weird proxy for excitement.

The restaurant was long and narrow and flatteringly lit with a sort of rosy, smoked-glass lantern light, the tables carefully choreographed and covered with heavy, expensive-looking linens. *Focus-group-tested*, Laura could hear Neil say. But she pushed the thought off—she was not going to think about Neil tonight. This was imperative. And the urgency with which she resolved this was actually quite relieving: an escape from that dark, creeping monster of guilt and confusion that seemed to be dogging her lately, running its chilly tentacles down her spine.

Mac arrived a little late, and watching him enter the place, Laura noticed the way people looked at him—men and women alike. He had an impressive dark head of hair that so many men his age envied, and the thickening square of his jaw and features hinted at satisfaction, even opulence; in the last five years or so he had acquired that particular solidity of form that comes with success in the field of money. It was as if the very substance of his body had changed from blood and flesh and bones to something more permanent.

"They have our table?" he said, giving Laura a quick kiss on the cheek.

"I think. I told her we were here."

Mac walked over to the maître d' and leaned forward in communication. The woman nodded rapidly and gestured at two available tables. How funny that this businessman in the expensive suit and Hermès tie was her husband. She was not dressed the part, she realized, looking down at the worn black flats she was wearing, and the cheap Banana Republic skirt she had bought last year. He was leaving her behind. The thought was actually kind of titillating.

Once they were seated across from each other, though, Laura's standby irritation at Mac stepped back in.

"A bottle of the Château Gloria," he told the waiter, without consulting Laura. Then he took out his handkerchief and blew his nose in that honking, graphic way of his that Laura felt was akin to farting.

"Actually, I'll have a glass of the Pinot Grigio," she told the waiter, who looked confused, but Mac just shrugged.

"We'll get the bottle too—you'll have a glass, won't you?" he asked.

He was so oblivious—it was impossible even to be passive-aggressive. The waiter scurried off to procure their drink order.

"I'm having the salmon," Mac said, shutting the menu after about two seconds.

"*English peas?*" Laura mused, still staring at the elaborately described list of entrées. "As opposed to what? American? *Cob-smoked bacon*? Why does everything have to be so precious—who really cares if its cob-smoked bacon or wood-smoked bacon or whatever? It's bacon."

"Mm," Mac grunted disinterestedly. "Silly." He seemed to be scanning the room for people he knew.

It was a very Neil-type of thing to observe. The realization ushered in a whole line of Neil-influenced thought that she would have done well to push away. But it was irresistible—or, holding it up to Mac, like a test of sorts, proved irresistible anyway.

"Doesn't it just seem so crazy sometimes that we live in a society where we can eat at a restaurant like this—with a fifteen-dollar mini–corn cake on the menu," she asked, leaning forward, "when you think about all the people in the world who would feel like they won the lottery if they got fifteen bucks? I mean, it would pay for, like, a year's worth of food and school for their kids and a new house or something."

"Where's that?" Mac asked, tearing off a hunk of the expensive "twice-milled" multigrain bread.

"I don't know—plenty of places—I don't have some particular place in mind, I just mean the *idea*—"

Mac shrugged. "So? Better that fifteen dollars go out into the world than sit in my pocket."

"Is it, though? I mean going out into the world—from *here*? I mean, doesn't it just do that much to make the price of corn more expensive and less available to whoever we're talking about in Rwanda or Bangladesh or wherever?"

"Ha!" Mac let out an insulting laugh. "I like that take on global markets, babe."

Laura frowned.

Mac leaned forward and rested his elbows on the table. "I'm not making fun. It's just, why are you trying to spoil a nice dinner? We can donate money to UNICEF or whatever. It won't make any difference to the starving kids in Ethiopia if you eat a fifteen-dollar corn cake."

There was nothing to say to this. She was being childish, in a way—she could see this. Here, in Mac's presence, the vast global discrepancies and her own privileged position in the spectrum of them seemed not so much *unequal* as *incomparable*—apples and oranges. And there was a surprising relief that came with this.

Since she had seen Neil, his voice, and his cynical, even jaundiced views, had risen to an almost deafening roar in her mind. It was as if the less she actually saw of or spoke to him, the louder he spoke in her mind. Washing the spinach for supper, she was aware of the sheer waste of potable water running down the drain; and changing Miranda's diapers, she was overcome by the guilt of creating so much waste for her own personal convenience—the convenience of throwing smelly toddler poop into a trash bag that could be cinched shut and carted off by men whose job it was to whisk unsavory things out of sight!

This afternoon, getting a facial at a fancy spa Jenny had given her a gift certificate to, Laura had been struck by the sense that the very existence of such a vain and unnecessary service was a sign of imminent apocalypse. Lying in the darkened room, her face slathered with expensive lotions, her fingers stuffed into what looked like giant heated oven mitts, Laura had been gripped by panic. The facial was an excess, just like the ridiculous, elaborate wigs and decadent balls that characterized the court of Louis XIV, or the fountains of wine and toiling slaves of ancient Rome. Here she was, having her very pores coddled by some poor Slovakian immigrant, while elsewhere in the world people subsisted on a handful of rice a month. Wasn't this a symptom of an imbalance that would surely be leveled by the equilibrium-loving sands of time? At least there were no slaves, she had tried to reassure herself, but Neil's retort occurred to her immediately. There *were* slaves! The distant, unseen slaves of the global economy, toiling in Chinese factories, splicing electrical wires, and melting plastic to make these ridiculous finger-warming mitts! They were probably living on lead-poisoned fish, raising children in shacks with no running water or electricity, facing a life expectancy of forty years and a high risk of succumbing to AIDS or malaria or some mutant new interspecial flu.

She had left the spa feeling chastened. And when she went to pick her children up from school she hugged them close, smelling their warm sweaty heads and exclaiming over their bizarre and fragile artworks with a feeling of nostalgia already for the easiness of this world they lived in, the unsustainable beauty and peace and abundance that they had so far known. She needed to prepare them for a rougher reality. For a time when Americans would know hunger and want and disease. But how?

It was not as though Laura had never thought of these inequities before, but they had not reared up in her head with such regularity or urgency until recently. She had become reflexively aware of the sheer luck of her existence, and the grand and disturbing scale on which she blundered through the universe.

But here at Clio, sitting across from Mac muted the volume on all this. He believed in possibility and hard work and the rewards of this. He never second-guessed anything in his life. There was something calming about this. Mac lived in the world of facts and figures distinct enough to be mastered, of worth that was measurable in coin, of talk that followed convention and conveyed surety. He was a man you would want at your side if there were a disaster—an earthquake or a terrorist attack. Neil, on the other hand, was not.

Tonight Mac was making an uncharacteristic effort to engage. He asked Laura about her work—about the books she had read lately, whether (this was what it always came back to) the *Beacon* magazine had given her a much-deserved raise. The proportion of hours spent to money earned in the world of arts and letters was appalling to Mac. Ungraspably disproportionate.

He asked about the children: *How was Miranda's nursery school working out? And was she worried about how sensitive Genevieve seemed to be?* There was something sweet about his foggy concerns.

And, prattling on while sipping her stubborn glass of Pinot Grigio, Laura felt an utterly unexpected swell of appreciation for Mac. He was a good provider. He worked hard. He was ambitious and intelligent, if not witty. He did not ruminate on the pain and absurdity and futility of human existence—in fact, he did not give much thought at all to the larger questions of life. Laura did not spend the meal registering the waste that went into washing the table linens and she got over the ridiculousness of the fifteen-dollar corn cake. She ordered the lobster and morel stew without a second thought.

But it was because of Neil that Laura could feel, for the first time in a long time, the chemistry of being a woman and Mac being a man. When she got up to use the ladies' room, she felt Mac's eyes on her and was aware of the flattering drape of fabric over her breasts and the strand of hair that had escaped to lie along the curve of her neck. The sting of Neil's radio silence made her hungry for Mac's admiration. It was perverse, even despicable, but true.

Two-thirds of a bottle of Château Gloria later on her part (of course Mac had been right, she would drink it) and two cognacs on his (Mac was a great lover of antiquated, after-dinner drinks), they made love for the first time in almost six months. It was a little clumsy—infused with shyness and a self-conscious sense of momentousness—but maybe because of this, a little bit exciting. They did not speak afterward, but lay side by side in the darkness, breathing, the room buzzing with everything left unsaid.

After some time Mac lifted his hand and took hers, lightly. The innocent childishness of the gesture felt horribly sad. Laura felt too ashamed and dishonest to squeeze his fingers in return. So she lay very still and pretended to be asleep while a kind of cold and dreadful panic overcame her: what had she done?

The next morning Mac did not leave for work at the usual crack of dawn. He was still in the shower when Laura began assembling the girls' breakfast—a chaotic, bleary-eyed routine for all three of them, characterized by Laura's frustratingly interrupted efforts to get coffee made, Miranda's quick and violent changes of mind about what she wanted to eat, and Genevieve's endless daydreamy dawdling.

Upstairs, Laura could hear Mac padding around in his study as she buttered toaster waffles and divvied out frozen raspberries, braided Genevieve's hair, changed Miranda's diaper, and let Cocoa out into the yard. She wrestled the full trash bag out of the can and scribbled a grocery list for Kaaren, who absolutely lived for trips to Whole Foods, but given no instruction would return with giant bags of bulgur and rye flakes and dried yellow split peas—none of the pitifully limited array of basics that the children actually ate.

It was in the middle of this that Jenny called. Laura greeted her coldly. She had been trying, unsuccessfully, to reach her friend for nearly two weeks. She had left messages twice volunteering to help unpack boxes and not heard so much as a polite refusal in response.

"Can I call you back?" she said. "I'm just trying to get everyone out the door."

"Oh. Of course—just—" Jenny cut herself off. She sounded a little strange. "Do call me later. I need to tell you something."

"Oh!" Laura's first thought was of Neil. That somehow Jenny had found out. And was going to . . . what? Press charges? This was what popped into her mind, although of course it made no sense. "Okay.

I will," she blurted robotically, and stood pressing the receiver down into its cradle.

"Who was that?" Genevieve wanted to know.

"Jenny."

"Where she?" barked Miranda, who loved Jenny and her loud, cheery, talking-to-kids voice.

"At home," Laura said. "At her new house," she was correcting herself when Mac appeared in the doorway. She had forgotten he was home.

"How are my princesses?" he asked. He looked a little uneasy, fresh-faced and damp-haired from the shower.

"Aren't you late for work?" Genevieve asked.

"No, I'm not late for work, miss," Mac said. "I can go in whenever I want."

"Shoulder ride?" Miranda asked, standing up on her chair.

"So you usually *want* to go before we get up?" Genevieve said.

"No." Mac scowled, scooping Miranda up. "I usually have meetings."

"Mmm." Genevieve looked knowingly down onto her remaining waffle, and Mac walked out into the yard with the squealing Miranda, little hands sunk deep into his plentiful hair.

"Kaaren says Americans work too hard," Genevieve said.

"She does?" Laura paused midlist.

"There's no balance."

"Mmmm." Laura nodded, though in fact she was still mulling over what Jenny could have to tell her. Something not good, she guessed by the sound of her voice.

"Except you," Genevieve said, bringing her plate to the sink.

"She said that?" Laura asked.

Genevieve shot her a sideways look. "No. I did."

"Why? Because I'm so balanced?"

"No." Genevieve looked quizzically at her. "Because you don't work very hard."

"Oh!" Laura exclaimed, as Mac and Miranda barged back in.

"Alright," Mac said. "Shoulder ride's over." He ignored Miranda's protests and set her on the floor, where she collapsed, wailing. "See you," he said, putting a hand briefly on Genevieve's head.

"Bye-bye," Laura said automatically. "What do you mean, I don't work hard?" she turned back to Genevieve, but Genevieve was already engaged in a heated argument with her sister.

And looking around the disastrously messy kitchen, her squabbling children, and her coffee-stained bathrobe, she felt the sting of recognized cliché.

It was not until after she had dropped the girls off at school, run a few errands, and settled herself back down in her little study that she returned Jenny's call, which was certainly going to be about Neil. She had spent the last few hours weighing explanations and excuses, apologies and defensive tirades (why is everything about you, Jenny? why should it even matter?), so when she picked up the phone and dialed the number her brain was abuzz with anxiety.

But Jenny was not calling about Neil.

"I haven't called you because Jeremy has cancer," Jenny said flatly.

And almost before sadness or worry or confusion, Laura felt blindsided by guilt, at the superficiality of her concerns.

17

JENNY HUNG UP THE PHONE and sat looking at the bright, cheerful pill that only a few weeks ago had seemed so full of promise and excitement. It still looked good. Even pretty. But the promise it held, right now, on the damp palm of her hand was of a different, more personal and less professional sort. She was tempted to pop it into her mouth.

For all of her time spent marketing antidepressants, she had never taken one. She could recite the benefits and drawback of this SSRI, she could explain in great and nuanced detail the effect it had on the pathways and chemistry of the human brain, could even list the possible side effects down to *itchy eyes*, and could certainly reassure and convince even the most reluctant depressive that it was worth a try. But she had no idea what it felt like. *Like nothing*, she told people. *It wasn't a high. It wasn't a rush. It was simply, over time, something that you might notice evened things out, enabled you to stop obsessing, make decisions with more confidence, sleep.* Her mind slipped immediately into the marketing pitch she knew so well. But what did it mean, really, to feel "more even" or "perseverate less"?

She had never before been tempted to find out. After all, she had already felt "even." She had never "perseverated." She slept like a rock. But now, in the last week, she suspected that she could use help.

Since diagnosis, Jeremy had been calm, even steadfast. It was not

good. It was advanced renal cancer—stage four. It had spread already
to his liver and chest. He would have surgery and chemotherapy and
a newer immunotherapy that would, in attempting to arm his own
body to fight the cancer, make him very, very ill. It was odd, though,
in the face of this grim prognosis, he had more energy than he had
had before. He searched the Internet exhaustively and set up interviews and appointments with preeminent doctors and acquaintances
or acquaintances of acquaintances who were researchers in the field.
He was on the phone for hours. And he ordered books from Amazon
by the truckload. They were the first things he filled into the void of
his cavernous office in the new house.

"Are you sure this is good for you?" Jenny asked. "All this information?"

Jeremy had barely noted the question, posed from the doorway
of his office, where Jenny leaned as though she couldn't possibly
hold her own weight upright. In her hands she cupped one of her
suddenly ubiquitous cups of tea. (Since when had tea seemed like
such a palliative? She was a coffee drinker, but suddenly she craved
tea, with honey and milk, lots of it, just as her mother had made her
when she was sick as a girl.)

Jeremy was determined. He had taken an immediate leave from
work—had literally, and uncharacteristically, gone into the office
only once since the diagnosis to wrap things up. The goal, as far
as his treatment was concerned, was to have surgery to remove the
cancer. But until the growth of secondary tumors on his liver and
his lungs was checked, this was impossible. And so first chemo—
and possibly some radiation. The order of treatments, in which
each next step hinged on the outcome of the previous, was like a
bewildering bog to Jenny—there was no map, no path, and certainly no guarantee of a way out. But somehow Jeremy seemed able
to comprehend it, or in any case to form a steadfast routine in the
face of the uncertainty.

The efficiency and discipline with which he proceeded through the day-to-day was actually more "Jeremy" than any behavior she had seen from him in what felt like years. He rose at seven, mixed up an unpleasant-looking spirulina shake, and went for a speed walk in the fancy, and up until now unworn, windbreaker and sweat suit Jenny had given him last Christmas. He came home and checked into the bewildering web of cancer sites he seemed to have sussed out and categorized in record time. Then he napped, ate lunch, and did two hours of yoga at a local studio that he had apparently been going to for months without Jenny even knowing.

The only unregulated activity of his day was the time he spent with Colin. It was, maybe, the biggest transformation of his illness. His relationship with Colin had changed from one of benign neglect to one of great engagement. Even more than engagement, love. Playing with him on the floor, making his toy monkey jump and making him laugh, building block towers and playing peekaboo, these became Jeremy's primary recreation. He wanted, suddenly, to put Colin to sleep, to feed him dinner, to take him for walks in the stroller. And the time he spent with the boy, for whom Jeremy himself was a delightful new discovery, was the only time Jenny ever saw him smile. It was as if his illness had suddenly awakened some playful, nurturing side of him that found its expression in the boy. It would have made Jenny jealous if—well, if it weren't so goddamn tragic.

Meanwhile, Jenny herself was unusually and uncharacteristically scattered. She was flummoxed by decisions. Should she order a sectional couch for the new TV room or two cushy sofas with a giant ottoman? Should she enroll Colin in a playgroup at the local nursery school or was it too early? Was Maria changing his diaper often enough?

At work she was distracted, and she tended to get in at eight-thirty as opposed to her usual seven forty-five sharp. That twit

Galena had noticed. "Would you like me to take over the Priorities Memo?" she asked with insidious sweetness. The Priorities Memo was something Jenny had always sent out by eight-fifteen. Was this an Eastern European thing? Was Galena's ambition a product of being free—finally—of the communist hangover that had dampened her country's progress and aspirations for so long? Or was she simply a born player—in the same way (Jenny did not dwell on the thought) Jenny herself was?

Jenny had not let anyone at work know about Jeremy's cancer. She needed to tell them. She could see that. Especially since Jeremy had already broadcast it in his own office, and who knew what sort of obscure overlap would turn up? Boston was, after all, a small town. But she did not want pity. Or gestures of helpfulness. And below this, she had the primal feeling that admitting weakness could be dangerous. Take Galena, for instance, waiting in the wings, teeth sharpened on Jenny's own tough diet of hard work and ruthlessness.

On the day of Jeremy's first chemo injection Jenny had told Violet, Eric's assistant, that she could not attend the monthly progress meeting because her mother was having an operation. Two hours later, she had gotten a call from Eric himself: Was her mother all right? Did Jenny need extra time to help her out? *Oh, no, it was just knee surgery, temporarily incapacitating but not dangerous,* Jenny had reassured him. She had worked this out beforehand, but she was flustered by Eric's kindness and concern. And now the lie, which had been conceived as a stopgap, had taken on a momentum of its own. On top of all the reasons she did not want to talk about Jeremy's cancer in the first place there was now, in addition, the fact that her initial weird cover-up would be exposed. It would draw attention to her own psychological weakness.

So instead she sat at her desk and considered the beautiful pill. Perhaps a dose of protease inhibitors was just what she needed.

There was a knock on her door and Jenny slid the pill off her palm into the drawer of her desk. It was Galena.

"Walk over to the meeting together?" Galena said, sticking her head just inside the door.

Jenny frowned. "Which meeting?"

"ZGames! Of course!" Galena said brightly. "Did you forget about them again? *Tsk, tsk.*"

"Right." Jenny smiled icily. "I guess they're not exactly top priority right now."

"Oh, but this will be big, if it works," Galena said, smirking. "All those depressed misfits out there."

"I'll meet you in the conference room," Jenny said. "I just have a few things to wrap up."

Galena shrugged and sauntered through the door.

Jenny called up the marketing plan they had presented ZGames with. *Shit,* it struck her as the logo unfurled across her computer screen—was this the company that Galena had told her Neil worked at? There were three game companies they were pitching, so she could not be sure, but looking at the dripping black "Z" of the title she felt it was. Of course it was now, with the world caving in around them, that Neil had to resurface, trailing mess and complication. And turning out to be such a weirdo! A computer game designer! It was like finding out an ex-boyfriend was bisexual—it gave her an unsettled, anxious feeling. Was Colin going to turn out to be a weirdo too? She should just turn the whole project over to Galena. Forget overseeing it. After all, how badly could the girl screw up?

But, of course, this morning there was no backing out.

With an almost frantic vigor she opened the drawer she had slid the pill into, hunted it out, and popped it into her mouth. It had a sweet taste on her tongue and slid smoothly down her throat. Twenty-five milligrams. A typical starting dose. She did not need anyone to prescribe. It was an aid. A crutch to help her through a hard time. Hadn't she been pitching this for years?

It was that evening, halfway through her second glass of Merlot, that the possible side effects occurred to Jenny. Was the Setlan making her drunk? She was at Cobblestone's, the kid-friendly restaurant beloved across the Boston area for its combination of sophisticated adult food options (Moroccan lamb terrine and sweet pepper fried cod cakes, for example) and the cheerful, germy play area for unruly toddlers. Beside her, in the restaurant high chair, Colin chewed intently on a spoon. Across from her, Laura sat with her hands folded on the edge of the table, looking painfully empathetic and concerned. All around there was the din of clanking plates and children playing and adults making loud conversation to be heard above the general racket. Jenny was not seeing things through particularly foggy or otherwise inebriated lenses this evening, was she? No. The grating clatter and wail of a fight breaking out at the train table settled it. If anything, she felt particularly flat. She gulped at the merlot hungrily, wishing for the relieving tingle of a buzz.

Laura, who had risen to make sure the scuffle in the play area did not involve Miranda, sank back into her seat across from Jenny and began tearing up. "And how is Jeremy dealing with it?" she asked, the tears spilling over and running down her cheeks.

"He's being just amazing," Jenny said firmly. Of course Laura was crying. She was almost too empathetic. Her tears made Jenny feel tough and weather-beaten—pitiably hardened. "He's being very, very strong."

In the back of her mind, the last few conversations she had had with Laura about Jeremy echoed shamefully: her complaints and frustration with his ailments, her irritation and lack of sympathy. Another person—Laura, for instance—might have aired her guilt over these and taken solace in confiding and being reassured: *How could you know? Who doesn't feel irritated at their husband these days?* But Jenny did not air her dirty laundry, not even with such a good friend. She would not take the bland and reassuring platitudes her own confessions of guilt would elicit.

Laura wiped her eyes and sniffled. "Well, you're amazing, Jenny," she said. "And you have to promise to ask for help whenever—I'll try to think of the right things, but I know I won't always, so promise you'll ask—"

"I know. I know." Jenny scooped Colin out of his chair and onto her lap. He was not going to eat any more. This was clear. "I appreciate it."

For a moment they were silent. From the play area, Miranda's voice could be heard making ominous *vroom*ing sounds with a truck. And on Jenny's lap, Colin began to squirm and fuss.

"Do you want me to hold him for a minute?" Laura asked. And as if in response, Colin lurched forward and grabbed at Laura's water glass, spreading a pool of liquid over Miranda's abandoned crayon scrawls and dripping down onto Jenny's lap.

She handed him over to Laura, who began immediately to coo and speak in baby talk that made him smile. Jenny dabbed a napkin at her wet lap. "So I'm sure you heard from Elise that Neil is back," she said.

"Neil? Oh, right—yes. Yeah." Laura tossed her hair and looked nervously over at the play area. "I know. I ran into him, actually. On the street a little while ago. I was going to tell you—I mean, that's part of why I was calling, and then I didn't hear back from you—"

There was something guilty and practiced in Laura's response. She was a terrible liar. She had probably had lunch with him or something. And suddenly, in light of everything, the whole situation seemed so maddeningly, humiliatingly ridiculous to Jenny— the idea that everyone was scurrying around behind her back in fear of upsetting her, and probably talking about what a stupid concept it had been from the start to use Neil's sperm and then expect him to remain forever out of her life, and perhaps worst of all the fact that it *did* upset her and it *had* been stupid, and meanwhile her husband had cancer.

"It doesn't matter, you know," she said frostily. "It's fine. Neil can do whatever he likes and see whoever he likes. I'm not some sort of monster, you know."

"Oh, I know!" Laura protested, looking even guiltier. "I just wouldn't want you to think—" She stopped and colored slightly.

Jenny looked at her expectantly.

"I mean—I know it's sensitive, your whole agreement, and it must feel weird having him just resurface here and not be in touch with you even though I know you don't really *want* him to be in touch with you . . ."

Jenny frowned and looked over at the play area. It struck her suddenly, as Laura said it, that maybe in fact she *did* perversely want Neil to be back in touch with her. That if he was going to come out of the weird incognito existence he had created for himself and enter problematically into the normal orbit of her life, of *Colin's* life, despite everything she had erected against this possibility—he might as well be in touch with her. She felt, in some deep-down way, betrayed because he hadn't.

"Honestly, Laura," she said, "it doesn't matter. And whatever Neil is or is not doing is really *not* important to me. I mean, he could come see Colin, for all I care."

"Of course! Of course! Oh, God. Jenny—I'm sorry." Laura's eyes welled up again, and on her lap, Colin looked up at her with a serious, searching expression. "Oh it's okay." She bounced him a little and tried to smile. "You're such a sweet little man and here I am upsetting you. Maybe you'd better go back to your mama. I'm sorry, Jenny." She shook her head, handing the still-transfixed Colin back over the wreckage of the table. "I just can't say anything right today."

Miranda chose that moment to come barreling back toward them, waving a dingy rag doll. "Look, look, Mama! Dora! I find Dora!"

"Oh, look at that, sweetie!" Laura said, scooping her up and burying her face in Miranda's hair. Miranda pressed her cheek against Laura's chest and held her as though they had just, together, emerged from some exhilarating and risky trial. Jenny felt an odd jealousy rumble in her chest—would she ever inspire such fierce love in Colin?

"Do you want to show it to Colin?" Laura said, when at last Miranda pulled away and squirmed to the ground.

Miranda stopped midflight and turned to look at Jenny and Colin doubtfully.

"What have you got, hon?" Jenny asked, forcing a smile.

"Dora," Miranda said. She extended the limp doll toward Colin, who turned his head away and made a whiny sound of protest.

"He not care," Miranda announced gravely.

At home, Jenny broke one of her major parenting edicts. She did not put Colin to bed "drowsy but alert." She rocked him. She held him in her arms and swished soundlessly back and forth in the glider, feeling the weight of his little head against the crook of her arm. It was almost pitch-dark in his room. The last light of day was obliterated by the powerful blackout shades on his windows, and he did not sleep with a night-light. There was only the glow of the humidifier power button, illuminating a circle of carpet in a bright ghoulish green.

Jenny couldn't make out her son's face or the contours of his little arms alongside his body—he was simply a small, solid mass with a round head pressing its new, soft spray of hair against her skin. She could feel the breath moving in and out of his body and hear the tiny purring, almost mewing sound he made as he fell asleep. And it was so beautiful. She felt she could sit there, in his room, in this chair, all night: why had she never done this before? She had been so proud of his ability to be laid in his crib wide awake and put himself to sleep with no more than a little squawk or two. Who had time to sit around rocking a baby in the dark? she always said. And in the early days, when he was first born, she had listened to podcasts while she nursed him so as to avoid the blank stretch of time this entailed. But right now, with Jeremy lying next door, the specter of death like a dark and inescapable balloon tethered to his toe, she wanted to just rock, thinking of nothing but the feel of this baby in her arms.

When she entered her own room, Jeremy lay reading a thick book, with a picture of a stern-looking Indian man on the cover, entitled *Heal Yourself.*

"Do you need anything?" Jenny asked, and Jeremy looked up, his reading glasses sliding down his nose.

"No. What happened? You were in there a long time." It sounded almost accusatory.

"Nothing—it's fine." Jenny turned to the wall and began to take off her clothes. "I just wanted to—" She cut herself off, shocked to find herself tearing up. Behind her, she could hear Jeremy pick the book back up again. She took a breath and stepped out of her skirt, pulled over her head the sensible nightgown she had bought when Colin was born.

Then she lay down and pretended to read while internally she ran through a litany of logistics until she had drowned out the fear erupting in her mind. She would need to hang the curtains in the bedroom for Jeremy's recovery—there was nothing colder than a room with blinds and no drapes. She should call Jeremy's mother and dissuade her from coming for as long as possible, and she would have to work out some new hours with Maria. Plus there was health insurance to be dealt with and follow-up appointments to be scheduled. Gradually the march of these details stamped out her gathering panic.

"What time did they say they would start the chemo?" she asked later, when they were lying in the dark, Jeremy on his side with the Posturepedic back-support pillow curled along his spine, and Jenny on her back. She felt unsure in her new role as cancer-wife, like a person with a prosthetic arm trying to make it normal, trying to think of it as her own.

"Sometime before noon," Jeremy said.

"That's helpful—" Jenny started to say sarcastically, but stopped herself.

There was a rustling of sheets and covers as Jeremy turned to face her. The pillow remained between them like a squishy cartoon fence. He had to lift his head to see over it.

"Have you told Eric yet? About me?"

"No." Jenny sighed.

"You've got to do it."

"I know."

There was the distant sound of wheels on the road below, at the bottom of the hill. It struck Jenny suddenly as lonely, even a little dangerous, how much space there was around them. It was so different from their place in the Back Bay.

"Do you like it here? Do you sleep better with less noise?" she asked, and she could sense Jeremy frowning beside her, noting the non sequitur.

"Sure." He rolled onto his back. But then, as if on second thought, he shifted and propped himself on one elbow again, facing her.

"It's good, Jenny," he said. "You did right to get us out here. It'll be a good place."

And in the moment that she let herself meet his eyes, she felt the movement of so many dark shapes and unspeakable questions between them. She wanted to take each and shine her usual bright light of common sense and optimism upon it. She wanted to speak of all these uncertainties and pluck them from the darkness where they lurked menacingly, waiting to be named.

But with what language? They were the province of art, music, literature, or religion. And these did not belong to her. Or to Jeremy, for that matter. So she just lay there. "I hope so," she said finally, and her voice was tinny and inadequate. But it was all she had. It would have to do.

18

IT WAS UNUSUAL FOR ELISE to find herself sitting on the ruched leather sofa in Harold Rangen's office. She had a great deal of autonomy in the lab, and Harold, who was the head of it, was more the type to drop in on people unannounced than to call "meetings" in his cushy *MTV Cribs*–style office with its huge, inelegant pieces of furniture and black marble desktop.

But this morning he had called her in.

"Licorice?" he asked, opening a wooden box full of fancy rhombus-shaped black candy. His nervous manner and lack of eye contact did not bode well for what he had to say.

Elise waved it away. "This is about Ula?" She had told Harold about her pet project from the beginning, and, while he had not been thrilled, he had agreed to look the other way. Now that she had succeeded—now that Ula was producing milk (and milk with a very high plasma protein content), Elise had entrusted him to offer the report to corporate.

"Well, it's about our research in general. And about Ula as it applies to that," he added as Elise frowned.

"Harold," Elise said. "I don't need a lot of frills. It's me. What's the deal?"

Harold's fingers hesitated over the glistening contents of the box for a moment and then withdrew, empty, having apparently reconsidered the effect of conducting the meeting with a two-inch square of bitter, chewy sugar in his mouth. He popped the lid shut with reluctant finality.

"Well, everyone is impressed by your research—and your dedication, of course. And they recognize that you have a real gift for exactly the kind of science we are all about here at the Pharm—"

"Mm-hm," Elise said impatiently.

"And they are eager—really, really eager—to encourage that— no, sorry, let's be real here—to *use* that to best advantage, but— but—" he held up a hand in anticipation of her interruption. "They don't see the development of this protein as the best use of that."

Elise had braced for this, but it did not render her any less annoyed.

"Do they understand the data? Ula's rate of production is off the charts—it could just be her, but — Do they get that? And the bare minimum adaptation of the formula it took to get—"

"They do." Harold nodded gravely. "The thing is, the data are not the defining variable for this decision."

"Ah."

"They have Genron's corporate objectives to follow and the company-wide protocol—I mean, you *know* this a supportive place for scientists, this is a *great* place to do truly first-in-field research, but—*but* there is a process by which that research gets directed— we're not a university lab. We're not just following whatever we want . . ."

Elise rolled her eyes.

". . . and we're working within a given space—"

"And this line of research is not in that space? It's developing a plasma protein—isn't that what we're all about?"

"I mean within a given *market* space. Look, Elise, Genron has no plans to develop the market for any drug using the protein Ula produces. It can be used to treat . . . what? A disease five thousand people worldwide suffer from? Mostly in third-world countries?"

"Oh," Elise said sarcastically, surprised by her own anger. "And so it's not worth it—not worth this *minimal* adaptation of our existing platform to help them. This no-sweat-off-our-backs—"

"Elise." Harold looked irritated. "I know it's hard to put aside something you have invested time and energy into, but to be honest, I'm surprised that you're . . . surprised by this. You know the rule— Marketing develops the market, we develop the product. Not the other way around."

Elise was silent.

Harold tipped his chair back and put his feet up on the desk in a stagy gesture of comfort. It did not look natural, or comfortable. It occurred to Elise, through her anger, that he might have taken a management class that instructed him to strike such a pose at a time such as this.

"I know this is your baby . . ." he began.

"It is certainly not *my baby*," Elise snapped.

". . . but the main thing is you're doing excellent work here. Top-notch. And they know that. Everyone knows that. And if you can keep it up"—he lowered his voice conspiratorially—"I think you'll be pleased come year-end."

"Mm," Elise sniffed. "Well," she said, standing, "I'm sure there are other labs that would be interested in using this research as a foundation."

"Elise." Harold dropped his feet to the ground, his face reddening. "That is absolutely not an option. Do you really think you could share research that rests on this much proprietary science? I'm letting you off easy here for having even started down this road in the first place, but if you"—he seemed to become slightly breathless in the heat of his urgency—"even so much as share one shred of this research, Genron will not hesitate to take you to court."

Elise could feel the blood mounting to her face.

"I have seen it happen, and it ain't pretty."

It took Elise a moment to regain her composure. She could feel her heart beating in her ears.

"I see." She nodded icily.

"You're a talented scientist, Elise," Harold said. "Don't turn into some radical over this."

Elise fumed the whole way home, stopping for gas and for flowers in order to slow her progress and give herself better recovery time. This would not be the right day to come home with a cloud over her head: they had a birthday dinner to go to—Chrissy's sister's. The whole Noyes clan in all its bustling good spirits would be there. But Harold's alternately apologetic and strong-arm tactics remained tangled around her like the beginning of an unraveling thread. Clearly, she had been naïve. She knew Genron did not support scientific digression. This was the difference between the for-profit and nonprofit world—Genron was driven, after all, by the bottom line. Somehow, though, Elise had imagined her own practical assessment of the benefits—the minimal adjustments to the existing science and the incredible promise of these first results—could be a proxy for the company's. But this had been hubris. She could admit this. And the self-delusion of this confidence was disturbing.

Ordinarily she would have called Jenny. *What is this?* she would have railed at her. *Bureaucratic blindness? This is why American science is falling behind—the great corporate quashing of innovation for the sake of profit.* Or she would have tried to persuade her of the benefits of continuing the research—she would have argued for the moral necessity of pursuing this research, and gotten nowhere. She would have searched for more practical-minded, innovative arguments for how, ultimately, even such a tiny market could be turned into a piece of the profit puzzle. Jenny had a powerful voice. If she could be swayed, she could sway others.

But given the present circumstances, Elise did not do this. And there was, in a way, some relief that accompanied this. Because if Elise really thought about it—if Elise *really* imagined the conversation they would have—she knew what side Jenny would take. It was the elephant that had stood in the room between them ever since Elise had joined Genron. And their friendship was the reason Elise did not want to look at it.

When Elise arrived home, Chrissy and the boys were ready to go. Chrissy had packed a bag of homemade sesame noodle salad, wine, and mini-Playmobil sets for each of the kids. And she had dressed the boys in their cutest Angela Noyes–knit sweaters and baby jeans, and put her own hair back in a pretty, turquoise-studded clip. The whole scene made Elise, on top of everything else, feel like resting her head against the steering wheel and going to sleep. But instead, she climbed out and handed Chrissy the flowers, scooped up the boys, and tried to be normal and warm and unembittered.

This did not fool Chrissy. "What's wrong?" She frowned. "I know my family can be—"

"It has nothing to do with the party," Elise said.

Chrissy raised her eyebrows. Nigel looked up at Elise searchingly. "It's fine, it's fine, it's fine, it's fine," Elise said, shaking her head against his warm, soft hair. "Just give me a minute."

Chrissy went inside and found a vase for the flowers with the definite attitude of someone who was hassled rather than gladdened by such a gift. Elise buckled the boys into their car seats and climbed into the passenger side.

"So what is it?" Chrissy asked when they were driving, her eyes darting up to the rearview mirror.

"No more 'off-target' research."

"Oh, no!" Chrissy gasped. "Why?"

"I don't want to talk about it."

In the backseat James began a sort of tuneless humming, the sweet childish notes of which sounded melancholic to Elise.

"What will happen to Ula?" Chrissy asked. And with a pang, Elise realized that this question—or rather, the answer to it—had been hanging over her all afternoon. Ula would have to be "sacrificed"—the euphemistic laboratory term for killed. This was a given. It was hardly the first time one of Elise's animals had met such a fate. But there was something more personal about it this time. More pointless. Poor Ula, after all, had done her part and the science had certainly done its. "The usual, I guess," Elise said, staring out the window.

"I'm sorry." Chrissy put a hand on Elise's knee.

From the backseat, James's singing turned to fussing.

Chrissy glanced back up at the mirror and then over at Elise. "Can't she just . . . *retire* somewhere?"

19

AS SOON AS THE TUICĂ came out, Neil knew he should have insisted on going out to dinner. That had been his plan: take Galena to some innocuous restaurant and delicately, but unsentimentally, end things with her. Because it was better to do this sooner than later. There was a kind of corrosive energy to their interactions— a mutual sharpness and derision, which he recognized from past mistakes. There was certainly no foundation of respect, to put it in the language of Oprah.

To be honest, he had assumed it would be easy. After all, Galena was not falling for him—she was as utilitarian as he was. But the conversation so far had been surprisingly bristly. She was prideful, and used to calling the shots, and his tack of assuming a mutual dilettantishness about the relationship ("So this has been a lot of fun, but I think its probably best to cool it") was greeted with hostility.

Oh, it's been "fun," has it? Galena had said in a voice dripping with sarcasm. And Neil had attempted to backtrack, but she had excused herself to go to the bathroom.

The length of time that had elapsed since then was making him nervous. He girded himself for a puffy-eyed, swollen-faced Galena returning to the table only to pick up her bag and go. This had happened to him before.

But when Galena came back, she did not look like someone who had been crying. She had applied a fresh coat of bright red lipstick and wore a kind of wry, crafty expression on her face.

"Well, I guess you should get the check," she said, smirking, "if it's best that we 'cool it.'"

Neil regarded her warily. "Okay." He lifted a hand to signal the waiter, a rotund Bangladeshi man who seemed, for some reason, to hate them. He yanked the oily remains of their chicken korma and mushroom paneer off the table with a scowl.

"You know I didn't mean that I don't have a lot of respect—" Neil began hesitantly.

"Posh!" Galena scoffed. "You don't have to bullshit me."

"It's not bullshit—"

"Sure, sure, sure." She waved this away and squinted up at him nastily. "You think you're some kind of rock star, don't you, Neil Banks?"

Neil sat back in his seat. "No. Believe me, I don't. I am not a rock star. *At* all."

"Right." Galena nodded sarcastically, as the scowling waiter presented Neil with the check.

"Do something for me," Galena said, leaning across the table toward him.

"What?" Neil asked, relieved.

"Come back and have some tuică at my place."

Neil's relief turned to dismay. Tuică was the traditional drink of Romania—a cross between ouzo and lighter fluid—which Galena drank with great gusto. "I'm not sure that's a good idea."

"Oh, shut up. Suddenly you're too good for tuică?"

And so, despite the strong conviction that it was a bad idea, Neil went along. After all, why stop making mistakes now?

Galena kept up a stream of derisive comments that pretended to be good-natured teasing on the walk back, and Neil entered her apartment full of self-loathing. Why the fuck had he agreed to this when he could be on a bus now, on his own, heading back to J.P. free of Galena's bullshit?

"To good times," Neil offered, with his own hint of sarcasm, as they lifted their second shot.

"You call those good times?" Galena asked.

Basically Neil could see what was coming, but still, the force of it took him by surprise.

Galena strode across the floor and planted an aggressive kiss on his lips, shoving his shoulders back against the sofa.

"I don't think—" Neil began to say, pulling his head back, but her knee dug into his hip and she leaned over his head, breathing warm, Thai-food-infused tuică breath into his face. "*This* will be a good time," she said, grinning, and Neil honestly felt somewhat afraid.

What followed was a session of some of the weirdest lovemaking, if it could be called that, that Neil had ever had in his life. Galena poked and prodded and bossed him like a bullheaded Soviet street cop. She wanted to be on top, and sideways, and upside down. Any protest on his part was greeted by dismissive snorts of laughter, or worse, taunting, on her part. *What, my rock star can't take the heat?* she jeered, wrapping herself around him and reaching a hand under his scrotum. It was a face-saving operation for her, he could see—a last kick in the balls, which she could be the one to turn away from. But all the same, he shouldn't have allowed it to happen.

When he woke up, he was sweating, and had the unrested, slightly achy feeling of a person who had not so much slept as hovered in some excruciating state of middle-consciousness. And in this state he had been dreaming—or worrying, really—about Laura. She had been sick. Or hurt. They had been climbing a dark stairway and he had been pulling her up. Or trying to, but she kept slipping from his grasp. He was full of the feeling of panic and responsibility. It was like 9/11 in reverse—he was pulling her up into the tower instead of down. *Why isn't there someone else to help her?* he had been thinking. *Where is her husband? Where are the authorities?*

Even awake, he was suffused with guilt. He had as good as dropped her hand in life. Left her halfway up some dark, menacing stairway. And this was wrong, even though she was not actually his responsibility. Was she?

Beside him, Galena snored lightly, sprawled across the bed, the tiny goose pimples that gave the backs of her arms a sandpapery roughness illuminated in the moonlight. He had not meant to go to sleep. The digital clock blinked four a.m. He certainly had not meant to wake up in her bed.

Carefully, he rose and picked up his clothes, wincing when his cell phone dropped from the pocket of his jeans with a thud. But Galena snored away, insensible. Out in the living room/kitchen zone of her apartment he realized he was burningly thirsty. His mouth tasted acrid and cottony. He flicked on the light in the tiny kitchenette and opened her cupboard to find a glass, which he filled with lukewarm water from the tap. He drank this down without pause and refilled, this time sipping more slowly.

It was standing here in the fluorescent light, the night stretching wan and not even fully black outside the giant, unshaded plate-glass window in the living room, that he saw it: a Genron promotional folder lying open by the phone. Inside there were a number of pages. On top was the "fact sheet" on Setlan he had been handed at their first meeting in the ZGames conference room: over thirty million users worldwide, used to treat panic disorder, depression, obsessive-compulsive disorder, premenstrual syndrome, post-traumatic stress disorder, and social anxiety. Was there any kind of emotional discomfort this fucking drug didn't treat?

Hadn't the "symptoms" Setlan aimed to smooth over evolved and refined themselves over millennia to serve some purpose? Weren't they, for most people, part of a natural system of checks and balances? And wasn't the fact of their rising prevalence a warning that this modern American way of life was unsustainable?

Underneath this folder full of standard Setlan promotional materials there was another folder. The blue cover of this one was embossed with the same Genron logo, but stamped with the word "Confidential."

Neil hesitated for a moment, not actually considering whether or not he would open it—of course he would!—but honoring the moment, the trope of human behavior in the face of such signaling words. Then, with a glance at Galena's door, he opened it.

There were only two pages inside it, the top one a glossy photo advertisement of a pretty woman lying on a field of grass, holding aloft a laughing baby, smiling up at it, the baby's chubby arms and legs flailing in delight. *Setlan PPD* was emblazoned across the top in a sunny yellow font, followed by, *You deserve a happy motherhood.* And then in smaller print: *You deserve . . . to enjoy the life you brought into the world, to feel good about yourself and your baby, to sleep when your baby's sleeping, to have energy, to feel less anxious.* Below this was a description of postpartum depression. *Postpartum depression affects one in three American women. Talk to your doctor about Setlan PPD if you are experiencing trouble sleeping, headaches, stress, unexplained mood swings, food cravings, sadness, or loss of appetite.*

You deserve? Was this what it had fucking come to? Who "deserves" to be happy? And the answer was this? Middle-class white American women, living in the richest, easiest, most spoiled country on earth?

At the bottom of the page was a Post-it. *Jenny—this is perfect! They really took notes!*—smiley face—*Galena.*

So *this* was Jenny's brainchild. The campaign she had been so impossibly distracted and consumed by, according to Galena. Neil had asked Gelena how involved Jenny was in the gaming industry promotion of Setlan. *She has no idea,* Galena had said with a shrug. *She's all wrapped up in this new postpartum drug campaign she came up with.* It had been reassuring to Neil, actually. He had chafed at the idea of being, in an indirect way, a henchman of Jenny's bidding, creating the in-game billboards or spaceship walls or what have you that would be emblazoned with *her* product promos.

But this took the cake! Here was what she had been working on instead: a campaign that rested on the notion of "deserving." And you had to give it to her. She knew her audience. But this made her not only complicit, but responsible. She was one of the wizards behind the national psyche.

"What are you doing?" Galena's voice assaulted him from the doorway. She was standing, with the blanket held up around herself, looking both incredulous and cross.

"What's that?" Neil said, raising his eyebrows, his heart pounding, less from the surprise of interruption than from the frenzy he had been working himself into.

"Are you looking through my papers?"

"I just . . . yeah. Well, no," Neil stammered stupidly. "I mean, I just wanted to see this."

Galena took a few steps closer, brown blanket trailing and eyebrows knit.

"What is it? Let me see it." She held out her hand.

It occurred to Neil that she was speaking to him as though he were a child. Or a dog, actually. A bad dog she was training.

Sheepishly, he handed her the paper in his hand.

Galena looked at it and then up at him in surprise. "Why did you want to see this?"

"I don't know—I just— Why?" he asked switching tacks, finally, affecting a kind of wide-eyed surprise and trying to preserve some shred of dignity. "Is it important?"

Galena frowned. "What about the word 'Confidential' did you *not* think meant important?"

"Oh, does it . . . ?" Neil was not a blusher, but he could feel the color flooding from his pounding heart up to his face. It was an asinine position to be in. "I guess I didn't really see that—I just . . ."

He stopped and Galena's eyebrows raised disdainfully.

"Liked it."

"You 'liked it.' "

"Whatever," Neil said bitterly. "I thought it was fucked up, actually. I thought it was a fucking mockery of human suffering around the world. I thought it was the biggest piece-of-shit idea I've ever seen—like anyone fucking 'deserves' anything. And you people sit in your plush offices coming up with shit like this, feeding it to people . . ." He was aware of the words tumbling out of his mouth and sounding all wrong. Sounding not interesting or true or profound, but crazy.

Galena stared at him. For the first time since she had emerged from the bedroom something other than anger and incredulity crossed her face. Was it uncertainty?

"I think you should leave," she said. And Neil realized the uncertainty was not intellectual, but physical. She was a little bit afraid.

They stood for a moment looking at each other, with the sound of a siren flaring up somewhere in the distance. All the blood rushed back out of Neil's face. "I'm not—" he began.

"Please leave," Galena repeated.

Neil turned and ducked out the door, closing it behind him and holding on to the knob for an extra moment as if to be sure Galena did not follow him. Then he started down the long corridor to the elevator, feeling weak, almost dizzy.

What exactly had just transpired?

Part Three

1

IT HAD BEEN SEVERAL WEEKS since their date (if it could be called that) at the wine bar when Neil finally called Laura.

"Can I take you out somewhere, Lo?" he asked. "To a nice dinner?" His voice sounded oddly quiet—even subdued. But there was no apology for his silence. No explanation for having dropped completely out of sight.

"Do you remember that I'm married?" she said coldly.

"Of course I do." There was a pause. "I'm sorry. How about lunch?"

Laura was silent.

"Please, Lo—I know I don't deserve it—and if you just want me to get the hell out of your life, I'll respect that—"

"I know. I know, Neil. You don't have to rub it in," she said with a sigh.

"Shit."

There was a prolonged silence. Laura stared out the window at a giant pile of dog shit Cocoa had left as retribution for not having been walked.

"Lo," Neil said finally, "please?"

It would have been wise to say no. To end whatever it was that was between them at that moment. He had frightened her at Patrick's that night: his urgent, obsessive, and self-defeating questions. His general air of being unbalanced. And the hint—had it been a hint or simply her own worry?—that everything that had transpired between them had, actually, at its core, to do with Jenny.

But then there was the feeling she had had for him: the incredible desire that had coursed through her in that dingy bedroom of his apartment. It was as if this existed separately from all circumstance—the memory conjured it back up. To never see him again felt suddenly bleak—and utterly, utterly disappointing. Would that last urgent kiss, that last burst of passion, be the last of her life? From here to eternity, would there be nothing like it again?

"How about the arboretum?" she said after a pause. "I'll pick up sandwiches and we can have a picnic."

The arboretum had always been one of Laura's favorite Boston places. It was so big and so pretty and yet so overlooked. No one ever seemed to go there, nothing ever seemed to happen there, and the wide, ambling paths and fields were always empty. This was maybe on account of its location, which was decidedly uncentral. But there *was* a subway stop right there. It was not difficult to get to. No, its air of abandonment, Laura felt, had more to do with the kind of pleasures it offered: quiet, beauty, and tranquillity, but unaccompanied by stateliness, or class affiliation, or history, that quintessential Boston signifier. The Arnold Arboretum could be anywhere, which was part of what Laura loved about it. It was like a pleasant backdrop you could paint yourself into, in any way you wanted.

And then for Laura there was also memory. It had been one of her mother's favorite places. The winding paths, the lovely old trees, the rose garden and old-fashioned gates, these had maybe spoken to Annabelle Trillian's English sensibilities. Laura had memories of coming as a little girl, for Sunday "strolls" with her parents before lunch at the University Club. It was one of the few places where she clearly remembered her mother as able-bodied, tramping through thickets to examine the leaves of some bush or tree, walking with her up to the top of the lookout hill. In those memories it was her father who had seemed old—which he was, a good seventeen years older than Annabelle, who had been just nineteen when she had married him! It was just her illness that had equaled them out, made her old before her time and, in comparison, made Adam seem spry and youthful. Driving there today, Laura felt gripped by a horrible sadness for her mother, who had known so little of life! Who had been scooped up and married by Sir Adam, turned into a wife before she was even twenty, and then a mother, and an invalid in short order. She had certainly had no opportunity to slip away and meet a lover *or* an old friend, whatever Neil was, on a warm weekday morning.

Did Mother ever date anyone before you? Laura had asked her father the last time she had seen him. It had been an uncomfortable question, both because it involved Annabelle, whom they talked about infrequently, and dating, which they talked about even less, or, in fact, not at all.

Before we were married? Adam had parried in his most quizzical, distracted way. *Oh, I don't know, I think she had other suitors.* But he offered her no names, no stories—nothing to build a picture of. Nothing that implied Annabelle Trillian had known romance.

Of course, Neil was late. Laura waited leaning against the hood of her car for a good twenty minutes before his ragtag blue VW rounded the bend and pulled into the parking lot.

"Sorry, Lo, I had this crazy thing with the laundry machine in my building—" he began to explain, but Laura waved his apologies away. Of course he'd had a crazy thing with the laundry machine in his building. Everything with Neil had the potential for being crazy. It had always been that way. Hadn't it?

"Let's go up there." She gestured. "There's a nice field on the hill."

"Shit—I didn't think—do we need a picnic blanket or something?"

Laura patted her bag. It was an unusual role for her—master of organization and foresight—but with Neil this was what she felt like.

They climbed the path without much chitchat and at the top of the hill, where one side of the path opened into a wide, slightly bald field, they spread the blanket at the edge of a cluster of poplars. The sky was pale and tufted with small white clouds that moved rapidly toward the west. Laura lay back against the old bedspread she had spread.

"Aren't you supposed to be at work?" she asked, shading her eyes to look up at Neil's face. He looked different somehow. Less attractive. Smaller. The rise of stubble on his face gave his skin a grayish hue.

"I'm taking the day off," he said, rolling a blade of grass between his fingers.

"Why?"

Neil shrugged jerkily. "Mental health, I guess."

Laura rolled onto her side. "Why? Is something the matter?"

"No," Neil said testily. He tore off a new fistful of grass and let it fall on his knees, retaining one blade to roll into a pulp between his fingers.

They sat in silence for a moment. Across the field, the wind swayed the tops of pines. She and Neil had not kissed. Had not, for that matter, even touched each other.

"Hey, how's the tapestry coming?" he asked, turning to look at her.

"Good." Laura smiled. "I really love it."

She had, in fact, been obsessed with it. Last night she had been up until nearly one a.m. working on the fruit trees in the background. Magenta and lime green were the colors she had chosen. She felt her mother would have approved. And as she stitched she had been overcome by a sense of how beautiful it was. A gorgeous, interesting object.

"I was thinking about it," Neil said. "I was thinking about that unicorn-versus-monk thing. Like maybe it's kind of like science versus the church. Or not science, exactly, but impurity. Mixing—the half-horse, half-rhinoceros thing. Like it has to beat the monk back to be free. And then the interesting thing is that it's more divine than he is. That the unicorn is actually the holy one."

Laura regarded him. Even a few weeks ago this analysis would have excited her: Maybe this is the key! she would have thought. Maybe this was what her mother was trying to tell her. But something had changed. She could register his idea as interesting. Possible. But it didn't matter. What mattered was the way the process of stitching turned her, for the brief periods of time when she was working on it, into her mother—pulling the needle, concentrating on the waxy lattice she was filling, losing herself in the work. "Maybe," she said.

Neil gave her a funny look. Then he sighed and lay down on his back, looking up at the sky.

"What kind of person do you think I am, Lo?" he asked. "You've known me a long time."

"Terrible," she said. "A very, very bad person."

"Really?"

"Of course not." She stretched back out and looked up at the sky too.

"Well, then, really. What do you think, really?"

"It's a silly question. Too open-ended."

Neil was silent.

"Troubled?" she offered. "I think you are a troubled person."

"Shit. That sounds bad."

"No. Not bad. You're not a bad person."

"But not 'good,'" he sighed. "I'm not good either."

Impulsively she sat up and smoothed his forehead. "What kind of conversation is this?" She laughed. "We're not in *Star Wars*."

Neil smiled wanly and shifted onto his side, curled himself around her knees. He looked so slight and so vulnerable, like a baby. She was reminded suddenly of Colin, his baby—his biological offspring, but a baby who would in all likelihood grow up to be very different from him. It made her think of Jeremy's cancer. Shouldn't Neil know about this? But she couldn't tell him: she had promised Jenny she would tell no one until Jenny was ready. It would probably just agitate Neil anyway. And their time together today had been so much better and calmer than the last few times she'd seen him precisely *because* they had not been talking about Jenny. But Laura felt a twinge of unease at dismissing the impulse—putting Jeremy and his cancer aside rather than telling Neil.

"Remember Tory Sasserass?" Neil said.

"Yes." Laura laughed. "Except that definitely was not his name."

"That guy was bad. Through and through."

"That's true." She had not thought of him for ages: an ex-boyfriend of Jenny's, an All-American running back, arrogant men's club enthusiast, notorious date rapist. It had been the early nineties, after all.

"I'm not like him, am I?"

"Of course not!"

A bank of blurry white clouds was moving into view over the treetops and the whir of rising wind grew. Neil stayed curled in his fetal position. And Laura stroked his head as if he were, in fact, a baby. As if he were as innocent and unformed as one of her own children.

There was no more spark, Laura realized suddenly. This was part of the nostalgia she had been feeling. Did he feel it too? For a moment she teetered on the brink of melancholy. How empty not to have lust, or that tingle of excitement, anticipation.

She looked down at her hand on his dishwater-colored hair. What did it matter? If it wasn't there, it wasn't there. And certainly, from a practical standpoint, from the standpoint of her life, this was for the best, wasn't it? For all she knew, in some twisted way he was still in love with, or at least obsessed with, Jenny. Where had she thought this weird passion she had felt for him was going to take her? Neil, after all, was incapable of any simple straightforward feeling of love or attraction. She had the best of what he could give her, which was his trust. And his friendship. What was it that had happened between them? It felt as though it had transpired in a dream, and here she was, wide awake suddenly and removed—slightly embarrassed, even.

Neil rolled onto his back and looked up at her. "What are you thinking?" he asked, smiling.

"Nothing!" Laura said, startled.

"What a schlub I am, I know." He poked her playfully in the knee. With surprising grace he sat up and onto his knees before her, taking her hands in his. "Someday I'll get it right," he said, kissing the tips of her fingers.

That night, Elise and Chrissy and the boys were coming over for dinner. Mac was out of town again. The brief lull in his work was over. And in the face of darkening news on the real estate pages, he was back to his old self: distracted, grouchy, and barely present. It made Laura nervous: last night she had woken twice to the sound of his teeth grinding.

"Why can't we have Chinese takeout?" Genevieve whined as Laura gazed blankly into the wasteland of freezer-bitten chicken nuggets and "organic" pizzas that populated the freezer.

Chinese dumplings were Genevieve's latest obsession and she had managed to beg and wheedle them out of Laura for the last three nights in a row.

"We can't just always get take-out food," Laura said. "It costs money, you know."

"So does everything," Genevieve retorted.

"Not as much," Laura snapped. "And anyway, it's not healthy. That's the point. We're having chicken and broccoli. And noodles."

"Yay!" Miranda chirped from the corner where she was cramming toilet paper into one of Genevieve's Barbie bags—a forbidden act (wasting rolls of toilet paper) that Laura was pretending not to notice.

"Well, then I just won't eat," Genevieve said stubbornly.

Laura glanced at the clock. Five-ten. Elise and Chrissy and the boys were due any minute. And it was after five anyway. She pulled a bottle of wine out of the refrigerator. She was a cliché. Her life was a cliché: the chicken nuggets, the saucy six-year-old, the five o'clock drink. Were all middle-class (a vestige of Neil's voice chided her for the self-abdicating misnomer: *Rich*, it breathed. *Don't kid yourself, rich and pampered*) mothers as sucked into this stream of commonalities, or were there some who managed somehow to put their own unique stamp on the experience of, for instance, fixing dinner?

It was after dinner, in the blissful (if guilty) lull of Disney-induced quietude, that Laura found herself bringing up Neil.

The children were snuggled under a sleeping bag watching *101*

Dalmatians—the one DVD that had proved uniquely capable of holding everyone's interest. Cocoa was snoozing on her stinky L. L. Bean bed. And Chrissy, Elise, and Laura were sitting drinking wine at the dish-strewn table. Elise and Chrissy had brought sushi for the grown-ups, and the remnants of soy sauce and black plastic take-out trays mingled with stray chicken nuggets, smears of applesauce, noodles, and wet clumps of rejected broccoli on the table.

Laura refilled her glass and leaned back in her chair.

"Do you think something is the matter with Neil?" she blurted out, apropos of nothing. This was a slip, she realized, but the wine and the revelations of the afternoon made her careless.

"Yes," Chrissy said emphatically, and at the same time Elise asked, "Why?"

Elise frowned and turned to her partner. "You do? You never said so to me."

Chrissy shrugged sassily. "It's obvious!"

Laura laughed. She loved Chrissy. Loved that Elise had ended up with someone so fun to hang out with.

"Okay," Elise rolled her eyes and turned to Laura. "Why do *you* think so, Lo?"

"I don't know—I saw him today and he just seemed so . . ." She searched for the word. "Unhappy."

"Well, he's always been unhappy, don't you think? I mean, at least sort of?" Elise said.

"Lost," Chrissy pronounced.

"You didn't even know him then!" Elise exclaimed.

"I'm talking about now," Chrissy said.

"Yes," Laura agreed. "Lost."

"Hm." Elise took a sip of her wine and caught Laura's eye. "Where'd you see him anyway?"

Laura averted her gaze and looked over at the children in the play area. "Oh, I had lunch with him," she said breezily.

"You have to admit his job is weird," Chrissy said. "You said so yourself, Elise."

Laura was grateful for this return to Neil himself rather than her lunch with him.

"True," Elise said reluctantly. But then, who am I to say so? I don't know anything about that business. It's probably very creative."

"Oh, *very*," Chrissy said. "There are so many ways to kill people."

"Chrissy!" Elise said testily. "We don't know anything about the games he works on. You've never even played a computer game."

"I just wondered if he was in some kind of trouble," Laura said. "But I'm probably just being silly."

"I hadn't thought about that." Elise frowned.

For a moment they were all three silent. The sound of Cruella de Vil's shrill voice drifted in from the other room.

"Do you think this will give the boys nightmares?" Chrissy asked sounding wholly unconcerned.

"I don't think he's using—" Elise said. "I mean, is that what you were thinking of? I didn't get that sense when he was staying with us."

"Oh, no!" Laura said. "No—I mean something else. Like more . . . spiritual. Or something," she finished lamely.

"Depression," Chrissy said. "Like he's depressed."

"I don't know." Laura sighed. Suddenly she didn't want to talk about it anymore. Why had she brought it up?

"I should check in on him," Elise mused. "I haven't talked to him since he moved back to his place."

Laura rose and began clearing the table. Her mind drifted involuntarily to what Neil was doing right now: lying on that depressing couch in his apartment, maybe. It gave her an anxious feeling.

There was a shriek from the other room.

"Ah!" Laura jumped, dropping the pile of sushi trays she was holding.

But it was only Miranda, jumping up and down and shrieking at the TV.

Nigel began to cry.

"She's just happy!" Chrissy explained soothingly, scooping him up. "Look at the doggies."

But Disney's spell was broken. Genevieve's leg hurt and James wanted quiet and Miranda was still jumping and shrieking.

Plates were piled in the sink, protests about helping clean were made and rejected, children's shoes and jackets and sippy cups rounded up.

As Chrissy and Elise were heading out the door, Elise turned back to Laura. "Do you still have animals on Scrubb Farm?" Scrubb Farm was Laura's father's country house, a rambling pastoral place in western Massachusetts.

"Animals?" Laura repeated blankly. "Chickens. But the pony died. I thought I told you."

"But that caretaker still works there? Takes care of the chickens?"

"Mm-hm." Laura nodded, frowning. "Why?"

Miranda chose that moment to race across the room and nearly bowl her over with a hug.

"Nothing," Elise said. "I was just wondering."

"Why?" Laura asked through the mop of her daughter's hair.

"I'll call you," Elise said. "Thanks again—and I will check in on Neil. Not that I have some special power to fix things."

"Who's Neil?" Genevieve's voice asked.

"An old friend," Laura said with a sigh, kissing Elise goodbye.

"That guy in the car?" Genevieve asked.

"What guy?" Laura stiffened.

"The guy you went to Patrick's with," Genevieve said, cocking her head and looking up at her mother quizzically.

"Hmmm." Elise raised her eyebrows.

Laura hesitated for a moment. "Yes," she said. "That guy."

And the look in her daughter's searching eyes gave her a chill. She felt an almost uncomfortable swell of love for her. She put Miranda down on the floor and bent to kiss Genevieve's forehead.

"Let's go get ready for bed. It's been a long day."

2

JENNY SAT BACK IN HER SEAT and tried to process what Galena had just told her. Why had Neil been in the girl's apartment at four in the morning? Or actually, she understood *why*, but *how* had this come to pass? Jenny blinked. This was not the point anyway. Apparently he was destined to reenter her life through every possible crack and crevice.

Before her, Galena Ibanesku sat very straight in the faux-Eames chair and even so her head just barely cleared the back of it. She was wearing a cheap-looking navy-blue suit and flats. But something about the effect was formidable. She looked ready to pounce.

"I just think it's very strange that he was trying to steal it," Galena said stubbornly. Maybe she had expected a more dramatic reaction from Jenny.

"It is strange." Jenny sighed. "He is a strange person."

Galena narrowed her eyes at her evaluatively.

Jenny was exhausted. She had been up until two with Colin, who had come down with a cold. And then Jeremy had tossed and turned beside her in bed, and they had both lain there, staring at the ceiling, unable to sleep. She felt like something ragged—a body in one of those action movies, being pounded, kicked, beaten to a pulp.

"Do you know what his previous affiliations are?" Galena said, cocking her head to the side. "I mean, has he ever worked for Genzyme? Or Novartis?"

"No," Jenny said. "I'm sure he hasn't." If she were not so tired she would have found the idea funny.

Galena frowned.

"I just don't think he's a corporate spy," Jenny said firmly.

The girl gave an insolent shrug. "Then why was he stealing the mock-up?"

Last night, while trying to soothe Colin and at the same time make something at least moderately appetizing from the macrobiotic cookbook Jeremy now wanted to strictly adhere to, Jenny had called her mother.

"I'm getting on a plane tomorrow," Judy Callahan had pronounced. And for once in her life, Jenny did not resist her mother's oversized, overbearing gesture. This meant she had now told three people about the cancer: her mother, Elise, and Laura. All sworn to silence.

This was because she had still told no one in her office. Last week she had decided to go in to Eric with the news. But then, sitting in his office, staring at the ostentatiously framed photograph of his own happy family—a big, jolly wife and three children, all rosy-cheeked and wearing windbreakers at the top of some mountain peak they had just summited—she froze completely.

"So there was something you wanted to talk to me about?" Eric had asked, after the usual introductory chitchat.

And looking at that picture, that happy, wholesome American Dream picture, Jenny had been gripped by resistance. Cancer had separated her from Eric forever. No matter what happened, she and Jeremy and Colin had just diverged irrevocably from the happy club Eric was still a card-carrying member of. Would he, from now on, see her as someone to be pitied? Her silence, she was aware, sitting there on the sofa in his office, was heading toward awkward.

"I wanted to talk about the Barkman team," she found herself saying. "They're not hitting their targets."

Eric blinked. There must have been something about her voice, her manner, or maybe simply the buildup toward this conversation that made this a surprising subject. But if he suspected a bait-and-switch, he did nothing further to indicate this. The conversation proceeded as usual. It was only when Jenny left and walked out into the carpeted, cube-lined hall that she felt the blood pounding in her ears and the gaze of the receptionists' eyes on her like X-rays.

That afternoon Jenny snuck out of the office on an impulse: she would surprise Jeremy by coming home early. She would pull him away from the computer and take him for a walk—maybe on the Wellesley conservation trails she had heard so much about, or into the city, to Newbury Street, where they had walked so often in the early days of their marriage, to Stefanie's for a drink or Starbucks for a cup of coffee.

But then, when she pulled into the driveway and started up the steps to the kitchen door, she could see inside to where Jeremy lay stretched out on the flower-print rug, making a spring-loaded caterpillar shimmy in front of Colin. The baby looked delighted with this—absolutely amazed at the movements of the fuzzy, shiny object, and Jeremy himself looked completely absorbed in the activity. There was a real closeness between them, and an intensity to Jeremy's movements, which stopped her in her tracks.

And she could not go in.

As she watched, Jeremy leaned forward and lay his head down on the rug, almost in the boy's lap, and Colin banged his little hands down on Jeremy's soft hair, excited by the unfamiliar texture. She could not see Jeremy's face, which was turned away from her, but the tiredness of the gesture brought a wave of grief through her unlike anything she had experienced yet.

What was he thinking about with those little hands on his head? Listening to the coos of a boy he might, in all likelihood, never see become a man?

She was suddenly overwhelmed by grief for this man she had married—for his old life and, with this, for her own. Crazy, animallike sobs started to burst from her. She bent over and held her breath, trying to rein them in. But she could not stop. And she could not go to him like this. So she pulled into the garage and sat there, sobbing for God knows how long, until finally, when she was spent, she slipped into the kitchen and Jeremy was gone. *Napping*, Maria informed her, and Jenny did not wake him.

When Jenny got back from her run that evening, her mother had arrived. She was standing at the kitchen sink peeling potatoes. At the table, Maria sat nervously trying to pry yogurt into Colin's mouth. "Do you have any pudding?" Jenny could hear her mother saying. "There's nothing like pudding for a picky child." She was speaking in the loud, clear, talking-to-immigrants voice that made Jenny cringe. It had, maybe, been a terrible idea to let her come.

"Ah, pudding! Yes! Very good, I tell Jeneefer to buy pudding." Poor Maria sounded downright panicky.

Jenny hurried to the kitchen to diffuse the tension. But weirdly, uncharacteristically, at the sight of her mother she burst into tears.

"Oh, honey," Judy Callahan said, taking her daughter into her arms.

3

ROD EMERUS TURNED THE LAPTOP computer screen around to face Neil and gave him a hard look across the conference room table. "What is this?" he asked.

The image on the screen was from the second level of *Promo II*. It was the slick, futuristic highway that the geologists in possession of the Sphinx had to traverse to escape their pursuers. On one side it was skirted by a vast purple oil spill. On the other it was flanked by billboards—a series stretching as far as the eye could see. Each of these was plastered with a bright, creepy photo of a woman's smile and the word "Setlan" printed in neo-Gothic lettering across it.

"And this?" Emerus typed a command into the computer and the same eerie smile appeared, this time on the side of the transport truck that was one mode of transportation for the geologists and their precious cargo.

"And this?" He typed another command, which called up the kitchen of the underground bunker in which the geologists lived. The creepy smile was everywhere: on the side of the box of cereal they would expend twenty-five monetary points on in exchange for energy, on the door of the "food safe," aka the refrigerator, on the place mats on the table. If you looked closely, you could even see it reproduced in nearly microscopic proportions on the side of their bottled water.

"This is some kind of joke?" Emerus said.

Sullenly, Neil shrugged. "Just following orders."

Emerus glared at him. "No orders you received here."

Neil did actually feel somewhat sheepish about it. He had written the images into the game before the incident with Galena, the thought of which still turned his stomach.

"Apologies," he muttered. "I'll take it out."

Emerus leaned back in his chair, putting his hands behind his head in a pose of self-conscious consideration. "I don't understand you, Banks," he said. "You took this job and from day one you've had a pole up your ass about it. And now—" He raised a hand to head off Neil's halfhearted attempt at self defense. "And now I understand you are in the business of stealing corporate secrets."

"What?" Neil was unsure he had heard the man correctly.

"If that was what you were after all along, why choose this job as a way to go about it? You could have saved yourself a lot of hassle getting a job as copy clerk with Genron."

"What the fuck?" Neil paled.

Emerus did not respond to this but instead rocked gently in the Aeron chair, keeping Neil fixed in his gaze.

"I think you've got a screw loose, Banks. You're an angry young man."

"I have no idea what you're talking about. Really," Neil said almost pleadingly.

Emerus sat forward in a sudden movement that for a moment Neil thought was an attempt to jump across the table at him. He flinched.

In fact, Emerus was calling something up on his computer screen, fingers rat-a-tatting on the keyboard like machine gun fire. Then he spun the computer back around and showed Neil the screen. Neil squinted at it.

It was an email.

Dear Rod, it began.

A troubling matter of professional indiscretion has been brought to our attention recently. As liaison between the Setlan marketing

team and your company, I have to report the inappropriate activity
of one of your employees, Neil Banks.

As a game developer at your company, Banks had access to
pertinent marketing materials for the drug Setlan. However, he
managed through his position as a ZGames employee to also access,
without authorization, highly sensitive marketing materials for a
drug still in development here at Genron. We are deeply concerned
about his motivations for this.

We put our trust in your employees to honor the nondisclo-
sure agreements you signed when we commenced our relationship.
We put our trust in you to appropriately vet your employees before
assigning them to the task of working with us. The Setlan marketing
team here at Genron has reviewed the situation with care and great
concern. As a result of this breach of professional conduct we kindly
ask that you remove the said employee, Neil Banks, from this project
immediately. Failure to do so will result in an immediate termina-
tion of our contract.

Neil's mind barely registered the words. His eyes had skipped
immediately to the bottom of the email, signed *Galena Ibanesku*.
Her name leapt out at Neil like a shot in the heart—of course, of
course. Had he not felt the premonition of this, whatever the hell
this was, in her apartment?

"Jesus Christ." Neil pressed his face into the palms of his hands.
He pressed hard enough that his eyes swam with tiny sparky stars.

"I'll tell you, I don't know what this is, Banks. And it smacks of
bullshit. But"—Emerus nodded gravely—"I'm going to have to take
you off the project."

"Christ," was all Neil could muster up.

"I can't afford to lose this account and they're on us about this
now. They can pull out in a second. And"—here he raised his eyebrows at Neil—"you haven't exactly demonstrated great enthusi-

asm for your work here. This garbage, for example"—he waved his hand at the computer, presumably to indicate the in-game Setlan placements—"begs a few questions."

"Man." Neil sat back. He felt sick. His brain struggled to process what was unfolding. Galena had gotten him, all right. She was a snaky little bitch.

But "the Setlan marketing team"? It made his blood pound heavily in his ears. Could this be true? That would mean that Jenny was aware of Galena's actions. Had "reviewed" them, even, whatever that meant. There was a part of him that balked at believing this. It was not possible, even from Jenny. He was the father of her baby, for Christ's sake! She *knew* him. And she *knew* he wasn't a corporate spy or whatever the implication of this garbage was. His whole self was suffused with a kind of dumbfounded rage.

Slowly, gingerly, Neil rose from his seat. "I'm not going to beg you to keep me," he said, and his voice sounded gravelly and thin in his ears. "But I will tell you this is bullshit."

"The world is full of bullshit, my friend," Emerus said. "You've got to learn how to keep it off your hands."

It was packing up his things—throwing CDs and papers and as much expensive level-building software as he could find into a ZGames duffel—that Neil thought of it: the creature. He was stewing with anger. And it was the one thing he could do—the one grain of dignity and self-respect that he could salvage. He was taking the fucking Sphinx. They could put Steven Closter back on the job, make the fate of the *Perfect Life* universe rest on his ugly, unimaginative, and graceless monster. But not on the beautiful, perfect life-form Neil had created. That was his idea, and it was coming with him.

His knock on Emerus's office door was too loud. He had not intended for it to echo so jarringly across the floor. Several of the programmers who sat nearby jumped in their seats. Emerus opened the door with a startled expression.

"I'm taking the Sphinx," Neil said.

Emerus raised his eyebrows. "Would you like to come in?"

"Not really." Neil's anger animated him, made his body feel wiry and sharp. He stepped inside anyway and Emerus shut the door behind him.

"What is this?" Emerus asked, sitting down behind his desk and gesturing for Neil to sit as well.

Neil remained standing. "I'm taking the Sphinx. You can use Closter's monster."

Emerus frowned. "The contents of *Prometheus Syndrome II* belong to ZGames, you know."

"Right. But not the creature. That's my idea. Before me it was just a fucking 'digital tablet.' I came up with the life-form."

Emerus looked over his glasses at Neil, eyebrows raised. It was a gesture that was both obnoxious and condescending. "Do you really think the employees of ZGames own their 'ideas'?"

"You know, I don't actually care," Neil said. "I'm just telling you that the Sphinx belongs to me. I came up with it and I'm taking it with me."

"You know, you're beginning to waste my time," Emerus said acidly.

Neil stared at him, his fingers spread in agitation. He was incredulous. But why? it occurred to him. Why should he be surprised? What was he, some idealistic moron? He stood there watching Emerus sit down at his desk and begin clicking through emails. The absurdity and helplessness of his situation washed over him.

"Fuck you," he said, in the only gallingly childish recourse he had. Then somehow he managed to turn on his heel and walk out the door into the cube zone. And he could feel the eyes of the room on him—all the peons of this despicable empire.

He had already exited into the slick, stone-floored reception area when Joe caught up to him. The kid was sweating, as usual, and breathing as if he had chased Neil much farther than the fifty yards to the exit.

"Neil," he said. "Neil!" and Neil whirled around to face him.

"I'm sorry," Joe panted. "I'm sorry, dude, you know . . ." He brushed the bangs off his face in a now-familiar gesture. "I'm sorry—it's really fucked up that you're leaving."

Neil nodded and started to turn again.

"I just want you to know I'll try to keep *Prometheus II* up to your standards. I mean . . ." He seemed embarrassed by the grandiosity of the statement—in all likelihood he would be demoted to intern once again, they both knew that. "I just wanted to say you were awesome, man—your ideas—"

"Thanks," Neil said curtly, and started toward the door again. But Joe was persistent. He kept pace, just behind him, like a heeling dog.

"You know, I feel like you kind of made me think about things, you know, even outside the game."

"Ha!" Neil snorted, and Joe looked alarmed. But it did not deter him.

"No, I mean like biology. And DNA. You know, I was thinking how it's true—in a real apocalypse, I mean in the real world, that'd probably be our key—just like in *Perfect Life*. Fusing and tinkering with genes, like retrofitting our species. And they'll look back at *Perfect Life* and be, like, wow, that was prescient."

They had reached Neil's car. "I just wanted to tell you," Joe said, still breathing heavily.

"Great." Neil thrust his hands into his pockets. He was too angry to slow down, but he understood, on some semi-inaccessible level, that Joe was a sweet young man. The boy's chubby face trembled slightly with the expenditure of effort. And out of the damp, jelly-fish mass of this, his eyes shone a bright pale blue—they were much sharper than the rest of him.

Neil climbed into his car and backed it out of the parking space. As he revved the engine and pulled out of the parking lot he could still see the kid standing there, watching him depart, one hand raised in a kind of static, almost militaristic gesture. And it did something—not much, but a little—to defuse Neil's rage as he angled the car out onto the road and watched the anonymous concrete box that was ZGames disappear from the rearview mirror.

4

"SHE DID *WHAT?*" Jeremy's eyes opened and stared at Jenny with a lucidity that she had not expected. He looked truly amazed.

"Nothing, nothing—no big deal," she said hurriedly.

They were sitting in a pleasant—by hospital standards anyway —room in Brigham and Women's, facing out over Olmsted Park. And Jeremy was hooked up to an IV, which was delivering his first dose of chemo. He had seemed to be nodding off, letting his mind drift while his body absorbed the poison that hope rested on. *Tell me about work,* he had said. *What about it?* Jenny had asked. It had been a long time since he had expressed any interest in this. *Anything. Whatever. Just talk to me.* And so she had launched into a description of the Setlan campaign: her inspiration, the mock-up the ad firm had come up with, the initial focus group results (overwhelmingly positive), the new sales strategy. Jeremy had not seemed to be listening. It was probably just the sound of her voice he wanted. And so she had rattled on and come to the sticking point—the "Neil Incident," as she had come to think of it. It was, she realized, why she had chosen this subject to prattle on about. It had been simmering beneath the surface of her mind, begging to be addressed. She had just had too many more pressing things, more immediate things, to think about (the logistics of Jeremy's treatment, of the move, of the Setlan PPD launch). But the situation was incredible, really—completely ridiculous—that

Neil Banks, the man she had chosen (impulsively, irresponsibly even, it now seemed to her, but still . . .) to father her baby, would be accused of corporate spying! Galena's email had come to Jenny's attention ex post facto. The girl had apparently gone over Jenny's head, straight to Eric, who had given her the okay to send it.

Jeremy was staring at her lucidly. His expression was horrified.

"I don't know why I'm blabbing about this," she said nervously. "It's the last thing you need to think about."

"Well, now you told me," he said, shifting against the gray vinyl of the reclining chair. "And I don't get it."

"Oh, it's just stupid. The girl was sleeping with him and it got ugly, I guess. I don't know why Eric even gave her half an ear on it."

"But you didn't stop her from sending this email?"

"I didn't know about it!" Jenny said defensively.

"You didn't *correct* it after you found out?"

"Correct it how?" Jenny stopped short as the simple moral imperative of what her husband was suggesting struck her. It had been her responsibility to undo it. Somehow. The accusation was false. The motivation behind it was impure. It had rested on her shoulders, however overburdened already, to say so.

"I'm planning to talk to Eric," she said, mustering a crisp, slightly defensive tone. "I'll straighten it out."

"When did she send the email?" Jeremy asked.

"I don't know!" Jenny said exasperatedly. "A week ago, maybe. I don't know!" she threw her hands up in the air. "I guess I fucked up. I guess I had a few other things on my mind and wasn't thinking too clearly." It was a low blow, she knew as soon as it was out of her mouth.

Jeremy closed his eyes. The bag of chemicals suspended on its delicate silver cross dripped steadily into his arm.

"I'm sorry—I didn't mean . . ." Jenny began.

Jeremy was silent for a moment. "You're right. I don't need to be thinking about this."

Jenny sighed and stood up in agitation. She was not used to the feeling of self-loathing that swept over her. It made her physically sick. She had been wrong not to address the situation as soon as she had learned of it. She should have been more forceful with Galena. She should have talked to Eric, issued some retraction . . . Was there some little part of her that had stood back simply because it would be easier—it would be better for her—if Neil was forced to go away? Back to that cave of a home in Los Angeles where she had found him? No. She was not that selfish. The idea was repulsive. No, she would go to Eric tomorrow, straighten out the misunderstanding, and hope it was not too late.

"Do you want more water?" she asked. "Or something to eat? I'm going to get some coffee."

Jeremy rolled his head *No* against the back of the chair, keeping his eyes closed.

"Music? Do you want the music?"

"Sure," he said.

Jenny slipped the CD into the compact Bose player they had brought with them. The sounds of Simon & Garfunkel filled the room. Jeremy's choice, not hers. It had been an odd thing, choosing the music. It was the hospital's suggestion and dutifully they had followed it despite the fact that neither Jenny nor Jeremy was at all "into" music. If someone had offered her a million dollars she wouldn't have been able to guess what her husband would pick out. And here it was: Simon & Garfunkel, John Coltrane, and less surprisingly, a classical "sampler" she put on when they had company for brunch or cocktails. These were the sounds Jeremy wanted to listen to while his body waged this battle.

Art Garfunkel's sweet choirboy-like voice was almost too much to bear. Lying against the gray vinyl of the hospital recliner with his eyes shut, Jeremy looked pale and fragile—his cheekbones sharp and the skin under his eyes especially purple.

Jenny planted a quick kiss on his cool forehead and blinked back the tears that were suddenly, newly, so accessible.

Out in the hallway, she let herself just stand and take a deep breath. She was losing her grasp. This was the distinct thought she had standing there in that terrible, Vaseline-and-liniment-smelling gray tunnel. She was just so tired. So goddamn tired. She did not feel like she had control anymore. Of anything. Uncharacteristically, it had not occurred to her that she could take control of the Neil and Galena situation. She had honestly not really considered herself in any position of power. What had become of Jenny Callahan?

Right now all she wanted to do was hold her baby. Her sweet little Colin, who had of late been doing so much smiling and chirping. But it was, unfortunately, only eleven a.m. It would be another hour before he and Maria arrived via an elaborate commute on the train and subway. Maria was terrified of navigating her way by car into the city. For the umpteenth time in the last two weeks Jenny felt a pang of regret about having moved. Maria would have been able to bring Colin back and forth so easily if they still lived on Clarendon Street.

Jenny herded herself into the elevator and downstairs to the Au Bon Pain, where at least she could get a coffee.

It was while waiting in line to pay that Jenny got a call from Laura. She was here, at the Brigham, she had brought them sushi—she hoped she wasn't imposing and she could just leave it with the desk if that would be best . . . Jenny's first feeling was of irritation—now she would have to deal with someone else's feelings and questions and worries. But then, crossing the lobby to meet her friend, who had made the trip all the way here from Cambridge via Fugakyu and was standing, nervously, in the center of the giant, glass-ceilinged lobby, she felt actually a swell of love for Laura and the sting of tears against her eyeballs. Old friend, who had known her for so long. She had an incongruous memory, suddenly, of a time she and Laura had driven all the way to Lake Champlain to go to her then-boyfriend's end-of-the-year summer house party. She had gotten violently sick and Laura had stayed with her in the dingy little motel room they had rented, making cool washcloths for her forehead and driving the remote control until they found reasonably cheerful things to watch, instead of going to the party. And more remarkably, she had not acted bitter or resentful afterward.

"How are you holding up?" Laura asked breathlessly, giving Jenny a big hug. "And how is Jeremy doing?"

Laura had brought him his favorite cookies from her local bakery and the delicious, fresh-baked smell of them wafted up from the paper bag.

"Oh, he's okay . . . ," Jenny said, shaking the tears off. "I mean, he's not too uncomfortable or anything. Right now. I'm just driving him crazy, I think."

"Why? I'm sure you're not."

"Oh, I'm just—" Jenny stopped herself. She wanted and didn't want to tell Laura about the whole "Neil Incident." Laura would be confused—and then ultimately appalled. "Talking too much about work," she finished.

"Oh, sweetie," Laura said, putting a hand on Jenny's arm. "I'm sure you're not—you're just doing what you can."

"Which is nothing." Jenny was surprised by the bitterness in her own voice.

"That's not true." Laura frowned. "You're being there for him."

They were silent for a moment in the bustle of the hospital atrium, the peeling sounds of so many medical shoes on the polished concrete, the echoing of nurses' chatter.

"How is little Colin?" Laura asked.

"He's good. He's coming soon." Jenny felt a little leap in her chest as she said it.

"Oh, good," Laura said. And then she reached into her bag: she always had some giant tote that looked like it could hold a week's worth of supplies—snacks and pens and changes of clothes and God knows what else. "I brought you these anyway—they might provide some distraction." She handed Jenny a pile of trashy magazines: *Us* and *People* and *Star* and even *In Touch*.

"Maybe you can read to him about Tom Cruise's secret obsession with clog dancing," she said, pointing to a headline.

Jenny took the stack with a rush of gratitude. Trashy magazines were actually exactly what she wanted.

Armed with these, and with the sushi and cookies, she kissed her friend goodbye and started back across the lobby to the elevators. She would straighten out the mess Galena had made of Neil's work tomorrow, absolve herself of guilt. She just had to get through this day and the next and the next and then this round of chemo would be over. And then—and then, somehow, things would return to normal. Or to what she told herself would become normal. A new, more uncertain, less comfortable kind of normal.

5

IT WAS AMAZING how quickly the smell filled the car: pungent, earthy, and slightly acrid. Within minutes the Volvo smelled just like the barn. It wasn't only the goat. Elise herself was drenched in a cold, nervous sweat that had soaked giant stains under the arms of her T-shirt and was prickling up all over her scalp.

She darted a glance at Chrissy beside her. Chrissy looked calm as always, her hair pulled back, her face especially pretty in that flat Norwegian way. Ula was sacked out on her little stretcher in the back, her sides barely rising and falling in the depths of her tranquilized sleep.

Chrissy turned and put a hand on Ula's just-reachable shoulder. (They had flattened the backseat to make the back of the car one giant goat bed.) "She's fine," she said, retracting her hand. "Don't worry." She put the hand on Elise's knee.

Something inside Elise had simply balked at euthanizing Ula. It was not so much about the goat herself as it was about the science. Elise understood the necessity of ruthlessness when it came to missteps: in an unsuccessful experiment the animal had to be dispensed with. A lab couldn't support all its mistakes. But Ula had not been a mistake. The science that had created her was sound and promising and full of potential. It was the market—that cruel and uncertain beast—that dictated she must die. And Elise had made no pact with the market. At least no pact she wanted to admit to herself.

Elise couldn't pin the idea of stealing Ula—of *saving* Ula, really—on Neil, because he did not even know of Ula's existence. But he had planted the seed. *That makes you those animals' creator,* he had said when she had described her work. *Man.* He had taken a big puff of the joint. Together they had lain there on the splintery deck looking up at the pale spring sky. *You think if there's a God, he's as utilitarian with us?* It had been a joke, kind of. But it had stuck in Elise's mind. She was like the god of her little goats. It was true. Which meant she was responsible for something bigger than the proteins they expressed. Not—she would never use the word—their souls. But something—some intangible quality of their lives that had meaning beyond the market she had produced them to supply.

It was nearly one a.m. and the turnpike was all but empty. Beside Elise, Chrissy began, improbably, to doze off, her head sinking off to the side. Lowell, Fitchburg, Gardner—the exits flew past, bright green and silver signs illuminated by the sweep of headlights, and then falling back into the black of the moonless night and dark hovering trees. At home, Angela Noyes would be snoozing in her old-fashioned curlers on the guest bed, and the boys—she hoped— were sound asleep in their beds. Back at the Pharm, the night guard they had lied their way past was probably sleeping too.

The turnoff to Scrubb Farm was surprisingly familiar. The giant, dilapidated old manor house on the corner, the stand of dark pines, the swamp on the left . . . And then the long driveway of the farm itself, winding through woods and circling up in front of the big, flat-faced, plain farmhouse at the edge of the pasture. It brought such a visceral rush of memory back—Elise felt almost as if she had stumbled upon some weird lapse in the space-time continuum where she could coexist with her old twenty-one-year-old self.

They had come here often in college: she and Laura and Jenny and Neil. Sometimes there had been an odd boyfriend along (Jenny's football player romance, or Elise's own slacker chemistry partner and bong-pal). Sometimes a "flavor of the day," as Neil would later call the various friends who dotted the roommates' lives, rising to prominence as one or another of the three girls warmed to them and then, usually within months, falling back into obscurity.

Scrubb Farm had been a kind of social sanctuary, a place that existed outside the college universe. A place where they could play at being real grown-ups—actually cooking their own meals, building fires, and drinking wine. Elise remembered clearly the room she had always slept in: a tiny, north-facing single bedroom with an old-fashioned dry sink and pale-green-painted floors. Waking up in it had been heavenly: unlike any other place she could think of, it afforded her a kind of luxurious privacy. So plain, so simple, it was completely undefined. And against this indefinite background, so unlike their dorm room, with its plethora of posters and CDs and articles of clothing, all proclaiming allegiances and announcing worldviews, everyone became more completely themselves.

But this was no time for such nostalgia. The car bounced over an enormous rut and Chrissy jolted awake. "Are we there?" she asked, rubbing her eyes. Chrissy had never been to Scrubb Farm.

Elise nodded, pulling the car up at the front door. She did not even have time to unbuckle her seat belt before Laura appeared, silhouetted in the light of the doorway, pulling a cardigan tight around her waist.

Elise leaned across Chrissy to unroll the passenger-side window and tried to smile, she hoped not too nervously, at Laura, whose own face did not even try to affect unconcern.

"Is she in there?" Laura asked, looking doubtfully at the blanket obscuring Ula.

"Sleeping," Elise said, using the euphemism she usually hated as a descriptor of the drugged state the goat was in.

Laura nodded and bit her lip as though considering some new and unwelcome information.

Elise had put her friend in an uncomfortable position, asking this favor. Laura was a reasonable person and a good friend, but that didn't mean she couldn't share some portion of the world's general revulsion at the idea of all things transgenic. "We'll give her a hysterectomy," Elise had assured her. "There will be no chance she could ever have babies or express milk." And Laura had agreed, but only because otherwise Ula's death would be on her hands.

Laura led the way to the stall—an old shed that had housed a pony and some chickens, cared for by the farm's caretaker, when they had come here in college. It was fairly dilapidated, but functional, and inside the caretaker had put some fresh bales of hay. Together, and in silence, Laura and Chrissy and Elise lugged Ula out of the car on the stretcher.

"I'll stay with her till she wakes up," Elise said impulsively, "You two should go back to the house."

Neither Chrissy nor Laura protested, and so Elise found herself sitting alone in the darkness with the "sleeping" animal. It was cold, and pitch-dark, and at first Elise kept her flashlight on, but then it was unclear where, in all this darkness, she should point it. At Ula's inert form? Or the door of the shed? Each of these was, in its own way, creepy. So she turned the flashlight off. She could listen to the wind, the occasional scrape of twigs against the side of the shed, and the skitter of nocturnal animals in the leaves and underbrush outside.

And as she sat, she felt suddenly aware of the myriad of life buzzing around her. The hay, the wood, the tiny mites and rodents and bits of mold and fungus and vegetation claiming this shed their own. And herself and Ula, right there among all the rest—not even all that different. Variations of the same basic elements—particles gathering, spinning themselves into living beings, spinning back off again. It gave the darkness an aura of happy industry. Things were growing under its cover. Creatures were molting. Life was whirling through its constant cycle of resurrection and decay.

Suddenly Elise was startled by a sound—a frantic snorting, scraping, followed by a sneeze. She had not even realized that she had drifted into sleep. And now Ula (Elise placed herself immediately in the present circumstance) was awake. The goat made an unhappy gurgly noise and Elise groped for her flashlight. When she turned it on, Ula's form was illuminated, struggling to get up.

"It's okay," Elsie said. "You're okay—you're just in a new place." Her voice sounded strange in the darkness, and Ula's scrambling stopped for a moment at the sound of it. "You're going to be fine—you're just a little confused, probably. But its going to be okay—you're going to like it here." Elise murmured away, unaware of exactly what she was saying, as she moved gingerly, crouching, to assist Ula, whose leg was somehow stuck under her. With a kind of slow deliberation that she had not realized herself capable of, Elise put a hand on the goat's bristly, heaving shoulder and half pushed, half pulled her up until finally she was standing. Elise scrambled to her own feet.

For a moment there was nothing but the sound of their labored breaths and then the cautious, dainty click of Ula's heels as she began to walk around, inspecting her new surroundings.

Exhausted, Elise began to smile. It felt as though she had just given birth to Ula. Or as if, more accurately, like a midwife, she had just wrested her out of the clutches of some reluctant womb. Which in a way she had, hadn't she? This was Ula's new life, different from the one she had been born into, perversely old-fashioned and yet radical: an experiment—a transgenic animal in the real world. Ula was an unwitting pioneer.

"Goodnight," she said aloud, and for a moment turned the flashlight beam to Ula's face—funny, pointy goat face with its eerie diamond-pupiled eyes. She blinked with a certain mysterious equanimity. What did she know of her unique standing in the world of animals and man?

Elise let herself out of the shed and drove back up the driveway to the house.

Elise woke to the same light and smells that had always greeted her on her trips to Scrubb Farm in college. Coffee and the faint dry mustiness of the mattress, the long-stored sheets, the brittle chipping paint of the nightstand. And the pale, inscrutable morning light through the white cotton curtains.

She swung her legs out of the bed and parted these to look outside. It was beautiful. Bright early morning sun sparkled on the leaves of the oak tree and slapped off the white clapboard surface of the woodshed. She let the curtain drop and, moving carefully so as not to wake Chrissy, who was still sound asleep in the other of the two twin beds, she gathered her clothes and tiptoed to the bathroom down the hall.

Downstairs, Laura was predictably awake already, standing out on the flagstone terrace, steaming mug of coffee in her hand.

It was at Scrubb Farm that Elise had first seen Laura as the mother she would become. She was always up early and unenveloped by the vague dreaminess that hovered over her at school. Here she seemed sharper and more directed: making pancakes for everyone, or returning from a trip to the market in town in the ancient Ford Bronco she had inherited. She had a crispness about her that seemed very English. And the death of her mother, who had decorated the house, moved suddenly front and center, and always gave Elise a protective feeling for her friend.

"Hey," Elise said, and Laura jumped slightly.

"God, it's beautiful!" Elise sank down onto one of the rusty wrought-iron chairs that sprawled like a set of harmless, spindly spiders across the stones since God knows when.

"Isn't it?" Laura said. "How's Ula? Did she"—she hesitated—"come out of it . . . okay?"

Elise shrugged. "She seemed happy as a clam to me."

"I want to go see her," Laura said.

"Right now?" Elise said. She was pleased to see that the skittishness and strain of last night seemed to have left Laura, who looked happy—even excited, actually.

"No, no," Laura said. "Let's eat—I'm hungry. I got eggs and bacon."

Already she was heading briskly inside—the efficient, English Laura Elise remembered so clearly from their college visits here. It made her smile.

"Want me to make the bacon?" Elise asked, trailing after her.

It was at the stove, looking over at Laura whisking the eggs, hair escaping from her ponytail, face squared in concentration, that Elise remembered the thought that had occurred to her the last time she had seen Laura.

"Laura," she said turning toward her, lowering the heat on the sizzling bacon. "I have to ask you something."

Something in her voice must have sounded alarming, because Laura looked up in surprise. "What?"

"What is up between you and Neil?"

"What do you mean?" Laura sat back, knife still clutched in her hand, and a flush of color rose to her face almost instantaneously.

Elise cocked her head to the side. "I can just tell. Something is up."

"What do you mean—did he—"

"No—I haven't talked to him in ages. You did. You do. I just know you. And you're so . . . agitated whenever he comes up."

"I'm not agitated." Laura bent her head and resumed chopping the herbs so that Elise could not see her face.

"I'm not judging," Elise said.

There was silence, and from upstairs came the sound of Chrissy's footsteps. *Take a shower*, Elise willed her. *Don't come down right now*.

When Laura put down the knife and lifted her face, the answer was written all over it.

"Wow," Elise said, and for a moment they were silent, just looking at each other. Elise had guessed it, but even so she was stunned.

Mercifully, there was the sound of water running in the upstairs bathroom. From outside there was the sound of a blue jay squawking.

"It's over," Laura said brusquely, rising with her minced herbs. "Whatever it was. I can't even reach him."

"Neil Banks." Elise shook her head. "Who would have thunk it?"

"Don't. Please don't . . ." Laura switched the burner on under a frying pan and it ticked angrily before bursting into flame.

"Does Mac . . . ? Of course not," Elise answered herself.

Laura stared into the frying pan before her, and then turned suddenly to face Elise. "You can't say anything to anyone—not even Jenny. *Especially* not Jenny. It doesn't matter—it really—I don't even know why—"

They both froze at the sound of footsteps on the stairs. Apparently the running water had not been a shower after all. "Not even Chrissy," Laura hissed.

The swinging door from the dining room opened and Chrissy emerged looking sleepy, the crease of her pillow still pink on her cheek. "I thought I smelled bacon," she said, reminding Elise of the crackling pan beside her. "What a gorgeous day—Ula must be pretty pleased with her new digs."

"That's right, the lucky bugger," Laura said, switching into a cheerful, normal voice with ease. She'd had practice by this time, after all. The meanness of her own thought startled Elise. She wasn't married to Mac, or even particularly friendly with him—who was she to judge? But Laura's revelation shocked her. And in some sour way she felt betrayed. Once upon a time they had all four just been friends. What impact Neil's return had had on her—her work, her home—seemed suddenly inconsequential, dwarfed completely by this. But why did this matter? It wasn't a contest: whose life Neil could most fuck up, who had the most connection to him, as if he were some celebrity, or youth itself.

"How was it?" Chrissy asked, resting a hand on the back of Elise's neck for a moment. "Was she totally freaked out when she came to?"

"Ula?" Elise said blankly, and then, under Chrissy's scrutinizing gaze, collected herself. "Oh, no—she was fine. I had to help her get up, but then . . . she was totally okay."

"Hnh," Chrissy said, narrowing her eyes for an instant and then walking over to the French doors.

Of course, Elise would tell Chrissy of Laura's confession. This was one of the many differences between being married to a Chrissy or a Mac: Laura did not understand that for Elise to keep something, even of much lesser significance, from her partner would be impossible. Laura had, after all, never shared that kind of closeness with Mac. It gave Elise a pang of sympathy—and forgiveness—for her friend. For her to have turned to Neil for closeness or connection or whatever it was! There was nothing, honestly nothing, he was in a good position to supply.

"Eat outside?" Laura said, scraping the eggs onto a plate.

"Perfect!" Chrissy affirmed, pulling silverware out of the drawer. "And we'll save some for Ula."

Feeling still slightly dazed from Laura's revelation and suddenly exhausted from the past few nights of no sleep, Elise grabbed the greasy plate of bacon and followed them outside.

6

THE BALL OF ANGER in Neil's chest was growing like a gradually inflating balloon. It gave him heartburn and took away his appetite. At night, it blocked his sleep for hours on end. And when finally he did doze off it gave him fitful, hyper-realistic dreams. He had been drawn into the all-American world of products and lowest common denominators that he had for so long despised, and then, on the ugly, corrupt terms of this greed-driven environment, he had been fucked. Not only by a vindictive and crazy woman he had been sleeping with, but also by . . . how was he supposed to even think of Jenny—an old friend? An ex-girlfriend? *The mother of his baby?*

It was impossible that Galena's actions were unknown to Jenny. She was Galena's boss, after all, and a control freak of the first order. She was also *Jenny*. The ludicrousness and injustice of her involvement in this debacle was appalling. Objectively. It had cost him not only his job but his dignity, and the one worthwhile creative idea he had had in the last ten years. The Sphinx became more and more beautiful, more and more brilliant and appealing as it receded from his grasp. To have squandered it in a stupid computer game! To have had to relinquish control of it—its milky threads of DNA, its careful symbolic heritage, its secrets. It should have been—what? A book? An artwork? The subject of some thought-provoking article? Something more meaningful and more his.

At two a.m. Neil was wide awake and sweating in the tangle of sheets he had scavenged out of Johnson's rudimentary linen closet. The moon was bright and full and shone through the tiny cracks of the venetian blinds with a splintery boldness. He had been up since five a.m. He had walked all the way to Roslindale in his brooding deliberations this afternoon. Didn't he deserve to sleep? The echo of the language that had so galled him on the Setlan commercial registered ironically. He was no better than your average American asshole, thinking about what he "deserved."

He kicked off the covers and sat bolt upright. Even Albert Sorenson Jones had never had trouble sleeping. And Jones was a twisted individual.

Neil stepped into his jeans, pulled on a T-shirt, and went out.

He did not know where he was going at first. Just out onto the street, which was as empty and, this being Boston, as shut down as a party bus on New Year's Day. So when he found himself in his car and driving west, he could still think, on one level, that he had no plan—just escape. Escape, escape, and escape. This was a ruse he kept up all the way to Wellesley, listening to an old Nick Cave CD he found on the floor of his car. It was warmer than he had realized and he kept the windows open and let the air howl through the car. When he turned onto Belleview Road he turned the music off. The gig was up. He was not just driving. He had driven *here.*

He pulled the car over to the side of the road, exactly where he had left it on his last little trespassing walkabout, and started up the drive on foot. The vision taking shape in his head was an act of vandalism: he would slit the tires of Jenny's car or scratch something hateful on that pretentiously grand McMansion door. But then, emerging into the open expanse of damp, impossibly even lawn, he saw it: an open window at the far corner of the house.

And it beckoned to him, presenting the deeper blackness within alluringly, a secret to be plumbed. He had never broken into anything before, but it seemed astonishingly simple. Why hadn't he? Neil crossed the lawn to the window, which opened over an empty flower bed, the earth freshly turned and mulched and redolent of sticky, fermenting pine chips. There was a screen, of course, but, breathing rapidly, blood pounding in his face and adrenaline coursing through his veins, Neil took the penknife from his key chain and sliced into this fiercely. It was harder than it looked, cutting a screen. He sawed away as if his life depended on it, expecting, at any moment, an alarm to go off. But there was nothing except the tinny squeak and scrape of his knife. Finally he managed to cut and tear enough of the screen away that he could reach in and slide the window all the way open. In a burst of unfamiliar strength he ripped the remainder of the screen away and hoisted himself up onto the sill, stuck his upper body inside, and pulled himself through.

He had entered the dining room. A formal table stretched out long and shiny in the moonlight. At the far end of the room there was a hideous framed modern painting—something full of sterile, geometric blocks.

There was a part of Neil that expected, at any moment, to see Jenny—that *hoped*, almost, to see her. He was so charged on anger and adrenaline he felt himself to be in a position of righteousness, even here, having broken into the sanctified and private terrain of her house. But she did not appear. He stood for a few long moments in that dining room listening and waiting, but there was nothing, just the oppressive buzz of closely attended silence.

He made his way through this and across a large, empty living room into the front hall, with its arched stairway and second-floor balustrade. A giant chandelier glittered faintly in reflected moonlight and Neil could see the dark shape of himself in a mirror on the opposite wall. He averted his eyes.

There was no squeak or groan of the stairs—the carpeting was thick and the boards beneath it new and probably treated with some rubbery and invincible synthetic that made them give under his weight. At the top of the stairs he stopped again, trying to listen. And there was a great relief that came with the ascent of the animal in him—a muting of all the garbage that usually filled his mind. Just basic instincts, purity of purpose.

And what was his purpose? He did not ask himself this. He did not tell himself this. But somewhere, in his journey through the house, it had taken shape in his mind. Unnameable and profound. He was here to reclaim what was his.

Stepping lightly on the sides of his feet, muscles taut, heart still pounding, Neil started down the hall. The door at the end of this was partway open and he knew instinctively what this was: the master bedroom. This was not where his business lay. It was the door to the left of this and closer to the stairs that he was looking for. There was, it turned out, an obvious marker on it: a pillow embroidered with the words "*Baby Sleeping*," hanging from the knob. He paused for a moment, listening to some sort of soothing electronic rush coming from within.

And then he opened the door—twisted the shiny brass knob and stepped in.

Immediately there was the palpable energy of another human being—a charge of breath and sentience in the air. In the darkness, the obscure shapes of stuffed animals, a beanbag chair, a rocker, took on a shadowy dignity.

There was a movement in the crib—a rustle of fabric and slight crackle of mattress. It sent a jolt of excitement and panic through Neil. What if the baby began crying? For some reason he had not considered this.

But the baby didn't. Slowly, carefully, Neil approached the crib, which was in the darkest corner of the room. At first he could not even make out which end of the little bundle was the baby's head, but as his eyes adjusted he could see the round, bald slope of it, the little hands clasped as if in prayer before his face.

And looking down at him, he was filled with a kind of wonderment. Out of some small sampling of his genetic material had come this fully formed little being, who would someday grow up just like everyone else and become a man. As he stared at the little legs encased in the soft cotton of the baby's sleeper suit, at the little dignified, peaceful face, he felt the pull of some strong attachment. He wanted to know what this little body felt like: he wanted to hold him like a father holds his son.

Gingerly, he reached his hands into the crib, slid them around the baby's back. It did not matter, he realized, if the baby cried. He had to hold him. It was the only thing that mattered right now. He had to know what holding his baby felt like.

And somehow, miraculously, the baby did not wake. He grunted and frowned in Neil's awkward clutch, and stretched one little arm up over his head, but he did not cry. It felt, at first, terrifying: the lightness of his body, the fragility of the little limbs. But gradually, as Neil held him, he became more accustomed to this. Began, even, to feel there was a contagious buoyancy to the baby, as if his lightness gave them both an ability to rise. With growing confidence, Neil edged toward the rocking chair.

Once he was seated, he could really look at the baby. It was evident, right away, how much the boy looked like Jenny. The tilt of his little nose, the wide-set eyes, even the dark hair, which already gave a hint of being curly. But there was, Neil thought, a grain of himself in the straight little mouth and the chin. He hoped, it struck him suddenly, he had not given him much more. The boy would be much better served by inheriting Jenny's uncynical view of the world and unquestioning taste for success. In fact, he would be better served also by her hearty disposition, athletic ability, and social skills. Jenny's way of life was not one that Neil admired. It was not a way of life he had faith in. But it was a lucky one to be born into.

And with this, the question of what the hell he was doing here, in the baby's room, reappeared in his head. He had arrived compelled by the impulse to get back at Jenny. To punish her for everything she had done and everything she was. For all she stood for and all she had taken from him. But did he . . . ? Had he come in to . . . ?

He had not considered the flesh-and-blood fact of this baby, now sleeping so sweetly in his arms: that he could cry, that he would need to eat—what did he even eat anyway? breast milk? bottled milk? oatmeal and bananas?—that he would need his mother. Above all. Below him the baby's little fist clenched and unclenched in his sleep. He was a *baby*, not a Sphinx, not some transparent catalog of DNA. Not a belonging. And meanwhile, he, Neil Banks, despiser of all things material, of the American obsession with property, of the bare-bones mine-and-yours atti-tude capitalism spawned, had come here to *steal* his child. The realization of his hypocrisy was like a physical blow. He had come with the vague urge to protect the child—from what? The answer presented itself clearly at once: he needed to protect his baby from himself.

It was in the middle of this horrifying recognition that the baby began to cry. The first bleat from his mouth sent a bolt of adrenaline through Neil. After this first noise the baby stopped short and stared up at him, his dark eyes—huge now that they were open—seeming to be taking in the very essence of Neil. Neil tried, shakily, to smile. But to his dismay this made the baby cry in earnest, a real blood-curdling howl that squinched his face up into an angry ball. And with this, Neil's calm, come-what-may attitude left him. He had to ditch this angry, howling little being and get the hell out. But how? The baby writhed and arched his back and Neil practically had to wrestle him into submission as he scrambled up out of the chair in a blind effort to put him back into the crib.

In his moment of hesitation (was it inhumane to put down a screaming baby? had he somehow injured him? or was his shaky smile simply an intrinsically terrifying thing?) Jenny appeared.

She screamed when she saw him—a guttural, instinctive cry every bit as horrible as the baby's wails.

"It's me—Jenny, it's Neil. It's okay—it's okay," he began babbling, holding out the baby, whose howls literally felt as though they might kill him. "Take him, take him—I just—I didn't do anything, he just started—"

Jenny grabbed the boy, wild-eyed, and pressed him against her shoulder and began murmuring soothingly into his ear and bobbing up and down, walking toward the door. Neil stood frozen beside the crib, listening to the faint murmur of her voice. What the fuck was he doing? Should he just leave? Clear the hell out and run for cover? But this would put his actions in not only a bizarre, but a malevolent light. And he had never wanted to harm the baby. He needed to explain this.

Jenny's footsteps approached again from the far end of the hall, and wherever she had gone, whatever she had done, had calmed the baby down. He was still on her shoulder, wide-eyed, looking around incredulously.

"What the fuck are you doing here?" Jenny hissed.

"I'm sorry." Neil shifted his weight. "I'm wrong. I'm totally in the wrong."

Jenny gave him a wincing, incredulous look at the understatement. In her fuzzy terry-cloth robe, with her wildly curly hair down, she looked young, like a teenager, or even a little girl. It was unnerving. In his mind she had become a giant—hard and impervious, perpetually in makeup and a business suit.

"But what are you *doing*?" she said.

"I just wanted to—" Neil became suddenly extremely, dangerously tired. Where to begin his explanation? "I wanted to see the baby," he said finally.

"To *see* him?" Jenny repeated. She hugged the baby's head to her. "Why didn't you just call? Or email?"

"I didn't think you'd want to hear from me." It came out sounding peevish, pathetic even.

"I'd rather *hear* from you than find you standing in my son's bedroom in the middle of the night," she hissed.

There was nothing to say to this.

"I called the police," Jenny said.

It was logical, of course, but the knowledge settled over Neil with a crushing heaviness. He crouched down and pressed the heels of his hands to his eyes.

"Are you okay?" Jenny asked. There was an edge of panic in her voice.

Neil nodded. It was silent for a moment—the thick rush of electronic white noise filling the air around them like some heavier medium than oxygen. For a moment he and Jenny regarded each other through the darkness like strangers. But beneath this he could feel the deep-down movement of the past—faint slides of their former selves playing against the rock wall that had risen between them. They had known each other in a more innocent time—had glimpsed and consorted with each other's more hopeful and promising selves.

"You know I lost my job," he said impulsively.

"You . . . ?" Jenny blanched visibly. "On account of that email?"

Neil nodded.

Jenny had been leaning against the doorframe, and at this she slid down until she was sitting on the floor, back propped against the wall, baby now sleeping in her arms.

And to Neil's great surprise, she started to cry. Her shoulders shook and a kind of gentle hum escaped from her mouth, but as far as he could see she was tearless. There was a kind of violence to her crying that made sense. Somehow, the baby remained asleep.

"Shit," he said, squatting down and resting his own forehead, for a moment, on his palms. He could hear Jenny's shoulders shaking against the wall.

"I'm sorry," she said, her face bowed, buried against the soft bulk of the baby on her shoulder. "I was going to say something tomorrow— I should have done it earlier."

Her voice sounded muffled, small, un-Jenny-like. It was almost eerie. And deeply unnerving.

"Where's Jeremy?" Neil asked. "Are you alone here?"

"Jeremy?" Jenny asked, raising her face. "He's doped up. You could set the smoke alarm off and he wouldn't hear."

"Oh." The extremity and, what was it—resignation? or defeat?— of her tone startled him. "What, is he sick?"

Jenny's gaze froze on him.

Neil felt his stomach drop.

"He has cancer. Advanced renal cancer."

"Jesus.

"I'm sorry," Neil added after a moment, the shock of the information sounding through him.

Jenny seemed to draw herself together and sit up straighter against the wall. "I'm giving him an arsenal of pills every four hours, and keeping track of the appointments and the insurance, and going to work every morning, and I can't—I can't deal with you going psycho. Look at me, Neil."

Even across the room, across the dark, he could see the steely brightness of her eyes.

"I'm sorry I didn't . . . prevent this situation with your job. I really, truly am, and I will do my best to undo that. But you can't do this. You can't show up in the middle of the night in Colin's bedroom. Whatever you want, Neil," she enunciated very slowly and deliberately. "Just ask me. Visiting rights. Money. Whatever. Email me. *Sue* me. Just. Don't. Be. Crazy."

Carefully, she rose and, with some struggle to make her motions smooth, slid up the doorframe just as she had slid down. On her shoulder the baby stirred—lifted his little head and made a whimpering sound.

"I will break, Neil. I will." And the way she said it—fiercely, hair wild, and eyes flashing—he believed her. And he was afraid. She was unbreakable. No one would want to see her fall apart.

The sound of sirens in the distance was growing louder. Neil stood, lurching slightly to his feet. And then suddenly there was Jeremy, standing in the doorway of the bedroom.

"What's going on?" he said, flicking on the overhead light, which threw the room suddenly into the weird relief of the ordinary. And at the threshold of this was Jeremy himself: shockingly gaunt and unhealthy-looking. He wore a gray terry-cloth robe that hung from his body, and leather slippers. He was still—as Neil remembered him—strikingly tall.

"Don't worry," Jenny said hastily, wiping a hand over her eyes. "It's okay—you should be sleeping."

Jeremy looked from her to Neil. And under his gaze, Neil was filled with an overwhelming shame. His own malcontent, his own sorrows and bitterness, and whatever else had led him here—what were they in comparison to this? The man was dying. He was standing there, knowing he would probably die.

"What are you doing here?" Jeremy said simply.

"I just—I wanted—" Neil began, the words sticking in his throat. "I made a mistake."

"He broke in," Jenny said, a certain hardness returning to her voice.

The blare of the sirens was approaching.

"To do what?" Jeremy asked, his eyes boring into Neil.

"I don't know. Just . . . to *see* him—honest to God. I just wanted to . . . see him."

There was the violent crunch of wheels on the gravel drive, and in Jenny's arms Colin began once again to cry.

"Tell them to go," Jeremy said, looking at Jenny, who nodded without blinking. She extended the crying baby to Jeremy. Despite his frailty, he held the child easily, and in his arms Colin hushed immediately.

There was pounding on the door downstairs and then the sound of it opening, the blare of police radios, and, quietly between these, Jenny's voice.

"I'm sorry," Neil began again, shifting his weight. "I'll get out of your hair—and you don't have to worry that I'll come back—that I'll—"

"No," Jeremy interrupted. "Let's sit down," he said. "When they go."

There was the sound of heavy footsteps on the stairs. Of course the cops would not just take off. Neil knew enough about cops to know that. And weirdly there was some part of Neil that *wanted* them to take him, lock him up, make him atone for his transgression.

"I think it's time we talked," Jeremy said, shifting the baby, who seemed suddenly preternaturally calm, looking around with wide eyes, almost, in fact, like the Sphinx.

7

THE FIRST THING LAURA DID when she hung up the phone was bend all the way over and let the blood rush to her head. Then she considered whether the horrible washing feeling in her stomach was going to make her throw up.

Neil was losing his mind. Clearly. But that was not what made her so sick. He was "sleeping with some twit" in Jenny's office. That had been only a grain of the outlandish events Jenny had relayed, but Laura had remained stuck on it. That, in all probability, while he was fucking her, he had been also fucking this other woman, or girl, really—Laura imagined a perky-breasted teenager, sly and blond and completely oblivious to the blights of stretch marks or cellulite. Or worse, he had *begun* fucking this girl in the middle of his affair with her and the comparative pleasure of her nubile young flesh had been responsible for his disappearance from Laura's romantic life.

In the face of this, the lull that had settled over Laura's own attraction to Neil seemed unimportant. She had been cast off, rejected, abandoned for someone with a better ass. It stung piteously.

Laura dragged herself upstairs through the suddenly very quiet, very lonely house to shower. It was midmorning: Genevieve was at her summer camp and Miranda and Kaaren were at the park. Under the steaming water Laura ran her hands over her body. It had borne two children and survived. Every month it readied her uterus for more children, dependably, even hopefully. And it was still beautiful—the slope of her breasts was longer, but still lovely, the nipples still small and pink and delicately ridged. Her hips were broader than they had been when she was twenty, but her legs were lean and strong and agile—from what? Climbing the stairs? Pressing the accelerator? In the face of vast neglect, they were holding up valiantly.

Neil had been fired. And he had broken in—broken in!—to Jenny's house to see the baby. Clearly he was losing it. She had been on to something when she brought this up with Chrissy and Elise. Even in her cloud of hurt, she began to feel worried.

She went through the day in state of distraction, picking Genevieve up from camp and facilitating a playdate with her manipulative friend June, managing Miranda's tantrums, microwaving edamame and mac and cheese. Kaaren had the afternoon off for the weaving workshop she was obsessed with and Laura missed her usual competent, if joyless, presence in the house.

Getting into bed alone—Mac was not due home until the end of the weekend—she tried to read the paper (never mind that it was yesterday's).

When finally she dropped the pretense of reading and allowed herself to simply lie in bed in the darkness and think, she was surprised at how quickly sleep overcame her. She was more tired, apparently, than she had realized.

She dreamt about Neil. An awful, unsettling dream in which he appeared on her doorstep looking like death: pale and gaunt and slightly wild-eyed. He seemed to have been stabbed or somehow otherwise wounded. *Let me see—can I get you something? A bandage? Should we call the hospital?* She had asked, but he wouldn't let her see what was the matter. He had made a great effort to see her, but was now frustratingly silent.

It reminded her of the dreams she'd had after her mother died—

dreams of return, in which her mother came back, hair hanging loose around her shoulders and exaggerating the girlishness that had clung to her even in the final days of her life. And Laura would be overjoyed to see her, but then would realize all was not well. That her mother was dying, or was already dead, and that the great, uncomfortable effort to make herself present had completely exhausted her. *Mama,* Laura would say, reaching out, trying to hug her, *please don't go. Stay.*

It was a worrisome version of this sadness that drove her, the next morning, to turn onto Storrow Drive after dropping Genevieve off at camp, instead of heading back home to finish her now-overdue contribution to *The Beacon.* She made her way along the wide, congested stretch of Brookline Avenue that ran alongside the big hospitals—Beth Israel, Children's, the Brigham—and had a flash of Jenny and Jeremy, up there somewhere, behind one of the giant floor-to-ceiling windows. What would Jenny do if he died? Would she meet someone new? Or go through life a single mother? And what about Colin? What must Jeremy think or feel when he looked at this baby, who in all probability would never really know him?

And then she was in Jamaica Plain. She parked the car opposite Neil's triple-decker, dug her hands deep into her pockets, and crossed the street. At the door, she pressed the buzzer and waited with a growing sense of anxiety. Neil's car was on the street—she could see it just a little way down the block. He was home—she was sure. What if— She did not allow herself to finish the thought. But then, just as she was groping in her bag for her cell phone to try calling as well, there was the creak of floorboards and, yes, it was Neil, traipsing down the stairs clad in jeans and a T-shirt and looking reassuringly normal.

"Lo!" he said, turning the multitude of locks and opening the door. "What are you doing here?"

"I just—wanted to see if you were okay," she said. It was cool out despite the fact that it was nearly the Fourth of July. The wan sun had disappeared behind a cloud and Laura hugged her arms tightly around herelf.

"Ahh." Neil sighed and ran a hand over his stubbly hair. "So you talked to Jenny."

Laura nodded.

"Come up." He titled his head. "I have . . . water I can offer you."

Upstairs, the sight of Neil's packed bags greeted her: two scrappy duffels and a backpack resting on the floor of the hallway.

"What's this?" she asked. "Are you going somewhere?"

Neil disappeared into the kitchen without answering. "Water?" he asked, when she followed him in.

"Are you leaving?"

Neil leaned against the counter—the same counter, it occurred to her, where they had had their first kiss. There was not even a vestige of that excitement left.

"Is that surprising?" Neil countered.

Laura accepted the water he held out and sat down. "Did you—you lost your job?"

"Nah—they apologized. Jenny called them or something. I could go back."

"But you don't want to."

"Fuck that."

She stared at him for a moment.

"Was this just a total disaster for you—this return . . . home?"

Neil looked back at her directly. "No," he said. "No it wasn't."

They were silent for a moment, and from down in the yard there was the sound of the dog—of Amos—barking his signature high-pitched yelp.

"He's not on your watch this time, is he?" Laura said.

Neil shook his head.

"What a drama queen."

Neil smiled. "You're a good person, to come check on me, Lo."

Laura squinted her eyes at him. "Especially since I heard about the marketing girl," she said.

Neil blanched. "Galena?"

"Is that what her name is?"

"God." Neil slapped his forehead. "That was a mistake. I'm an idiot. It meant nothing, you know—just—"

Laura waved this away. "Don't. Don't."

"Lo." Neil crouched down in front of her, reminding her again of that first afternoon, what seemed like so long ago. "If I were another person—"

"Stop."

Neil hung his head and then finally rose and then dropped into the other green and chrome dinette-set chair.

Laura smiled. "So were you even going to say goodbye if I hadn't come here?"

Neil hesitated. "I wanted to write."

"Of course." Outside, Amos finally stopped yapping.

"And Jenny?" she ventured. "And Colin—are you going to try to get some kind of custody . . . ?"

Neil shook his head. "Look at me, Lo. What would a baby want with me?"

"*Anything*, Neil. You're a good—"

"Jenny's a good mother," Neil cut her off. "You were right. She's . . . Jenny, but she loves him. And he already has a father. I just wanted to see him."

Laura regarded him closely. There was something different about him. He looked sad, but also calmer somehow—less animated by reaction and impulse.

"Will you keep in touch with them—with him?"

"Yeah," Neil said thoughtfully. "I want . . ." he seemed to grope about for a moment, and then looked squarely at her. "I want to make something out of myself—do something he can be proud of."

Laura nodded, the thought of her own girls—her own sweet babies—creeping in around the edges of her mind. "That's a noble idea."

For a moment they were silent.

"He's of the future, Lo. I'm of . . ."

"The past?"

"No." Neil shook his head. "The sidelines."

Laura considered this. "Where does that leave me?"

Neil regarded her carefully. "The past."

She had asked this lightly. But it ushered in a crushing sense of sadness. *The past.* She was like Laura Ingalls Wilder or something, the typewriter, the phonograph, a ghost . . .

There was screech of brakes outside the window, followed by shouting.

"Well. I should be going," she said, standing, when she was sure her voice would not fail her.

"Thanks for coming, Lo," Neil said, as they walked down the long creaky hall to the door. "Thank you for everything—I'm sorry I dragged you down with me—because you deserve—" He smiled and shook his head inscrutably. "I mean, I *want* you to be happy, I *wish* I could have made you happy."

And in one of those rare moments of grace that usually only arrived to her afterward in the form of regret, Laura put a hand to his lips. "You did," she said, half truthfully. "Take care of yourself." She looked him full in the eyes. "You're worth it."

Letting herself into her house, she was surprised to see Mac's briefcase and suit jacket in the entryway. It was only Friday—she had not expected him until Sunday. A rush of guilt and the fear that somehow she had been found out darted through her, quickening her heartbeat. From upstairs there was the sound of Kaaren reading a story to Miranda before her nap.

Laura walked down the hall into the kitchen looking for her husband. She had been doing errands, she prepped herself guiltily. No—there was nothing to show for this—she had had a doctor's appointment. A routine checkup.

But Mac was not in the kitchen. He was not in the living room either. He had gone upstairs, maybe. Laura was starting toward the stairs when she saw a movement from the library—the darkest, most unfinished-looking room in their house, embarrassingly light on books. Mac was standing just inside the threshold of this, his back to her.

"You're home!" Laura said nervously, and he turned. There were deep circles under his eyes—he had been working hard. And the fatigue somehow made his face softer, or more thoughtful than usual.

"The deal collapsed."

"With the developer?"

Mac nodded.

"Oh, no! I'm sorry." Laura rose onto her tiptoes to give him a kiss.

"It's bad," he said. "The market's collapsing all over. It's not just us."

Laura felt a chill of premonition. Was this how the end began? Bad news in the paper. Bad news from Mac's work. Mac home at noon. Was this the beginning of that time she had become convinced was around the corner—that time when they would need to grow their own food in the backyard, and use their fireplaces for heat rather than pleasure? When even Americans like the Eliases would know insecurity and want?

How bad? she was about to ask Mac. *What kind of bad?* when he spoke.

"It's really coming along," he said. And Laura followed his gaze to her tapestry. She had forgotten it was there. Last night when she had finished her obsessive work on it in the wee hours of the morning she had spread it over the back of the library couch.

"Kind of," she said. And for a moment they stood side by side, looking. It was beautiful.

"Kind of funny to think of why your mom picked that out, isn't it? That picture?" Mac said thoughtfully.

Laura looked up to read his expression. It was genuinely contemplative.

She put a hand on his back, which felt warm and firm through the thin shirt cloth. "I guess it was just what she wanted to look at," she said.

And for a moment she felt as if she and Mac were on the same side of a great divide, looking across. In a flash she recognized how strange this was—how usually she felt she was on the other side of this chasm from him, not alone, but with her mother, the two of them a unit sufficient enough to render real connection with anyone else unnecessary. It was like discovering that the person you had been talking with, you had been thinking was right beside you as you walked down a crowded street, had somehow ducked off and been replaced by a stranger. But this stranger had a trustworthy face. Reliable, strong, beleaguered.

Tentatively she reached over and took his hand.

8

THIS WAS WHAT JENNY HAD PICTURED for Colin's first birthday party: fifty or sixty people, a giant lion-shaped cake from Party Favors, mimosas and Bellinis, and a paid performer of some sort— the guy who played ukelele or that guitar-playing clown. There were going to be gold and silver balloons (the Mylar kind that were *not* a choking hazard) and flowers from Winston's.

Instead, the party consisted of Elise and Laura and their families, Maria, and Jenny's mother. The cake was one she had snagged last minute at the Market Basket. There weren't even balloons.

From up here at Colin's changing table, she could look out the window onto the back lawn, where everyone was hanging out. Maria was setting out paper plates and plastic utensils, Elise and Laura were enmeshed in conversation, Mac was on the grass, crawling around with Miranda on his back. In the corner of the terrace, Chrissy sat at the edge of a chaise lounge, elbows on her knees, leaning into her conversation with Jeremy. Jeremy himself was reclining on the matching chaise, a light blanket over his legs. Jenny could not see his face, which was hidden under a baseball cap. The chemo had given him an awful raised and pimply red rash: he had to block every possible ray of sun.

"Mamamamama," Colin began to chant, twisting suddenly to sit himself upright.

"Excuse me, young man!" Jenny said, reminded of the task at

hand. "No partying without a diaper!" She pushed him back and Colin wailed indignantly. He was impossible to change lately, lying still for a few moments and then suddenly, just as she was about to slide a new diaper under him, scrambling in all directions, forcing her to pin him down or change him while he stood pulling at her hair, thumping on her shoulders, threatening at any moment to fall off the table.

Jenny was actually fine with this development. In the last weeks Colin had begun to come out of his shell. He smiled more often and made crazy little shouting sounds whenever he was allowed to indulge his new obsession: crawling. And his crawl itself was just about the cutest thing Jenny had ever seen. His hair had come in too—the softest spray of brown curls, a daintier version of Jenny's own.

She pulled his little jeans back up and leaned down to kiss his belly—that smooth, slim little plain of perfection, still devoid of baby fat. "Let's go, birthday boy," she said, scooping him up.

"Mamamama," Colin chanted again, craning around to look out the window now that he was upright.

"See?" Jenny said. "Your friends." Together they watched as Mac foisted Miranda from his back and replaced her with one of the twins, both of whom were yelping with delight. It was an unusual scene—Mac at ease, playing with the children, and automatically Jenny filed it away to trot out in response to Laura's next round of husband complaints. Colin put a hand on the window and began to bang.

As of two days ago, Jenny was officially on leave from work. Finally, she had told Eric. She had coaxed, cajoled, and ultimately whipped herself into his office with the confession. The speech she had planned, the explanation of not only the cancer but of her own secrecy, was crisp and thorough, but once she was in Eric's office, the facts had burst out of her completely unscripted, and in the most unprofessional way.

"You've been sitting on this for *how* long, Jennifer?" Eric had asked, laying his giant football player's paws flat on the desk.

There had been silence for a few moments, punctuated only by Jenny's sniffling, and from far below the rush of city sounds.

"You know your job here is secure," Eric said. "You are the best talent we have here—you take a few months off if you want, you take a year off—your job will be here. Waiting for you to come back."

The gravity of his expression, the genuine sadness, and beneath this, the *remorse*, were affecting. Eric Watson felt not only sorry, but responsible for her silence. "I don't know what kind of place I've made you feel like you work for"—he shook his head—"that you would keep quiet about this for so long."

Jenny had wanted to reassure him that it was not him. It was not Genron. It was *her*—but she found herself uncharacteristically unable to speak. It was maybe his likeness to her father—or if not actual likeness, the equation she had created between the two men in her mind. She just sat there in his office like a little girl and cried. It was mortifying in retrospect. But at the moment it had felt almost joyous. The relief of giving up her secret had been physical. Her whole body felt like a collection of brittle sticks turned suddenly to light, flexible liquid.

So now, when Jeremy went in for this next round of chemo, Jenny would go with him. *And* she would come home for the afternoon and take Colin out in the jogging stroller and give him dinner and a bath. It would not be either/or. She would not oversee the launch, next week, of the new national Setlan PPD ad campaign. It was out there. And she had conceived of it. Now, as Eric put it, it would have to walk on its own two legs.

She had wrangled one thing out of Eric: an okay for her to call off the dogs on poor Neil Banks the "corporate spy." *I just know he isn't,* she had explained. *I've known him a long time. Look—it's been four weeks now, and what news is there about anyone else launching a copycat campaign?* Of course, it was too late; he had already been fired. But she had done her best to rectify the wrong. She had suffered through an awkward, tail-between-the-legs conversation with this obnoxious Rod Emerus and done her best to make things right. And the company had offered him his job back. But Neil was not going back to work. He was leaving the country. He had told her this when she called to invite him to the party. She and Jeremy had offered him an agreement: visitation rights with Colin and recognition as the boy's biological father. He could do what he wanted with that. At the moment that seemed to be very little, but he had been happy with the possibility and the openness. It had felt to Jenny herself like a relief. The truth was out. Now maybe somehow, it would set them free?

Back downstairs, Jenny kissed Colin on the soft crown of his head and handed him to Maria. As usual, he let out a cackle of delight. It didn't matter how little time had elapsed since he had last seen Maria—fifteen minutes or a weekend. He was always overjoyed to reconnect. Jenny had gotten over her jealousy of this. She was his mother, after all.

Maria whisked him off to go play with the other children on the lawn and Jenny began making Bloody Marys. She had never been much of a bartender—or a drinker, for that matter—but this left her unhampered by some sense of how to make the drinks right. She filled a few glasses with ice cubes and splashed a liberal amount of vodka over these, poured in the cloudy red mixer, and as an afterthought grabbed some wilted celery stalks out of the refrigerator to stick into each glass.

"Sweetie?" she said, stopping first at Jeremy's side. "I made this one extra light."

"Thanks." Jeremy extended his hand for it distractedly. His face bore the focused expression Jenny had come to recognize as his disease-talk look.

"Are you okay over here? Are you warm enough?"

Jeremy nodded his head. "I'm fine. Did you know Chrissy's cousin had renal cell cancer?"

"No," Jenny said, looking over at Chrissy. It was the last thing she liked to hear about: more cancer. Other people's cancer. Other people's miraculous recoveries and strategies and treatments. But Jeremy thrived on it, sucking information out of the tiniest scraps of narrative, gleaning data, conducting his own surveys. Jenny recognized that he needed to do it. This was how he had always succeeded in business—his drive, his thoroughness, his one-track mind. He was going to outmaneuver this disease.

"Where was he treated?" she asked, forcing herself to engage.

"Johns Hopkins," Chrissy answered. And in the moment that their eyes met Jenny could see that Chrissy understood. She understood what Jeremy wanted, and she understood what Jenny didn't want, and she would supply both. Jenny was grateful.

"One for you?" Jenny asked, holding out her tray.

"Why, thank you." Chrissy batted her eyelashes. "That looks just perfect."

And Jenny was free to continue her rounds.

Elise was now leaning against the stone wall of the terrace beside Genevieve, deep in conversation. The little girl had her hair in braids and was twitching the paintbrush-like tip of one of these over her cheek.

"You two look serious," Jenny said, and both of them looked at her as if she were an unexpected stranger, someone who spoke a different language.

"I was just explaining photosynthesis," Elise said by way of explanation. "Genevieve asked."

"Ahhhhh, very important." Jenny raised her eyebrows. "Bloody Mary? For grown-ups only, sweetie, sorry," she said to Genevieve, who gave her a withering look in return.

"I *know*."

"Oh, I'm sorry—sometimes I forget that you're seventeen."

This elicited a giggle from Genevieve. It was their running joke. She was such a pretty girl, with her pale hair and slim bones and Laura's big gray eyes. And leaning there against the wall with Elise, she really did look like a little adult. Some waify, thoughtful-looking supermodel who would do ads for perfume or one of those ethereal designers.

"No, thank you," Elise passed on the drink—so sensible, as always —and Jenny continued her rounds.

Laura was now out on the lawn with Mac and Miranda and the boys. She was sitting, her cotton skirt spread over the grass and legs extended, with Miranda hanging around her neck. And she was talking to Mac, who had paused, head up and eyebrows raised, with Nigel on his back. Jenny could not hear what Laura was saying, but it was punctuated by the bark of Mac's laugh.

"Onward!" Mac bellowed, charging forward on his knees. On his back, Nigel shrieked and gripped his little fingers tighter into Mac's hair. The easy luck of the scene struck Jenny: Mac and Laura playing with the children, a husband and wife and their progeny romping on the green grass, all laughter and good health. Never mind that this was not a scene she and Colin and Jeremy would ever have enacted even before the cancer. She felt the ice-cold tentacles of envy rise in her throat. But she blinked and forced herself to swallow them down. She would not allow herself self-pity: that was not a Jenny Callahan approach.

Instead she hoisted the tray of drinks—now down to two—aloft. "Want one?" she said, approaching Laura.

"Mm, delicious!" Laura laughed, peeling Miranda's arms from around her neck and scrambling to get up. "But I've been so unhelpful! What can I do?"

"Sit down, sit down," Jenny commanded. "Nothing. Have a drink. The food will be ready in a minute."

"Let me help—"

"My mother's in charge. Just sit. Really." Below them, on the sunken terrace, Judy Callahan was bustling around with a platter of quiches, a giant bowl of fruit salad, and—her own insistent contribution—a bowl of "ambrosia": mandarin oranges, coconut, and Cool Whip.

"Well, where's *your* drink, then?" Laura said.

Jenny shrugged. "Right here, I guess."

Laura patted the lawn beside her.

"Let me get Colin," Jenny said, and returned in a moment with the happy, wiggly birthday boy, whom Maria had crowned with a sparkly blue and silver cardboard hat. Jenny took a sip of the Bloody Mary, which was outrageously strong, and let Colin scramble off her lap and onto Laura's skirt.

"So Mac is quite the Pied Piper today," Jenny said. "To what do we owe the honor of his presence?"

"The market crashing?" Laura said.

"Is it that bad?"

Laura shrugged. "You know I think the apocalypse is coming, so I'm not the person to ask."

"You do?" Jenny asked, genuinely surprised. Laura had always been sort of softly, uninformedly liberal, but not actually engaged in the state of the world in any concrete sense.

"Kind of." Laura sighed. "But that's not birthday party talk, is it?" she smiled down at Colin, who was busily trying to remove her bracelet.

"Since when did you become some sort of doomsayer?"

"Me?"

To Jenny's surprise, Laura colored and looked, almost nervously, down at her hand in the grass. "Oh, I don't know, just reading the news . . ."

And suddenly Jenny understood. Laura's recent skitteryness, her aura of contrition, her reclaimed flush. She had slept with Neil. The revelation was stunning. Jenny stared at her.

"What?" Laura said. "What's the matter?" She lifted a telltale hand to her throat.

Jenny shook her head, feeling suddenly dizzy. *Laura was sleeping with—or at least had slept with—Neil.* "Nothing," she said automatically, scrambling to her feet. "I'll be right back."

"Are you okay?" Laura asked.

Jenny nodded without looking at her. "Just watch him a moment, will you?" She gestured at Colin, who was still entranced with Laura's necklace.

"Of course—but— " she could hear Laura saying, but she kept walking, putting one foot in front of the other, into the house, blood singing in her ears.

"Grab the ketchup while you're in there," Judy Callahan called merrily, obliviously, after her.

Jenny walked past Elise and Chrissy and Genevieve and Jeremy, huddled still in his somber place on the chaise. Through the French doors and across the sleek hardwood floor of the sunroom, over the Persian-style carpeting, and up the stairs. Vase, mirror, carpet, photos, she took in the objects fervently, using their familiarity to press all else out.

Until finally, sitting on the foot of her own bed, facing the dressing room mirror, she allowed herself to *think. Think!* She had only a few moments before someone would come looking for her. The urgency of the predicament made her sweat.

She had been betrayed. That was one thing. Her friend, one of her two best friends, had slept with . . . what was Neil? Her old boy-friend? Her baby's father? Her *enemy*? Whatever he was, he was *hers*. Jenny's brain faltered a moment over this: wasn't he? She pictured Neil as he had looked standing there when she had last seen him, hands shoved into his pockets in the moonlight, uneasy, shifting his weight from foot to foot. He was—it struck her suddenly—still handsome. He was still attractive, despite his failures, despite his squandered promise and derelict lifestyle.

And for a moment she felt an unexpected jealousy claw its way up in her—as if Neil were someone she was still in love with but had only just recognized. Too late.

But no—she rejected this. She could not see him that way. Certainly not after the other night. It was the utter foreignness of the whole experience—the complete impossibility of doing something as careless and foolish as having an affair—that hurt the most. Not that she cared so deeply about the behind-her-back circumstances of it—but almost precisely that she didn't. It didn't matter. It served only to emphasize the stark life-and-death difference of the planet she now inhabited. A planet in which such frivolities as sex and marital strife and attraction had no place. It filled her with a desperate sense of sadness for her old life.

In the mirror across from her, her face looked wooden, unchanged despite the enormous currents rocking through her.

Now there *were* footsteps on the stairs. Laura.

"I brought you a glass of water—are you okay?" she asked. "What happened?"

Jenny stared at her friend. "You slept with him, didn't you?" she said. It came out with remarkable dispassion.

"With . . . ?" Laura colored, and then darted a glance at Jenny's eyes. "Shit!"

For a moment the room filled with silence.

"I was going to tell you—" Laura said. "I kept meaning—I just didn't know if you would be . . . mad. It was stupid—I mean, I don't even know why—"

Laura's distress calmed Jenny. "It doesn't matter," she said flatly. "It doesn't matter to me."

Laura crossed the carpet and sat next to Jenny on the bed. She took her hand and, predictably, there were tears in her eyes. "I should have told you."

Jenny shook her head, her composure growing with Laura's discomfort. "I made a mistake," she said.

"A mistake?" Laura looked taken aback.

"Creating the situation I did with Neil. Making him stay out of our lives."

From outside there was the sound of voices—Chrissy, Mac, Judy Callahan . . . Miranda. Behind them, the alarm clock ticked.

"You did what you thought made the most sense," Laura said finally.

"Did you know—did you think it was stupid all along?" It was possible, it occurred to Jenny, that this was the first time she had ever asked Laura's opinion of the matter. Their conversation had always involved telling—Jenny *telling* Laura what she was going to do, Laura listening, nodding, reflecting back.

"Not stupid, no." Laura sighed and wiped her nose. She stood and walked over to the window.

"For him?"

Laura looked back at her. "For everyone."

Jenny nodded slowly. It *was* difficult. It was unrealistic. How could she, in this of all things, have had such a breach in judgment? She, Jenny Callahan, whose fiercest skill in life was to estimate and plan correctly?

"Jenny?" Judy Callahan's voice banged up the stairs. "Everyone's waiting for the cake!"

"Coming," Jenny called back through the closed door automatically.

"Shit." Laura sighed. But then she grabbed Jenny's arm with a sudden fierceness. "It'll be fine, though," she said, looking directly into her eyes. "Everything will be fine."

"Will it?" Jenny asked.

"It *will!*" Laura said, drawing her friend into an embrace. "I promise. It will be all right."

Later, when the quiches were portioned out, the Bloody Marys drained, the ambrosia (who would have thought?) finished, Judy Callahan brought out a bottle of champagne and a tray of fancy crystal flutes that Jenny herself never would have taken onto the flagstone terrace, though she did not protest. The party was unfolding around her as if on the other side of a thick, muffling blanket. Judy handed the bottle to her daughter proudly. "Can't have a birthday without champagne!"

Jenny untwisted the foil and wire dutifully and then handed the bottle on to Mac, who was standing beside her. In one smooth motion, his big thumbs pressed the cork out and it popped against the house with a dramatic bang.

Jenny held out the first flute for him to pour.

"Toast!" he demanded rollickingly, reminding her of the cocky business school student she had first known him as.

"Toast?" Jenny echoed, and as she said it, she felt panicky. A toast? To what exactly?

She looked around at the expectant faces—some (like Laura's and Elise's) displaying comprehension of the uncomfortable challenge of Mac's demand, and others (her mother's and Chrissy's) simply smiling enthustically. Jeremy, it seemed to her, was actually paying attention, for once. He was looking at her, his expression expectant—neither joyful *nor* afraid. Just waiting.

A warm wind rustled the treetops, and from the grass behind her

Jenny could hear the buzz of insects. The plastic Elmo tablecloth trembled.

"To Colin," Jenny said, forcing herself to move her lips. "To turning one. And"—she hesitated, waiting for words to save her from this precipice, "to this moment. All of us. Right here—" *Before.* She stopped the word on her tongue. It was not to be spoken. But it was the point, wasn't it?

And as she held it she felt focused on exactly what she had just named: this moment, these people in front of her, this place. It filled her mind completely, pushing out all the chatter of doubt and ambition and fear.

"Hear, hear," someone said. There were exclamations of "That's right!" and "Happy birthday!"

Jenny felt dazed. She could see Laura wiping a tear away with the back of her hand and Elise picking up Nigel. Jeremy tilted his head and something in his solemn face conveyed . . . was it approval? Or simply understanding? Looking into his eyes, she felt their connection.

"Mamamamama!" Colin babbled as Maria handed him to her. He was beginning to look tired and irritable, his face covered with vanilla frosting and crumbs of birthday cake.

"Hi, my big boy," Jenny said, pressing his warm, straining little body to her, feeling a foot dig into her belly, a shoulder squirm against her arm.

"We brought you something," Elise said, as she and Laura deposited a giant blue-and-green wrapped box on the table in front of her.

"Mamamama!" Colin cried.

"What on earth?" Jenny said. "It looks heavy!" And looking at her two friends she felt a glow of love spread over her.

"Well?" Elise said. "Are you going to open it?"

Shifting Colin over on her hip, Jenny tore in.

9

LIFTING OFF THE GROUND, the plane wobbled, groaned, and creaked. For a moment it was still the heavy, earthbound collection of steel and fiberglass it had been born as. But then, as always, the physics of wind and speed took charge.

It was a modern-day sacrament, really, Neil thought: the leap of faith that enabled all these passengers to sit reading their magazines, sipping their bottles of water, tapping away on their computers, full of blind faith in the science of aviation. If there was a God out there, he certainly had not designed the human body to fly. But possibly he was on to something in witholding this. Possibly humans never would have achieved so much if they had started out with more than this paper-thin coat of skin, this collection of breakable bones, these teeth no sharper or more dangerous than a pig's. If they had been stronger and more physically capable, they never would have embarked on the trajectory of scrappy resourcefulness, big dreams, and constant self-improvement that had led to such inventions as skyscrapers, cars, and airplanes. They never would have made self-invention a stick they measured their success by.

Neil pressed the metal button on his arm rest and reclined his seat despite the still-glowing "Fasten Seatbelts" sign. Boston was receding in the darkness, an uneven collection of lights glowing like the embers of some deep internal fire. Below the plane was ocean— dark, cold, and theoretically terrifying. Neil considered reading the magazine on his lap, but settled instead for closing his eyes. Already news media seemed irrelevant to his new life.

Neil was going to Africa. A graduate student at the University of Pennsylvania had accidentally uncovered two volumes of what turned out to be Albert Sorensen Jones's own travel diaries. Neil had driven through the night to see them—the unusually neat, back-slanted script he knew from forms and insurance records. He had gotten special dispensation to photocopy the pages and create for himself one thick, semi-indecipherable file. Now he could travel in the man's own footsteps, something no one had ever done before.

What was he looking for? Would it help him finish his dissertation? These were Jane's questions for him when he had called to say goodbye. But he was after something bigger than this. He was going to write a biography of the man's life, something that did not yet exist. He was going to write the story of Albert Sorenson Jones. And he would accompany it with a juxtaposition—the Africa Jones had traversed over 150 years ago and the Africa he, Neil Banks, would walk through now.

Why did it matter? What was the use of this? His knee-jerk cynicism supplied the questions, but this time he had an answer. This man's small, complicated, and imperfect life mattered. Because if it didn't, what did? It was his *life*. He had tried to make something of it—had tried to build something and had failed, but there was meaning in the effort and there had to be meaning in its chronicle.

In the last few weeks, a new freedom had come over Neil. He was done with ZGames, with all its inherent compromise and market pandering. He was leaving Boston, a place he never should have come back to. And now he was leaving his country—a place he was too pessimistic, too unambitious, too *unpragmatic* to belong to. It felt like shedding cumbersome layers of clothing. He was naked, going out into the world. He could afford to. There was a portion of himself—a little boy named Colin (he had resigned himself to the name)—who would bring the Banks DNA into the bright bold future that had already left Neil behind.

What do you want? Jeremy had asked that night after the police left. He asked it not with anger or rebuke, but with frankness. And the question had flooded Neil with a kind of panic. What *did* he want? The anger and resentment that had driven him down Belleview Road at two a.m. were gone. *Paternity? Visitation rights?* Jeremy had continued in that reasonable, sonorous voice that Neil could imagine reassuring investors in his companies, constructing complex business arrangements involving millions of dollars: he was a man whose judgment you could have confidence in.

And so it was Jeremy himself who had translated the engine behind Neil's actions into the concrete language of concessions and demands. He and Jenny would give Neil an open place in the baby's life. He would become a *known* biological father—known to Colin himself as well as to Jenny and Jeremy. It was both minimal and profound. Neil certainly would not have paternity, or even explicit visitation rights. But if he wanted to, he could get to know the boy, just as any family friend could. He would be invited over for dinner if he was in town—and he could make as much effort as he wanted to be in touch.

But he would not be a "father" and bear all the weight and authority and complicated baggage the term implied. Jeremy was the boy's father. For better or for worse, dead or alive. As Neil watched the baby fall asleep in Jeremy's arms that night after the police left, this had been totally clear. There was a calmness to Jeremy's movements, and a knowledge—the intimacy of which Neil had no frame of reference for. Jeremy *loved* the baby. Not the idea of him, or the DNA he was composed of, but the little boy himself. Sitting at their stark white kitchen table, observing them together, Neil himself had been rendered almost mute with humility.

And watching Jenny flitter with uncharacteristic nervousness between the teakettle and the cupboard, the baby and the teacups (when had he ever seen, or even imagined, Jenny Callahan doing something so prosaic and homey as making tea?), his bitterness and skepticism about what kind of life his child would lead dimmed. So the boy was born rich. Born into blessings Neil himself had never had. Was that so terrible? Did he want his child to grow up with the same sense of want and otherness that he had?

And if there was one thing Neil knew Jenny Callahan would do, it was protect her child.

Neil opened his eyes and looked out the window onto the black sea. There was a distant light. A boat of some kind, a small beacon of fire in the heart of the sea. Neil tried to make out what it was—giant tanker or cruise ship or little sailboat. But it was impossible to tell whether it was big or small from up here. It didn't matter. He closed his eyes again. He was glad it was there.

10

IT WAS THE FOURTH OF JULY, and even Boston had finally entered summer. The air was not just warm, but humid. The trees hummed with crickets and cicadas. And the bay beyond Lynch Park was thick with sailboats, windsurfers, and even a few kayakers heading ambitiously toward a picture-book-perfect lighthouse.

Elise pushed the double stroller up the hill intrepidly. Beside her, Chrissy looked anxious. Her face was frozen in a distracted, searching gaze as if she were looking for a lost child or runaway dog. A strand of hair had blown across her cheek and stuck to the corner of her mouth.

"They're probably over there," Elise said, gesturing at the array of picnic tables to the right.

"What?" Chrissy said jumpily. "Oh, I know. Do you have the diaper bag?"

Elise patted it demonstratively.

"Wait a minute," Chrissy said, stopping short and clutching at Elise's wrist with a cold hand. "Do you think this is a bad idea? I mean—do you *still* think so? Have I just been totally stupid?"

Elise stared at her and started to laugh. "Are you kidding?"

Chrissy shook her head and looked so miserable that despite Elise's innate shrinking from public displays of affection, she drew her into a giant hug. James twisted around the side of the stroller to look back at them.

Chrissy pulled away and looked at Elise searchingly. "What if they're awful?" she whispered.

"Who—the mothers?"

"The children."

"Ha!" Elise let out a shout of laughter. "They won't be!" She reached down and tousled Nigel's hair. "And if they are, we'll know we got lucky."

"Okay," Chrissy nodded like a brave child persuaded to walk into an intimidating classroom. "Okay."

It was Elise who spotted them first—the balloons and, more prominently, Claire Markowitz and the inimitable Justin.

"I'll get us settled," she offered. "You go help her set up."

And so immediately Chrissy was whisked off into the world of anxious preparations Claire Markowitz lived in. Elise, meanwhile, steered the boys over to the shade beneath a giant oak tree and spread their picnic blanket on the ground.

Slowly the women and their children began to arrive. It was an eclectic crew: lesbian couples, single straight women, even one transgender lesbian couple. Chrissy had given Elise the run-down when the picnic planning was still in its infancy. If Chrissy would calm down enough to come and sit with Elise and the boys, it would be fun to wage bets on who was who. Elise introduced herself agreeably to anyone who approached, but tried to remain genially apart from the hubbub of Donor #176's uniting progeny.

She did sneak glances at the children, though: this mess of little ones, all half sprung from the same set of genes. They were dark-haired and brown-eyed, and although some were chubby and some were slim, some were big and some were small, there were certain striking commonalities. There was a little boy who had decidedly the same wide-set eyes as the four-year-old twins at the cupcake table and the little girl with pigtails. And four of the children (Nigel and James included) shared the same wide mouths and bumpy little noses they got so many compliments on.

Elise, who rarely drank anymore these days, felt the sweet tingle of alcohol wash over her and turn the whole event into a sort of interesting anthropological experiment. Shouts of laughter rang out from neighboring picnic sites. The air smelled of charcoal fire and grilling meat. It was a beautiful park! In a beautiful country where healthy, happy people could make children out of vials and beakers of biological fluid.

And it was Independence Day, that curiously fitting all-American holiday that celebrated not just victory, or heroism, or the birth of a nation, but independence itself: that peculiar American value that had spawned everything from the two-car household to the Unabomber. Wasn't that, in some way, what this gathering was all about? Independence from the constraints of nature and corporeal function?

She watched Nigel and James navigate the scene—James boldly engaging in a silent grappling match with one of the other twins, pulling at his end of a plastic dump truck with determination, and Nigel standing more anxiously to the side, observing his brother's antics with a furrowed brow. Elise felt a swell of love for them that was, she realized, decidedly parental. How could she have questioned that? She was proud of them— of James's toughness and Nigel's sweet thoughtfulness. As she watched, James let go of the dump truck and toddled off after another cupcake. And Nigel, seeing his brother safely extricated from the tug-of-war, looked around as if wondering what to do next. Brightening, he took a few steps up the hill and dropped to his hands and knees on the grass. Then he sat back holding something up triumphantly: a fluffy dandelion pinwheel. "Li li!" he called out, looking around with an expression of total amazement and joy. "Li li!"

Elise started toward him, grinning herself. This was something she had taught him last week. They had picked the delicate white globes and blown on them, watching the tiny filaments disperse, *seeds for next year's dandelions*, she had explained. His deep brown eyes had taken this in with a kind of gravity, absorbing it into his understanding of the world.

"Li li!" he chirped with delight now as she sank down beside him. He took a deep breath and blew. "Seeds!"

Acknowledgments

SPECIAL THANKS TO MY EDITOR, Jill Bialosky, and agent, Eric Simonoff, to my readers Risa Miller and John Shattuck, to Jay Bradner for showing me around his lab and letting me ask a million stupid questions, to Jennifer Egan for writing the article that got me thinking, to The MacDowell Colony, Richard and Linda Fates, and Ann Hersey for loaning me the rooms in which this book was written, and of course to Preble Jaques for his love, support, and encouragement, as always.